JANE BORODALE studied site-specific sculpture at Wimbledon School of Art. She was recently Leverhulme writer-in-residence at the Weald and Downland Open Air Museum in Sussex. Her first novel, *The Book of Fires*, was shortlisted for the Orange Award for New Writers and she lives in the West Country with her husband, poet Sean Borodale, and their two children.

# Also by Jane Borodale

*The Book of Fires*

# JANE BORODALE

# The Knot

FOURTH ESTATE • London

Fourth Estate
An imprint of HarperCollins*Publishers*
77–85 Fulham Palace Road
Hammersmith, London W6 8JB
www.4thestate.co.uk

This Fourth Estate paperback edition published 2013
1

First published in Great Britain by Harper*Press* in 2012

Copyright © Jane Borodale 2012

Jane Borodale asserts the moral right to
be identified as the author of this work

Frontispiece portrait of Henry Lyte (held at the Somerset Heritage Centre, Taunton)
reproduced by kind permission of the Maxwell-Lyte family

Illustrations by Andrew Pinder,
redrawn from the *Cruÿdeboeck* by Rembert Dodeons

A catalogue record for this book is
available from the British Library

ISBN 978-0-00-731333-4

Printed and bound in Great Britain by
Clays Ltd, St Ives plc

MIX
Paper from
responsible sources
FSC
www.fsc.org   FSC™ C007454

FSC™ is a non-profit international organisation established to promote
the responsible management of the world's forests. Products carrying the
FSC label are independently certified to assure consumers that they come
from forests that are managed to meet the social, economic and
ecological needs of present and future generations,
and other controlled sources.

Find out more about HarperCollins and the environment at
www.harpercollins.co.uk/green

Henrie Lyte Esq; the eldest son of Iohn
Lyte Esq; first ma: Agnes ỹ da: of Kail
way of Cullumton Esq: his 2 wife was
Frances ỹ da: of Iohn Typtoft a Citizen
of Londo. his 3 wife was Dorothy ỹ da
of on Iohn Gouer He died at the age of
78 and was buried in
ỹ North Ile at Charl
ton Mackarell
Anᵒ 1607.

*For my grandmothers, who both had green fingers*

*The good and vertuous Physition, whose purpose is rather the health of many, than the wealthe of himselfe, will not (I hope) mislike this my enterprise, which to this purpose specially tendeth, that even the meanest of my Countrymen, (whose skill is not so profound, that they can fetch this knowledge out of strange tongues, nor their abilitie so wealthy, as to entertaine a learned Physition) may yet in time of their necessitie have some helps in their owne, or their neighbors fields and gardens at home.*

HENRY LYTE, *A Niewe Herball*

# Acknowledgements

GRATEFUL THANKS to my agent Sarah Ballard, Clare Smith, Essie Cousins, Kerry Enzor and Jo Walker at HarperPress, and Sarah Castleton. I'm indebted to many people who so generously and patiently shared their scholarship, time and expertise: historian of science and medicine Deborah Harkness; medical herbalists Christina Stapley and Ruth Mannion-Daniels; legal historian Christopher Whittick; historian Danae Tankard. Also very many thanks to Barbara Wood and the National Trust; Nancy Langmaid and Celia Mycock of the Lytes Cary Landscape History research project volunteer group; Peter and David Maxwell-Lyte; Richard Harris; Jon Roberts; Hannah Tiplady; George Boobyer; Yaniv Farkas; the Old Deanery Garden project, Wells; Rebecca Board; the British Library; Somerset Heritage Centre, Taunton; Somerset Library service; Jon Hill; Valerie Hill; Sam Hunt; Annie Hunt; Marie-Thérèse Please; Lydia Dickinson; Dr Tom Hutchison; Esther Lewis-Smith; Lorelei Goulding. Special thanks to Sean and the boys, for all the love and for not minding about the weeds, which were very important; and most particularly and respectfully to Henry Lyte, whom I hope can forgive me from beyond the grave for making so freely with the fragments of his life that are known to us now, and for inventing the rest.

There are many books I'm grateful to have been able to refer to during research, but some I couldn't have done without: Henry Lyte's *A Niewe Herball* (1578), and his own copy of Rembert Dodoens's *Cruÿdeboeck*, translated by Charles l'Ecluse into French as *L'Histoire des Plantes* (1557), and annotated throughout in Henry Lyte's hand; his son Thomas Lyte's commonplace book, held at the Somerset Heritage Centre, and also transcribed by Nancy Langmaid; *The Lytes of Lytescary*, HC Maxwell-Lyte (Taunton, 1895, reprinted from *Proceedings of the Somersetshire Archaeological and Natural History Society*); *A New Herball*, William Turner (first published 1551, ed. G Chapman and M Tweddle, CUP, 1995); *The Jewel House: Elizabethan London and the Scientific Revolution*, Deborah E Harkness (Yale, 2008); *The World of Carolus Clusius: Natural History in the Making, 1550–1610*, Florike Egmond (Pickering & Chatto, 2010); *Medieval English Gardens*, Teresa McLean (Barrie and Jenkins, 1989); *Herbals: Their Origin and Evolution*, Agnes Arber (CUP, 1953); *Medical Authority and Englishwomen's Herbal Texts 1550–1650*, Rebecca Laroche (Ashgate, 2009); *The Gardener's Labyrinth*, Thomas Hill (first published 1577, OUP, 1987); *Encyclopedia of Herbs*, Royal Horticultural Society, Deni Bown (Dorling Kindersley, 2008); *The Tudor House and Garden*, Paula Henderson (Yale, 2005); *The Old English Herbals*, Eleanour Sinclair Rodhe (Dover, 1971); *A True Report of Certain Overflowings of Waters*, E Baker (Weston-super-Mare, 1884).

# THE FIRST PART

## *The Place*

# I.

*Of BORAGE. Which endureth the winter like to the common Buglosse. The stalke is rough and rude, of the height of a foote and halfe, parting it selfe at the top into divers small branches, bearing faire and pleasant flowers in fashion like starres of colour blewe or Azure and sometimes white.*

TWO HOURS OF DIGGING, and Henry Lyte still feels that unrecognizable discomfort.

Like a slight tipping, washing inside him, a darkish fluid lapping at his inner edges as though in a dusk, yet when he turns to it; nothing, nothing. Perhaps he is about to be unwell. Perhaps the Rhenish wine last night at supper was old or tainted, or he had too much of it.

A man of nearly thirty-six with all his health should not be troubled by sudden, unspecifiable maladies. Being at work on the garden out in the fresh air should be enough of a wholesome antidote to sitting hunched and bookish in his study, over his new, impossible manuscript that is going so slowly. There is satisfaction to be had from being outside instead, slicing and turning the light brown, clayish soil, breaking it into the kind of finer ground he needs for planting. The day has been good for October, bursts of rain giving way to bright sunshine, yet still it is not enough to distract Henry Lyte from being so ill at ease. He decides that as he can't place the sensation, nor what provoked it, he will try to ignore whatever it is. Probably nerves, he thinks. It is not every day that a man is due to ride up to London to collect his new wife. His second wife, and they have been married for three months already, but she has not been to Lytes Cary yet. Within the week her postponed marital life and duties with Henry are to begin. He leans on his spade and considers the hulk of the manor house, the sky to the north dark behind, and wonders what she will make of it.

Lytes Cary Manor is made of limestone, a modest huddle of yellow gables and chimneys embedded comfortably on a mild slope of arable land where the Polden hills begin to rise up out of the damp flatness of the floodplain that is the Somerset Levels. The estate itself spreads down onto the damp moor in several places, but most of it sits on higher ground over a knoll in the crook of a bend in the river Cary, as far as Broadmead and Sowey's Fields, then out onto the lower, uncertain ground of Carey Moor. Lytes Cary stands on the very brink of the Levels, and in winter these marshy acres to the south-west are inundated with shallow salty water from the sea and can be traversed only by boat. The Mendip hills are high and blue in the distance to the north, to the far south-west are the Quantocks, and to the near west, at about seven leagues off lies Bridgwater Bay, with its bustling port and the wide murky sea that stretches to Wales.

About the house sit diverse barns, the malthouse and dovehouse, and tenants' cottages, many put up in his father's time. Henry can still remember improvements being made to the house when he was a boy. The adjacent manor of Tuck's Cary is almost uninhabited, just a handful of tenants, since Henry's brother Bartholomew died of a pleurisy four years ago. There is also a hop yard, two windmills and several withy beds.

The new garden project here, however, is of his own devising.

To his knowledge, this part of the grounds has not been cultivated for at least two generations, though it lies alongside the kitchen garden that feeds the household, and the little plot in which his first wife Anys grew a few of the most vital herbs. Sheep have been folded here right up by the house on this grass during summers for years, so the soil has been kept fertile with dung, and it is level, south-facing, and as well-drained as any of this clay country is likely to be. Now the earth needs to be prepared and opened up, so that the frosts can penetrate the clods and break it down over the winter months.

He likes digging. He likes the pull of the spade against the earth, the tilting strain on his back, the mud drying on his palms. More accustomed to directing men than taking up the tools himself, he is always surprised at how much you can be changed by working physically till you ache. The world seems more vivid, more manageable. He does not feel it is at all beneath him as a man of status to be at work like this, instead he imagines his guardian spirit glancing down approvingly from time to time, saying, *look, see how he takes charge of his affairs*, because that is how it feels to be digging into the good soil with the iron spade and mattock.

And then of course he remembers that guardian angels are no longer the stock in trade of any churchman worth his salt, nor any true believer, and are resorted to only by those such as his cook, Old Hannah, still cutting her surreptitious cross into the raw soft dough of every loaf on baking day. At thirty-six, Henry Lyte does not practise his faith in the way he was instructed as a boy, nor as a youth, because the world is not now as it was, not at all. It has changed, and changed again.

While he digs he is free to let his mind wander, and he dreams his kingdom of pear trees in the orchards across to his left, growing skywards, gnarling, putting forth fat green soft fruits with ease each year. The trees that already grow in the orchards he loves almost as women in his life; the Catherine pear, the Chesil or pear Nouglas, the great Kentish pear, the Ruddick, the Red Garnet, the Norwich, the Windsor, the little green pear ripe at Kingsdon Feast; all thriving where they were planted in his father's ground at Lytes Cary before the management of the estate became his own responsibility as the eldest son. So much has happened these six years since his father handed over and left for his house in Sherborne: there have been births and deaths – Anys herself was taken from him only last year. But the pear trees live on, reliably flowering and yielding variable quantities as an annual crop that defines the estate, and he has plans to add more.

He wonders – as he does at some point without fail each day that passes – whether it would have been better if his father had, despite everything, attended his wedding to Frances. Three months have passed now since the ceremony, and the fact of his father's deliberate, calculated absence on that day is a smouldering hole in their relationship, there is no doubt. Henry had stood with his bride-to-be at the church door perspiring with anxiety and the heat of July, in the hope that his father would appear as invited, despite Henry's letters having met with a deafening silence. After almost an hour the chaplain could wait no longer, as he had others to marry at two o'clock, so he garbled through the litany and vows, and the thing was done without his father being there. Henry would have liked his approbation, but there was nothing to be done about it, for his father, when he gets an idea into his head, is a stubborn man.

That in itself was an inauspicious start, and then suddenly Frances was burdened with pressing, unexpected matters to attend to in London because by great misfortune her own, beloved father had died on their wedding night. Her mother had needed assistance with probate, which proved a terrible family tangle that Henry was unable to involve himself with. After several weeks he had returned to Lytes Cary alone to deal with his own estate that could not, after all, run itself, and sent up diffident, occasional letters to his new wife as though to a stranger. Now her brother has come to the aid of their mother so that Frances's presence is no longer essential, and tomorrow at last he goes up to London to fetch her.

Henry digs on to the end of the row, straightens up and looks south, and finds now that evening is already creeping up the hill from the west, that the large, yellowing sun is close to the horizon. A green woodpecker flies to a branch of the tallest willow at the end of the bank and squats back belligerently on its tail, the slope of its red cap bright in the grey of the tree. Henry always calls that bird the Sorcerer, it has a menacing, ethereal presence he would rather do without. From there the bird has a commanding view of its surroundings, it knows more than he does about their mutual territory.

The sweet savour of dug earth is all about, and yet for a moment Henry Lyte thinks he can smell the sea – a weedy, salt smell of unwanted water. Then it is gone – perhaps it was a draught of air drawn over the half-completed brick wall from the heap of rotting compost in the kitchen garden, some stalks of greens maybe, or kale. But Henry Lyte pauses, and for a moment has a strong thought of the sea itself wash round his head – the great blank sea that lies in sheets of water against the low shoulder of the land at Berrow, the wide strip of coast where the mouth of the river Parrett coils its way out across the mud flats at low tide below the dunes thirty miles from here.

It must be explained that the sea there is held back by only the thinnest strip of land at high tide, and with the highest tides in winter the sea wall is often breached. But these winter floods are to be expected; they are planned for, understood by farmers, eel fishermen, migrating birds. Unseasonal deluge has never happened in his lifetime; that would be more of a threat to human life than he would care to think of. Nevertheless, it is said that a true native from these parts, with marsh-blood going back centuries, is always born with webbed feet, because nothing can be taken for granted in this precarious world. Unusual weather stems from unusual circumstances. It certainly felt that way just after the death of Anys, the winter that followed – last winter – was the coldest and deepest he could ever remember. And there are plenty who believe that bad weather is a punishment from God.

Downwind of the chimney, Henry can smell what might be supper and the unaccustomed exercise has made him hungry. He props his tools in the outhouse and bolts it tight, goes into the house by the back door. His blisters sting satisfyingly as he washes his hands in the ewery. The dog in the porch beats her tail without raising her head, a young mastiff bitch called Blackie who has developed a reciprocal loyalty to this half of the house rather than to her master. He puts his head in the door to his left. The kitchen at Lytes Cary is high and cavernous, the rack over the broad fireplace hung with hams and sides of salted beef and bacon, gigots of dried mutton, stockfish, ropes of onions and long bundles of herbs. On the east wall is the great oven, and ranging off to the west are the pantries and buttery and dairyroom, and all of this is Old Hannah's dominium, filled tonight with meaty steam and the fatty goodness of something fried. Three blackened cauldrons sit at the hearth, beside a stack of gleaming earthenware and a basket of scraps for the poor as it is Tuesday tomorrow. One vast wet ladle lies across the mouth of a brown pot, and a row of pewter plates laid out indicates that serving is imminent. He won't disturb her; if she gets talking things might go cold. Old Hannah has a rolling walk, it is always alarming to watch her crossing the kitchen carrying a large pudding basin filled brimful, or a cleaver for chopping the heads off plucked fowls. Tom Coin who works in the kitchen with her is a gangly sprout of a boy with a long, earnest face and hair of the soft brown sort that grows very slowly. Through the door in the cross passage Henry can see that Tom has set the trenchers in the hall, cut up the maslin bread, lugged in the pitchers of the small beer that is suitable for hindservants, and is just about to call supper for the household.

Tonight though Henry thinks he will eat with the children separately in the oriel. A speech that a father must have with his girls before the arrival of their new mother – *God knows but he never thought he'd ever have to say such words to them* – must be done in private. As he walks through the hall the armorial glass in the windows above to his right glows with the setting sun outside, casting a ruby-coloured light of the ancestors over the swept floor and the plain trestles. There is no escaping the ancestors, and they observe – as God does, but with perhaps more vested interest – his every movement through this place.

# II.

*Of BISTORTE. They grow wel in moist and watery places, as in medowes, and darke shadowy woods. The decoction of the leaves is very good against all sores, and it fastneth loose teeth, if it be often used or holden in the mouth.*

I T IS LATE, BUT HENRY LYTE can never sleep easily on the eve of a long journey. He sits with the trimmed candle burning low and ploughs on with his translation. He is an orderly man who likes to work in a state of neatness, which should stand him in good stead for the task ahead of him. There is, after all, a place for brilliance of mind and there is a place for method, and he feels he may have enough of the latter to complete all six hundred pages. He has ink of different colours ranged in pots on his desk; red, black, purple, green and brown, for different types of fact or notes, and he likes a sharp nib. Surrounded by other men's herbals for ease of cross-reference, he is working directly from the French version as *L'Histoire des plantes*, which is itself translated out of the Flemish by Charles l'Écluse, or Carolus Clusius, as the great man prefers to be known. He hasn't decided what his own is going to be called. A title is crucial and difficult to decide upon, he's finding. The original work, startlingly detailed and scholarly, was published in 1554 as the *Cruÿdeboeck* by the learned Rembert Dodeons, a master of plants and medicine, whom Henry himself had met when he was in Europe as a young man all those years ago. Sometimes Henry blushes with embarrassment to think that he has been so audacious as to consider himself man enough for this enormous undertaking. Why him? Not a physician, not an expert in anything. It is almost ridiculous, but the project is well underway now, too late to turn back.

He has finished *butterbur* and begun *bistort* today, which is a familiar kind of herb to him. Some plants are easier to render quickly because it is very clear from their descriptions or the Latin what their equivalents might be in English. Others are not, and he will have to return to those later, get specialist opinion, exercise extreme caution and assiduousness in applying names to them. The excellent plates by Leonhard Fuchs are also of considerable help in identification, but grappling with the French is his own charge entirely. He hovers over a disputable word. What is *ridée* in English? He thinks. He notes down *rinkeled, folden, playted or drawn together*. He considers his sentence, and then writes *the great bistort hath long leaves like Patience, but wrinkled or drawen into rimples, of a swart green colour*.

He can hear from the creak of boards upstairs when Lisbet leaves the children's room and goes off to where she sleeps in the chamber over the dairy in the north range. With her departure all four children settle down in their beds and a quietness conducive to writing subsides throughout the house. For two full hours Henry works hard enough to forget most of what weighs on his conscience, though it is a temporary displacement. When the second candle is burnt about halfway down its length, he retires to bed to dream of nothing.

# III.

*Of PAULES BETONY. The male is a small herb, and
créepeth by the ground. The leafe is something long, and
somwhat gréene, a little hairy, and dented or snipt round
the edges like a sawe.*

HIS NEW WIFE FRANCES, daughter of the late John Tiptoft,
London, distant cousin to the Earls of Worcester, is standing
for the first time at Lytes Cary in the hall. It is a wet blustery autumn
day. The highways from London these past six days have been very
bad for mud and their passage was slow, beset with driving rain and
herds of animals on their way to market; broken branches and at
least one diversion to avoid hazardous bridges. Henry loathes driving in a carriage as it is painfully cumbersome, and makes a man's
limbs sore and stiff, doing nothing on a lumpy, jolting road for such
a distance, but Frances had refused to ride on horseback so far in
weather like this. They might have been better hiring a horse litter
for Frances, with Henry riding alongside, as even with allowances
made for the sluggish nature of progress by carriage, the journey
had taken a day longer than it should as a wheel was lost and they
had to put up overnight at the inn in Stockbridge whilst the axle

was repaired at the wright's. But now here they are. This feels momentous, her arrival here; perhaps more so than the marriage itself. There is baggage due to follow when her mother comes next month.

Four o'clock in the afternoon, and the fire has been lit with all speed to honour her entrance and take the chill off the hall. Someone has swept out the leaves and dirt that sift into the porch on windy days and has left the besom propped in the passage. All of the household is gathered here to glimpse the new mistress; John Parsons his bailiff; Old Hannah, Lisbet and other servants; the dairymaid; Richard Oxendon the horseman; various farmhands, and several tenants' children clustered at the door. Frances removes her chaperon and cloak, goes straight to the hearth and stands shivering against the yellow fire. Her black hair is in rats' tails from being blown about. She says nothing at all. Old Hannah mutters something to someone Henry cannot see. Henry tries to be jolly, stands beside her feeling stiff and damp and out of sorts and makes an awkward joke about the countryside, whilst all the time trying to recall how she'd looked when he saw her last. She seems very different here. Her skin is unnaturally white and smooth. He has a strong impulse to touch her cheek to see if there is any warmth to be had from it. She is like a doll, a figurine. He had wanted, expected her to look about and take in her new surroundings eagerly. She had been so pleased to see him, so chatty for much of the journey, pointing out distant spires of churches and asking questions. She must be feeling the very great difference of what she is now, he thinks, and is occupied with that. She is anxious, perhaps, or very tired. Yes of course, she needs hot food to eat and then her bed should be warmed. It must be that she is white with exhaustion, quite blanched through with it, indeed he can see now that she is almost swaying on her feet. Henry Lyte feels guilty that he hadn't thought of that more promptly. She looks ready to faint.

'Lisbet!' he claps the servant over to take his wife to her chamber. A boy is dispatched to the carriage to bring in her first of many bags and cases.

'Send up a caudle,' he tells the cook. 'Or a dish of eggs. Something hot and quick. My wife is tired.' He is annoyed with himself for not having sent word on ahead to have a spread of food prepared ready for her arrival. Clearly he is out of the habit of being married to someone younger. The crowded hall filters away to usual duties, until it is very quiet in here, just the spit and crackle of the freshly lit fire.

His girls, all stood beside it in a row, are watching him like little owls. Edith, at twelve years old the eldest, opens her mouth to speak but then closes it again. He looks at her, and then at Jane, who is nine, with baby Florence on her hip. At Mary, six, then back to Jane again – and is baffled.

'What?' he says.

His new wife is asleep in the very middle of their bed by the time he goes up to see how she is, a plate of half-eaten tart and an empty mug on the floorboards at the end of the bed. He parts the curtains and holds up the candle but she does not stir in the pool of light. Her face is fine-boned and angular. Her breathing is deep and even, she lies with the cover pulled up over her chemise and one narrow wrist flung out. It seems bad-mannered to climb in and push her across, so he takes a blanket from the wicker coffer and retires for the night to the dressing room, where he does not sleep because the owls are so loud on the roof above him.

In the morning he goes to his study to give his wife time to get ready in their chamber before coming down. He is not going to be a stranger in his own house ordinarily, but this is, after all, the first day:

the first day of his new life. He stands at the window that gives onto the garden and watches a fine rain coming down and the green Sorcerer out on the grass, up-loping toward the ants. He sees Tom Coin coming back from the fishponds with a large carp flapping so much he can hardly keep it in the basket. Henry opens the window and leans out, and the noise of chopping up in the coppice tells him that the woodman is not idle, despite the weather. There is nothing seemingly wrong at all, and he should be glad for it. Why then does he feel so angry? It makes no sense. The Sorcerer puts his thick head up and seems to laugh at him as it flies away towards the wood.

'I had no choice but to marry, I have four surviving daughters to consider. Four, dammit! They cannot run free in the mud like dottrill or little urchins. They need a woman's hand to oversee their maturation, to bring them up in a civilized way until they are of age and can enter the world as wives and then mothers. They need to know French, totting-up, how to stitch, how to make sweet malt, bind a man's wound, how to be in charge of the kitchen. Not everything can be taught by a nurserymaid.' He indicates out of the window at the rainy scene. The grass is sodden and deserted, though to the far left a cow is being driven into the yard from Inner Close for milking.

'Look at it out there,' he demands, to the empty room, 'what civilizing influences will be had by them if I do not seek it?'

He regrets that there has been no time for grieving – practical matters to attend to when a family member dies seemed on this occasion to take all his vigour for months afterwards, he has felt blank and sucked dry of any melancholy or other emotion. He does not mean he didn't suffer pain but that he felt it like a physical blow to the body, so that he sat by the hearth alone at night aching as though he'd been in a fight. Yes, it was just that he'd been in a fist-fight with death on behalf of his wife and had lost. It is all perfectly normal. Doesn't everyone suffer deaths within their close family circle?

In the year that his own mother Edith died, coffins went up the road to the church almost every week. There had been fair warning that death was to be afoot that year – in March around Lady Day there had come a great comet, reddish like Mars, half the size of the moon in diameter, with a flaming, agitated tail that stretched itself across the night sky and scorched a rightful terror into the hearts of those who looked upon it. There were many who said it was a clear token from God that the end of Catholic rule was near, and that Queen Mary's tumour may have begun with its manifestation. A comet is a sure sign of change, or death. He hopes never to see another body like it in the sky. His mother had died in exceptional pain, drenched in sweat and gasping for air in what had been the hottest summer for eleven years, as she clung to his hand for those last dreadful days. Sometimes across his knuckles he feels the grip of her bones still, has to flex all his fingers to free himself of it. And sometimes when his eye catches at the horizon just after sunset, the first bright sight of Venus makes his blood pound momentarily, mistakenly. It is surely unthinkable that another comet of that stature could appear twice in a man's lifetime.

His father, remarried himself after Edith's passing within two years, has no right to listen to any bad claims against his character. It's just the usual way of things, to marry again.

'Everybody does it,' Henry goes on aloud to no-one. 'Hadn't I waited a decent length of time since Anys was taken from us by the will of God? *By God's will alone.* It had been nearly a year.' With this last thought, a draught blows under the door, and for a second he almost thinks he can catch the scent of her brushing against him like a substance.

Anys smelt of leather polish and warm skin and oats. She smelt of hard work and prayerbooks and children and bread. He is sure he has remembered that right. He is sure she knew how well she was esteemed by him. He swallows. The whole business is unavoidable. He leaves the study hastily, goes to the last of his new wife's boxes stacked in the hall, and carries them up.

❧

He had lost two servants soon after the funeral, but they'd each had good reasons, as they explained, for their change of situation. Lisbet is the new maidservant, she replaced Sarah who was a diligent worker. He had let her go with regret, Anys had thought so well of her. Lisbet is tolerably good, but he did wish he couldn't hear her feet slopping down the corridor all the time when he is trying to concentrate. Why does she never pick them up when she walks? It occurs briefly to Henry Lyte that her shoes might not fit properly. She has a pleasant enough face. There is even something quite appealing about the crooked tooth that juts out a little over her lip, though it is the kind of countenance that will not age well, and of course he knew her mother. He prefers to hire local girls like her, they stay for longer, ask fewer questions, and he doesn't think she can have heard anything of what happened. The misunderstanding will all simmer down and be forgotten. He hopes that Frances herself will never hear what people have said of him. It is just a matter of time. People forget so easily; memories are flimsy, friable things that get buried and mulch down into the past like vegetation. A few will stick, of course, inevitably. His memory of what happened is already concentrated to a few sparse images that he cannot shake off. One can be forgiven for forgetting a detail here or there – even though details, the little unimportant daily things amassed together over time, are what makes up most of living. What does his own life add up to, he suddenly wonders. In forty years, a hundred years, three hundred, what will be left of him?

He recalls a distinct, disturbing sensation he had once in his early days as a student a long time ago, in one of Oxford's many bathing houses. It was not the sort of place that he was to frequent very often, but he was a young man missing home, missing his mother, and had gone for comfort, a little bit of human warmth that could be bought straightforwardly with sixpence.

A pretty doxy by the name of Martha was rubbing at his back with oil, plying her knuckles to his spine, to the very bones inside his muscles, and smoothing backwards and forwards across his shoulders in a shape like a figure of eight, her breathing ragged with exertion. There was a good savour of flowers or resin all around. Afterwards she was friendly to him, and didn't seem to mind that he had fallen asleep.

'How was that?' she'd asked, prodding him gently and pouring a drink from the jug. He'd thought carefully, yawned and sat up. He examined the back of his hands, turned them over as if seeing them for the first time.

'It was like … being rubbed out,' he'd said eventually. It was the only way to put it.

'Out?' she'd queried, her brow wrinkling up as if she hadn't heard this one before, and pouring herself a measure too, just to take the edge off. She had a busy night lined up.

'Like being erased,' he'd said, 'quite worn away into nothing. No trace of me left at all, not a bump or ridge to show I'd existed.' As if it were his history that was being smoothly abolished with her accumulating, efficient strokes, in just half an hour. He had an image of himself face down in the earth, being slowly flattened and absorbed into its clayish mass, and it had felt inevitable, nothing out of the ordinary, as though this was what happened to everyone. Which it does in the end, of course, for who gets remembered? Almost all of us go back to the earth to be worn away into nothing again.

She hadn't laughed, he recalls, but pursed her lips as though it was not at all the answer that she'd wanted. She stood pinning up her curls and ducking in front of the polished plate that served as a glass to catch her reflection. 'You should go to church more if you want that kind of talk.'

'I don't mean my soul,' he protested, confused that she was so offended. 'I mean my presence on this earth as we know it.' But she had a customer waiting, he could hear his shoes scraping outside on the boards, and she'd gone to the door and held it ajar for him to depart.

# IV.

*Of CELANDINE. The small celandine bringeth forth his*
*fleure betimes, about the return of Swalowes in the end*
*of Februarie. It remayneth flouring even untill Aprill,*
*and after it doth so vanish away.*

I T HAD BEEN SHORTLY AFTER THE DEATH OF ANYS that he'd
begun planning his Knot garden in earnest. On paper at first,
endless sketches and discarded ideas that he would pore over by
candlelight in the evening when it was too dark to see anything
outside. He made occasional visits to costly gardens in London, and
drew on recollections of aromatic, unattainable gardens in Europe
that he'd seen as a youth. The ground itself here needed preparation.
There was a lot of dross to get rid of on the site, including a defunct
fallen-down building where his father had reared pigs before the new
sties were built. This was removed, piece by crumbling, splintery
piece. It is always surprising how small the footprint of a demolished
building appears. How could so little space have enclosed so much?

'Much faster to take down a building than to put one up,' one of
the labourers had informed him, as though Henry had no sense of
practical matters. It took little more than an afternoon to do. There

was a lot of other debris to clear away, an old trough, piles of inexplicable rotting logs and branches, crawling beneath with worms and woodlice.

'Look at that. A garden is teeming, isn't it,' Henry had said, brimming with cheerful purpose in the fresh air, as he squatted to examine a yellow centipede, rippling in kinks against the damp earth. 'The very stuff of life itself.'

'If you're lucky,' his gardener Tobias Mote remarked, straining to lift something into the barrow to take to the bonfire. Henry looked at him to check he was joking. 'Seeing as the job of nature is to feed on death.'

Sometimes Henry wishes that Mote's voice wasn't so dry, so opposite to what he hopes for.

The pegging-out of the borders and the Knot, however, had been one of the most exciting moments so far in this process. The simplicity of unwinding each ball of twine in the hand and walking backwards, squinting, squaring up and measuring sideways with the feet, pushing in the stake like a New World explorer with his claim. Mote worked alongside him, scratching his head, making unhelpful, tardy suggestions where none was wanted, because everything was decided now in terms of form and symmetry. The garden was like a grid for days from the upper windows before they took the twine away, making last-minute adjustments to the guidelines they'd whitewashed. It was a sheer delight to see it stretched out down there. What had existed previously only on a small piece of paper as the final meticulous inked plan for the structure has now been unravelled from inside his head, squared up and made manifest.

Now he has the shape out there, but what he will plant is still to be decided upon. Roses, definitely roses. He also has a master plan for content, and marks in his choice of plants and herbs as they occur to him. This plan by contrast is chaotic, filled with crossing-out and scribbled re-inking. He paces about outside making mental lists to write up later, checking up on the bricklayers putting up the new walls course by course which will shelter his tender specimens from the winter harshnesses that they will have to suffer, looking over the work of the men he has hired in for the week because there is more digging than he and Mote can manage if they are to get it over with in time for planting. Today the four of them work steadily across the earmarked areas; Thom Pearson from over at Tuck's Cary Manor just a stone's throw from the stables here, William the oldest son of Hunt of Podimore who leases the windmill, Ralph Let, and some other man from Devon who was passing through and had asked for work.

'Lucky to get Ralph,' Tobias Mote says with a wink. 'He's good at that, being parish gravedigger he's had a lot of practice, brings his own spade, just never mind what that spade iron's gone through; very full that graveyard is, a lot of folk dead these days, begging your pardon. Just don't turn your back on him – he'd nimble you in.' Mote laughs with his face like a weasel's, his eyes closed to slits.

The diggers have broken the persistent turf all down what will be the raised border. It's coming along. To anyone else the scene looks like chaos, but Henry Lyte is beginning to have it all mapped out in his mind's eye, the raised square beds, the enclosing walls, the espaliers, the roses, the medicinal herber. And close to the house, this garden will have at its heart a perfect Knot; green, intricate, fragrant, a convergence of senses.

Henry is not in favour of the kind of closed Knot currently fashionable that he has seen so many times in London, laid out to weedless, barren segments of coloured sand in red and yellow and other garish hues, intersected by rigid, close-clipped hedges, the whole intended to be amusing from inside the house, or along the gallery or walk, like a dead kind of outdoor carpet. He has no wish to go about decorating his land like that, but hopes to coax from it an exquisite, flourishing entity; something wholly alive and changeable, a place where man and nature can meet and within which he and others will be able to study the riddles of botany. He knows his ambitions for it are high, that it will be hard work.

He goes on considering. Espaliers there against the warmth of the bricks, he decides, and perhaps a further row of espaliered trees at right-angles to the wall itself – offering glimpses through the layers of branches, as into green and fruited chambers.

But what kinds of fruit? He would like very much to be bold enough to try to grow apricots. He has eaten them abroad straight from the tree, the warm, furred skin of them bursting under his bite, the juice running in his mouth. He has eaten them in this country at other men's tables, both the tender yellow kind and the tougher sort, flavourless, the green of raw turnip. He has enjoyed dried apricots too, shrunken to a brown leather of sticky molasses sweetness. His mother used to call them St John peaches, ripe only in June. Of course she would remember when monks once sold them from the Abbey, when their walled enclosures were secure. He can just remember the day that the Abbot of Glastonbury was hanged on the Tor. He remembers particularly because his father owed the Abbot money, and there was uncertainty afterwards with what to do about the bonds. *Don't worry, the Crown will be hounding me for it soon enough*, Henry recalls him soothing his mother. The King's agents had moved in and taken the Abbey and all the contents. Henry had ridden past Glastonbury a few days later with his brother Bartholomew on an errand, and seen the distant sight of the Abbot's misshapen figure up there, swinging by his broken neck. At the time it had felt like the world was ending. It was hard to know which God to turn to, He seemed to differ according to who one spoke to about Him. Henry had dreamt constantly of brimstone, smouldering deadly, choking fumes, all the terrible punishments his grandmother had warned him about if he strayed from the good path laid down by God. He must have been about eight years old, sat between his parents at the hearth, his mother's anxious face rosy on one side from the heat of the fire. His mother loved all fruit, of course.

And what else should he grow here? Perhaps there could be an entirely separate plum orchard. Imagine the tiny stellar blossoms appearing in early spring, before the apples and pears. One fruit that can be simultaneously green and sweet is the greengage; perfect greeny globules of juice, almost gelatinous with being ripe, melting to fibres that lodge between the teeth. He too loves all fruit, but thinks perhaps the greengage is his favourite *prunus*. A plum orchard should be near the house, because the blossoms, coming early in the spring would be so cheering. For the other orchards, there are sixty new apple trees of sundry sorts on order, mostly whips and maidens because they will take to the soil better than if their roots were already more developed.

For the far end of the walled gardens, he thinks a vine. Sweet grapes gladden a man's heart. And a peach tree. Voluptuous, fat-bottomed velvet fruit of heaven. A fig, fibrous juicy threads, cool seeds cracking delicately between the teeth, at their very best when they are oozing resinous juice. He would like to eat every one of them, *a fig pig*, he thinks, but they will be laid in the sun to darken and dry. Walnuts, for pickled walnuts of course. There are walnuts in the woods nearby but the squirrels always strip them bare. Nut trees are lucky, perhaps he will have two or three.

But what he knows best and what will do best on this difficult clay ground of theirs are pears. The orchard is already filled with almost forty varieties of pear but there are many more to choose from that he has not tried. Perhaps having one here against the lea of the sunny-sided wall might bring even an early variety forward in the fruiting season. Imagine that – the first ripe pear in the borough.

He ducks through the space where an oak door will sit on the hinges to be made at the blacksmith's just as soon as he can get into Ilminster, and checks the wall from this side. For a moment he is dazzled by the low sun.

'Master Lyte?' a voice rasps.

Henry almost jumps out of his skin. He blinks and sees that it is Widow Hodges, sat almost under his feet outside her dilapidated tiny cottage on a low stool, silently working withy into baskets as she does on most days when the weather permits it, though rarely in winter, when weeks can go by without her emerging as if she were dormant, or dead. To be frank he usually takes care to avoid chancing upon her, as most people do. He can never tell if she is merely old, or ancient, but she has struck an unreasonable fear in him since he was a child. Perhaps he should know more about his tenants, but there are exceptions to every rule he makes for himself.

'I saw you knocked down those pigsties, Master Lyte,' she grates out. Her voice is cracked and tired, like something left at the back of a cupboard and never used properly. 'You're not going to be doing away with my cottage?'

Henry assures her that he plans no such thing. Childishly, he tries to avert his gaze. Her wrinkled face is twisted into puckered lines and dots where her eyelids meet her cheeks. She is blind, and the eyelids themselves are flat, grotesque.

'We are going round you with the new garden wall, dame, no cause for worry,' he shouts cheerfully, backing away as if very busy with something. 'The wall runs to the back of your dwelling.'

'I heard all the noise,' she goes on saying. 'And I've been thinking about it these weeks since. It's just I've been here a long time, Master Lyte. A very long time.'

❧

It is almost All Souls', he thinks, as he goes back to his study to note down the last of his financial outgoings before the end of the month. October has flown by. There is little of note for the rest of the afternoon, bar a brief flurry of noise from the other side of the house when in the kitchen one of the servants scalds her hand on a kettle, and then the boy comes with the packhorse for his father's grain. Henry Lyte has to pay his father two bushels each of wheat and dredge malt every week to supply their household brewing and bread over at Sherborne. Sometimes he wishes that they would take a fortnight's worth at once, or more, and leave him in peace. His stepmother Joan Young (he will not call her Lyte, nor mother; she is no blood of his) declares that there is no provision for storage at their house, but Henry knows it is an excuse to keep a weekly eye on proceedings at Lytes Cary. She is becoming far too interested in it.

After this he is able to be utterly absorbed in his accounts. Henry puts aside what he needs to pay the tithingman of Kingsdon for the queensilver, which is sixteen shillings the quarter, and works out what he is owed himself on the field rents since Lammas. These accounts done, he is free to return to his work on the herbal.

As a grey evening draws in again, earlier and earlier now it is so close to Hallowtide, there is an interruptive, particular tap on his door that has become familiar to him this last fortnight, and Frances comes into the room.

'You have not lit the candle yet, Henry,' she says.

'I can see well enough.'

'They have been calling supper.' She sounds annoyed, but goes to her husband's side and touches him lightly on the shoulder. He puts down his pen and a sentence hangs unfinished; *Medewort doubtlesse drieth much, and is astringent, wherefore it restraineth and bindeth …* the word *manifestly* floats newly inked, untethered to any other on the page. It can't be helped. Her fingers are indeed very pale and smooth. What she lacks in warmth of speech, he has decided, she makes up for in other ways. Her presence glitters softly out of the corner of his eye as she picks up a pebble on his desk and turns in the gloom towards the light to examine it idly, puts it down again. She smells of subtle things, something like damask rose perhaps or musk ambrette, a dusky, milky scent that he presumes she must buy from a London perfumier in a bottle, though he likes to think it is her skin itself that secretes such promise, such difference from what he is.

He has a sudden thought of her fingers as they would be if closing round his own, against his limbs. He finds that he understands her with more clarity once the matters of the day are over. He likes the silences produced at night – the dwindling need for words and explanations. A silence lit by daylight has to be used fully, taken advantage of, but at night a silence could be simply encountered, dwelt in, quite for its own sake. He wishes that on balance it might not be unreasonable to dispense with supper altogether and suggest the bedchamber. Of course it would be very unreasonable, but he admits her presence excites his senses, distracts him.

When he lies with her at night, she does not envelop him as Anys used to, with gentle arms and her eyes appreciatively closed. Frances keeps her eyes open and fixes him with a gaze that he cannot read or enter into. He thinks it is curiosity that makes her do this, but he can't be sure. Her body is very different from Anys's, too, more taut, rawboned. She does not seem to object to him paying her proper attention in bed; indeed, more than once he has had the distinct sense this gives her a gleam in her eye, but again it is hard to be sure. His father always told him that whores are the only women who enjoy their carnal duties to the husband, and he would not like to think badly of her. For himself of course he prefers to think of it as natural procreation rather than venery.

'But what will you do with all this effort, this … learning, Henry?' she asks unexpectedly, as if puzzled. She has never asked a thing about his work before.

'Do you mean my book?' He lets her wrist go and begins to gather up the pages that are dry into a bundle.

'I mean the book, the time in the study, those letters that come, the exertion generally.' He can't see her expression.

27

'I don't have a publisher yet for my translation, but I have high hopes. My dear,' he adds briskly, as she stifles a yawn. 'Is it late? Is it white herring for supper again? No doubt it can't be helped, on a Friday. When a thing is plentiful there is always so much of it.' He wonders why his habit is to speak so loudly when he talks to her.

'Could we go up to London before Christmas?' she asks.

'London? Certainly not. There is too much to do. The roads are a nightmare.'

Neither speaks for a moment. Outside by the gate a dog is barking. A dog barking at dusk always sounds louder, he thinks, than during the day. A log slips on the fire irons, and a shower of sparks flies up the chimney.

'Why do you suppose that old woman never does her work indoors?' Frances asks.

'What woman?'

'Whom you spoke to this morning, the old basketmaker.'

Henry frowns. 'What makes you mention that?'

'I've been watching from the bedchamber window, she sits out there all day.'

'Perhaps her rafters are too low – those rods of willow reach very tall at the beginning of a basket. And you will have seen how they take up room to the sides as she weaves, her cottage must be too cramped for such activity.'

'Or perhaps she needs the brighter daylight to properly see what she is doing.'

'She is blind. Her eyelids have been sewn shut for nearly thirty years.'

'Oh!' Frances flinches at the thought.

There is a silence. Really he'd prefer to start a new page of his translation, but he cannot do it with Frances standing by him. He cuts a nib for later. He might get up to *fleabane* by tomorrow. *Hote and dry in the third degree.* It is going to take him ten years or more at this rate.

'How did she become blind?' Frances asks.

'Mmm?'

'The old woman.'

'I've no idea.' There is something vaguely tugging at his memory as he says that, something odd and unpleasant from way back when he was a boy, but then it is gone. He does remember the talk around the time that they sewed her lids shut to cover up the mutilation.

'I was away at school but they said her screeching was heard right down on the Fosse Way. After that when I was disobedient I thought that the redness I saw when I shut my eyes was God showing me the colour of blood, a warning not to cast my gaze unheedingly upon wicked things. I always thought she must have seen some wicked thing to get like that.' He shrugs, looking at his manuscript. 'The savage, unfair minds of children.'

'I can't imagine a noise like that coming from her.' Frances is still at the window.

'She's got a stone's silence about her most days. Squatting there in the middle of her webs, though like most old women she can also pounce on a man with unsolicited speeches, if he should forget to go by the other path. How she knows who it is that's passing is any man's guess, but she always does.'

Once a month Henry sees Widow Hodges at the market in Somerton, selling her baskets. He's seen her struggling up onto the cart pulled by a decrepit skewbald that another old woman, with whom she shares profits, drives over from Kingsdon. Years ago, he used to see her plying her wares further afield, such as the St Paul's Day Fair at Bristol, but she is too old now for such distances.

'Maybe she does need the light to work by. I've heard some can see the brightness of the sun. There are degrees of blindness, Henry. Many different kinds.'

'There are many different kinds of spider.'

He thinks of her as sat at the heart of a web. He can't help it. Even though she is blind, when he goes by her cottage he has a suspicion that she has an inward eye on him, some kind of sentient finger or whisker stretched out to feel the twitch of his passing. There is something about the way she cocks her head as he approaches that makes him shiver, without a pause in the rhythm of her fingers catching the withies, knotting them down, netting his details.

# V.

*Of MOUSE EARE. A man may finde amongst the*
*writers of the Egyptians, that if a bodie be rubbed in the*
*morning early, before he hath spoken, at the first*
*entrance of the moneth of August with this hearbe, that*
*all the next yéere he shall not be grieved with bleared or*
*sore eyes.*

**H**ENRY LYTE HAS GONE OVER TO WELLS to buy various items. He wants to go himself rather than send a servant, for he has heard that his old friend Peter Turner is in town staying with his father – the radical Dean of Wells Cathedral, and botanist of note, Dr William Turner. The ride over is back-endish, yellowing stalks collapsing over the paths, the sweet smell of fruit and rot everywhere, too many insects. He is glad that he still has the Turners to discuss matters of botany with. Another good friend Thomas Penny – in whom he had a fellow fieldworker, together scouring the West Country and elsewhere thoroughly for plant specimens – has just gone to Zurich because Archbishop Parker believes him to be too outspoken against the church. Dr Turner is outspoken too, but somehow retains his position here as Dean of the cathedral since his return from exile in

Germany during the dark time of Mary. 'So far, so good,' he'd grinned the last time he'd seen him, as though it was all a conspiracy, or luck.

As Henry winds through the busy, dirty marketplace, the booths, the standings, flesh shambles and fish shambles, towards the cathedral, the clock strikes ten and he realizes he's going to be too early. He scratches his beard, which feels itchy and unkempt, and decides to go to the barber for a trim. He dismounts and turns his horse around. The sky to the west is dark with impending rain, though the sun is out, so that the stone of Penniless Porch shines yellow by contrast. A beggar is lying inside the arch, his face blotched with sores and clutching his stomach as if he had some griping torment there. Henry hopes it is not dysentery. A woman passing by grimaces at her companion.

'Look at that, poor man, he is in pain,' she says.

'But they are used to being like that. Quite accustomed. I need to get a pigeon before we go back. Or two. Do you think we need two?' She checks in her basket then looks down at the beggar. 'It is different for them. They don't know any better, just as well. They are like animals in that respect.'

'It is a shame.'

'One must pray for them,' she says brightly. 'There is nothing else anyone can do about it.'

'Nothing,' the other woman concurs, and they glide on towards the market and the pigeon stall. Henry feels the blood rushing in his ears. He has an urge to run after them and try to make them see how they are wrong, but instead goes swiftly to the beggar and on the same, furious impulse gives him the first coin that he fishes from his pouch, which is a half-sovereign, a great amount of money to give to any man in the street or otherwise, more than a skilled mason earns in a week. The beggar's eyes widen, and even as he puts it into the outstretched bandaged, filthy hands Henry has a spasm of doubt, but it is too late.

'Bless you, Master, it is a sign!' The beggar mutters, rubbing the coin against his cracked lips. He jerks a finger at the sky, and to the west now a rainbow is stretched inkily over the whole of the town, so vivid with colour it almost fizzes in the sky. He must be right. Surely this must be a good omen.

Fat drops of rain begin to spot the dry compacted earth of the thoroughfare as the sunshine fades. People jostle to take shelter under the porch, and when he turns about, the beggar has vanished.

Half a sovereign.

He had better not mention that to anyone, not Frances, not Dr Turner, he decides. But by the time he has arrived at the house, it is already weighing so heavily upon him that he must say something. The boy removes his horse to the livery and another poor man follows him up to the gate and pulls at his sleeve most insistently until he finds a coin to make him go away. He is more careful this time, makes sure it is a penny.

Turner's naughty little dog comes to greet him, yapping at his heels. Turner has trained it to jump up and remove the corner-caps of bishops at table. Turner hates ecclesiastical trappings; the pomp and ceremony of the high church. He also hates his bishop, which is making life difficult in Wells, but Turner has always prided himself on his ability to thrive on controversy.

He rises from his desk to kiss Henry.

'You've missed Peter,' he says. 'Oxford drew him back a day early, as he leaves very shortly for Heidelberg and has things to wrap up before his departure.'

Henry Lyte is disappointed, everyone is going somewhere, it would seem, and he is sorry not to have the chance to say adieu to Peter. But it is always engaging to spend time in William Turner's house. There is always something very obstructing to debate, some nuisance ignorant with a bad opinion holding his own torch wrongly.

'People are so easily offended,' William Turner complains, waving a letter. 'Do they have no resistance of their own that my view can rake up theirs like ponds so hastily?' Henry Lyte smiles. He has many a time had his own self raked over by Dr Turner, but he has learnt to live with it; there is too much to gain from being with him.

Dr Turner peppers his speech rapidly with Latin and Greek, so that Henry, who is much more comfortable with French, has to concentrate hard to keep abreast of him. Often in Turner's company he wishes he had paid closer attention to his studies whilst at Oxford. University is wasted on the young, he has decided, without strict guidance. He was too occupied with pacing between the taverns of the town in a long coat drinking malmsey until the small hours of the night and sleeping with doxies, though he did read every volume of Dioscorides, Matthiolus, Galen, Pliny that he could. A normal existence, anyway by all accounts. 1546, when he left and married Anys, daughter of John Kelloway of Cullumpton, was the year in which all that ground to a halt and his responsibilities seemed to begin, sharply.

'Have you begun that work you crow so often about? Your *opus de singulis*?' Dr Turner is a demanding man, who will not let a thing pass once mentioned.

'You mean the translation of Rembert's herbal? I have started it. It is quite slow to get going.'

'I am waiting for the competition!' His laughter is hoarse but not unkind. He considers Henry when the mirth has left him. 'You will need to be very contained to write that book, young man. There will be times when you must shut your ears and eyes to anything outside the vessel of your undertaking. And once you are done, the dissatisfaction with it will pour in from all sides. Easier to find fault with a wheel already rolling than it is to build one up from raw timbers.'

Dr Turner's eye has a little more white about it than one might expect in a calmer man. He is old now, but they say he was once very handsome, like an ox in his prime.

'I think it will take me a long time. It mentions eight hundred varieties of plant. Not only does it have to be translated accurately from

34

the French, I shall need to seek out every single name in English, which part I believe shall be the hardest.'

'There will be much scholarship in its making. You may achieve it.'

'I don't know, Doctor, I—'

'You will need to be tenacious. But there is something of the limpet in you. Not a fast mover on your rock, but you cling on tight.' Henry bridles, quick to sense criticism where perhaps none is intended.

'Should I speed up, Doctor, how should I do that?'

'Drink more hare's piss.' Dr Turner's back is to him as he searches for a book he needs shortly for a service, then starts away down the corridor.

'What kind of advice is that?' Henry calls, aggrieved. His diminishing back looks square and spiky in its black church garb that doesn't fit about the shoulders. He has no patience for a tailor fiddling about him, and it is clear his wife has but hasty measurements to pass on for an impossible task. Dr Turner is not a man who glides his way to anything. His sermons are punctuated with enraged jabs as though even the air itself between him and his congregation needed prodding into discipline. He is not a man with whom you'd dare to share a lukewarm half-thought unprepared, unless you felt like being torn into tiny pieces for the evening's sport.

'Come,' he says, and beckons Henry Lyte to follow him downstairs. 'There is something I must show you.'

The doctor is showing signs of his age, and stumbles on the path out into the garden. This labour of his latter years has paid off in the shape of a most glorious plot to the south of his house, with a small orchard of the choicest variety of fruits, and a horseshoe of beds laid out to herbs and flowers in the final states of blooming, though most are tatty and seeded into heads or fruiting now. In a few days there will be frosts and all will be blackened, but for now these latter-end herbs still cling to their season.

Dr Turner stops by a low wall and points into a browning, damp tangle of small climbing herbs that have colonized the stones over the summer and are dying back.

'What do you see there, Henry? Does a thing strike you?'

Henry Lyte gets down on his knees and obligingly blinks and peers. 'Well, Doctor, I ...'

'No doubt you see remnants of pennyroyal, *Pulegium*, and mosses of various sorts and a little bit of old unwanted yellowing *Aegopodium podagraria* that I must speak to my garden man about, and something else, Henry.' His voice drops. 'What is it?'

Henry Lyte is aware that the knees of his hose are very wet now from pressing at the lawn. A small fat spider, her belly full of eggs, is climbing up a crown of murrey-coloured stalks. 'I see herb Robert,' he says eventually. 'Flowering late, in your sheltered haven.' Dr Turner cackles then and rubs his crabby hands together.

'You do! *Geranium robertianum* is a humble little herb that, as Dioscorides has told us, is to staunch the blood of green wounds and is used against corrupt sores and ulcers of the paps and privy members. And here, nestled as to its custom against the wall, and its purple-pinkish five-fold petals ... Ah! And you have seen it for yourself at last.' Dr Turner's face is shining at the sight of Henry Lyte's astonishment. He squeezes his hands together now as if in fervent prayer, and cocks his grizzled head on one side to hear the answer. 'What is its difference?'

'This flower is white, where it should be purple. Every single flowerhead upon its stalks is white as snow. I cannot believe such a deviation is possible without intervention, a natural anomaly.' Henry Lyte cannot take his eyes away from it. 'What does this mean, for scientific study, for our understanding of the way that nature takes its forms?'

'It means that the Holy Spirit takes many guises, and does not eschew a humble weed to show that the power to change things takes many forms, and can begin in simple ways, in obscure corners. Not for nothing do the country people call this plant *poor Robert*. I say it is God's way of showing how nothing is fixed – that this earth is *in fluxus*: a constant state of being made, of being in change. This is a glorious thing, yet found in a moist and shady corner which our eyes are trained to overlook. The same ignorants might say this is the work of malevolent, unchristian spirits such as Robin Goodfellow, appearing in disguise to mock God's choices. You and I, Henry, are here to prove that this is never the case. We do not deal in falsehoods, you and I. We are true scientists, *physicus*, studying the work of God. Only what we see before us can be verified, with the exception of the will of God itself. Nothing is to be taken for granted. Only God's will is absolute.

Henry feels a flicker of doubt.

'But, if—'

'It means, take nothing for granted, Master Lyte. Apply all your powers of observation in your work. If you do it thoroughly, your work will be of use to someone.' Dr Turner's outsize, drooping sleeves hide knobbled, twisted hands with fingers like root vegetables, and when he prods one's chest to instil a point, it is almost painful. Henry Lyte tries not to flinch or rub the spot.

'I am worried, Doctor. I saw a beggar in the porch as I came here this morning and—'

'What use is that, Henry?' he barks. 'Whether or not you worry about some man in the street you saw in passing makes no difference. It is what you do next that counts. Otherwise it is a form of vanity and odious self-reflection.'

'I did worse than that, I gave the man a large quantity of money, and then he disappeared. I can't explain, but I do feel very bad about it,' he says. He know that sounds weak-willed. He is irresponsible, a bad citizen, worse than those women for at least they, in their ugly, easy complacency, did not actually go out of their way to court trouble for the man. He pictures the beggar made vulnerable with that gold in his hand, killed for it by other beggars, vagabonds or lawless rufflers. He pictures him in the tavern drinking it off in a night, and dying of drink. And who would know?

Dr Turner leans forward on his stick so that Henry can see up close the very substance of his face. It is like a natural exclamation of rage. Hair sprouts from his nostrils, his eyes are red-rimmed. 'It is not about salving your conscience, Henry. It is about changing things. You have been blessed with certain privileges, and in the eyes of God you must employ them in ways that create a change. I was brought up where the stink of the tannery permeated every crack of life, every breath, each mouthful of food. I was inured to its poison, and yet I never wish to forget what poison is or what it does to men. There are many different kinds of poverty, Henry,' Dr Turner says. 'Who are you or I to say that one man's suffering is worse than another man's. It is not our task to judge between sufferings, only to help where relief can be given. Your man may well have made those sores himself by laying irritants like spearwort or crowsfoot upon his members, a known practice in these parts amongst their kind. But what else is he to do, being whipped from parish to parish? With no home to speak of. Poverty is the visible, residual poison of a bad society, it eats away at the lives of those who have little or cannot help themselves.' He pushes his cap about on his head.

'These changes in the Church are not moving fast enough to reinstate an antidote. All this mealy-mouthed absolution and confession that we've lived with for too long has made us lazy.' He snorts. 'That's not a way to improve the world, is it? People don't like to hear that. How much easier it was to go to a priest, smell the frankincense, bleat unworthiness and be absolved like infants. Cut into a Catholic's flesh and be warned, you may see whey running from the wound instead of blood.'

Henry looks shocked.

Turner flaps his hand dismissively. 'There is still too much Romish pox about.'

'If a man has to make amends how can he properly go about it, if he is not to just hand out bits of gold?'

'By making an *effort*.' Never had such a simple word sounded so menacing and unachievable.

'God gave you hands, didn't he?' Turner holds open his own palms skywards as if to be inspected.

'Use them!'

Henry's ears are ringing all the way home.

# VI.

*Of TUTSAN or PARKE LEAVES. At the top of the stalks*
*groweth small knops or round buttons which bring forth*
*floures like St Johns grasse, when they are fallen or*
*perished there appeareth litle small pelets very red, like*
*to the colour of clotted or congealed dry blood, in which*
*berries is contained the seede. The roote is hard and of*
*wooddy substance, yeerely sending forth new springs.*

THE GREAT FROSTS HAVE COME. The fields and hedges are white and the early morning air in the ribbon of valley beneath the slope is quick with birds. The redwings are here, getting down to the business of stripping the last of the haws, and filling the hedges with a gregarious, weighty presence that sets the squirrels chattering angrily. Crisp, seeded heads of wild angelica are spiky with crystals.

Henry walks down to Broadmead to cast an eye over the cattle. They should be brought in for the winter now; they stand cold and miserable in the hoary grass, breath in clouds about them. He must talk to his stockman. He walks on and stops by the Cary, the little course that runs down off the Mendip, through Somerton and winds out across the Levels. There is vapour rising from the river. One

40

moorhen nervily shrugs itself through the water at the edge near the overhanging reedy bank, black plumage against the blackish water, a faint wake the only clue to its movement.

He calls in at the barton to see it is ready for cows, and then goes back up the hill to eat with his family. He takes a shortcut across the back of Horse Close, and then without thinking turns past Widow Hodges's place. Rounding the corner of the new wall he comes across her suddenly, weaving a wide-mouthed, greenish basket in the cold without looking at her hands, as if they had a way of their own and could work on without her.

'Good day to you, Master Lyte,' she says. Her nose is running. Her hands are very pale in the November light, almost flashing as they move, twisting withy against withy. The flickering lids of her eyes are very dark and seem to latch on to his movement as he passes, as a hawk's gaze might, fixing to the warmblooded gait of rabbits. He is unwilling to put his back to her, and turns once to raise his hand absurdly as he bids her good morning.

It is warm in the hall by comparison. He stamps the frost from his boots. Hannah has boiled black puddings and somehow the cold makes them all seem even more delicious.

'That woman gives me the shivers, Frances,' he complains.

'Your Widow Hodges? All men find old women disconcerting, Henry.' Frances is amused. 'Once past childbearing age, a woman's use is ill-defined even if working, particularly if she has no husband to tend. Men are unsettled by their ugliness. They are afraid of withered things.'

'Gardeners are afraid of withered things,' Henry concedes, going off to his unformed Knot.

It is good to stand up straight after two hours' digging and to quench his thirst with a long draught from the flagon Mote's boy brings him, instead of waiting, tetchy, inside at his desk, for the slop-slop of the maidservant's stepping up the corridor. The lawns are steaming where the sun hits the frost. He wipes his mouth. He needs to decide what shrubs to plant for the low, trimmed hedges that will form the body of the Knot.

He has considered the cost of bringing down from London some of the newly introduced box-tree. They say *Buxus* is best planted at this time of year, and he is tempted, because the hedges of box he saw in France and Holland were firm and densely foliated, and agreeably disposed to being clipped into shapes. But they also say it has little use in medicine, and with its reeking, astringent smell like cat's piss it could prove a mistake for his garden. Hyssop, though apt to grow straggly, has a mildly aromatic charm of its own, and many virtues.

Henry sits down on the upturned new waterbutt, just delivered from the coopers, and examines the progress so far. The bricklayers finished their final course last week, and the garden wall stands ruddy and crisp. Tobias Mote's children are clearing up the hardened bits of lime mortar all along its base. The joiners over at Kingsdon are measuring up now for the pair of doors.

Henry calls over to Mote. 'Has the smith sent in his bill for the ironwork?'

'Not yet. I can fetch the hinges in the afternoon if you're in a hurry for them.'

'I'd like to get them as soon as possible because the trees will be in soon and those doors will keep out nibblers.'

Mote crosses the sea of opened earth.

'I've been thinking,' he says. He takes off his soft cap and scratches his head. 'It's only that there are a few things we should mind.' He pauses.

'Like?'

'Like we're getting a bit forward of ourselves.'

'Are we?'

'That plot needs a lot of husbanding before it's fit. If you want the handsomest plants you'll need, well, diligence.'

'What are you saying, Mote?' Henry sighs inwardly. 'I sense a dampening of enthusiasms coming on.'

'It would not be seemly to start planting this year.'

Henry raises his eyebrows.

'It wouldn't harm to put in some trees, perhaps, come a month or two, but we ought to be getting the soil in better fettle and, as it is, that ground is overbound with clay. There's still thorough clearing to be done, look at that ashweed, and setting our minds firmly to the shape of it all. We can't do that if we're fiddling around with plants already put in, and bits of earth already committed over to being sown or set with slips. It'd be an evil mess in my estimation.'

Henry is thinking that he couldn't remember asking Mote for his thoughts on the matter.

'It's a big job, Master. It's not just a few dainty pot-herbs in a frame.'

Henry doesn't need reminding of the scale of his task. He sighs again, louder this time. It's just that the idea of a desolate unplanted mudbath outside the house for a twelve-month is not appealing. He pictures the rainwater puddling on the walkways and the creep of the most voracious sort of weeds colonizing the blank spaces; thistles, docks, running grasses. And then after almost a year's worth of decrepitude and neglect, once everything was waterlogged and become prone to yellow mosses and vermin, the frost would descend, unmitigated by any sheltering stalks or the overreach of wintered shrubs; needling down with violent, icy precision to split the lias paving slabs asunder, the earthenware pots he hasn't bought yet, this very waterbutt.

'It'll fly by,' Mote says, rubbing his hands together, as if it were all settled. 'Time won't lie long on us, as for the while we can hoe what comes up, and we'll get the gang back to turn in the dung after St Martin's feast in a two-week's time. We'll still need a fair portion of the dung over in the kitchen garden as well, remember, Master. It's what's needed most for a fair, well-dressed earth.'

'Are you saying there may not be enough?'

Tobias Mote shrugs cheerfully. 'And that all depends.'

'On what?'

'On whether you carry on with all those roses you've got a mind for is the truth, Master. They're hungry buggers for the dung.'

Henry winces. 'I see. Well we can buy in more from somewhere, can we?'

'Probably.' He chuckles. 'Though that'll get them talking.'

He can see that it would. He imagines the gossip at the market; *have you heard? They're buying in shit up at Lytes Cary.* He imagines the sucked-in breath and shaken heads. *Whatever next? It'll be all over anyway, come the frosts, for those fancy plants.* It makes him annoyed, the way he cares about what other people think.

'But it's not just the roses, Master, is it. It's that we've got a ground here that is cold and stiff, which we can make more lively by the digging in of hot dung.'

'Not near the rosemary,' Henry adds.

'Nor the carrots,' Mote says, thinking of all his duties, 'the carrots most particular. But the nature of this closed-up soil will be warmed and loosened if we keep on with it. If we can find more dung to see us through this year at least.'

'I may send word over to the Lockyer's. They have so many horses at livery they are bound to have a surplus to requirements.'

'Horse dung is only any use if it has stood a year.'

'I know that.'

'Or it burns.'

'Yes,' Henry says. What is this goddammed habit Mote has, of trying to teach him all the time.

Over where the plum orchard is to be the Sorcerer shrieks manically, and it still sounds horribly like laughter.

'We'll turn in that dung, like you say, and we'll be half-there already.' Henry says, and then feels suddenly nettled into resolution.

'You know what? By spring we'll be planting in it.' He claps his hands together. 'Let's get cracking.'

Tobias Mote looks startled. He chews a corner of his grimy thumb and then nods secretly, imperceptibly to himself as if it was all to be expected.

'I've a lot on my hands, then. I'll need at least another boy to help me, if that kitchen garden up there is to feed more than a nest of starvelings,' he says. 'And if it gets too much, well.' He spreads his hands out wide to show the true reach of his feelings, and pretends to yawn, his grey teeth showing. 'There's sundry other gardens in the parish could do with tending.'

This is certainly true.

'Blackmail,' Henry says. It's not as though he hasn't already considered the situation he could find himself in without a competent gardener. He can't do this thing on his own. But Henry is definitely bothered by Tobias Mote. He does not match up to expectations. He does not pause between spadefuls of earth and consider the weather evenly and at length. He laughs too much. He has opinions.

Yet he has been here for very many years and knows the soil like one of his family. His father had been stockman here for most of his working life until his death, and Tobias had grown up running in the meadows with the kine. He knows what the very grass on this clay soil tastes like from field to field. He knows about the particular way of the wind here, and the likely pattern of rain and the sheltered places. He'd first learnt his gardening from his mother, whose patch was the most burgeoning in the village, and a husbanding man called Colleyns, who he had gone to as a boy about sixteen when he knew he preferred pears to driving cattle down to the other side of Pricklemarch Bridge, say. Tobias Mote has been gardening this soil at Lytes Cary for nigh-on thirty years. Henry knows that he would be foolish to deliberately lose a man's skills just like that.

'Would another four shillings a year make all the difference to your sense of optimism about this project?'

'It would,' Mote says to the sky in general, without a trace of irony, without turning round.

Some little brown thing is flicking up leaf mould – a wren, a mouse – they look the same sometimes from the corner of one's eye. That reminds him, he needs to set traps tonight. As soon as the cold weather comes, mice are all over the house, getting into the pantry, the stores, behind the panelling.

'Master?' Tobias Mote scratches his neck, then stops.

'What?' Surely to God he won't ask for more.

'It's just that there's a bit of talk going about. Not much, only a word or two. I just was wondering …'

'What?' Henry says coldly.

'If you knew of it, and if there is a way it might be stopped.'

Henry is in no mood to discuss family matters with his gardener. 'I have heard nothing about anything,' he says, 'and do not care for it.'

'You don't care to know what they are saying?'

'I do not listen to the wigwag of idle tongues.'

'Alright.' Mote shrugs in a way that suggests he will try again later, and carries on with his spade. 'It's just that—'

'No!' Henry rounds on him. 'There is too much to do today for all this. Far too much.'

'I'm going for my dinner soon,' Mote warns him, unnecessarily. 'It's already late.'

And so it is. The day passes very quickly, and it seems no time at all before a fat, white moon has shot up into the sky with startling rapidity, shrinking as it does so, and its gaze seems harder, more judgmental, up there above the alder, than it had all vastly soft and gaping down on the horizon. Tobias Mote goes off down the path towards Tuck's, he is small and spry and lithe. He is not at all what Henry imagines a gardener to be. This vexes him more than he can put into words, but he tries anyway, complaining to his wife over meals and in bed.

'A gardener should be big-handed, slow, move steadily like a root moves in the soil, not flitting quick and tense between the beds, perspiring freely, energy bounding out of him with every springing step. Damn it, Frances, that man almost *crackles* about the garden. Will that be bad for the plants?'

He wants Frances to laugh then, and get up from her chair and go to him to soothe his troubled feelings and gather him into her fine encircling arms, and suggest an early retirement to bed for the night, but she does not; she is playing at being the dutiful wife. Instead he watches her bite a length of her thread from the reel and hold the needle close to her face to see its narrow impossible eye in the candle-light. He feels desire kindling in him as she puts the end of the thread in her mouth and makes it firm and damp between her lips, and then the thread is through. Henry looks despondently at the interminable hem she is stitching along, and knows there will be no consolation to be had from her tonight. It is not that she is shy, or reticent about her new role as a wife, and she even listens to him as she works, something it must be admitted that Anys did not always do. But he is finding that her poise and coolness disconcert him on a daily basis.

She has very good teeth, he thinks, looking into the fire, at least he has that to be grateful for.

# VII.

*Of SHEPHEARDS PURSE. It hath sound, tough and pliable branches, of a fote long, with long leaves, deeply cut or jagged. The floures are white, in place whereof when they are gone, there riseth small flat cods, or triangled pouches, wherein the seede is contained.*

C HRISTMAS AND TWELFTH NIGHT have been and gone, but scraps of ivy and mistletoe are still up in the hall. They drive Henry mad, everywhere he treads, little, limp leaves beneath his feet, but it's been a pleasure to have a reason to open up a vat of Gascon wine, and make spiced hot hippocras by the fireside, share it out on those cold, stark nights. They all survived the tenants' feast and there were no disagreements. The girls enjoyed the juggler that came on Boxing Day and Old Hannah surpassed herself with tarts, roast meats and suckets, though Frances didn't seem to enjoy the Christmastide victuals as much as he did. He hopes she is not sickening for something, as wintertime is not ideal for having doctor's visits in the night, the roads can be treacherous.

No word though from his father during this time, which is a source of great sadness to him. He had sent a fat goose over to

Sherborne, but received no word in return. He always misses his mother at Christmas, and he observes the girls and knows how much they must miss theirs, too, though they never complain. Anys loved games at Christmas. Of course after she died Mary in particular was inconsolable, crying for hours on end, clinging onto her poppet. Florence was just a newborn. Jane did not speak. Edith, the eldest, bustled about the younger ones, in fact he hardly saw her, but even she has a look in her eye still that he finds hard to describe, except that it is like a dullness, as though some essence in her had died away.

The memory of his own mother Edith is now so eclipsed by the disagreeable nature of his relationship with his father's second wife Joan Young that Edith Lyte appears only occasionally as a kind of improbable saint in his imagination. Sometimes he dreams of her as a white, cloudy horse leaping over his head, and the leaps are like steam pouring through air. In these dreams his horse-mother never lands, is always vaulting the hedges, legs stretched mid-jump, so that he sees the underbelly, the pale unshod hoofs. In the dreams he does not know if she can see him standing there below her, his small boy's face tilted up to the dark sky, studded with stars. Sometimes he knows her view of him would be obscured by trees even if she should look down, he netted in shadow, rooted in shadow, his leather boots sunk an inch into mud on the track so that he cannot move from the lea of the withy hedge, its overhang.

His father is becoming a stranger to him. In the last few months they have exchanged cursory messages about land matters, church dues, administration, crops and tenancies, but not a word between them about family life, no ordinary pleasantries. He has never asked after Henry's new wife's health, and never refers to her by name, in fact Henry is not sure he has ever mentioned her at all. He has many feelings about all of this, most of which he pushes to one side and declines to think on. But when he receives word to expect his father on Tuesday next he has no choice but to recognize the state of things between his father and himself.

It has to be said, he is not sure of his motives for coming. John Lyte's health is not good and the ride over from Sherborne may not be comfortable for him, but according to the short letter he has sent, he insists on coming to discuss the proposed sale of various cows while prices are strong. Henry knows that he wants to check on the estate, make sure that Lytes Cary is not suffering in his son's hands. In turn, Henry is looking forward to imparting good news about the ditches, which have been cleared already, and have him savour last season's cider, which is exceptional. Henry always strives to please his father: this time it seems vital, and as a small chink of light falls onto that ignored, closed corner of his life which his father occupies, he begins to wonder. He wishes … oh, it is no matter what he wishes. No doubt it will all die down or be smoothed over and forgotten before long. The childish dependent part of him hopes the visit is a reconciliatory one, in which his father plans to apologize for not attending the wedding.

At the same time he resents the way this makes him feel. He wants it all to go away and leave him to get on with the real project in his mind; his garden, his pride. He wants to talk of it with his father but something prevents him, and he thinks they will not walk around to that side of the house to show off the new walls and ironwork and open beds. Though every other ounce of him cries out to try to impress his father, he would prefer to wait until the garden has found its balance, until its own presence has become distinct. He does not want his father's disapproval spoiling his enthusiasm, and most of all he does not want Joan Young prying into the cost and workings of it all, criticizing his choice of rose, his taste, his usefulness, his ambitions.

Indeed he is hoping that Joan will stay behind, because her presence in the house makes the servants behave erratically in front of his father, which makes it seem as if he cannot properly restrain his household. At least that is what occurred on the last occasion that she came, over a year ago. It had been unfortunate, for example, that a large, black fly the size and furriness of a bumble bee had drowned itself in her glass and bobbed unnoticed all the way from the kitchen to her place at table.

In his reply to his father's letter he had not extended a courteous wish to see his stepmother. For several nights he lies in bed at night agonizing over whether he might be making a mistake by not inviting her, and then again, is he making one if he does?

All this browbeating proves to be a waste of time, because even as he spies the newfangled, painted carriage that she insisted that his father purchase lurching up the drive, he can see from the dark, malevolent shape wrapped beside him that they will not be left alone together, that she has come. It is St Vincent's day; the patron saint of drunkards, he thinks wryly, and as they approach he steels himself for the abomination of her company, summons the cheerful greeting he has rehearsed.

'Father!' he calls up, but he can see the discomfort all over his face already. His hand raises stiffly in the air, more like a warding-off than a greeting.

When he descends they embrace briefly, but then his gaze looks everywhere but at Henry. Blackie runs round the horses, barking, providing distraction.

'Madam,' he bows to his stepmother.

Their distaste for each other is entirely mutual. When she smiles her ghastly wooden teeth at him, it is more as if she was grinding them together. A very fast, small woman, she clambers unaided from the carriage and beetles straight across the porch threshold and disappears into the passage towards the kitchens, her sleeves trailing. No one has worn sleeves like that for twenty years. Dressed in cloth of that inky purple hue, and with her nose turned blue at the tip from the breeze on the ride, she has always looked to him like death on legs; cadaverously alive. He had detested her manner from the moment she entered their lives when he was younger; she would coil herself around his father like she owned him, in an offensive way his mother would never have wished or dared to do. In his blackest, most resentful moments, he has thought of her like rootless Devil's Thread, wrapping its strands about the crop plants in the fields, strangling all hospitable life from them. Now though he knows to call her parasite would be disrespectful to his father. She is kin.

'Henry?' He can hear her shrieking for him. 'Henry! Is this beef we are having today?'

'I hardly know, madam, I—' Henry stands awkwardly at the kitchen doorway, trying to avoid the glower of Old Hannah, standing by the fire with her basting spoon in hand. 'It is not my business to poke about in there.'

'It won't be done on time, you know we're hungry after the ride. Look at that fire.'

'You are very early. Perhaps—'

'Where's that wife of yours?'

'She is … upstairs, madam, and will be with us shortly.' Henry knows that Frances will be in her chamber, staving off that minute when she must glide down the staircase like the lady of the house she is, and greet her mother-in-law with gracious if entirely feigned obeisance.

He goes to the foot of the stairs and looks up but does not call. He is not sure but thinks he hears a door being slammed at the end of the corridor. He hopes there might be a kind of unspoken solidarity between them both now that Joan Young is in the house – perhaps the only feeling that they share, but some men would have less to boast of. He takes a deep breath and goes back to the hall, to seat his father according to the rules of honour. He feels stifled with anxiety, his throat so tight he can hardly get simple niceties and phrases out. His girls appear one by one and curtsey properly before they take their places, which is a relief, and even though the guests have arrived so appallingly early Old Hannah manages almost immediately to produce a first course of roast fowls and salad, but after this it is unfortunate that the beef takes a long time to appear, and so does Frances.

'Where is that wife? Does she exist? Of course she does, I can *smell* there's a woman about the house,' Joan says, pushing her plate about impatiently.

'I do dislike a hiatus in a meal,' she hisses to Edith, sitting next to her at table. 'A gap can feel so dissatisfactory. It is fortunate that nobody important dines with us today.' She casts her eye glassily round the hall, though as Henry Lyte knows she is short of sight, she will not have focussed much on anyone.

After all that fuss, she doesn't eat much, helping herself to meat but draining the juice away with the edge of her spoon against the bowl as though the dish is too watery, turning the loaf suspiciously to check the underside for mould, rifling through a salad of winter cresses to find the choicest pieces of bottled artichoke, only to fling them back with a bitter little sigh and eat nothing. Though she does like bones, sucking the last little fibres of meat from them, snapping them to get at any traces of marrow concealed inside.

When Henry enquires after the journey, she runs through a tedious itinerary of the way they had taken, and how poor the roads in this part of the country, how hopeless the route chosen and how slow the horse.

His father, who until this point has not uttered a word, puts his knife down.

'That carriage was a mistake,' he mutters.

'No John,' she snaps, in front of everyone. 'It was that the horse was inadequate.'

Nobody else seems to blanch at the way she speaks to her husband before company. For a second he catches Jane's eye, and then when he looks at his father he sees a small red patch, the size of a coin, flare up on his left cheekbone. Even when the conversation veers towards the matters of local taxation that usually rouse his father to table-thumping vehemence, he toys with his table knife in silence. Either he is feeling unwell or he, too, has something heavy weighing on his conscience or his family affairs. Henry looks across at his own offspring and tries to imagine their roles in reverse. He is a very different kind of father, isn't he? But after all, children rarely consider the innermost feelings of parents, indeed they do not seem to have them, which is the natural order of things.

The girls are very quiet during this visit. Jane in particular says not a word, she sits still through the meal; bowing her head as they say grace, eating neatly what is put on her plate, dabbling her fingers clean in the waterbowl. She is occupied in watching, taking in what-ever strangeness it is happening just under the surface in all of them, her eyes flicking between the adult faces as they speak. Henry wonders how she can be aware that something is wrong. On the surface this is a perfectly ordinary family day. After all, nobody else could possibly know that there was such a storm swilling inside him. Why should they? Any guilt or resentment is entirely his own, entirely invisible.

Joan Young. Even her name is a contradiction, she is the furthest from young a body could ever be, representing for him all that is shrivelled, bitter, hardened. There is a shallow stream he knows up on the Mendip which, if one drops a stick or small object in its flow, with alarming rapidity will grow a crust of greyish lime about it, as hard and coarse as any stone. He imagines that someone caught habitually in her presence could suffer a similar fate, because stoniness exudes from her very soul, like a contagion. He can see it slowly afflicting his father, a callous skin edging across his being. Looking at his father is like looking at himself as he would appear in twenty years if he had a crust of stone grown over him.

Frances is the last to join them at the table, in fact she is distinctly late by the time she glides into her seat. Henry is not sure if she has done this on purpose, even though she is very pale. He hopes she doesn't have the green sickness, from which his sister used to suffer.

'Ah!' his father says, rising briefly as she takes her chair beside Henry.

'I've always been a good riser,' Joan Young remarks.

'Even when expecting, madam?' Frances smiles sweetly at the nearest child and takes some bread from the basket, and then the long-awaited beef course arrives and there is much chatter and diversion.

Henry looks at her astounded.

No-one else seems to have heard what she said. What is the matter with everyone, are they deaf? And though he keeps on staring at her through the rest of the meal she does not speak again after that, and the conversation veers towards his father's lawyer who is unwell. When they have finished eating Henry follows her down the corridor into the kitchen and closes the door.

'Madam, did you mean to—'

'Shhh.' She puts her finger up to her lips and smiles, her eyes dancing.

'That's all you can say? You can't leave a man unsure over something like that! I beg you!'

She touches his arm. 'We'll see. I am rarely so late with my courses, and I have begun to feel sick these last few days. But it may be nothing.' She will say no more.

Henry's heart is racing inside his chest with familiar apprehension and hope. 'A child!' he whispers to Blackie, who thumps the stub of her tail once on the flagstones. This time it will surely be different. His new wife's first baby.

Henry pays slightly less attention to the rest of the day than he should. Ignoring his father's reticence, he goes with him anyway to examine his windmill up in Cowleaze field though the tenant is out, then they skirt across to Inmead. Though they stand and look out at the view to the wet moorfields, they do not speak, and as his father does not ask about the trees he does not tour the orchards with him as Henry had planned. Indeed they do not do anything he planned; he feels rather superfluous, as though he were following his father about in the same, slavish manner as Blackie, trotting at his heels. His mind is elsewhere now, though, and he is almost grateful when the horses are got ready early and his father and stepmother leave despite the special supper being prepared.

The very house itself seems to let out a sigh of relief to see Joan Young gone, as the carriage containing her pulls mercifully out of the yard and onto the track towards the road, trundling back off to Sherborne again where she belongs. His father had not mentioned, Henry realizes, any sale of cows.

He goes straight to the parlour to find Frances, to examine her closely for clues.

'Well,' he says. 'That was not a complete disaster, was it.'

'Is there no stone which that woman will leave unturned?' she exclaims, quite amazed at Joan Young's rudeness even though she had been warned.

'Probably not. But she is your mother-in-law, and there is nothing to be done about it,' Henry says.

'Why is she like that?'

'Because she had seen herself here, upon marriage to my father. Here at Lytes Cary. She believed that she would be first lady of this manor, did not anticipate that he would stand aside and allow me to manage the land, while he retired with his new wife to an unimposing though pleasant enough house in Sherborne. By virtue of my being the sole heir to my father's estate as eldest son, I have ruined her plans – and she is always reminded of this on coming here.'

# VIII.

*Of CINQUEFOYLE, or Five finger grasse. The great
yellow cinquefoil hath round tender stalks, running
abroad. The roote boyled in vineger, doth mollifie and
appease fretting and consuming sores.*

I T IS THE TWELFTH OF MARCH, and the second week of Lent.
Outside in the last of a spring frost the plants are made of glass,
the sun full upon them, a few melted drops catching light and winking colours. Henry walks the edge of the estate, steam rising from the
river like a pan seething. The wood is a theatre, cutout black twigs
shot through with vapour and diffuse beams of light against which
birds flit, softly translucent. The willow's tawniness is flaring to orange
with the year's growth, a supple bristle of shoots. Coming back
through the garden Henry watches honey bees among the snowdrops,
their legs fat with yellow catkin pollen. He remembers to avoid the
upper garden door, so that he does not have to speak to Widow
Hodges.

Today Henry takes delivery of seeds.

Looking through them when the man has gone, he has to admit
that he's probably bought too much. There are others on order, too,

but the seedsman doesn't pass through very often and Henry was keen not to overlook a chance to buy many sorts. The man had parsley and radish which he said had come from nearby, and endive, cucumber, anise, lettuce, purslane and pompion from further afield, mostly London. Henry also took pear kernels brought from Worcestershire, and he was tempted into buying fourteen liquorice plants, even though he suspects they will not do well on this kind of soil.

It is like a banquet, a seed banquet at his desk as he sits there opening the little packets one by one and relishing their differences: pale seeds of angelica like discarded shells of dull, brown beetles – flat and ribbed as if each one had been squashed in the overcrowded seedhead. He puts one into his mouth for that explosion of resinous savour, harsh at first then with a distinctive soapy undertow. Astonishing, he thinks, going on chewing, his tongue tingling and numb, how such insignificant, woody flecks can unleash such potency. He has seeds of ammi, too. Horribly dry and bitter. Smallage lives up to its name; the seeds are minute, scarcely bigger than grains of sand or mites. Alexander seed is black and large, like fat rat's droppings. Gromwell is of a cold dense grey like that of tin-glaze china, quite startlingly like the eyes of cooked fish – with a high shine on each, and a faint patch of yellow blush. Not perfectly round, these seeds are mobile, free-flowing on his hand.

He also has dill, vervain, motherwort, thlaspi of Candy, sanicle, dittany, thyme, aristolochia, pennyroyal, calamint, centuary, alecost, herb of Grace, and wafer-thin moons of lunary; some call it Honesty but what is truth or honesty or lies to a plant? Such riches at his fingertips!

Of course for years he has bought in seeds for the vegetable yard, but this year his enthusiasm bubbles over even for them, as well as the seeds for the Knot, as though he is seeing them anew. He already has plenty of onion seed bought locally in March – maybe three pounds in weight. He digs his hand in and lets the seeds run through them in his delight as he opens each little sack and examines the contents, sniffs them, cracks a few open with his teeth. There are various peas, and borlotti beans in their stiffly undulating parchment pods.

He pours a mixture of some of the peas and beans into a pot to gloat over at his desk. They are soft red and brown and green, silkily dry, wrinkled. They are the colour of dried blood, tallow, bone, fresh larder mould, lichen. They are as hard as shingle, as light as buttons. And they are all – he feels quite overwhelmed with the sheer mass of them – waiting. He puts his forefinger to them and stirs them about. He rattles a handful from palm to palm. They are extraordinary – how has he never heeded it so well? And the promise they contain. These things seem dead, and yet … A few drops of water, the enclosing dark earth with its minerals, the warmth of sunlight; and each of these desiccated, mummified little bits of toughness will hydrate, fatten and burst into vivid miraculous sweet shoots, climbing, sinewing towards the light.

❧

Tobias Mote looks at them doubtfully, when Henry takes a fair selection out to show him.

'That's a fearful lot to be grown from seed,' he says, scratching through his rat-coloured, curly hair. 'We'd be better off buying in little plants already set from Mistress Shaw in Wells. Only so much time on a man's hands. Can't produce a nursery out of thin air in a year's stretch.' He points with a blunt, grimy forefinger at the dug turf around them. 'Not with all this going on.'

Henry's good mood is unshakeable. 'But they'll last, even if we can't get round to sowing everything this season.'

'If they don't get mildewed, or eaten by mice, or stolen; or so long as they don't sprout untowardly.' Tobias Mote chuckles with more glee than Henry wants to hear. 'There's a lot can go wrong with seeds stored badly.'

Henry stops listening to him.

For a second he thinks he hears something else behind the garden wall, strains his ears, his heart beating, but it is the low noise of ravens up in the woods that sounds like men talking.

'Anyway, I've been thinking, we'll be needing a bank,' Mote is saying. 'We can cast up one here where it should catch the sun alright.'

'And grow a soft kind of cover over it – then I must add grass seed to the list.' Henry is making notes on a board propped on an over-turned cask.

'And grass it.' Mote repeats. Henry finds this is an annoying habit he has, of saying again what has already been said; not as if he is committing it to memory, more as if he is weighing up the readiness of what has been decided upon, as one might judge a fruit in the palm of the hand during the course of a tour of the orchard. It is not that Tobias Mote is rude or disrespectful, just that he seems disconcert-ingly his own man, that won't be bidden.

'So that it can be used as a seat for contemplation amongst the calm of the plants, facing the Knot itself.' Henry goes on regardless, still pleased with the idea. 'I imagine in June it will be popular.'

'Folk can sit and kick their heels, when they've little to do.'

Henry Lyte looks sharply at Mote, but he can't see any evidence of sarcasm. Mote's countenance is fixed always either to the far distance of the horizon, detecting the weather, or straight down to the soil to the matters in hand. He digs very fast and straight, as though he were racing. Only for trees, it seems, does he make an exception and look out to the middle ground. Once Henry saw him watching a fox cross-ing Easter Field with a hen from the yard in its jaws, a ruddy streak trotting diagonally, its brush out straight and triumphant.

'See that devil go,' he'd muttered grudgingly to no-one in particular.

But on the whole, Tobias Mote seems to know what is going on around him without looking, without ceasing his thin, see-sawing whistle, without raising his eyes from the ground as he digs or rakes. His ears are small and pricked, perhaps their bristle of hairs makes his hearing more acute than other men's. Mary calls him the troll, because she is afraid of him. If she is naughty, he only has to mention his name to make her squeal and comply with parental requests.

'Does he do magic?' she'd whispered once in awe, when they were discussing the crop of skirrets laid like dead man's fingers buttered on the plate at supper, but her stepmother dislikes that kind of talk and made her get down from the table. Frances applies herself with scant duty to prayer and worship at the appropriate moments of the day but has a horror of talk of spirits and the afterlife, that makes Henry suspect that her beliefs run wilder than some. Of course he can't be sure of this as they have never discussed it, not being something a civilized family should concern itself with. His first wife Anys, he can't help remembering, was devoted to prayer.

'And on the shady slope behind the bank, for who ever thinks about what is behind them, we can set primroses, or violets as a surprise, and other little shy flowers that do not mind a lack of sunshine – all in due course,' Henry adds hastily. He is determined to remain enthusiastic about remembering details, even in the face of cynicism. He paces up and down the length of land, which Mote is now raking finely, slighting the soil in preparation for the sowing as soon as the weather seems suitable.

Henry has hired a weeding woman who lives at Tuck's, called Susan Gander. She has been pulling out neat, tender bits of dandelion, jack-by-the-hedge and long, easy roots of withywind, so that the beds are smooth and clear, and everything is ready for committing the seeds to the earth. Some areas are sown, and some left bare for pricklings to be set out later. Susan Gander is an odd woman, Henry decides. He has caught her staring at him when his back is turned, and when he speaks to her to give instruction, she doesn't say much in return, just nods, staring all the time even as she tosses weeds into the basket, so that she sometimes misses. He knows she's not a half-wit, she is the wife of John Gander who is the most reliable carter round here. He thinks perhaps she may be put out because at first he found it hard to remember her name, but now he has it, and still she goes on, which is making him feel almost paranoid. It happened when he saw her at church on Sunday, he swears he saw her surreptitiously turning round and watching him out of the corner of her eye, nudging her neighbour. Her behaviour proves to him something unpleasant he has been suspecting for a few weeks now.

There can be no longer any doubt that something has begun to quietly, insidiously, circulate the district about the nature of his first wife's death. No-one has mentioned it to him, not a single mortal soul, but he hears the whispering and sees the glances, and slowly the whole ghastly mess is rearing its head again in an unformed, pliable version of itself like a bad dream.

He goes inside, and watches the sowing of seeds from the study for a while, with more than a touch of jealousy. Mote somehow knows he's watching, brazenly raises his hand once to him. *See?* Henry mutters to himself, *even his own gardener prefers him not to dig in the garden.* He seems to regard it mostly as his own domain. But he does trust Mote sufficiently to carry out what they have agreed. The progress is invisible from here.

Henry prays, then goes to his manuscript, though it is hard to put his mind to it. Every day as the season draws on he finds it more of an effort to apply himself to its difficulty, tinkers with what little there is of it so far. He feels mired and tense.

The next day is grey, and the lesser celandines have kept their petals half-shut. A small brown hawk with pointed wings, not from round here, has been flying between the pear trees and making the blackbirds jittery. By midday the pale sky has lowered and dissolved into a mizzling fine drift of rain that is perfect for moistening, nurturing those seeds laid already in the earth. Tobias Mote says that a successful life for any seed is determined in the first day – the first hours, even – of being planted.

Watching the hawk whirr up to the edge of the copse, Henry is reminded of a reddish-brown moth and thinks it softly beautiful, until he sees its decisive landing in the ash tree, cruel feet outstretched and latching onto the bough so swiftly that he flinches. It is a meat-eater, through and through.

# IX.

*Of PLANTAINE, or Waybrede. The third kind of plantaine is smaller than the second, the leaves bee long and narrow, with ribs of a darke greene with smal poynts or purples. The roote is short and verie full of threddie strings.*

F RANCES QUICKENED TODAY. Henry can't feel it of course, though he puts his hand dutifully on her belly, but he praised God for it; another healthy child kicking in the womb. He can never picture a miniature human in there, like those shown in the diagrams in medical books. His mind's eye suggests rather that it is a pinkish kind of grub or caterpillar, that will later transform into something more recognizable, when it is pressing tiny feet and hands against the inner side of her belly skin. He is after all an experienced father. There were the births of Edith, Mary, Jane and Florence, and there was the other birth too, but this is too painful for him to remember. This last memory is the one that is slippery, evasive, so deeply interred that he can't even acknowledge it. He is adept at forgetting; extremely adept.

'Come and see the garden today, Frances!' he says, on impulse.

'Then you must wait while I find my old shoes,' she says.

64

'No, now! Come at once! It is the end of April and you have not seen what has been happening out there,' Henry makes himself laugh, tugs at her hand. And as they go out together to see the progress of the Knot and its surrounding borders, Henry begins a descriptive verbal tour for his wife, so that she can imagine how it is to grow. What will be here and here. What will be high, what will be climbing. He ignores Mote, who is grinning to himself as he listens to Henry's enthusiastic, expansive rendition of how it is to be.

'Picture its frankness,' he entreats, 'fat and green. Here will be the gillyflowers, and these little slips of lavender will have grown into plants by then, and see all these frondy bits of dill coming up, and these are the apothecary's rose, and these the damask. What do you think?'

'I do love roses.' Her tone suggests that there is doubt involved in all of this.

'The beehives are at the far end by the garden. If you sit up here by the house they will never bother you, and here is a good corner where the sun warms the wall. Even the little rock lizards bask in this spot.'

'It really is quite hard to picture, Henry.' He knows she is only allowing herself to see the mud, the parts that are not finished.

'Think of a lily. Think of breathing in the plant's waxy freshness like a draught of vital spirit.'

Frances does smile politely.

'Think of a rose, then, think of bringing a fresh pink rose up to your face and drinking in its scent. It will have opened that morning and you will have your basket with you in order to gather many more, perhaps to make an aromatic water in your stillroom that very day while the blossoms are wholly fresh. If you like there could be a seat here for you to sit on, by the roses.' He fetches a cask for her. 'Try it!'

'And my face won't catch the sun?'

'Your fair white skin would be shaded by the briars overhead.'

She looks suddenly keen. 'And could we have that by the week in July when my mother comes to visit for my lying-in?'

'Well, no, it may take a couple of years to reach overhead.'

She looks back at the house. 'Everything takes so long. Can't you just buy bigger roses, more full-grown, and get the men to twine them up as if they'd been there months and months?'

'Roses do not like being moved – better to wait and coax them up the wires at their natural pace if you want them to last their proper lifetime's span.'

Frances is becoming concerned for the state of her shoes and the mud that she will be treading into the house.

'Every time I come out here, Henry,' she points out. She knows perfectly well that one cannot rip up roses by the roots at whim. She is being wilful in her lack of interest. Henry cannot understand why she does not enjoy the garden more. To be sure there are many bare patches and places where herbs are not added yet, but he has described to her the wholeness of it, its beauty that by next June will surely dazzle her.

'And is it all very costly, darling?' she adds lightly. He looks at her. In the sunlight her straight black hair shines as though it is polished. She is not at all like a flower, he thinks. She is mineral, crystalline, waxy, brittle. The cost of his garden is not something that he wishes to discuss, he realizes.

'How you can spend so much time inside the house without fresh air is quite beyond me,' he retorts instead, as she walks away. He is very annoyed that she is blind to the garden's soft growth, its promise. Mote smirks at the masterwort in the bed behind him, saying nothing.

He opens the garden door and leaves the neat, planned, incipient beauty of his Knot and strides off to inspect the orchards and the wilder, rampant plants in the wayside. He will clear his head, stretch his legs, shake off that disappointed feeling that comes from not being able to rouse enthusiasm in another being for something that one loves.

As he walks about, gradually and in truth for the first time in his life he begins to see the plants around him in terms of both their particularities and their potential. He begins to examine them all with a mounting respect and excitement for their distinctions, going from plant to plant, getting lost in their worlds, making mental notes, determined to write down what he's observed when he returns to his study. Next time he will bring a notebook outside, and something to write with. He looks closely at the yellow loosestrife with its expanding, hairy, silky, fat stem, a plain-looking plant. He admires a specimen of elecampane; muscular in its softness, stiff with preparing to grow. He sees wild feverfew, with its almost sticky leaf; comfrey, a foot tall now, relaxing out of its growth into a soft almost reptile skin; and there is lady's smock; pinkish, wavering in the air as though alert or tense. In the orchards the Dunster plum tree has rounded leaves peeping from the smooth twigs. On the greengage, tight waxy points are bright yellow-green, thin and strong. The apple leaves are opening raggedly on the branch like a conjuror's flourish, and the quince is decked with little piles of hairy leaves, long pile like the hair on a young woman's jawline. On the medlar are mild, elegant fingers of leaf and pinkish buds. Those leaves are fine in texture, rippled. He applies most observation to his favourites in the pear orchard. Their white blossoms are open like hats, and the leaves silver-soft, with a white-green tip that is crisp to the touch, and shedded brown husks at the base where it has sprouted. He watches a metallic green beetle clinging and clambering inside a blossom, and sees the boughs are dripping with mosses and crusted with three kinds of lichen; bearded, creeping, yellow. He wishes he knew more.

He wishes he could have some word from his father, who has kept up a resolute silence although Henry has written to share the good news about Frances's condition. It is often surprising when a man gets what he hopes for, but so rarely does it come in a guise that one could have predicted. For a moment he has the most peculiar, overwhelming sensation that something vast is creeping up on him, drawing nearer. He turns around in alarm but it is only Blackie, trotting over the wet grass towards him, blunt tail in the air.

# X.

*Of BLOOD-STRANGE, or Mousetails. It floureth in*
*Aprill, and the torches and seede is ripe in May, and*
*shortly after the whole herb perisheth, so that in June yee*
*shall not finde the dry or withered plant.*

H E NEEDS TO GO AND COLLECT A HUNDRED ready-set slips of
gillyflower, on order from Mistress Shaw, an old woman of
some sixty years that lives in Wells. At its best her garden is a fat,
colourful kerchief of blossom, and the children always vie to come
with him in the cart when he goes to her for plants and seed. Rumour
has it that as a young girl she was a Benedictine novice in a London
convent, but that she left the calling and walked south-west long
before the upheavals in the Church began. They say that she was never
wed, yet everything else she plants springs eagerly to life.

Once they arrive at her garth, which is a square of land that sits
beyond the town on the flat beyond the Bishop's palace, Mary and
Jane run off to hide and reappear later with the stains of strawberries
about their mouths, oozing fistfuls of redcurrants, though they swear
they were not thieving. She never chastises them, which he suspects is
not only because their household provides good custom for her

business. On occasion he has caught that raw, hungry glance that the barren can sometimes have on seeing children, but she seems to take some pleasure in cultivating their sound running full tilt in her garden.

She has narrow shoulders, but these days a protruding abdomen makes her very wide about the middle under her gown, and walking makes her lean a little as if one side of her were puckered up. Henry Lyte sees that she must suffer from some kind of growth inside her, but knows he cannot mention it unless she does. But on this visit, which is about his fourth or fifth already that season, as he is ducking out of the gate in her garden wall, he turns back to her. Checking that the garden boys are out of earshot, he asks very quietly, 'You have been seen by a physician, madam?'

She looks down at her hands. The knuckles are shiny with the swelling of old age, and the nails green and split and grubby with work. When she speaks he smells her breath has the unmistakable unsavoury sweet smell of rot, and he is sorry for it.

'There is no need, Master Lyte, no need at all.'

'A doctor would give you physic to ease your suffering, and he can prepare you for what you might have to expect.'

'I go to church to know what there is ahead of me. And beyond that I do not want to know. I pray. I try to sleep at night.'

'Do you sleep easily?'

'I do not.'

Henry tries to think what he can usefully do to help her. 'I shall have a boy ride over with a bottle of aqua vitae for you, for the pain,' he says.

Mistress Shaw's eyes widen. 'No! I can manage, thank you, Master Lyte.'

'Or I can leave half a crown and you could order some yourself.'

'No, really, but I thank you anyway.'

He smiles, will not be put off by her firm demurral. 'I do insist,' he says. And when he gets home he dispatches it immediately, a corked brown bottle wrapped in cloth.

But something very strange happens, which is that Mistress Shaw sends it back unopened with the boy that very evening, and with it is a little note. *I thank you again Master Lyte, but I will not take strong drink. I hasten to assure you how this has naught to do with what they say of you, which wickedness I shall not believe.*

What they say? Precisely what is it that they *say*? He must find out. He calls his bailiff but he is still out at market. He begins to asks Lisbet but before he reaches the crux she finds a pretence to vanish away to the kitchen. There is someone else he could ask, but something makes him hesitate. In the gloomy distance, he can see Mote's form on the edge of the garden, digging, digging. He considers sending the boy to call him in. He delays lighting the candle, so that he can keep an eye on his progress. But in any event he does not need to make further enquiries, because by tomorrow forenoon a letter from his father comes.

# XI.

*Of HORSETAILE. It is good against the cough, the
difficultie and paine of fetching breath, and against
inward burstings, as Dioscorides and Plinie writeth.*

H E IS NOT SURE WHICH IS WORSE, the fact that he has disappointed him, or believing that his father would allow himself to be manipulated into this position by that woman.

He stands, transfixed, in the hall. Across the passage he can hear Frances giggling in the kitchen over the clatter of pots. Her condition is softening her, she has begun to waddle very slightly as she moves from room to room, and listening now to her voice like that makes him feel protective. It suits her, this temporary relaxing of the rules she has set herself. He hears footsteps approaching from the kitchen, towards him standing there. The smile dies on her face.

Frances sees he has a letter in his hand. 'What is it, Henry?'

'From Sherborne.' He is smarting.

Frances snatches the paper from him. 'What does he say? I cannot make head nor tail of your father's hand – it's like cobwebs.'

'Here.' Henry directs her to the passage.

Her mouth opens a crack in disbelief as she takes it in.

'How can he even suggest such a thing? And then *seamlessly* he goes on to talk of picking up the barley malt on Friday. It's scarcely credible.' Disparagingly she turns the paper to see if there is anything of worth to be found on the reverse. 'This cannot warrant a reply,' she says. 'Do not even give him the pleasure of watching you put your attention to it.'

'But does it sound like his usual way of speech?'

'I scarcely know him, Henry.'

'It is that viper woman, hissing in his ear. I know it.' Henry bites at his thumbnail. 'Coiled in the sand over my father's money like a clutch of someone else's eggs.'

'It's just the words of a bad-tempered old man. Pay no heed. Parents can be cruellest to their children, but they may not always mean it.' Frances pretends that it is of no consequence but her cheeks have flushed scarlet with offence. She stands for a moment, rubbing the mound of her belly and looking at nothing.

'But to say that God will *punish* me,' Henry says. 'And that my conscience will be nothing if not tainted. This is like a curse upon us!'

'What has provoked it?' she asks.

Henry does not know where to begin to answer. 'The imminent arrival of a child can bring on … change, bring unsaid, underlying matters to a head. There is nothing like new life to unleash the past,' he says.

'But what underlying matter could that be?' she says, bewildered.

Above them there is a crash on the floorboards, one of the children starts to cry and she has to rush upstairs.

❧

So certain things begin to make sense. Here is the vile rumour laid out in black and white upon the page, in his father's hand. He is the very source of it, the wellspring, and it is unthinkable. A more bitter blow could not be had, he thinks, than being struck down maliciously by your own father. In great anguish of mind Henry sits down and attempts a reply to his imputation. *My good father*, he begins. Then comes a torrent of opening lines each crossed out in favour of the next.

*With deep regret I received your—*
*I beseech you to reconsider the harshness of your—*
*I cannot know by what false informant you have arrived at this—*
*I am sickened by your—*
*It is an injustice, sir, that I shall not swallow—*

Henry crumples up the sheet of paper and finds a fresh one. There is black ink all over his fingers, his face. He must keep to the point, he thinks, pacing about, phrasing and recasting over and over in his head until all is garbled and makes no sense even to him. What were the circumstances of his second marriage? It is hard to remember. He takes more wasted paper to the grate and burns the pieces into flakes of ash. He will try again later.

He goes out to find solace in digging at the garden. He fetches the iron spade from the shed and chooses a difficult, untamed corner to confront, where even the most persistent robin leaves him alone. By noon, he is drenched in sweat and goes to the ewery to wash thoroughly before coming to dinner.

Frances has a great liking for eggs at the moment, so they eat white-pot alongside the meat today. Usually it amuses him to see her eat such quantities, her fine frame dominated by the firm round belly so that she puts away great slices of custard pie and boiled beef in large, eager mouthfuls with uncharacteristic speed. The baby has also meant that she cannot abide the smell of green vegetables, so has to excuse herself if salad or greens are to be served. But today he does not notice what Old Hannah brings out for her, and they avoid all mention of the letter's content before the servants, indeed they hardly speak at all.

In the afternoon he still ignores the unwritten thoughts running through his head, and goes to work out the quarter-wages for the household staff. He notes that where last year there had twice been a change of dairymaid, Bridget had been with them now since before last Michaelmas, with a marked improvement in the keeping qualities of the butter.

His hand is uneven as he sets out these figures in his ledger, he makes several mistakes, but it is evening before he permits himself to return directly to the matter. Joan Young is very clever, he thinks, to have turned his father so hard against his own flesh and blood. He shaves a new quill to a satisfactory sharpness and sits down again to set it out clearly.

> *Father,*
>
> *You hold that I have married another man's wife and you intend to disinherit any issue we should have. You may cut off whom you choose, but remember that Frances carries this child as my lawful spouse without dispute. Should it be found, if it please God, to be a boy, he shall bear our family name, and through me prove ultimately to be your rightful heir as a Lyte of Lytes Cary – our shared descendance. Once this child is born of my wife's body and cries within these four walls, in law and life Frances is bound to me in property and God's eyes. I beg you not to go against the way of natural succession without good cause. I entreat you for your blessing, pray for your good health, and remain your obedient son.*
>
> *Father, never did I wed another man's wife.*

He makes adjustments, shakes the castor and slides the document across the desk to dry. Outside in the dark a nightingale pours out its ceaseless, bubbling song. He has an incongruous recollection of an evening spent once in a garden in London. The garden itself was plain and empty, the company laughing and playing a game of lawn bowls, with wild nature just visible on the surrounding hills.

# XII.

*Of SOPHIA or Flixweede. Groweth alongst bywaies in*
*untilled places, and specially whereas there hath bene in*
*times past any buildings. The séede drunken with wine*
*or water of the Smiths forge, stoppeth the laske.*

H ENRY LYTE WAKES IN A SWEAT, and lies there on the bed with
his heart racing. Joan Young was in his dream again like a long
red tendril coiling up and up towards his neck. He looks toward the
thin strip of light from the window.

The moon always makes him dream badly. Weeds in the Knot
garden make him dream badly; running grasses, bittercress, nettles,
sinister little towers of horsetail. It is the time of year for such things.
Early summer with its abundant froth of blossom and greening fields
looks idyllic to the untrained city eye, delighting in the sight of cows
dotted in the meadow and nice asparagus to eat at lunch – but to be
inside the working countryside is a different matter. He rubs his neck
to be rid of the tight sensation he still feels there. Arcadia it is not, and
no-one feels this more strongly than his wife. Frances knows that a
walk in the fresh air is good for her but refuses to go out on more
occasions than not. There are several types of weather that she does

not tolerate – fine rain because it presents a dilemma about whether to go out, heavy rain because obviously one will get soaked, thunder because one may be struck by lightening, icy because one may slip and break a bone, damp and warm because one may catch an ague, windy because one may catch a chill, too late in the afternoon because one may get lost and not have enough time to discuss supper with Old Hannah. It is beginning to be clear that Frances is not wholly suited to the countryside. Which is why she asks again this morning if they can go to London this month.

'London?' Henry looks up from the book in which he jots down market matters. He thinks of the annual tasks for the land and almost laughs.

'Impossible.'

He makes a note about the price of raw wool in his meticulous hand, and flips the pages to examine the same for the previous year. He calculates what kind of profit might be expected from his flock, how many hoggets should be sold off, how many kept. His shepherd William Warfyld has a plan to use the unclaimed field known as No Man's Plot, which means he could afford to raise the numbers unless someone places an objection. He wonders though whether that field is just too wet. When he looks up, she is still in front of him, waiting for an answer.

'Besides, what would you do there?'

Now it is Frances's turn to be amused. 'Do? Master Lyte, what do you suppose I spend my time at here that I should miss? I must run the household but it can manage without me if we are not here. After all – if we are not here, there is much less to do. We can stay with my cousin, now that mother has remarried and gone to Devon.'

'Surely there is plenty to do wherever we are; it should make no difference?'

'I do not mind hard work, but in London there would be less weather and more people,' she replies. 'And we can bring Lisbet.'

Frances, when she chooses, can set quite a stubborn line to her jaw. 'I lack for just one thing, Henry. Fun.'

'You'll have plenty on your hands soon enough,' he says, indicating her belly.

'There are *months* left to go,' she protests.

This really is very tiresome. He has several sorts of account to pay today; tailors', mercers', smiths' and chopmen's bills. He waves his hand vaguely at the door. 'Go for a walk. Learn an instrument.'

'An instrument?'

'Yes, a lute. No! Perhaps the virginals.' Reverend Tope says that a lady should only ever learn an instrument that does not cause her to spread her legs. He agrees with very little that Reverend Tope opines on, but today he is in a hurry, and other people's thoughts can provide an occasional shortcut to thinking for oneself, can't they? And in her condition … He is sure that one could sit at the virginals with one's anklebones neatly together, though at this very moment he does not much care.

'I don't know, Frances, you are a grown woman with an entire household to run, and in the unlikely event that you have an ounce of spare time you can occupy it for yourself. Learn ballads. Anything! But London this month is out of the question.'

This afternoon Henry receives another letter from his father. There have been many sent between them now, their dealings with each other becoming at best unkind, at worst hostile, a volley of fire. But this letter, it becomes clear as he breaks the seal, is the most poisonous of them all, one that at all costs Frances must never see. This letter summons every evil that his father has been alluding to over this horrible month, but never yet dared to mention outrightly. And here it is, set down as if it were a truth, a twisted fact. If it were so, why does he not make his accusations in public? Why does he hide his venom in a letter, yet leaking breath and whispers of his intent all through the borough so that it comes to his ears slowly from all directions. His claim is that Henry himself was to blame for the sickness and death of his first wife Anys. *Death*. The man claims he is a murderer. *Murderer*. Odious, odious lies.

'I am a good man, am I not?' he says to himself, his carefully nurtured world falling apart inside him. 'How can I clear my name, when there has been no fair trial?'

# XIII.

*Of MULLEYN. It hath great, broad soft and woolly
leaves. It sheweth like to a Waxe-candle, or Taper,
cunningly wrought.*

WHAT THE HELL IS THIS *SATYRION*, a kind of orchis? He has never seen one for himself, nor even had it verified, and he will not write about a kind he does not understand. He puts that section of the translation aside and waits until the simpler calls by again. In the meantime he finds he cannot respond to his father's letter. He will. He will write soon, but not until his head has cleared. It is like a fog in there; remembering anything is more like groping about and stumbling by chance upon fragments.

When the simpler comes, he calls her in.

'Does my lady yet need hart's tongue or camomile for her limbick as she used to before?' she bleats. 'She were always such good custom off me. She'll want a good few handful.' She starts pulling bundles out of her pack and spreading them across the table. 'I have a quantity and can get more. Plantain, as you call it here? Sorrel? Betony?' The simpler is a thickset, wall-eyed woman with black fingernails. Her one good eye roves the carpet as if looking for herbs.

Henry Lyte clears his throat. 'What do you know of standegrasses, orchis?' he asks her.

The woman looks blank.

'I'll know the plants I know of, and that's flat.' She is not inclined to be helpful, in fact she is distinctly disgruntled. Since the death of Anys, her sales of flowers and other necessaries up at Lytes Cary have been minimal. Anys used to order roseheads by the bushel to supplement those grown at the edge of her little plot, which was eightpence a time.

'They have two roots in the soil like a man's cods,' he explains. 'One fat, one shrivelled. Spotted, fleshy leaves, thick upright stems with—'

The woman's face clears. 'You means butcher flowers, long purples. Too late for them now.'

'But there are others like them—'

'Ah! Like maybe fools ballocks, or sweetheart's, you mean?'

'Possibly, it's just that—'

She looks sly. 'I may have been approached by several gentlemen in London and once a lady for the same before. I may know of a place where they grow. In confidence, you'll want them, like they did.'

'In confidence? Why?'

Her eye fixes abruptly on a spot upon the floor and does not waver. 'It'll cost.'

Henry sighs. 'How much?'

The woman's good eye briefly meets his own then slides away. She shrugs. 'If you want 'em I can get but it'll be sixpence. Each,' she says flatly. 'There's not so many of them and with my sight I'll be scrabbling all over the hillside up off for too long before I'm spotting any. Got to make it worth my while.'

'I shall need a variety of specimens. Whatever you can find.'

'What did you call it? Stander grass? Never heard that. Don't know that I call it anything much, any old name'll do half the time, and the other half I calls 'em nothing.' She perks up suddenly, having got her price.

'And just the fat cod out of the two roots it has, Master? You'll not want the slack one with nothing in it? That's no good to Venus, Master, is it.' Her lopsided wink is a peculiar sight and Henry Lyte looks at her uncomprehending. Surely the wretched woman doesn't think he wants them for a provocative to venery. He has seen a recipe called a diasatyrion that mixes orchis cods with grains of Paradise and nuts and Malaga wine and candied eryngo root among other things, a sweet electuary. But he needs to *observe* them, and then if still fresh enough he may set them in the garden when he is done with that. He is irritated to find that his face is flushing.

'No, no, I'll need the whole plant, my good woman. Bring me the various sorts you can find. And try to remember where each specimen comes from. It is for my research. They have … they have no practical application whatsoever.'

The woman smirks. 'Whatever you say. No doubt there are *no* other uses a man could find for them.'

She goes off into the corridor just as Lisbet passes by with a besom.

'Several sorts of dog's testicles for you then, Master,' the simpler hisses out noisily, winking. 'No bother at all.'

Lisbet drops her brush on the flags with a clatter. As she bends to retrieve it Henry Lyte sees the disgust on her face, and he is sure that by the evening the entire household will be discussing his business, as if he was practising witchcraft in addition to everything else, damn it! He slams the door behind the simpler's squat retreating figure, behind everybody, and stands with his back to it.

'God's wounds! I do not have to explain myself,' he says angrily, to the empty room.

But of course he must. First he puts his mind to other things for several days more, thinks instead of the confusion caused by too many diverse names. This is always the difficulty with employing simplers, they all have their own aberrant, singular names for a herb or plant.

It is, he believes, one of the obstacles for a sharing of knowledge, or any collective progression, it is also a source of mistaken identities and the reason for many a wrong or dubious leaf finding its way onto an apothecary's shelf by another name. Ask a local where a particular plant may be found and he will look at you blankly unless you can name it as he was taught it as a child, toddling at his mother's knee in the grasses. But if a proportion of those who can read would learn from or recognize what they know in print, set out clearly, consistently in black and white, *and in English*, then a hoard of particulars would be transformed into knowledge. Misbeliefs, wrongnesses and ill-used wisdoms could be set right, and many lives saved. This thought breeds hope and frustration mixed up in him.

Increasing age is supposed to make a man grow more contented with his lot, with what God has bestowed upon him, but some days Henry Lyte can still feel something like the rage of youth inside him at the slowness of progress, at the satisfaction with the state of stupidity the world is so often content to live in, himself included.

*We are so ignorant, so coarse in thoughts and knowledge!* he rages at the pear trees that afternoon, stretching his back between batches of summer pruning. *Our aspirations should be high, higher than they are.*

But then when he goes to his pages spread out, he finds that he takes a very long time to write a sentence, to think through anything. This is the real trouble, the gap between what is needed, wanted, and what is possible for the ordinary man.

It is high summer now, brutally hot when a man has been working. When he goes back to the garden, the hot green smell of it is like a smack in the face. The annuals they grew from seed are now clambering up the walls, the stakes, thick in the beds, covered in bees.

Indoors, Frances is vast and panting, drinking quantities of buttermilk, writing lists, preparing herself for any outcome as her confinement draws near.

'I must write to my father,' he mentions out loud when he goes in to see her.

She sits up on her elbow. 'Do not write, Henry. Let him stew in his own juice for a while yet. Leave it a month or so. You are his son. Make him suffer for the hurt he causes you. Besides, you may just make it worse.'

Henry does not think he has her steely reserve. But then again, she does not know the full extent of it, that last letter which she did not see was by far the worst. Every night he prays she will not hear what his father says of him. But although he can feel himself yielding, as a son, and it is natural enough to want to be on good terms with one's father, it is easier to go along with her suggestion. Women can be very wise, he thinks. His mother was.

'Leave it awhile. Be strong, Henry! Let it lie, just a little while longer,' she says.

'I shall do it soon,' he concedes. But a day passes, and then another, and still the letter is not sent.

The orchis arrives just over a week before Lammas. He unwraps it fully and pays the simpler. A dug-up plant is always disconcerting. It is limp on his desk, an unhappy, naked tangle, dried mud everywhere as he examines it closely in order to be able to properly describe it to others, making notes. It is only later that he remembers one other characteristic ascribed to the orchis. Too late now, he thinks, with Frances approaching the time of her lying-in. It would have been worth a try. Anything would. *If men do eat of the fullest and greatest rootes … they shall beget sonnes.* Of course he has been blessed with many daughters. But is it not the truth, he thinks defensively, that in this world a man needs a son?

# XIV.

*Of ARCHANGEL, or dead-Nettle. Is of temperament*
*like to the other nettles.*

**I**T IS NEVER GOING TO BE GOOD NEWS when an urgent letter arrives on horseback in the late evening. Henry has not yet retired for bed and is already halfway across the hall when he hears the knock, a familiar dread already tight in his stomach when one of the kitchen boys opens the great door. As soon as he has it he recognizes the hand – it is from Nicholas Dyer, his father's friend.

He thanks the messenger, who is sweating and thirsty and covered with dust from the late summer roads in riding from Marlborough at speed, and orders his horse be watered in the yard. Henry waves him into the kitchen for a drink and bite to eat, and still does not read the letter for some moments because he has a sudden urge to urinate, and goes hastily up to his room to use the close stool. Frances is sitting in bed sewing in the hot July dusk.

'What was that rapping?' she asks, pulling her thread through its length, and tucking the needle in again. The sound of the thrush's song from the ash outside drifts in through the open window.

'A letter from London. I haven't read it yet, but I know what's in it.' He does up his breeches and sits down on the end of the bed with a creak of rope. The evening has taken on a horrible significance. He knows he will remember forever the particular sight of the loose weave of the bedcover, the smell of the half-used washing ball on the form by the bed, the ordinary aftertaste of the wine from supper in his mouth.

He breaks the seal and the stiff paper unfolds unwillingly for him, and then he reads the scant, crabbed lines three or four times over, as if there was not enough there on the page to tell him what he already knows.

He puts the paper aside and lies flat on the bed with his shoes still on.

'What? What is it?' Frances says.

'He is dead. My father is dead.'

*Silence.* Frances puts her sewing in her lap. Outside even the thrush is quiet. Henry can hear no noise from any quarter. Not a whistle, not a breath, not a creak of anything. Then he hears his heart, going on beating.

'What is the date?' he asks.

'July the thirtieth. The eve of St Neot.'

'As I thought. I cannot even pay my due respects because today they buried him at the church of St Botolph without Aldersgate. But I must ride to Sherborne to help tie up his affairs. There will be the inventory to sort out, and many papers …' *There is no air in here.*

'If Joan lets you set foot over her threshold.'

Henry sits up abruptly and swings round to face his wife. 'That woman may think she has a life interest but my father's business is my own. It should all be made clear to her at the reading of the will.'

# THE SECOND PART

## *The Time*

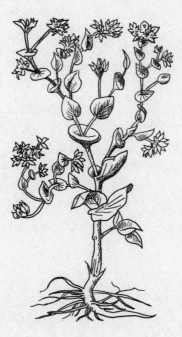

# I.

*Of THOROW-WAX. It floureth in July and August.*

THE ANCESTORS ARE WAITING in the hall with him, all about like silver smoke or fog. A dissolved airborne, sense-borne host of tiny flecks or particles of the continuity of living. They have his face, his hands, his eyes, they all speak at once as if from a great, hollow distance away and they have his voice, and his father's voice, and his father's before him. There must be hundreds of them waiting here, a faint, infinite crowd lightly shifting and jostling in the atmosphere as a shoal does.

He paces the length of the hall, waiting for the noise of hooves outside the porch. He has had no choice but to send for Goodwife Dutton and let her into the house, despite everything that had happened with Anys.

She greets him sternly, untying the panniers and bringing them in.

'Mistress Dutton, I—' he begins, waving at the boy to take her stocky little mare off into the stables.

'We'll bury our differences shall we, Master?' She begins to unpack right there in the passage. 'There is not much time for messing about with life, I find. Your wife is within due season? And how long has she already been travailling? Two hours, four? And the fluid humours have left the matrix? Then I must not tarry.' She bustles past him, laden with rolls of cloth and a brazen pot from which she produces a bewildering variety of dried and fresh herbs. Without appearing to do so, Henry edges closer and tries to identify what she is about to give his wife. He thinks he can see a packet labelled *Elleborus*, which would make sense, and maidenhair, aristolochia, motherwort, fenugreek, but what is—

'Hands off for gentlemen,' she remarks, slapping his hands away with astounding rudeness and gathers them up to go into the birth chamber. She believes that nothing good ever came from books.

'If you can bring the birthing stool,' she orders.

She points into the kitchen.

'Water boiling?'

'Yes, Lisbet is—'

'And her mother is here?' she says over her shoulder as they go up the stone stairs.

'Yes, Mistress Marwood is with her, and other kinswomen come up from Devon.' They reach the closed door of the great chamber and can hear them murmuring inside. 'What virtue does the oil of white lilies have?' He can't help asking.

Goodwife Dutton looks extremely disapproving. She lowers her voice.

'Lily does make the privy parts wont to slipperiness, Master. Better than duck's grease or the white of an egg together with the yolk, which I use on ladies of the poorer sort to loose the straits. Now, if you don't mind? Gentlemen engender babies and then they are to leave the rest to those who know what they're at. That's the rules, the way of the world. You need something to do? See the maidservant has the kettles always at the ready, bolsters, hot white wine and more clean cloths. Send up caudle for the ladies. Your wife may need refreshment of good meat, but never anything with oatmeal for it will clot viscosities.'

She twitches a smile at him. 'Then I should retire for the night, Master, if I was you, after your prayers. We can wake you if need should arise, which it will not. I'll pass on your wishes to her for a speedful deliverance, Master.' And with that she shuts the door in his face.

Henry Lyte closes his mouth and can do nothing but wait. He remembers now why she makes him grit his teeth, cocking her power deliberately beneath his nose because she can at times like these. Everybody knows what happened when she did not come to Anys. If she had come … well, there is no use dwelling in that, is there.

Through the muffling of the door he can hear her speaking firmly to Frances. 'Up and kneel on the bed Madam! Kneel! In the country way! You can pray later. Your matrons will pray for you. There, you see. Good girl, good girl.'

Frances has prepared for death.

Henry fully intends to sit up all night on his chair in the corridor listening to Goodwife Dutton barking demands. For what seem like hours he strains to hear Frances's responses but cannot hear his wife at all, no cries, nothing. All he thinks he can hear is the brush and hiss and breath of the ancestors, amassed in the draughty air just beyond the reach of the guttering pool of light cast by the candle at his feet. The dark tonight is all uncertainty, but he feels time rushing in to fill that newly opening potential. The first confinement is so often long and arduous and filled with peril, and though Henry Lyte has had other children born to him, this is the first by his new wife Frances and her strengths and weaknesses in that respect are an unknown quantity. But somehow he jerks awake and it is the grey of morning and Goodwife Dutton is before him in the empty corridor, a bundle of bloodied cloths in her arms. The ancestors have gone, their interest sated, for of course now they already know what he does not.

His heart contracts. Her face is unreadable as she tells him the news that he can hardly hear for the beating in his ears.

'Today your wife is delivered of a strong child, Master, born at full time. Of sound limb and lungs.'

'And is she—'

'She laboured sore for twelve hours and is tired from her travail.' She walks on. 'But sitting up and doubtless will be glad to see you when she's cleaned up well enough and has had a bite to eat.'

'Thank God, Mistress, thank God.' He tries to keep his voice from shaking. Henry can hear a thin, vibrating cry now from behind the door. His child! He cannot bear to wish. He must not, for it will be God's judgement upon him if it is otherwise to what he hopes for. He goes to the chamber next door and opens a window, looks out without seeing and breathes the late summer air in deeply, his hands still trembling and sticky with sweat. What is the date? The nineteenth of September; cradled just between Ember days following the Day of the Holy Cross. A sacred day indeed!

One hour later and he is permitted to enter the room and see his wife and their new infant. He holds onto the tiny, swaddled bundle with an inexplicable mixture of relief and numbness.

That the bundle has a son inside, is beyond his comprehension.

Holding onto it gives rise to the most binding feeling he has ever experienced, as though his heart were being wound round and round, lashing him to this infant, squeezing his heart almost tighter than he can bear.

The baby's head smells sweet and clean, almost like flowers. His eyes, when he opens them, are dark.

'You are born into a house in mourning,' he says, 'and we shall name you John, after my father who has missed you in life by only six weeks.'

For that, and for other reasons, Henry's joy combined with his grieving is complicated.

'You know nothing of what families cause,' he says quietly. 'As God is my witness I shall try to do my best for you.'

Just for this moment, he tries to put from his mind the trouble brewing down at Sherborne. Only a very old and outdated will has come to light, drawn up by his father the year that Henry married his first wife Anys. Henry's mother Edith was alive then, and naturally it makes no mention of any Joan Young, whom he married twelve years later. With no will, there is no executor appointed. Henry had hoped to do that. He would like this business done properly, because in truth he is not sure that woman could be trusted to do it right. He is sure it will prove to be a technicality, that it will just take time. It will not be difficult to keep her at arm's length. John Lyte died in possession of a small rural manor known as Mudford Terry or Woodcourt, near Yeovil, that he held of the Earl of Derby, and Henry believes that it was his father's wish that a good portion of this should be Joan Young's jointure for life, as his widow. After her death of course Mudford would simply revert to the Lyte estate. Henry will see that she receives fair terms, with some kind of annuity to add to the considerable wealth she has already from her previous marriage. Henry knows it is his duty to do so, because he is the sole heir to Lytes Cary and the rest of his father's legacy.

'The wet nurse is sent for,' Goodwife Dutton says, coming into the room and taking the baby from him. 'She will arrive sometime this forenoon.'

Henry's eyebrows rise. Anys had fed all her daughters herself, discreetly, up in the nursery, facing the window and singing under her breath. Sometimes it felt that he scarcely saw his first wife whilst she was nursing; just the back of her shoulders, her head tilted towards the baby.

Frances however had looked mildly disgusted a month ago when Henry mentioned that she might do the same, as though he had suggested rolling up her sleeves and emptying the cesspot into the foulwater herself, instead of leaving it to Lisbet.

'No! I shall hire a wet nurse like anyone else,' she'd said. 'It's perfectly safe if the nurse lives in and an eye is kept on her. Besides, I've far too much to do than be sitting about giving suck all day.' Henry had read in the medical books that he'd seen on the subject that a mother's milk was the most natural substance for a child to feed upon, but what could he do, it was none of his business.

'Hannah says that the goodwife will send up a woman,' she'd said, as if it were all settled.

'Make sure she is of a suitable complexion. Too choleric and the infant will have hiccups. Check the milk.'

'*Check the milk?*' Frances had burst out laughing. 'And how do you know so much about women's matters?'

'I have read many sundry texts on medicine, many learned, some quackish. And just very occasionally, what I have read might be put to use.'

Frances, her hand on her belly, had worn a look on her face that he couldn't decipher.

'What?' he'd said, but she'd shaken her head. All of which seems irrelevant now that the child is actually here. The woman arrives from Ilchester, her shift wet with ready milk after the long journey and she is neither a shrew nor a dumb woman. He gives Mistress Dutton five shillings in addition to her fee.

❧

Henry stands in the great porch and looks out at his fruitful land, subsiding readily into autumn; thick reddish ropes of drying ferns at the base of walls collapsing to the grass. He walks up to the orchard in the morning light, his shadow bouncing alongside him, and he sees the last pinkish-orange windfall apples lying cupped amongst the ribby waybroad leaves, and a crawling, humming, leggy patchwork of insects rises and falls giddily, drunk on fermented juice and the approaching lateness of the year. He wishes he could show this beauty to his tiny son; sharp points of rainbow light see-sawing along the threads of gossamer between the hedgerow stalks; the shining cranes-bill and the straggling brambles laced together with cobwebs, collecting damp. The hornet's flight is heavy, an alarming swoop like a swung weight.

He must get some women in for picking crab apples and then two men for grinding into verjuice. He makes a quick calculation; maybe eleven days to make three hogsheads.

Henry goes back to the yard and orders the wood in to be stacked after the summer's seasoning. Its greyish stiff pieces are ready to be cut and laid into a weathered mass against the side of the outhouse for the winter. He looks up at the window of their bedchamber, open a crack to the fresh, sweet air. *He has a son in there!* It's good to be laying on stock for the months ahead, keeping the house warm, well-fed, in a state of progression.

# II.

*Of SANICLE. Who so hath Sanicle, néedeth no Surgean.*

LITTLE JOHN IS TO BE BAPTIZED ON SUNDAY. That evening Henry is on his way to Charlton Mackrell to make arrangements for it with Reverend Tope, when he passes Widow Hodges' cottage.

'Master Lyte!' she rasps out from inside the door. It is evening, he is a little late for his appointment and his heart sinks when he hears her, so that he is ashamed when next she says, 'hold fast a moment! I have something for the baby. Come in, Master, while I find where I have laid it.'

Henry ducks into the low interior and lets his eyes adjust to the gloom.

'Strike a light, Master, if you will, it makes no odds to me.' The flame grows in strength and steadies, revealing a surprisingly orderly space crammed with new baskets of all shapes and sizes, and long bundles of withies laid across the open beams above. Henry is intrigued, despite himself.

'You have been busy, Dame.'

'You'll see how little room is left for living.'

'Do you not worry that there will be a fire in here? One spark and it could all go up.'

The old woman shrugs. 'Where else would I keep them?' He holds up the candle and stares in admiration at the stacks of fishweir baskets, flat winnowing baskets, dossars.

'Mind the trough, Master!' she says, and he sees the dark rods soaking at his feet. The sharply dry, smoked-fish smell of wet willow is strong at the back of his throat. Above his head the roof space is filled with finished baskets, panniers and traps, hanging out of the range of rats and mice. At the back of the room behind a partition, great bundles of willow rods stand upended.

'That's the store stock,' she says, hearing his step. 'It's good and dry in there. That side is where I keep plain withy, dun or white, which they say is not white at all, and on the right the red, though there's less call for that, only for baskets. Fish don't care much what their trap looks like and nor do fishermen.

'You'll excuse me but I just need to reckon for a moment, Master, I'm tying in the slathe and can't let go. Then I'll be able to lay my hands on the gift I have for you ...' Her fingers work around the cross of the pierced sticks three times, and then she splays open the eight sticks that will make the base. 'It'll be a big one, this, Master. There's a deal of reckoning in making baskets. Not a lot of people know that. I have to pay more attention than most basket makers need to bother with, as I can only see what I have with the ends of my fingers ... thirty-four, thirty-five. There.'

She gets up from her low stool with a cracking of joints and shuffles to a pile of rods that are mellowing under sacking. Her stiffness of gait is at odds with the lithe strength of her knobbled fingers.

'It's under here,' she gropes about. 'Or here. Mistress is well, Master? And the baby; is he fat and pretty? I am glad for it, Master, very glad. Always an anxious time, childbed. You are off to the church? When my own little girl was born I remember how fervently we too thanked

God. My husband, rest his soul, hastened straight to the curate as you are doing. Already we had a boy named Richard with a robust pair of legs and a will to match, and the girl's arrival was like a light had come to all of us.' The old woman's face crinkles.

'Was of an evening, the last quarter in August just before the corn was to be cut, and as the last part of her was born from me the lowering sun came streaming in across the sill.' She's rambling now, and Henry takes a step towards the door but he cannot get away. 'The midwoman held her up all red and glistering with fluids in the light that flooded in and it was like the baby had a force of life about her. If I said that everywhere was like the reddish light of jewels was cast in it – garnets, or plum syrup, or the Master's wine (for when I had my sight I'd served at table) – it sounds outlandish, Master. It was all bodily riches like I can't explain, and it came to me as I lay there that it was like she was the living heart wrenched right from my body, the very pulsing heart or kernel of me. She was glossy with redness, remember, all four limbs. Even the lumpen bloodied cord that yet held her to me; all gleaming. But you'll perhaps grant that a woman's thinking straight after her time is not quite of this world.'

A cock crows over by the barton. 'If it sounds like I have relayed this overmuch in detail, you'll remember too that I have had much time and cause to think upon it since, what with all that followed.' There is a silence, and then she tries to change the subject. 'The wasps are very bad this year, aren't they, Master.'

'So did she—'

'I'll come to what happened shortly, if I can bear to, or if you can bear to hear it, for it's not a pretty tale. My travail this time had not been difficult as she'd clambered from me lustily and as I lay back as they dried her, I breathed out gratitude that God had seen fit to bless us with a thriving daughter. I had thought to name her for my mother, but of a sudden it did not seem unmeet to call her Benet, which means blessed as you will know.'

'*Benedictus qui venit in nomine Domini* – blessed is he that commeth in the name of the Lord. They have left this out of the new edition of the prayerbook.'

She beams. 'That's it, well I could never tell a word of Latin, but in those days at church it was the words of God just come down pure from heaven. I loved the sound of them, they gave me a seemly peace and fear at once inside myself.' She scratches at her arm. 'But often I wonder if we had not chosen such a name, things might have turned out otherwise. I'd swear, Master, it was that strange reddening sun laying its spell over our humble chamber that caused me to forget my course.'

'And how did it turn out, Mistress Hodges? Was she—'

'Suffice to say I was to discover for myself how it is not wise to tempt providence like that, in naming carelessly. My happiness for her was short, for as she was put to me, and she opened her pert and rosy mouth to take the pap I saw what no-one else had seen, and my heart did plummet like a stone inside me, and icy cold I felt, with beads of sweat that broke out over me though I didn't breathe a word. It was a dreadful thing for any woman to meet with after childbed. But, God forgive me, the motherbond itself is fierce, and I vowed to shield her from the consequence of what she had been born burdened with. Even monsters, mistakes or freaks, or so my thinking ran, were they not God's own creatures?' There is a long pause, and taking Henry's silence to be disapproval she hastens to recollect herself, fumbling for the picking knife that has dropped out of her apron. 'Here I am going on, Master, and you off to church with happy news. What am I thinking.'

Henry bends for the tool and knows he must be on his way. He feels a morbid curiosity about the fate of little Benet Hodges, but it is late and the Reverend may not wait for him.

'Your gift, Master,' she says, out of breath but finding it at last. It is a baby's toy, made exquisitely from fine, knotted withy, a curious gourd-like shape evenly wrought and balanced as it sits in his hand, with cobnuts rattling inside its hollow.

'You are too kind, madam,' he says, examining the skill and fineness of her craft with genuine respect. He fishes in his pouch for sixpence. Any gift from the poor carries a reward.

'I don't want nothing for it. It's no trouble, for I can do several in a day. Forget my babblings, Master,' she adds, as though apology was needed. 'I'll not say a word on it further,' she calls after him.

The wind shakes every leaf on every pear tree, so that the whole orchard seems to shimmer against the sky.

Frances eyes the rattle suspiciously when he shows her later.

'It is from that old woman?' she says. 'It is made from withy?' She shakes her head. 'I'll not have it in the house.'

'But it is a gift, Frances, a perfect thing, a blessing made for John! It would be bad luck not to accept it.'

'It will be worse to have that object in the house, made of the wetness of this place, the dead marsh. It has something about it.' She shudders, picks it up gingerly on the end of the poker as if it is cursed.

'No!' he says, realizing what she is about. But before he can stop her, it has gone to the back of the fire, damaged, then spitting and crackling until there is nothing left but strips of ash.

The christening is a sober, happy service. Frances's mother and her cousin have already returned to Sealake in Devon, but afterwards a number of people from the parish come back to Lytes Cary to bestow good wishes. Frances remains upstairs according to custom but the girls come into the hall and pour wine for the company. Reverend

Tope is the only one who waits on, in order to be invited for supper. Even at this distance Old Hannah can be heard clattering the pots in the kitchen, as the fowl she has ready will not be enough.

The Reverend Tope is the kind of man whose breath smells of meat even in Lent. The minor challenges of his life have been knocked back and rearranged into place as a series of weekly hurdles of sermons and tedious parish business to do with the poor, to which he occasionally sends on his curate in his stead and returns home to snore, face downwards on the feather bed that his satisfactory incumbency affords. He has not the least interest in wielding the power that he has on a local level, preferring to bask in it and partake in the polite, steady flow of its offers to dine. He is an unavoidable fixture at most occasions held by the better sort.

He does not have much to lose sleep over and like many men in his position has a little too much to eat, and every year that goes by swells a little more into his clothes. He is harmless, only slightly irritating, and tonight, with his new son christened in the eyes of God, Henry is more than usually happy to spend an uneventful evening listening to his opinions that stream steadily forth, demanding little of the listener.

'And will yours be a *fashionable* garden, Master Lyte?' the Reverend says hopefully, dabbing himself with his napkin. He has after all, like everyone, heard something of the gardens of Lords Dudley and Cecil. 'Perhaps people will flock to this one too from far and wide, for the marvels and novelties it presents?'

'Fashionable gardens bore me,' Henry says patiently, 'with their stranglehold on growth and natural beauty. Fashionable gardens are everything about order and symmetry and nothing about plants. They are hard, measured battlegrounds against nature, as though it was the enemy. Sometimes it is even enough for whole areas to be eradicated of foliage and filled in with coloured sand or gravel, and triumphal gaudy flags and emblems set about the site, as markers of the inexorable march of civilization eating up the wildernesses.'

He turns to check that the Reverend is not disappointed, but he has fallen asleep.

Edith leans over and delicately moves his cuff out of the gravy with her fingers before the garment is ruined.

# III.

*Of SARRASINS CONSOUND. Hath a round, browne,*
*redde, hollow stalke, three or foure cubits high, as Pena*
*writeth.*

J OHN IS LESS THAN ONE MONTH OLD, not yet out of swaddling.
The wet nurse, a bulky, talkative woman, has overslept and the
infant is shrieking and hungry.

Frances is churched today, after the uncleanness of birth she must
be made pure either in the sight of God or of the parish, it is hard to
know which. He arranges the carriage, uncomfortable though it is, as
she is not up to walking, and travels with her to keep her company,
though it lurches about so much halfway he gets down and walks
alongside the horse instead, watching the square jut of the church come
into view as they approach the village. The children enjoy the ride.

Watching her veiled figure kneel before the altar, Henry can't help
but think instead of nature's gift to women in labour that is motherwort, aristolochia, myrrhis, oil of white lilies. Reverend Tope has gone
to Shropshire, so his curate takes the service. Henry looks at the font,
thickset pale yellowish limestone; where his fine, sturdy son has
already been baptized, squalling with a healthy fury at the cold water

being poured upon his warm, fat little body, and Henry can hardly keep still upon his seat, such sudden joy and pride washes through him.

It is a shame that there is one uneasy matter that he cannot put off bringing up with Frances. He has kept it from her long enough now, for fear of causing her untoward disturbance.

They are home and alone in the parlour when he broaches it. He clears his throat.

'Frances, my love. You remember how we plan to build the long gallery on the other side of the courtyard, to look west and have somewhere to stretch our legs on wet days?'

'I do,' she says.

'Well, it seems that we must put that plan on hold for some time. My father died intestate. At least, that is how it appears. They are still searching for a ratifiable will.'

There is a pause, but she does not break into the childish fury that he half expects. Instead her first thought is much more level. She puts her palms flat to the arms of the chair. 'But without the surety of his will, you stand to lose—'

'Unlikely. We could not lose Lytes Cary. Joan Young has made it very clear to me that she will fight my position, if it comes to that, but having no children with my father her counter-claim would be feeble at best; I would say spurious.'

'You are your father's eldest son and legitimate heir. Your younger brother Jack is feckless and liable to debt, he will not offer useful advice. You could write to my mother's husband John Marwood. You have consulted your lawyer? What does he say?'

'Simon Cressing says that it could be a long haul, but should not be a source of worry.'

'She would not turn us out?'

'No, she cannot.' He gives his wife a kiss on the cheek. 'We are safe here. It is all in hand.'

# IV.

*Of GOLDEN-ROD. This hearbe groweth in Woodes,*
*uppon Mountaynes, and in fruitfull soyle.*

WINTER COMES ABRUPTLY. The drop in temperature on entering the bedchamber is like a jolt, and he does not fall asleep for at least an hour because his feet and hands are so cold, but lies there feeling bad tempered that there is no more heat to be had from anywhere.

In the mornings his head aches tightly with the cold, as though it is shrinking. He parts the bedcurtains, crawls to his outer garments and does not wash because even the wash cloth hanging over the basin is frozen stiff. His breath clouds in front of him. Outside he can hear the cattle bellowing in the barn closest to the house, but he can't see out because the windows are coated with a fine growth of ice, whorled like ferns.

Mary is in bed with her wheezing for almost a month. It is hard to believe that she is seven years old now. At night she sleeps in the nurse's bed for warmth and for her to keep a watchful eye, so that if the wheezing grows too bad they can get her out of bed and put her face over hot steam to loosen the coughs.

He looks in on her from time to time during the week; a white face peering out of a mountain of bedclothes.

'I have been learning my letters, Father,' she says, the breath rasping in her throat. She smiles. 'Lisbet says I can have sippets of toast with my broth.'

Henry digs up elecampane root for her and has Old Hannah boil it to an aromatic, resinous white syrup. Mary does not have a strong constitution, she was a sickly baby who rallied when she entered girlhood, but her vigour lapses sometimes in winter.

Downstairs Frances is moaning about her situation, the dampness, the dreariness, the provincial company. She dislikes these cold, hard months in the country with a vehemence bordering on hatred. She does need a distraction, or some self-control, something to wholly occupy her mind or hands.

Regretfully he remembers how Anys spent so much time in the stillroom that her clothes often smelt of herbs, her hair and skin. It was her tiny kingdom, it was useful, delicious; she was very good at running it.

He sighs. 'The trouble is that you don't appreciate the place you are in,' he says. 'I am weary of this discussion. Doesn't the word *Eden* mean anything to you, or sound a warning note?'

'And you are Adam, I suppose, out in that muddy patch of yours, delving away.'

'Some husbands beat their wives,' Henry remarks.

'What is that supposed to mean?'

'That you could try to be more grateful for what you have, it could be so much worse.'

'I would never have married a wife-beater,' she flashes.

'You would have had no choice, if that was what your father bade. Besides, how would you know one?'

'By the marks on his first wife.'

Henry looks up sharply. But surely the rumour had circulated and then died away without a whisper before she heard it. Gossip is like

that, no matter how close or authentic the source, if nothing transpires or develops within a particular duration, it vanishes. Doesn't it?
*Everyone asking about what really happened up at Cary, at the time of
Anys Lyte's sad passing? And then: nothing at all.* People have short
memories. Nevertheless, he prepares to defend himself.

'There is a world of difference,' he begins, 'between making one bad
decision as a husband and sustaining brutal, unchristian behaviour.'

'I don't know *what* you are speaking of now,' she snaps. He is reas-
sured by the confusion and annoyance conflicting in her face.

'Are we having a quarrel?' he says, with sudden relief, and scoops
her towards him. 'Please say we are not. When the garden has sprung
to life, you will see how beautiful it can be here, you will see its value.
I will take you on a tour and show you every delightful little flower,
every blossom with its lips newly parted. You will smell the fragrance
of the air, eat ripe red berries from the bush. The air will be thick with
bees and birds. You will be amazed by the change that has been
wrought on what you call my muddy patch. It will be transformed.'

She struggles free from his warmth.

'I can't breathe, Henry. Let me breathe. You are too strange tonight.
I am missing London, that's all.'

## ❧ 1567 ❧

# V.

*Of YARROW, or common MILFOYLE. The floures grow
in faire round tuffets or bushes at the top of the stalke.*

ONE DAY IN FEBRUARY SOON AFTER CANDLEMAS, Henry has
to ride over to the Quantocks for the christening of his sister's
child, to whom he is to stand godfather.

'You have the gift?'

Henry pats his waistcoat. The silver porringer is wrapped in a strip
of linen.

'Don't forget to enquire whether she has heard anything about the
will.' His sister Alice is on better terms with Joan Young than Henry
is, at least face to face. Behind her back, he had once heard Joan
Young remark, '… the manner in which that woman just goes on
breeding like rabbits is extremely vulgar to be sure, but we can overlook it in this instance because Alice *clearly* cannot help herself. It is
most fortunate,' she'd added darkly, 'that she married a gentleman
of ample means.' At the time her acidity seemed almost amusing, an
outsider's unwanted commentary. Now though those accumulating
irritations seem more embedded, each one working closer to the
heart of him.

110

'I won't forget. While I am gone,' he says, 'you will put your mind to what I ask and keep an eye on the progress of the garden?' He kisses his wife's cheek. 'By which I mean putting on your overshoes and actually crossing the grass, even if it rains, which it may well do?'

'You are worrying too much. Mote will manage perfectly whether you are there or not.'

'That is partly why he needs supervision. He has … ideas.'

'You will be late,' she says.

And if he could see round the other side of the house – as the Sorcerer can, from his vantage point in the ash tree – he would have found that Tobias Mote is also up early that morning, already at work on the pruning of the apple trees while the sap is down. It won't be long now before life is shifting in the earth again, turning over. Down by the river the new growth of the willows is bright as flames against the rest of the winter-dark foliage.

Henry is over at Alfoxton for two days, and returns to Lytes Cary refreshed by his ride and by the foreignness of the hilly Quantock landscape, which is covered in lovely specimens of ling, and stunted oak trees in shallow coombes that smell freshly of leaf-mould. Alice's kitchen served venison which is a treat, and he has enjoyed the elevated view of the flat Severn estuary, purple with mud.

He goes back to his study after breaking his fast with the family in a sanguine humour. He sits down at his desk and opens several letters, one of particular interest from a scholar he met at Oxford about a rare plant he is interested in obtaining for the garden, which he puts aside to read closely later. The last letter is addressed to him in a puzzling, unknown hand.

He breaks the seal and to his astonishment sees he has received an invoice from a merchant in London for a very expensive item. His good mood evaporates as he goes to find Frances.

'Madam do you not think this is a little extravagant? How did you get this man to deliver an item like this without my authority. I did not sign anything for it. You are not permitted—'

'Henry, you told me yourself to learn an instrument.' There is a sharp glint in her eye as she bends over the new box.

'Isn't it a beauty?' she says. The sides are inlaid with slices of walnut wood; rippling tabby marks with a yellow sheen like honey. He looks in incredulity at its foreign name embellishing the front in gilt letters.

'It won't like the damp,' he says. The virginal's bone-and-polish smell has changed the nature of the room. The keyboard is like some kind of insect, very square, very alien. It is ridiculous. There has never been a thing like it in this house. He objects to it on grounds of … what?

'Well at least put a piece of baize under the box so you do not spoil the surface of that table which was my father's.' He can't think of anything more to say about it. It had, after all, been his own suggestion. As he leaves the room she taps her fingers sharply over the keys and hums something under her breath that he can't quite catch. He has no idea whether she can already play.

§

In his study the manuscript has sat untouched since Christmas. Henry thinks perhaps he should get it out and do a little work on it, every little part done is a step towards its whole completion. But it seems so much trouble, such a tedious chore, and instead he goes to the window that gives onto the garden and stares outside feeling irritated and sorry for himself.

He hears noise at the gate and remembers it must be Tuesday, when the poor come for scraps and broken beer. He has no idea who these people are, nor could he say if they are the same each week, just the poor at the gate, banging their bowls together. Old Hannah has spotted them.

'Are the scraps ready?' she is shouting. 'Can someone bring the jack to pour the dregs? No, not you Lisbet, I need you to start the pies and your fingers are clean already, that man was crawling with lice last week.'

'I'm not going to *touch* him.'

'Don't cheek me,' she says energetically. Then Henry sees Tom Coin go out to the gate with the alms basket, and the poor cluster round. Why is it, he thinks idly, that they never enter the yard – why do they not burst in and take what they will? Why do they not help themselves to grain, poultry, tuck a hen under their ragged arm or newlaid eggs, barge through the dairy door and scoop out salty butter from the crocks and put their chapped lips to the jugs of thin winter milk and drink it down? It is fear keeping us all in our places – fear of the law, of the dogs, the sheriff, the stocks, fear of consequences and pain, of being accused of things we did in a state of being stretched to our outermost.

He watches their retreating, shabby figures head down the track. An unspoken, invisible line is drawn across the entrance that they would not traverse. But still, he wonders, what is it stopping them from doing so. Is this what it is to be civilized?

The inequity of life is breathtaking.

In the parlour Frances is playing the instrument relentlessly, as though she is hammering at rock. When he passes and stops at the doorway, her face is blank with concentration, looking down at her hands.

The following Tuesday, by chance, Henry intercepts the kitchen boy before he reaches the gate and he examines the contents of the basket. It contains: eight stale rounds of rye bread left from the servants' table, two pieces of white merchet loaf green with mould, a ribbon of malodorous bacon and a wedge of cracked, translucent cheese. Under these articles lie several bruised apples from the store, including one which is brown with rot and clearly inedible.

'And they like this, do they?' he snaps at Tom Coin, as though it is his fault.

'They take it,' he mumbles, shrugging more from bashfulness than any opinion. At the gate three women and a man stand waiting, looking toward him. Even at this distance he can see that the man has a open, livid sore on his forehead.

Henry Lyte turns sharply on his heel and goes in to find Frances.

His wife is sewing with his eldest daughter in the great parlour. There are pieces of Holland cloth laid out all over the carpets.

He gestures at the gate through the window.

'They are supposed to feel grateful for what we throw out there. Worse than what we give to pigs. Surely we are obliged to provide proper nourishment in the sight of God, God help us!'

Frances looks at him as though he is mad.

'But if you do that there will be more next week and hundreds here the week after, once word has got round that there is a soft touch up at Lytes Cary manor. Then your own workers would be asking *why do I labour when you give these wastrel folk good food for nothing*? And so the stability of our charity would be lost, for want of a little restraint.' She squints at the needle. 'Where would it end, Henry?'

He turns to his daughter. 'What do you think, Edith?' he demands.

'I don't know, Father,' she says politely. It is very quiet in the parlour, just the fibrous sliding crunch of her scissors cutting across the Holland, and a sparrow piping mildly somewhere.

'The man had a festering wound, Frances. We should do something about it.'

'I have three chemises to stitch here before the light fades, Henry, and the clouds are banking up so the sun will set early. Your girls are growing. If this is all pricking at your Christian conscience so much, why don't you simply go into the stillroom for that jar of St John's oil that sits there and decant a little to put out for his use next week.' She smiles firmly. 'Now leave us in peace!'

Henry cannot bear to go to the stillroom. He avoids going there at any cost. He will send Lisbet or a sensible child into its cobwebbed, dusty interior to fetch the healing oil for him, he cannot enter it himself. Frances has been in there briefly a number of times, has probably rummaged through Anys's careful array of labelled pots and bottles to find what she needs, but she has no interest in it. His feet take him there almost against his will, he unlocks the stillroom door but then he wavers outside, his hand on the latch. Because nobody comes out of the kitchen and sees him there, it is easy to give up after some minutes and walk away down the passage. The nausea that has started throbbing in his head lasts all day, even once he has called Lisbet and had her bring the brown jar and set it on his shelf in readiness.

# VI.

*Of MARCH-VIOLETS. Violets are cold in the first
degree, and moist in the second. The syrupe good against
the inflammation of the Liver and all other inward
parts, driving forth by siege the hote and cholericke
humors.*

I T IS NOT LONG UNTIL LADY DAY and Henry is in his study with
the bailiff running through estate matters.

'Who is still due to pay rent this quarter?'

'Cooke, Hyll, Hunt,' John Parsons says, scanning down the list.

There is a scraping outside and Henry starts as Tobias Mote sticks
his head in at the window.

'I'll be going over to the edge tool mill at Middlezoy for those
shears, Master,' he booms. 'I've left the weeding women on their own
sowing in the vegetable plot. It's no good us all struggling along with
the one pair of shears. And if there's hoes, what about it? There's the
ones for out in the cornrows but they'll be needing those just as we
do, weeds sprouting everywhere.' He lets go of the window ledge and
rubs his dry palms together briskly, enjoying his enemies. 'Lord –
when I was a lad I'd go to sleep and dream on and on about darnel

and corncockle I'd hoed away, with them still come back choking the crops dead, crawling up the hoe, up my arm.'

'Nothing like a dreamt weed's vengeance to get a hold on you,' Henry says.

'Sorry, Master?'

'Yes, get the hoe blades,' he says loudly. 'And next time you want to speak to me, come down the corridor like any normal man.'

'Saves the carpets,' Mote says and vanishes. Henry finishes up with John Parsons, closes the rent book and pulls out his manuscript.

The noise of the music from the parlour is distracting him. Its silvery staccato is like the very opposite of what he's trying to say. He dips his nib into the ink again, taps a drop back into the pot and tries again. *Water sengreen*. No good. The metallic notes are like rows of stitching at the back of his head. Needling in and out, in and out, the silver chords bristling into hard clumps of sound at the end of each phrase. He wishes Frances wouldn't play with such prevailing rigidity. About mid-morning there is a merciful silence during which he can hear the birds singing uninterrupted from the orchard, an ivy leaf brushing against the opened window in the gentle March breeze, and then it begins again. This time it is worse; the taut and stilted cadence of an unlearnt tune read newly from the sheet. He must either interrupt his work and go down the corridor, or ask her in future to shut the door before beginning.

In the end he does neither, but decides that as Tobias Mote is away for the morning and the weeders behind the wall in the vegetable plot, he will take advantage of the uninterrupted peace out there and do some weeding of his own. He begins to cheer up as he changes into rougher clothes. He could have two hours out there in the spring sunshine getting his hands muddy, his thoughts roaming freely.

Firstly he looks over the seedlings in the medicinal bed. The baby gromwell he planted yesterday has perked up – its leaves full again and radiating from the stem. The root was beet-red and fine, with little dark crooked hairs from it. The ground the rows of calendula seeds are in is a little dry, there has been no rain for several days. He fetches the heavy earthenware thumbpot and souses along the row, releasing a rain of water by raising his thumb from the aperture, sealing it to stop the flow from the holes in the base. He enjoys its cool quenching glug, its glazed weight. A thin, coral pink earthworm stretches and compresses itself fleshily across the bare soil, and then disappears. He looks about. What else? Frondy stems of tansy laddering up. Small unfolding fans of lady's mantle, spiders scurrying away from the fall of his shadow as he inspects the beds. The honeysuckle is offering up tiers of new greyish-purple leaves along its stems. In the medicine bed, knobs of pink rhubarb shine rudely from the crinkled uncompressing leaves. Rhubarb is a faithful plant, it never fails to come up, year after year, its magnificence begins surprisingly early in the spring.

He begins weeding in earnest, around the base of the fruit trees, then about the early shoots of mallow like fingery, outstretched hands, the low growth of betony and calamint, the fat spikes of peony pushing up the soil at the back of the bed. He shakes soil from the clump of buttercup he has uprooted and a fat earthworm falls out, coiling and uncoiling itself in the sun, its saddle grey and ridged. It feels good to be opening up the soil, clearing it, letting his precious plants breathe and spread and prosper. But the ground is riddled with pests. Henry turns up some leatherjackets, some greyish grubs like soft crayfish, and balled-up slugs – he tosses them sacrificially onto exposed soil a short distance away in the hope that the robin that is following him about will eat them up. It goes without saying that anything that destroys his plants is unwelcome.

He doesn't hear Tobias Mote return through the open garden door. He observes Henry weeding for a few minutes.

'Mind how you do that,' he says eventually, going to the outhouse with the new hoes and shears. 'You'll enfeeble the plants if you go on so roughly.'

Henry straightens up, his legs set far apart over the new hedge, and frowns into the sun.

'Purge them up tenderly,' Mote spells it out for him. 'Winkle them loose, not ripping. Not for love of the weeds themselves but so that by coming up whole they do not leave anything of themselves behind, and so that you do not disturb the threads and roots of those plants you're tending.'

Henry does not say anything, but bends to his task and goes on weeding. He plucks off rooted runners of buttercup, mugget, cinque-foil, tiny isolated nettles with their kink of root, and easy rosettes of bittercress. Two tough seedlings of alder. Several dandelions in various stages of growth, some, it must be admitted, broken off at the taproot. Deadnettle leaving bits behind. Never-ending lengths of grasses.

Tobias Mote looks over. 'Dainty, that's the word I'd be looking for if I was trying to think how best to weed, Master. Daintily does it.'

The rain comes the next day, too much of a downpour for any sowing of annuals. The week goes by, church on the Sabbath with the family and servants, and then it is Tuesday again. He has not been at home on a Tuesday for a while, and so the little pot of St John's wort oil is still beside him on his shelf. He decides he will take the medicine up to the gate himself. When he can see some people and a child by the basket Tom Coin has at the gate, he goes out to meet them. He can't see the man.

'Wait, where is the old fellow that goes with you?' he calls out to the woman. When she turns he sees the skin of her face is puffed up and her eyes are red-rimmed, though she holds his gaze steadily, and he sees that she is not as old as he'd thought.

'That man? My husband was taken on Friday forenoon,' she says.

'The man who went with you? By whom?' Henry Lyte thinks of the sheriff. He himself has served as undersheriff and no-one has observed more closely how his men can be a bit pugnacious. Only last week he saw officers dragging a drunken ne'er-do-well by the hair from the inn at Kingsdon.

'Taken to God,' the woman says, 'by the poison got into his flesh on account of some canker was worming away at him.' She makes the sign of the cross against her filthy kirtle. 'I'd talk longer, Master, only I am bone-tired and do not want to stand, begging your pardon.'

She steps stiffly down the track, her gait jerking carelessly as though she was walking with her eyes shut, and Henry goes back to his study in dismay and puts the redundant little pot on the shelf. He should have given her some money. He settles to work again … *hearbe which fléeteth upon the water. By the sayd shorte stemme grow long thréedes like to verie fine and small Lute-Strings, stretching themselves even to the bottom of the water.*

He occasionally glances up at it.

Perhaps it would have been too late anyway, if the man had been offered help last week, or the week before.

He does not see the woman again, because on the following Tuesday he is called to Somerton on county business; and then later that month, when he glimpses the poor gathering at the gate as is their habit, she does not seem to be out there amongst them, though it's hard to be sure.

# VII.

*Of WILD-CAMPION. The séed are verie good against
the stinging of Scorpions, their vertue is so great in this
behalfe, that this hearbe onely throwen before the
Scorpions, taketh away their power to doe harme.*

FOR TWO DAYS NOW THE SUN HAS SHONE right through from
dawn to dusk, no clouds at all. Henry stands at the base of the
hill and drinks in the good noontide smell of the spring grass. The
scent rolling towards him is like hay and promise, it fills him with
pleasure.

There is a fresh molehill in the orchard, the fine, processed earth
loosely, airily mounded where it has been cast up overnight. As he
always does, he pokes through it with the edge of his boot and then a
gloved finger, searching the perfectly damp and crumbled soil, for
what? For treasure of some kind. He's always half in hope of something intriguing – an ancient shard of pot, a gleam of metal from
antiquity. Moles are the soft-footed enemy of gardeners, rummaging
out tunnels at the speed of lightning, ruining the grass, chewing
through roots and eating the good pink earthworms. Nonetheless he
has a fleeting gratitude, excitement, on catching sight of a new

molehill, a reminder of the life beneath our feet. So many secrets buried under the soil's surface may never find their way upwards into the light. Fragments of other lives broken into hard little pieces of inorganic matter that lie embedded in the earth, the context of their use eroded away – decayed, rotten, rusted.

Today's molehill yields nothing but the whorl of a snail shell, light with age, that he puts absentmindedly into a pocket.

The next day there is no rainfall either, so that the winter's waterlogging of the meadows at last begins to drain away, and by the third day the growth of the grass itself has soaked up the residue, so that the ground is bouncy to walk on.

'Plush, that is,' Tobias Mote says, coming back from eating his midday bite in the upper part of Broadmead, with spots of bacon grease over the bib of his shirt where he has taken off his tunic. 'The lusher the growth the squeakier it is underfoot. Have you ever noticed that, Master?'

Henry wishes Mote would wipe his mouth after eating.

But later he calls in his stockman to decide on a date, weather permitting, for the cows to go back out to grass.

In the parlour Frances is sewing dried rushes into a new busk for Edith who is becoming a woman and growing so fast that her child's size does not fit. That's the thing with girls. One day they are running about playing with their toys and then overnight it seems they are flourished into women. Henry does not think Edith has started her courses yet, but it won't be long.

Frances is a good seamstress, and clearly takes some pleasure in the clean kind of accuracy that is demanded by the task in hand, her eyes narrowed with concentration. She has the busk nearly finished, most of its ribs are stitched into the linen piping now, each set of rushes tamped down into a long strip with the firmness of her rows of stitching. The length of the garment is opened out in four flat scoops across the table in front of her like a pliant, unbleached musical instrument. Maybe three more narrow bundles to work in, and then the hems, holes for the laces. She hums as she works, and eyes the virginals more than once as though she were promising herself half-an-hour's scales or exercises later. Henry quite likes the tune she has been playing recently.

She glances up and catches his eye. 'What?' she says.

He clears his throat. 'It's coming along.'

She flexes the garment to hear the rushes' dry squeak. 'There's no doubt that a new busk is always noisier than the old one.' She does not add, because it is not the kind of observation she would make, *whose ribs have settled into the shape of the wearer over time; through habit, sweat, warmth of use.*

'Where did the rushes come from?' Henry asks suddenly. 'Did you pick them yourself?'

'Down on Eight Acre Mead.' Henry knows the surprise is evident on his face because she adds hastily, 'I sent Lisbet, I knew she'd pick well.'

Frances does not like the Levels. She complains that the soft, unsteady ground makes her uneasy.

'It's like walking on bodies,' she'd said one day after her first winter here was over. Henry asked her not to say that in front of the children, or Old Hannah, who was born at Huntspill and would be offended by that kind of talk.

'But it seeps up your clothes, its sucking grip tries to drag you down with every step into its jelly of rotting roots and worms and softening twigs. Man was not made to walk in marshes, it is perfectly clear. The moor is a place for ducks, fools and the lonely. God does not accompany men out onto the marshes. He stands at the edge and waits for their return, when they've come to their senses, if they're lucky that is, and aren't being drowned in the decay, the indecisiveness of it all, by increments.'

Henry had thought of George Colt the wildfowler who works the sluices, and his flimsy house far out on the moor on the other side of the river.

'If that is true then why did God provide George Colt with two webbed feet? Ask him to unstrap his boots next time he comes so that he may show you.'

Frances had grimaced.

'And everybody knows he was made that way because of living on the moor, it's peatwater in his veins instead of blood,' he'd said.

'Well it gives me the creeps, Henry, and it's just,' she'd nodded, 'out there. The truth is I try not to think about it being so near.'

Frances hooks her needle into her needlebook and puts the reel of thread away and shuts the basket. At the virginals she drums four or five scales up and down and then plays a brisk passage from a lavolta he recognizes as one that he likes.

'Don't feel you have to stay,' she says, striking the chord of G major, then D. 'I know you have so much to do on your book.'

In some ways she is right, Henry thinks later. The moor can be insidious, wet, treacherous. It does lure people to their death each year, as though, as everyone says, it needs souls to feed on. And yet it is so much more than that. The richness of the flora in the summer takes his breath away. At its best in those months it is a green bowl of God's abundance, every tiny detail perfect. And then by the winter it has drained back, collapsed into itself, allowing itself to be taken by the sea, by water. Its flux is its beauty. There is a bargain being struck each year between the sea and the land: submission, return, submission, return. Waterbirds see it as their right and arrive in thousands and then leave in thousands. The eels go back to the sea. The crops and meadows are enriched, because in return for being taken, the soil is nourished by the winter silt and inundation. And then every spring the zone is given back to the rest of the land, newly baptized. The year is divided in half in this way. Part water, part land, and several states in between.

# VIII.

*Of COW-WHEAT. This plant groweth among wheat
and spelt. The séed taken in drinke, troubleth the
braynes, causing head-ach and drunkennesse, yet not so
much as Muray or Darnel. Vaccis pabula grata &
innocua.*

WILLIAM TURNER OPENS HIS HERBARIUM and lifts a few of
the loose pages and places them aside one by one until he
finds what he wants. Henry pores over them eagerly, knowing this
may be the last chance he will have to see them. He has never got to
look at this collection of dried plants as often as he would like, perhaps
because of the fragile nature of the specimens, or perhaps because he
has not yet proved himself worthy enough to have the privilege for
granted.

Dr Turner cackles. 'Take a look at that.'

Henry carries the sheet over to the light and peers at it.

'Centaury?' he hazards, although the stalk seems somewhat thicker
than it should be, and he can see that the flower, even in its dried state,
is bluer and slightly larger than the common reticent pink of that
familiar plant.

'This is *seaside* centaury,' Turner says. 'Very rare. It seems to grow in only a handful of sandy, salty places in England.' He beams, his dried lips cracking. 'Of course I have called it *Centaurium littorale*. And the good Christ knows how glad I am to have been made aware of its existence. How we must treasure these precious jewels as they come to us. Think of all those other plants growing in our native soil that we do not have a name for yet, and yet here is this singular specimen plucked from the dunes.' He takes the page and lies it tenderly back in the box. 'Ah, how I loved the sea when I lived in Friesland. And what future delights hitherto known only to God will the sea present to us? Or in other tucked-away or modest habitats; in marshes, behind walls, on windy screes where no-one goes. Their local flora may go on yielding unfamiliar, unrecognized varieties for generations. We know a lot about the plants growing about the villages of London. But there are other places to explore. Remember Henry, what we do not yet know may prove as vital as what we do. And there is so much to be done! At the moment I have my boy ring the bell at four in the morning so that I rise with enough time to work before prayers. It is God's work that I'm doing, and yet it makes so many people cross.' He picks at a ring of spilt wax on the table with his fingernail and adds under his breath, 'It is a wonder that the bishop does not complain of my bill for candles. He complains of so much else. It is time I was gone back to London.' He goes to the window and looks out at his garden. 'I do like daffodils.'

For a moment Henry feels a flash of envy for Dr Turner's disregard for his own body's needs over the demand of work and scholarship. What did sleep and comfort matter when vast and urgent matters of humanity are there to be solved? Here before him was a man who had suffered for his beliefs, suffered exile, illness. He thinks of his own uncomplicated path, as though he had lived his life so far unheeding of his fortune, like a spoilt child. Tomorrow he will seize the day, ride to the coast and gather specimens, apply himself to study.

'There is something rather pathetic about a man arriving somewhere from inside a carriage,' Turner remarks, looking out of the other window and down at the street at the sight of the bishop drawing up and being discharged onto the pavement in all his red robes. 'Ridiculous novelty. Travelling by carriage one is blind, helpless, unobservant. I dislike being entrapped and made frail by my mode of transport.'

Henry laughs. 'How then do you prefer to arrive?'

'On horseback; in this way a man is already well-adjusted to his new environment, because he has approached it with his eyes and senses wide open, at a natural pace.'

'So your fear is one of being surprised, is it, of ambush?'

'My fear is luxury,' he raps out. 'For myself, for anybody.'

Then his faces eases, and he smiles. 'I shall miss your visits, Henry, when I am in London. I shall be glad to hear how you are working hard still on your translation.'

'Are you packed and ready to go?'

'I have little to pack, the books are already there. The most vital manuscript to me now is the third part of my own herbal, that describes plants not mentioned by Dioscorides nor other writers of old.'

'Is Peter's help hastening it?'

'It is done! Peter has been sending sensible suggestions from Heidelberg, and the printers at Cologne expect it *imminently*.' He rubs his hands together. 'Just as soon as I can let it go.'

'I shall look forward to seeing it all set out in folio. But I will miss you being here, Doctor. Come down and stay with us sometime. We'll have Lisbet make up a bed for you in the little chamber.'

'As long as you do not have that fat toad with us over supper.'

Henry smiles. There had been one distinctly awkward occasion when Dr Turner had been seated opposite the Reverend Tope by mistake. They had not been courteous to each other.

'He is not so bad, he means well.'

'He's a hypocrite, Lyte, and a soft, indolent one at that. It turns my stomach just to think of him – like a bad cheese, any sort of overripe fruit. I'd sooner choke on my meat than hear him going on and on again.'

'You shall not have to,' Henry assures him. His own memory of the night aside from the argument flaring to his left was that it had been a very fine piece of beef brought to table, some brawn and a roast capon. But he knows that Dr Turner does not tend to look at what he puts in his mouth, let alone actually taste it.

'I must beg you to excuse me now,' he says, embracing Henry warmly, almost like a father would.

When he gets home Frances and Jane are dipping chemises into a large, strong-smelling vat. They are dyeing them with meadowsweet for a darkish pink. Henry sees one finished article dripping from a line strung up. He makes a mental note that meadowsweet boiled with white silk gives the colour of old blood in water.

'It is five pints of liquid to a wig of roots, Father,' Jane reports.

'A wig?'

'See it in the basin there, the roots are like witches' hair.'

'Medusa's head,' he agrees.

Both of these women in his life look at him and, seeing he is superfluous to their experiment, he withdraws to his study.

The next day he holds to his vow to collect more specimens, pay more attention to what he passes, and rides to the sea at Berrow for that purpose.

Beyond the glitter of mudflats he sees the purple green cliffs, Brean Down is vertical stacks above the horizontal dunes.

The compacted sand on the beach by the church is tawny, littered with many-coloured, cockly shells spatchcocked open like pairs of lungs. This seaside is the river Parrett's emptying bed, until the turn of the tide; and then it will begin to disappear once more under the creeping incoming weight of muddy saltwater. In, out, in, out. The water is calm today, seems almost benign. Gulls squawk overhead.

By the late afternoon Henry's bag is filled with eryngium, glasswort, thrift. His head is filled with salty air and open space, which makes a change. Out here on the edge of things he can think more clearly, or rather he can allow himself the luxury of no thought at all. There is no doubt that he needs to work harder. Dr Turner is right. He needs to make a difference in whatever way that he can.

There has been no recent news about the unresolved matter of his father's estate. Last month Joan Young sent a succession of letters penned by her lawyer William Phelips, declaring herself furious at the ill-treatment that Henry proposes for her. Mudford, she says, is a damp, poky and unpleasant dwellinghouse fit only for peasant stock. Its environs are most aptly suggested by its name, and there is no ounce of civilization possessed by any of its neighbours. She will not go there willingly whilst there is breath in her body. Any notion that it was her departed husband's wishes that she would be installed at Mudford until her demise is an affront to her decency and genteel birth. She has said she will never accept it.

But for several weeks now there has been only silence from Sherborne, where she has insisted on staying, at Henry's ongoing expense. No poisonous little missives, sent by special messenger, no lawyers' letters armed with Phelips's ostentatious seal. Perhaps it has occurred to her that Henry has a son and heir of his own, and that she should not interfere with the natural order of things. She is a widow twice-over now. Perhaps grief has mellowed her a little. She must be given time to arrive at the right conclusion, of her own volition. Henry's lawyer Cressing tells him that he must be patient, that it is a waiting game.

Today at least he does not feel any threat, and it is a great relief. God is good. Henry smells the sea air and feels braced, throws a shell to the sky and catches it. And he has a son!

# IX.

*Of LARKS-SPURRE. Whereof one kind groweth in gardens, and the other is wild.*

MAY, AND HENRY LYTE IS OUT IN THE ORCHARD. The grass under the pear trees is dewy against his shoes. The day is warm and pleasant, the light dappling on the leaves, and he sees that the fruit has set – tiny, long, rosy pears behind the contracting flowers, and these fruitlets are covered with rough down like a newborn baby's back. He checks the grafts on the younger trees at the end of the orchard, more out of habit than anything else, and stops to admire the bearded clumps of lichen dotting the older specimens like an airborne seaweed. He bends to pinch at the purplish leaves of alehoof clustered in a mat at the roots of the tree, and sniffs his fingers for the pungent aroma that is so good in beer. Idly, he watches red ants hurrying up and down the trunk.

Even on such a calm and peaceful sunny day, he thinks, ants keep up that frantic business. He smiles. And what is it all for?

He decides to return to the house via the garden, to see how the new growth on the hedges is doing, and have a look at the beds. Every day like this brings inches of new shoots. He can hear Tobias Mote rummaging about in the outhouse against the garden wall, and whistling a buzzing tune between his teeth like a large kind of insect. The tune stops and he emerges with a stack of redware crocks that he puts on the ground with slightly less care than Henry would like, and straightens up.

'Morning, Master,' he says. He has cobwebs in his eyebrows.

Henry Lyte greets him cheerfully. 'Magnificent day.' Mote squints up at the sun as if to judge for himself, and gives an indeterminate chuckle, but Henry rubs his hands together and looks around at the garden's progress in some satisfaction. He rocks on his heels at the edge of the bed and it feels like a kingdom rolling out around him, all according to plan. The blue haze of stubby bugle on the lawn, the square, hairy stalks of wood betony with its leaves like paddles, held back like wings poised for flight or a dive, and when he touches them, like rasping fur. The giant yarrow is covered with greenish heads of buds, like brains, and the stalks are as thick as his little finger. The honeysuckle is almost ready to flower, its little reddish knobs of bud like blind fingers in clusters.

He notices three wooden trays of seedlings laid out in a row on the path, basking in sunshine.

'Are these the lupins we sowed last month?' he enquires, squatting down on his heels beside them. The finely sieved soil they are grown in is perfectly moist and smells wholesomely of mould and minerals and promise. Each tiny forest of seedlings quivers in a breeze, their stalks like pale threads and their seed-leaves being superseded by new growth on every tip. He looks at them and longs for them to have more space for the roots to spread, for them to be able to burgeon.

'They should be pricked out soon enough, or they will be too large and crowded.'

'They'll wait a day or two,' Mote says easily.

'The weather looks good, they would do well to be bedded out.'

Tobias Mote taps his thigh with the handle of his knife.

'Sometimes waiting is better, Master, if there's a shadow of doubt as to the state of the weather.'

'Doubt?' Henry laughs. He gestures up at the clear blue sky. 'But look at it!' High above them a single rook or raven crosses the expanse with a lazy, muscular flight and then disappears behind the house.

'The bed is prepared,' Henry adds, 'as I directed the weeding women yesterday, while you were out. Look! Not a stone or lump left on the surface, it's broken up and picked over, and all that bittercress cleared away.'

Mote steps into the outhouse and returns with a bundle of dry willow.

'Still, best left for a brief while yet.' He ignores the seedlings and begins to cut pea sticks. 'There'll be a plummet of rain tonight, and if they get put out, they'll be drummed about something painful, if not washed away. They'll not stand a chance.' He is whistling again, and Henry wonders whether this baulking at his wishes is some kind of test of his own authority, and suddenly the sunshine seems a little less bright, a little less promising. It is only a small thing, but it is clear that Tobias Mote has no intention of following his instruction – and not a cloud in sight.

'See what the pismires are up to?' Mote says, slicing into the sticks.

Henry looks down at the paving slabs where the ants are scurrying to and fro, in disbelief.

'What have the ants to do with it?' he demands. The ground is crawling with them, now that he looks more closely. He must have stepped in the nest.

'They tell better than you or I that tonight'll be bad.' Mote is emphatic. 'When they're all about like that for no reason. Besides, can't you smell rain on the way yourself?' He sniffs the air. 'Lovely.'

Henry stands up. Here is the day, all balmy around him, and a wave of annoyance at the contradictory stubborn nature of the country mindset with its mishmash of unscientific hunches and piecemeal folklore dictating the course of the day's work in the face of the obvious is more than he should have to bear. He opens his mouth to point out exactly what tasks are to be done today, when Mote adds briskly, 'and there's no need to go wasting good seedlings just on our whim, Master, is there.'

Henry turns on his heel very abruptly, leaving his gardener and the wretched ants to go on with their day just as they please.

❧

At ten o'clock, long after supper, he looks out at the night and cannot tell if he can see the stars, but it is still mild enough, with no wind to speak of.

'Ridiculous,' he mutters, closing the window against the dark and getting undressed for bed. Frances is already asleep and as it seems uncouth to press himself upon her he lies awake for some time listening to the uneventful silence of the night broken only by her rough breath and a mouse scratching in a corner over by the chest. Later that night he dreams of foreign armies marching in from the sea and setting up camp at the head of the valley, red flags streaming out, crackling in the wind, and felling large swathes of the forest on the side of the Mendip to feed their vast, all-consuming awful fires. And of course when he wakes the first thing he hears is that there is a fierce, breezy rain beating the panes, and when he looks out, he is not sure which is more depressing; the sight of the waterlogged garden or the fact that Tobias Mote was right again.

# X.

*Of GOAT'S BEARD, or Joseph's floure. The saide roote*
*also is very good to be used in meates and salades, to be*
*taken as the rootes of Rampions.*

JANE SHADOWS EVERY MOVE HER STEPMOTHER MAKES. Over
the past two years since Frances arrived Henry has seen the
conflict of feeling inside Jane rising and waning as she follows her
about like a watchful spaniel, checking, making comparisons with
what she can remember of her mother.

But that is fading daily now, in favour of a grudging admiration for
her stepmother's crispness, her stylish dressing and her firm, if slightly
capricious will and method.

Though she doesn't speak languages herself, Frances is keen for
all the girls to keep up their Latin, and some Greek, and hires a
timid governess that Henry rarely sees but at mealtimes. Of all the
girls Jane shows real aptitude for learning, and has also begun a
study of local plants in paints, which she brings to him to identify.
She will be a capable wife to someone one day, he thinks, watching
her write the names painstakingly beside each little colourful sketch
once it is dry, though she may always have green stains on her

136

fingertips. She has a healthy, enquiring demeanour and is not one to be told what to look at. If he is out in the field with Jane, collecting specimens, she will be the first to turn something over to discover what it looks like underneath. Her scrutiny is nothing if not thorough. He likes that; his second eldest child with her empirical mind will be an asset to any man's endeavour. Because before long he must begin the process of finding her a husband. The right match for her and for the family is crucial for so many reasons. She is his daughter, and in truth he can't imagine what it will mean to hand her over to another man. Wherever she goes, it will not be an early union.

Today they are to go across to the bottom of Sedgemoor, in search of some unusually large butterwort that he saw there last year. He stands in the porch waiting for her, facing the orchard. It annoys him, the way Mote persists with calling the bark of trees 'rind', like his father used to. It is the modern world, for goodness' sake. Trees are trees and cheese is cheese.

'Sorry, Father?' Jane has appeared from nowhere. Henry clears his throat.

'Right!' he says, hastily gathering up his coat and hat.

It is only occasionally that she comes with him on his shorter botanizing trips down onto the Levels to look at water plants, or simply for the pleasure of seeking out a good specimen of bog myrtle or bogbean. She does not talk much, she is like Anys in this respect, and so there is also hope of chancing upon interesting birdlife, tiny waders such as stints startling up from the reed beds, or dabblers flicking cautiously amongst the knotty textures of the alders. He doesn't think it does her any harm. It means she will be able to teach her children of the world about them.

Frances is less sure, and on their return today after a particularly wet afternoon spent looking at water-spike, with its resultant wet shoes and hems, begins to put her foot down.

'It really is not seemly for her to jaunt about in mud like that at her age. She is too old now to come home soaked up to her elbows in putrefaction.'

'It is hardly—'

'No, Henry!'

'Then I shall just have to start training up Florence to be my companion, she could wear breeches,' he jokes sadly, trying to make light of it, for he knows his wife is right.

'It is not a suitable activity for girls. It is too damp, too … odd.'

'Then I shall wait until Johnny is a little older. You can never start young enough—'

Frances takes a deep breath. 'I am quite resistant to the children going onto the marshes at all,' she says.

'Why?' He laughs. 'It is hardly a site of iniquity. It is a very mild place, brimming with—'

'There are agues in that slack water.'

He sighs. 'You are a city woman at heart and do not understand the nature of the moors, for they are not stagnant at all but renewing themselves over and over. If you came down with me more often you would see for yourself how glorious it is, how fertile. Your objections are,' he tries to think of a polite word, '*unfounded*.'

She shivers perceptibly. 'No. If I look at my feet as I am walking there I shall see drowned faces staring up at me, under that brown water.'

'Your imagination does you no favours, Frances.'

What is the matter with her? She is so coldly logical about everything else. 'And I hope you do not put ungodly ideas into the children's heads about their home when I am out of earshot.'

'But it is a place of drownings,' she persists, though keeping her voice down. 'That ground is saturated with death. It is rotten with dead and dying things, and creatures that feed on that. Eels, shelduck, whatever they are, scavengers all, their bellies filled with pieces of greying, swollen, flaked-off flesh.' Her eyes are wide with fright. 'And their nights lit by the bobbing greenish lights of spirits drawing off the unwary.'

'Oh for heaven's sake, woman. Enough!' He can't stand this melodrama, she is unnerving him. 'It is all superstitious nonsense. If you keep up with this I shall have to call for Reverend Tope to talk sense into you.'

She retracts in an instant, begins gathering her sewing together, then gets out her ledger for the kitchen accounts and smooths the page flat. *Look at her now, sharpening her quill.* She must have been play-acting. She must have been making a huge fluster out of what seems after all to have been a passing anxiety. His palms are sweaty. What a peculiar thing.

'As you please,' she says, frostily, into her ledger. 'It is your decision.'

# XI.

*Of CANTERBURY BELS, or Haskewurt. There be divers*
*herbes which have floures like Bels, whereof this*
*Auicularia may be very well a kinde, the floures of a faire*
*purple colour, fashioned like a Bell or Cymball, with a*
*small white clapper in the middle.*

JOHN HUNT'S DOG IS BARKING out at the front of the house, which could mean either that a barn cat has streaked across the yard or that a visitor has arrived. Henry likes the fact that his study does not overlook distractions but he suspects this may be a visitor that cannot be ignored. He prays it is not bad news, or Reverend Tope. He looks at the page. *Prunus*. He has not even begun to describe the virtues. *The great sweet blewith plums*, he writes, *doe cool and moisten the stomach and belly. The snags and cat sloes are cold, drye and astringent*. It is hard not to be always reminded of jobs on the land just lying undone. He should get the men down to the blackthorn encroaching onto the sheep pasture, and do some grubbing out while the bushes are manageable. Next year is too late. The thorns can drive deep into a man's foot through his leather sole, and cripple a sheep. *For they stop the rheume, and flowing down of the humours*. He pauses to listen. The dog is still barking, though muffled as though it has been put inside. Regretfully he wipes his nib clean and leaves it to the side of his pages. Old Hannah has already set the door wide onto the bustle and the sun streaming in.

'Lyte my friend!' a young male voice shouts, a trim, black silhouette against the brightness. For a moment Henry cannot think who this person is and then a brisk delight rises in him. Thomas Moffat is a staunch ally whom he rarely sees except in London. He is more than twenty years younger than Henry, but they get on very well.

'I was in Bristol with Bredwell on a rare botanizing trip. You know how I hate the fresh air, it was a torture. And once we were done and had dropped him back in the arms of his long-suffering lady wife I hastened here before I go back to London. My Christ but that man is a drop of ice-cold water to the soul. I have something to show you.' He tugs baggage from the pannier.

'Everywhere I look is insects now, Lyte. My brain is crawling with them so that I cannot sleep, my wife tells every company that I make rasping noises like crickets with my teeth the whole night through. It's all carapaces, and light stalky legs articulating, chattering, inching through my dreams. They're everywhere, man – you only have to—' Henry Lyte pulls his arm in time to stop him overturning the large stone by the great door, and asks, 'How long are you staying?'

Moffat turns his round, heavy-lidded eyes upon him, and narrows their beam.

'I'm not disturbing the penman at work?'

'Anyone else would have been,' Henry Lyte says, 'but you – I am extremely glad to see. The scribbles are amounting to something, I think. And you must inspect my garden's progress. Stay all month if you like.' They go into the hall.

'I have something from Garet's garden that may interest you.' He roots in his enormous bag and begins to unwrap a woody plant. 'Not crushed at all! A very rare sort.'

'What is this obsession the Netherlanders have for rarity?' Henry Lyte is quite delighted at the thought. 'Look, Frances, at what we have here.' His wife, who has put on pomade, brushes by him.

'Do you mean Thomas, or this little shrub in his fist?'

'Oleander, madam, or rose bay.' Moffat bows low with his hat off.

'*Oleander*?' she pronounces the words delicately, almost in a whisper as if she has never heard the name before. Henry Lyte had forgotten how flirtatious his wife can be. He likes the smell of the pomade, it reminds him of when they were first pledged to be married, when her lips were always rosy red.

'Let me guess. Is it for pottage? Or sauce?' She teases.

Moffat pretends to look wounded. 'No madam! For every part of this is poisonous to man and beast.' He laughs. 'A pottage would be no worse a fate for it than one of your dreadful winters, Lyte. All that water, swilling about and nowhere to go. It's a wonder any plant lives here and is not choked to death by damp.'

'We'll air your bedcovers this time, Thomas,' Frances says, and Henry sees her squeeze his elbow. 'Sit in the hall and I will bring the travelling man a drink. I see the oleander has buds, are the flowers very pretty?'

'The flowers, madam, and this is why I bring it to you today, are as rosily pink as your maiden's cheeks. You shall fall in love with this plant as your own child.'

'And what are its virtues?' Henry asks, knowing the answer, for he remembers now that he has come across this plant abroad.

'They are … yet unknown,'

'It has no virtues Moffat. Not one. If you or I were to swallow any part of that plant we would drop dead of a stoppage of the heart. Supposing it gets in with the cattle fodder? Or one of the children tastes it? Or even a dog? There is no place for needless poisons on farming land. I shall extend to you no thanks at all for bringing it into Lytes Cary.'

Moffat looks mischievous. 'Not at all.' He winks at Frances. 'This plant is *pretty*, madam. Love it for its wicked beauty. It will irradiate like a veritable witch in your sunny border.'

Henry is not at all pleased about it. It will not come out of its pot. Henry hopes that if he ignores it, it may be ignored by others and then by fault of no-one or everyone, it will quietly expire. But of course it is very popular. It is given abundant water by its admirers and begins at once to thrive in its own sunny spot.

# XII.

*Of CAMOMILL. Especially the white, is hot and dry in the*
*first degrée, and has power to dissolve, and make subtile.*

THOMAS MOFFAT ENJOYS ASPARAGUS. They dine in the hall, then go on sitting there in conversation, although Moffat believes that a man should never be at table for more than an hour.

'I can't believe you burn this miserable stuff, Lyte.' He pokes a foot at the stack of peat.

'It does well enough, doesn't it? A steady heat.'

'But where's the blaze? I feel like a peasant at your hearth, choking and gobbing at the shadows in the corner. What's for supper? Don't let me guess it will be herring again, or some cheap fish hung too long in your chimneys. Or mallards,' he adds, thinking of last time, when they'd gone wildfowling and he fell in the sodden moor and had to be hauled out with the ice cracking round his knees and one boot lost.

'I seem to remember we went out at your own insistence,' Henry says wryly, 'that there was a particular kind of teal you very much wanted to get acquainted with.'

'The truth is I find ducks less than fascinating these days.' Moffat empties his glass.

'For a puritan you're remarkably inconstant, not to mention partial to a bit of comfort. And for a naturalist, you've a staggering aversion to the countryside.'

'It is just that your countryside is so damn chilly, Lyte, even now when June is nearly upon us here we are hunched over the fire and the draught at our backs.' He stands up and opens the door a crack onto the screens passage. 'See? Even your sun has gone in.'

'You'd like Italy. It's warmer there.'

'And sweet deuce but the insects would be plentiful. I can hardly sleep at night for thinking of them. One day I'll have finished my degree and shall leave Cambridge and traverse Europe, the sunny climes.'

'Will you bring me back some good plants for the garden, little slips or seeds?'

'What kind of thing?' he asks, suspiciously. 'I'm not bringing bulbs, they cause too much trouble.'

'Anything that looks fascinating … aromatic, vigorous and not too tender.'

'And the foreign moon thrown in for good measure. I'll do my best. You'd better write it down, make a list. Once I've had a glimpse of *buprestis* in the flesh, there's no knowing what will happen to my memory. I may never come back.'

'Insects have no flesh.'

'Oh, you writers; so over-cautious with how you speak.'

'It's our natural humour, we revel in it.'

Thomas Moffat returns his attention to the peat stacked up by the side of the hearth. 'Look at you, burning your primitive slices of earth to keep warm. The absurdity of the rational mind in his lair.'

Henry Lyte grins. 'I like a guest like you, Moffat. The start of summer and here you are to keep the grim realities of our English climate alive and kicking. A more cheerful aspect would just make a rural existence seem all too tempting – one might even start enjoying life.' He holds up a slice of peat as dark and dense as spice bread. 'It is a rich kind of heat it offers,' he protests.

'My grief, man! And you are too serious about your fuel.'

'It's more than fuel – the very Levels themselves are made of this – no bedrock or clay to hold the world up there, just this halfway stuff a rich life-giving layer between sea and sky. It is soil in the making.'

Moffat is unconvinced. 'Rotten stalks,' he says.

'I can see you've yet to realize the marvels of its nature. Tomorrow we'll go out to the moor and watch them cut the peat and you will see just why it is a miracle.'

'That will be damp.'

'It will. And then, our expedition done, we can return to the fireside and bathe in its intrinsic warmth more gratefully.'

Thomas Moffat shifts his chair closer to the hearth and looks sulky.

'But it's the kind of flame for small, low spaces, Lyte. It's not proportional.'

Henry Lyte bursts out laughing. 'So that's your trouble with it! I had no idea your principles of scale were so easily affronted. I'd have put it down to your devotion to comfort and maintaining that city-spaniel softness about the ears.' Thomas Moffat's hair is as lush and shiny as a maid's, fanning out like a halo.

'There are uncommon sorts of dragonfly down there,' he adds. 'Which you would never see in London.' Henry always feels more rough about the edges when Thomas Moffat visits. They share a similarity in interest but their work unfolds in vastly different contexts. It cheers him up, seeing Moffat, but it does remind him of his preoccupation with working his land, his manorial duties; all making a difference from those on Lime Street with nothing to do all day but advance the cause of science, be it as doctors or botanists or etymologists. It is not that he is jealous of their intellectual freedoms, but there is always a quantity of flax seed to get in for Ridgeway Close, say, or debate needed with his bailiff over the new tenant at the upper mill. What they might not understand is how much enervating *time* a man has to devote to estate matters here, and of course there is the garden. The garden. For a moment his mind strays outside and wonders how the hyssop hedge is faring. Some lower leaves had begun yellowing and some had dropped, but the rest seemed firm. He must remember to direct the women to water all along its length before they leave. There will be no rain tonight. He should check the level in the butt by the east gable and consider drawing something from the brook. Mote's boy if left unsupervised will just take the drinking water from the well. There is so much satisfaction to be had from watering plants, those roots all drinking, filling up their skins with liquid.

'And?' With a start he notices that Thomas Moffat's boyish face is all agog in front of him – demanding, 'Where shall we walk, Lyte, if you say we must get out in that cold wind? Let's get it over with. I shall want to see everything.'

❧

After a tour of the gardens and orchard they stroll downhill, cross the river and stand on Carey Moor considering the layers of peat that they stand on.

Moffat is as morbid as Frances about it. 'All that life, so green and various and changeable, composting down to a black and crumbling soil, to nothing.' He rubs his hands on his smart breeches.

'But it is not nothing,' Henry points out. 'It contains another kind of life, another energy, and it will change yet.'

'But it is stagnant, dead stuff,' Moffat looks almost horrified, gazing about him as though he has never seen it like this before. 'It is huge, quivering slabs of … death.'

'Is it?' Henry asks. He bends and breaks off a great handful and smells it. 'But it does not smell of death to me. It is sweet, Thomas. It smells clean and wholesome.' He holds it out to him. 'It is land in the making, it is new.'

As they turn to make their way back to the house, Moffat examines the ground by his feet. 'What is that plant, with this woolly stuff about it?'

'Cudwort. Turner says it is good sodden in tart wine against the bloody flux.'

Moffat laughs. 'In every corner of his mind there is some cure for something ghastly.'

They come back by way of Sowey Wood and stop to examine a specimen of burdock; giant's leaves made of elephant hide, holey, tough, reddish veins, opaque, a landing place for solitary bees. They glance up to the purplish-red of squirrels, chattering and bushy in a walnut tree.

'I know I'm a naturalist,' Moffat says, sidelong, 'but why does my mind always hiss *fur coats*, when I see them?

'It's your upbringing,' Henry says, as if that explained everything. 'I have my father's best black cloak still, with its good trim of wolf ...'

At the word 'wolf' the squirrels freeze, as if noticing the two men for the first time. They eye them beadily, one red tail twitches, and then they scramble for safety.

'I like it here. Your bees have a lot to celebrate,' Moffat smiles, showing green-stained teeth where he has been tasting the garden.

# XIII.

*Of WILD LILY. Fleshie leaves, of an old purple or*
*dimme incarnate color, powdered or dasht with small*
*spots. The wild Lilly is not used in medicine, and*
*therefore his nature and vertues are as yet hidden,*
*and unknowne.*

I T IS MOFFAT'S LAST DAY AT LYTES CARY, and they are walking in the breeze, discussing in the garden as the day draws towards a close. The air feels turbulent and changeable. Henry will miss the flood of debate and stimulation that Moffat brings, he feels enlivened and motivated by his visit, but he is also looking forward to settling down with his manuscript once more.

They walk past the basketmaker's cottage by the garden door.

'Evening, Master,' she calls out.

'And to yourself, Widow Hodges. How are the baskets today?' he asks cheerfully.

'That's never a basket, Master, that's eel traps.'

He looks more closely and sees that it is. There are finished eel traps on the ground by the door, and the unfinished shape between her knees has a tall, bottlenecked height.

'How can you know who approaches on the path?' Henry can see that Moffat is curious. 'You knew it was myself?'

'It's your step, Master. Every soul has their own particular way of stepping on the earth. I know Master Mote from the manner of his cludding along. Master Oxendon is plunk, scrape, plunk, scrape. I can't put it rightly into words.'

'And my own?' he can't help asking.

'It's rude to say so, but I know your walking from its neatness. There's a strong noise to it, but not loud, and you don't make a big fuss out of walking like some do.'

Henry is amused by the detail of her scrutiny. He winks at Moffat. 'How about my friend here, what is his step like?'

'Slithering.'

Moffat roars with laughter.

'And my wife?' Henry wishes immediately that he hadn't asked this. The old woman frowns. 'I'm not sure that she comes by this way so often. I suppose she'll be mostly inside, is she, up at Lytes? Not like your other wife, Master, begging your pardon.' Her face creases with anxiety. 'By which I mean …'

'Your eel traps are very fine, Widow Hodges,' Henry reassures her, not wanting to sound brisk. 'Good day to you.' And with that they move away. Moffat wipes his eyes.

'I knew your mother's step very well, Master,' she calls after them.

Henry turns swiftly back. 'My mother?'

'A woman light on her feet.'

'Do you remember much … of her?' he asks, his throat tightening.

'She was kind to me at the time of my second husband's passing, and sometimes as I worked alongside of her would tell me all sorts about the children and their growings-up. In those days she'd have me about in the kitchen and malthouse, until the day I fell against the brewing lead and broke my foot and was no use to no-one. And that was when she set me up with a load of withies and a new sharp pick-ing knife and bodkin, just to start me off. She was a good woman, Master Lyte. She'd think much of you and your endeavours here, if you'll forgive me. She's no doubt watching over you. A good woman,' she repeats.

'She was,' he says.

When the wind blows from the north-east, the lea of the hill becomes unusually full of birds, sheltering from its chill. It's blustery enough down here, but up on the ridge there is a roar of wind. Out of the corner of his eye, as he thinks of his mother, Henry can see a mistle thrush, a pair of jays, a whitethroat, a spotted woodpecker, and a host of long-tailed tits flitting confusedly from bush to bush. These hedgerows are crawling with a medley of bird life.

Was this woman trying to tell him something? Why did she mention it like that? Despite the freshness of the wind he feels very itchy in his waistcoat suddenly. Much to Moffat's relief Henry decides to go home at once and change into something more comfortable.

Crossing the hall, he is surprised to see that Frances has put a jug of newly cut flowers from the garden on the high table. It must have been Frances, nobody else would have gone into his garden and cut so many blooms without asking permission. He bends over and takes a deep breath of rose and lavender, nestled in a froth of lady's mantle. The jagged edge of catnip runs crisp and hairy under his fingertip. Campion, cornflower, ox-eye daisy, pellitory of Spain, lovage, honey-suckle. Ten varieties of plant and he didn't see her out there, picking. He is sorry to have missed it. At six o'clock they sit down to eat, a second sitting after the household has finished their pottage. The flowers are bright and fresh on the edge of his vision, through grace, through the rest of the meal.

It is Moffat's last supper, and the genial sadness produced by a visi-tor's imminent departure pervades the hour.

'Did you have a good day, Mistress Lyte?' Henry wants to ask about the flowers, but finds he cannot.

'I did,' she replies. 'Mary, will you pass the sauce to your father? No, no, *with* the spoon.' There is a babble of family matters and one of the dogs steals a piece of beef from Jane's plate and has to be banished outside, so that there is no appropriate time to drop his query into their fragmented, mundane conversation over the children's heads, and then supper is over and Moffat goes off to pack. It is probably for the best that he didn't bring it up. He doesn't want to be misconstrued, nor to spoil the enjoyment of the flowers.

# XIV.

*Of the HYACINTHES. The common hyacinths do grow*
*about the borders of fallowed fields and pastures, and are*
*found in many places, especially about Wincaunton,*
*Storton and Mier, in the West parts of England, etc.*

**H**ENRY LOOKS OUT ACROSS HIS UNFOLDING GARDEN and tries to remember how it looked, so recently, when it was untoiled grass with just an unkempt kitchen patch exposed to too much wind from the north-east. Now, he has a walled sanctuary and bee garth; filled with blossoms, aromatic herbs, young trees being trained into a compliance of shapes, and a developing Knot. The hedges of the Knot are still young and thin, not quite the fat, lushly clipped quadrilateral that they will surely become, but the green bones of it are all there now.

He loathes the oleander. It sits with a ridiculous Mediterranean incongruity in its leaden pot close to the house, covered in those showy, acid-pink flowers like paper that Henry dislikes intensely. Frances loves it, for all the wrong reasons, waters it herself, turns it in the sun to keep its thriving growth even. It is brash, poisonous and useless, the worst kind of plant imaginable. He looks forward to the cold season when it will surely perish and Lytes Cary will be rid of it.

Jane comes into the room behind him, carrying little Johnny on her hip. She has been painting flowers again and has streaks of colour on her cheek.

'Would you like to come with me tomorrow on a field trip? This breeze should have died down by then,' he suggests. 'We could buy some gingerbread in Langport on the way back,' he adds, her face showing no expression at the prospect. She sets the boy down unsteadily on his feet, saying nothing.

'If we don't go soon we will be missing so much detail, Jane. This month is perfect. There are plants down there you could only dream about.' But she shakes her head earnestly.

'No thank you, Father,' and she takes Johnny by the hand and leads him away to play in the nursery.

He can feel Jane growing up and away from him a little more each day, like clematis or bryony climbing the trees, towards the light and out of reach. It is only natural, he supposes. There is nothing to be done about it. But what on earth is the point of learning all that Latin, he wonders, if she's not going to apply it to botany?

Henry can hear Lisbet grumbling to Frances outside in the hall about the wind as she still has a lot of wet washing to get dry somehow and if she puts it out on the hedges by the stable today it is all going to blow away, isn't it. Their voices drop and Henry wonders if they are not speculating on the likelihood of him allowing them to use the sheltered hedges of the Knot for draping garments over.

'No! Is the short answer,' he says flatly, when Frances knocks and pokes her head around the door. 'I am not having that prime hyssop made buckled and drooping for the sake of undershifts and aprons.'

No-one takes his garden seriously. Do they not *realize* that it is an exemplary herbalist's plot, filled with choice cultivars and several rarities that would be the envy of any good apothecary with ambitions for his own fresh supply of almost anything, that is bar resins, ground-up tortoises and rhino horn and other nonsense that good medicine should have no time for. His garden is filled with all that is fresh, potent, useful. He goes to the window again to check that the women are not eyeing up any other drying possibilities within his encircling garden walls, the espaliers come to mind with their few, newly set fruits behind the pink and white blossoms that are flaking softly away now, but neither the women nor their big, damp laundry basket are anywhere to be seen.

He doesn't particularly like washday at the best of times, it's the smell of bleaching linen; collars, ruffles and embroidery laid in warm urine for half an hour, after which boiled in hot water or liquor, and it all stinks. The dirt itself must be better than this? The drying ruffs on sticks outside look very sinister, like empty white flowers. Turner disapproves of ruffs of course.

'But my household uses cuckoopint to stiffen linen, sir,' he'd said once, 'not corn. Not something that would be used for food. I am not depriving a hungry child of bread by starching my ruff, sir.'

'Not directly, perhaps.' He shook his greyish, untidy head, so that dandruff showered down. 'Nevertheless,' he'd said. 'There is politics in every little aspect of your day.' Turner does not make allowances for anybody, and neither should he.

The next morning of course he cannot find clean clothes.

'Where are my shirts? There is not a single one in here.'

'Damp still, Henry. Too damp to wear.' Frances is busy folding the covers back to air the bed.

'Oh.' Outside he notes the weather is still blustery, clouds scudding across a scoured blue sky.

'Lisbet can lay some of the washing on the sheltered side of the kitchen garden wall, if she needs to. Don't let her make a habit of it.'

He is annoyed that he has to be involved at all with their domestic minutiae. Frances is still in the room, expecting some kind of answer to something. Can't she see he is soaping his face?

'What?' He is tetchy. She hands him the towel.

'I was wondering whether you had taken any time yet to consider moving to London for the winter, just for the winter. A long visit.'

'Ah,' Henry says, puts the towel aside on the bed.

And that's how it starts off, any row between them is always some insignificant domestic difference that swells instantly to something bigger and more troublesome, as if waiting beneath the surface of their conversation all the time.

'It is all layers, layers, layers in a marriage,' he grumbles, 'and no sure footing. I just want to get on with *living*, Frances.' He knows that he sounds plaintive and that makes him more annoyed with her, for asking such a thing, putting him in the position of having to argue his case. 'To want to be living here, in the house of my forefathers, is a perfectly reasonable intention. I do not want to feel like a visitor in my own home, being here only when the sun is more likely to be shining. To know a place deeply is to see it in all its aspects. And as any husband should be able to expect as a matter of course; when you married me you were wed to Lytes Cary.'

'You struck that bargain with my father and I am not responsible for it,' she retorts, under her breath.

Henry blinks. Does that mean she did not want to marry him? But she will not elaborate on this, she has flounced out of the chamber.

Dear God. When his own father John Lyte swore at Henry that he had taken someone else's wife, perhaps then he was right. Those bitter letters sent from father to son over whom he had married, at the time Henry had dismissed them as jealousy of his own happiness, fuelled and stirred up by Joan Young's viperish whispers in his ear. But, now that he puts his mind back to this uncomfortable topic, yes; what on earth was it that made Frances choose him over someone she was already pledged to? At the time she had assured him that her previous engagement had been only a verbal agreement between her father and someone – Henry cannot recall his name at all – made long before she was consulted. She had sworn that, though verbal contracts made

between prospective bride and groom were as binding as any ceremony, there had been no such thing between them, and her conscience
was clear. John Lyte did not believe her, and declared her already
wedded in the eyes of God. He was an old-fashioned man, he'd said,
from an age when principles were stood by. But maybe Henry was not
her choice at all. Maybe, just for example, his request for the marriage
portion was more agreeable to her father than that of some other
man. He was merely the cheaper option for the Tiptoft family coffers.
That couldn't be true, could it – that her father preferred his hand
over that of another man's for the relative cost of the portion alone. It
is not as if he could ask him, for peace of mind. The man is dead, with
Frances's mother married again, to John Marwood.

He wants to please her, he really does, but he will not be made to
choose between his home and his wife's whim. The final decision
about such things rests with him. And surely a man's home and his
wife should be one and the same?

Nothing is ever simple. He knows it is childish to wish for simplicity, that there is no such thing when it comes to matters between a
man and his wife, be they alive or dead.

# XV.

*Of MARJEROM. A delicate and tender hearbe, of a
sweet savour. It loveth fat and well maintayned ground.*

J ULY TIPS INTO AUGUST, and it is harvest time. As the oleander's
lavish flowering season draws to an end, Henry watches in fear,
and writes vehemently in the herbal, *it is time to supplant it: for it hath
alreadie floured, so that I feare it will shortly seede, and fill this wholesome soyle full of wicked Nerium.* He considers whether the bonfire, or
a slow death by frost, would be the best end available.

But Frances preempts him, and one afternoon Henry discovers
that she has had Tobias Mote trundle the pot and its loathsome
contents into a corner of the hall to overwinter out of the frosts.

'See!' she says, 'Isn't that a good idea? I do take an interest in your
garden after all. And when spring comes, we can wheel it back out
again.'

The miller is busy, the mice are plentiful, pouring out of the shrinking cornfields, he goes down to oversee the men bagging up and loading the corn stores with sacks of yellow grain. The grinding noise of the stones at the windmill up on the hill, going round and round, goes on into the late evening each day of the week but the Sabbath. There is a dry dust on everything, on his sleeves, on his boots, on the horses' sweating flanks; the air shimmers with it at midday. There is dust churning up at the gate where they come in and out of the field, there is dust on the fruit in the orchard, on the green glazed flagons the boy lugs back at sundown. Everyone has the thirst of an ox on them and the estate drinks gallons of beer. Lisbet can hardly keep up with the brewing, though she did plan ahead. Frances remembered from last year how stocks got low, and made sure that enough dredge malt was ready beforehand. Harvesters drink. They like it strong and the stronger it is the harder they work – or so the saying goes.

'It's the way it's always been,' Henry shrugs when Frances queries it. Hind servants usually drink small beer, but harvest, that's different, it's hot, hard work from dawn till dusk. The beer is as strong out there as at sheep-shearing time, but the drinking is more good natured, no fights breaking out as they can between gangs at shearing. But harvest, everyone is hot and dog tired, and for Old Hannah there are many mouths to feed.

Henry comes into the kitchen.

'Extraordinary good luck, Frances,' he says, waving a letter. Frances is inaccessible on the other side of the long table, rubbing pastry crumbs together in a big basin, she pushes hair out of her eyes and smiles expectantly. Tom Coin is grating bread into a pile, sweating as he does it and Old Hannah is standing on a stool reaching a ham down from the rack.

It seems that nobody has a care for little Johnny, who is asleep and tied into his cradle to stop him falling out and set at a sensible distance from the hearth, so that any passerby can rock him a little with their foot. Henry frowns. Is that how his son and heir should be looked after during the day?

'Where is the nursemaid?' he asks.

'She went off to her mother who is sick but will be back by eight o'clock this evening.'

Henry turns to leave, he can see everyone is busy.

'But wait! What is your news?' Frances calls after him, eager for word of something good. 'Did an ancient aunt die and leave us a fortune?'

'Almost as good. An eminent botanist called Mathias Lobel, whom I had the great fortune to meet when I was in Montpelier, is shortly moving from Flanders to England. He was a pupil of Guillaume Rondelet, no less. And will you hazard where he plans to take up residence?'

'I can't imagine.'

'Bristol! Isn't that magnificent. Our corner of the countryside suddenly does not seem so barren of scientific thought, despite Doctor Turner's departure to London.'

'Good, good,' she says, distractedly. He hardly ever comes into the kitchen. It does not feel at all like his kind of territory, and Old Hannah finds this suits her very well. He picks up a spoon and points at the saucepan.

'Is that for dinner?'

Frances looks disappointed. 'For a moment I thought you were going to say that you'd had word of your father's will, that it had come to light. You looked so excited.'

Henry is about to say something encouraging but Johnny wakes up and begins bawling by the hearth, so that she has to pick him up.

He goes outside. He watches a yellowish, skulking chiffchaff in the alder, and a perky Jenny wren flicking its tail. The harvesters are dots up in Ten Acres field, the bailiff is there, they will be fine. Just as he decides to ride over to Bristol tomorrow, he hears a tapping on the path and Widow Hodges comes into view. She has a long stick with which she feels her way forward, and a basket over her arm, which as he approaches he can see contains two brown eggs and something greasy in a piece of cloth. He doesn't mean to startle her, but she stumbles as she hears his voice so close beside her, and he is sorry for it. She looks bedraggled in the heat, her eyelids flickering.

'Didn't hear you there, Master, nor anybody. Nobody's ever stood there as I come by, I was elsewhere in my thoughts.' She is disorientated, her chest rising and falling with the effort of shuffling home, and he takes her basket and walks with her to her dwelling. She sits down and catches her breath. Her skin is grey.

'Could I trouble you to pour me a sup of wellwater from the jug?' she asks.

'Are you well, dame?'

'I do not like the heat,' she says. 'Nor do I like the smell of harvest.' She drinks it down.

'Too many thoughts and recollections in it, this time of year.' She wipes her mouth on her sleeve. 'I look forward to the frosts, where there is no such abundant smell.'

Henry smiles at such a notion. 'People need to eat. Men, women, children.'

She seems about to say something, and he remembers all those months ago the day that Johnny was born, when she did not finish her story of her daughter Benet. Hadn't she said she was born at harvest time?

'You are kind to ask after her, Master,' she says, after a pause, but there is apprehension in her voice.

'Did she live?' he asks, quite gently, sitting down beside her in the gable's shadow. 'What was it that you saw was wrong?'

But this time Widow Hodges begins a slightly different kind of story. She picks up a basket and her finger traces the spiral of the withy's progress backwards.

'I do not think it blasphemous to say that we felt blessed to have her, despite everything,' she says. 'Benet suckled well and by the time she was near to her second year she was speaking in little tumbles of words and able to carry a crock to table without spilling a drop. Indeed I felt there was nothing amiss with her at all. Her chubby hands grew long and fine of finger, with a strength in them, so that she was set to be a boon to us inside the house and to herself and in time to her husband when she came of age. By her sixth year she was very deft with the needle and with dibbling seeds and anything that needed straightness, pointedness and being in rows, and she began to show a gift for working withy, making baskets alongside me which I did oftentimes for a little earnings on top of what we had, which indeed was adequate.' She suddenly turns and faces him.

'I have heard say you are writing a book of healing cures for every disease and affliction?'

'I am, dame, I—'

'Well I should make sure you look after every one of your kin, every one of them.'

Henry is taken aback at the turn this has taken.

She tilts her face up to the blue sky. 'I saw my daughter once with the stars lodged in her eyes, Master, lodged deep down as if two yellow stars were there, winking at me.'

The woman is mad, Henry thinks, she is a mad old woman with her head spinning in the heat. She rambles on. 'It was a strange sight I have not been able to forget.'

He gets up to go.

'How can you bear to spend so much time talking with that old woman?' Frances asks, in the bedchamber as they retire together. There is no need to light a candle. In these light, balmy August evenings it is easy to believe that summer never ends.

'She is lonely, she has no-one to talk to,' he says. 'I find her mildly entertaining.' He hesitates. 'We share interests in common.'

Frances raises her eyebrows.

'She knew my mother,' Henry adds, more accurately. 'It seems she knows a lot about this family.'

And then he goes to Frances and holds her at arm's length in order to look her over, carefully, tenderly, searching for signs in the dusky light, and he can't help smiling.

He does not mention to Frances what else Widow Hodges had said as he walked away from her, so quietly he almost couldn't hear.

'The next one will be a son, too. You didn't know she was with child?' she'd laughed, hoarse as a toad. 'Trust an old woman to smell out the truth of things.'

# XVI.

*Of OKE of JERUSALEM. The same dried, and
layd in presses and Wardrobes, giveth a pleasant smell
unto clothes, and preserveth them from moths
and vermine.*

IN THE END HE DOES NOT RIDE OVER to meet Mathias Lobel
until the autumn. It is the last day of October when he goes,
Hallowtide again, and outside the world is disintegrating, a blur-
ring of boundaries. Everywhere is desiccating and sticky,
threaded with cobwebs, laced together with dryness and nothing
and falling apart. The leaves that are left are shivering on their
twigs and the tock-tock of yellow is everywhere as the leaves
come down. He enjoys the coarse textures of this time of year,
looks forward to November, but he arrives late for dinner as the
roads are difficult. There is boiled beef left though, and the servant brings good wine.

Lobel is earnest and self-important. His friend Pierre Pena, also a
pupil of the great Rondelet, is at his house and they are talking
endlessly of their project, which they call the *Stirpium adversaria
nova*. It sounds like a mishmash but very learned.

Lobel is giving a detailed account of a botanizing trip he made last Saturday with a local man called Stephen Bredwell, whom Henry has met perhaps once in Moffat's company.

'My Christ but that man is a climber,' Lobel is saying. 'No qualifications to speak of and there he is, practising his medicine as he pleases, undercutting my charges.'

'I thought he was admitted to the College of Physicians last year?' Pena says. 'And you don't like field trips,' he adds. 'I'd stay at home if it makes you crabby.'

Henry says nothing. In fact the image that springs to his mind as he hears Lobel say *climber* is of a particularly fragrant climbing rose that he has seen in the garden of Mistress Shaw, and he intends to ask for a slip. Its modest blooms have a blush like the palest of maidens and the leaves are notched very fine and close cut, like sweet briar. He hasn't had much success to date with taking slips of rose, but has come across a new method he would like to try. A good rose is a delight.

Lobel is asking something.

'What?'

'I said, do you think you will be done shortly with your translation?' His tone is rather cold. Henry wonders if Lobel might not be a little annoyed that he did not think of doing it himself.

'No,' he says cheerfully. 'I am a long way off. Besides, I am liking it too much to let its time run short.'

'What will your market be? By which I mean, who will purchase such a thing?'

'Those who are not doctors,' Henry says. He is slightly irritated by their attitude.

Lobel and Pena crane forward as if seeing him for the first time.

'But are you not concerned for the evil that may be unleashed by knowledge being used badly, by those who should not have it?' Lobel asks.

'Not at all. The true evil is the *withholding* of knowledge,' Henry says. He does not mean to be so outspoken but he can't help it if they ask.

'If there is a man called a doctor who knows certain things which can relieve pain or cure disease, but only administers his knowledge on receipt of a fat fee from the more privileged amongst us, then that is the kind of complacency that incubates evil. The state in which we live needs to be stirred up, doesn't it?' Henry has Turner's voice ringing round his head, and for once he agrees with him. 'I'll tell you this. God's gifts to the world, in the form of potent roots, seeds and herbs are not there to be misappropriated. They are not a doctor's to keep secret for private profit, he has been merely entrusted to properly, responsibly dispense them to those in need. The doctor is entitled to his decent living, and respect afforded to him, but the path of wealth and glory should not rest on the converse, unsavoury truth, that those who lack the means to pay him for what he knows will suffer and die.' Henry scratches his beard. 'I can see you are shocked by my putting it so bluntly, but I believe this is the case.' He grins, wondering what Moffat would make of their faces. 'Besides, I rather like the idea of merchants' wives passing my book down from hand to hand, consulting it for remedies, understanding why this plant works or that plant, saving ordinary people from a bit of discomfort.'

It is a mark of Lobel's greatness that he does not take offence at Henry's opinions.

'We shall see,' is all he says, and asks the servant to bring more wine and the rest of the afternoon is passed very pleasantly.

# XVII.

*Of RUE, or HERBE GRACE. This rue lasteth both winter and sommer, and dieth not lightly.*

'HAVE YOU EVER DONE A TERRIBLE THING IN YOUR LIFE?' The oddness of the voice jolts Henry Lyte awake, so that he lies with his chest pounding. The moonlight is stark in the chamber, lying in slant bright strips across the inky blackness beyond the bedcloth. He can hear breathing, and of course it is his wife who is lying beside him in the bed. He stares up where the cloth above them must be, but can see nothing.

'Have you?' she whispers again.

Henry clears his throat. 'I was asleep, I ...'

'Because when I hear of some men's deeds – running a man through in battle, say, with a sword or cutlass so that his blood and bowels spill out – I find myself wondering if even an ordinary man is capable of wickedness in extraordinary moments.'

He struggles to focus on her peculiar question. She must have been lying there thinking for some time. But why disturb his sleep? He rubs his eyes. Henry can't tell what kind of tone of voice she is using, when he can't properly see her face. Then she rolls a little on the mattress, and her eyes are gleaming in the moonlight, and that is almost worse. As if she could read his mind he tries not to think of terrible things, tries to empty himself of the faint creeping fear he can feel in there unasked for. When she speaks he can also see her white teeth.

'Or abandoning his infants in a time of need.' Did Frances say that? Why in heaven is she lying here thinking of all these things? Is she fully awake? It must be the baby inside her belly making her strange. He feels as if he were struggling to free himself of weeds in an obscure pond, and begins to actually rise in the bed to defend himself.

'But those are very different instances.' He sits right up into the stream of moonlight and blinks. He can feel his chest tightening with that familiar anxiety.

'The moral conflict that a man must suffer before or after going to arms …' he stops and tries again. 'Often a man has no choice but to go to arms. And the wounding and slaughter of men is an unfortunate objective in time of war.' Henry has a sudden image of a field of grass being scythed to the ground. How different a man's death is to a plant's, he thinks. There is strength in a plant's system of life, where it might be cut asunder but still sprout from the roots again. And by contrast how weak and vulnerable we are, walking the earth like meat.

'What?' Frances says, as if he had spoken aloud. He lies back down in the darkness and squeezes his eyes shut. She is hard, coldly cerebral. He can't quite explain what he means but there is definitely something cold about the mechanisms of her mind, as though there were small cogs in there, going round and round.

'Do try to rest, darling,' he says. 'For the baby's sake.' She is such a strange woman.

An owl wavers its call quite close to the house, then there is silence, just the rushing of blood in the ears that is like the far-off hiss of a flat expanse of sea.

Frances raises herself on her elbow, the ropes creaking.

'But you did not answer my question, Henry,' she whispers insistently, and there is no answer. When she bends over him her hair hangs down like willows in darkness at the edge of water so that it brushes his skin once, twice. She can surely see that he has fallen asleep and her question must wait.

In the morning at breakfast after prayers Frances looks across at him. 'Last night you were restless, Henry.'

'I was?'

'You spoke and muttered in your sleep, and churned the sheets.'

'I'm sorry, I …'

'All sticky with sweat.'

He tries to smile. 'Not a crime, I hope.'

'Were you dreaming?'

'I'm sure that I was,' Henry says. He really doesn't like it when she is digging in his head. He hears himself add inexplicably, 'I was dreaming of things that have no bearing on things that have happened.'

Frances yawns.

'I wish something would happen at Lytes Cary, frankly. If I have to stay in that kitchen boiling one more batch of fruit I will die of boredom. Is that possible? My own dreams are populated only with bobbing roundels of sour purple fruits in vats. It's like staving off death, that kind of preserving, Henry. Holding off the inevitable rot, at arm's length. Fancy having to labour for every little luxury in this way. And all for a bit of change in the cold season,' she grumbles. 'I'm sure my own mother simply bought these small things when they were needed.'

He doesn't like this childish spirit of discontent to be displayed in front of the servants, and tries to be brisk until all the plates and fingerbowls are cleared away. 'And no doubt if we were in London and not the countryside that would be the case. However,' with an effort he does not leave the hall before he's finished his sentence. He is already thinking of the translation of a particular word, the subtle variance that would distinguish it from another meaning altogether. He turns at the door onto the passage.

'You are, after all, the wife of a country landowner at home.'

'My point exactly, Henry. If we were in London everything would be very different,' Frances says, as he pulls the latch and escapes, but after some minutes she pins on her sleeves and goes to the plums in the kitchen anyway.

That afternoon he hears from Mote that Mistress Shaw has passed away in Wells. With regret and sadness he thinks of the loss of her climbing rose, the hunger in her eyes for children, all those plants that will not be propagated this year.

Here in the orchard he watches the black pin-bright eye of the wren absorbing the tiniest details amongst the nooks and crannies of the wall by the medlar, the rotting leaf-mould at its root, a world invisible to his own eye. He feels large and clumsy in his clothes today. An oaf. These new padded trunk-hose that he is wearing make him far too obvious to the eye. Frances had made him have them made up in London. *But how can I do anything in these? I can't bend or walk properly. They make me strut like a farmyard goose*, he had protested at the time, as she and the polished little tailor man bustled round him with tape and pins, and he was right. What seems right in London is rarely suitable for Somerset, and vice versa. He doesn't go as far as extending this comparison to the chief components of his marriage, not even privately.

Even this far from the house he can hear Frances playing at her instrument, the acidic ripples of her notes.

# XVIII.

*Of FENELL. The gréene leaves of Fenel eaten, or the séed thereof drunken with Tutsan, filleth womens breasts or dugs with milke.*

B Y APRIL THE MARSH IS LIKE A MANGY DOG'S BACK; brown, uneven tufts of rough sedge and rush. Henry and Jane are sent out walking by the goodwife who has come again because Frances is in labour and she doesn't want them hovering outside the door. A jack-snipe flies up as they approach the wood. Henry picks his way across, checking for eggs underfoot at every step.

The copse is filled with points of birdsong. If they listen they can hear the shape of the wood.

'Will the baby be all right, Father?'

'I hope so.'

Yesterday was Good Friday, and tomorrow will be Easter Sunday.

They watch the first, fat bumble bees scribbling their furred and cranky plans in low flights all across the grass, from here to there.

'What are they looking for?'

'For holes.'

'Not flowers?' Jane says. 'Why?'

JANE BORODALE

'I don't know. But they are queens. That's why they're so large and out so early. Ask Master Moffat next time he comes – he's good at insects.'

When they return to the house, they find that today is the day that Thomas Lyte is come into this world of sorrows, born with the caul over his head. Frances looks relieved. 'That will protect him from drowning,' she says.

# THE THIRD PART

## The Kinds

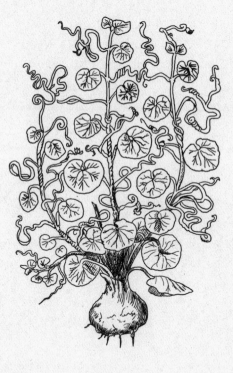

# ❧ 1568 ❧

# I.

*Of CORIANDER. Coriander is a very stinking hearbe,
smelling like to the stinking Worme. The juyce layed to
with Ceruse, Litharge, or scum of silver, cureth
St Anthonies fire, and swageth and easeth all
inflammations that chance on the skinne.*

ON AND OFF ALL MORNING he has been hearing a puzzling and intermittent tapping from the garden, like the noise of someone making a fence without his permission, for example. But each time that he goes to the window to peer outside, the noise stops and nobody is there. It is only later when he gets up to take a stretch in the garden, standing stock still and lost in thought that he sees the culprit – a mistle thrush beating a snail against a stone, smashing the brittle whorls of shell to get at the pulp of its sticky flesh inside. What we would do for our offspring, he thinks idly, as the bird flies to the hedge with the soft, grey contents dangling from its beak. What horrors we undertake without a pause for thought, because there is no time to question what we do. He would do anything to shield his children from peril. He would jump in front of a running cart, starve so that they could eat, face a rabid dog, so that they could be saved. Disease is what he most fears for them.

The scattered bits of shell on the edge of the path crunch underfoot for days, until a late April downpour washes all away.

Frances has indigestion. Since the birth of Thomas two weeks ago she has had varying degrees of appetite, with Old Hannah making small tasty dishes to nourish her. Today she sent up a piece of gently boiled young pike, and a broth of lettuce, but Frances stirs the spoon about listlessly and lies back in the bed.

'I can make you up a digestive powder,' he offers, it is the least he can do for the mother of his two sons. Thomas is asleep next door with the nurse. 'It's very warming; lovage root, caraway, white amber, fennel, peel of citron, rosemary flowers and sugar.'

'I'll take none of your witches' brew, thank you,' Frances says, opening her eyes. 'I still have some proprietary pills made by Dr Madox that I brought from London, they'll do nicely.'

Henry does wish she would have more interest in the herbs.

'I am the one with the stomach ache, Henry,' she says, rubbing the front of her chemise. 'There's no need to sigh like that.' She looks at him curiously. 'Besides, I thought you did not like to go in the stillroom.'

'I've never said that, have I?'

'Oh, all right then, let me try the powder, as long as it is not disgusting, and does not make me choke.'

❧

The stillroom is at the far end of the kitchen offices. He hasn't been here since Anys died – and has discouraged anyone else from taking it on, even Jane, he thinks perhaps he hasn't had the heart to begin to face it. Occasionally people have gone into the stillroom if it has been necessary to fetch an ointment for a wound or bruising, or a powder for a headache or sickness or cough already ground up, but otherwise nothing has been disturbed or prepared in there, nor replenished, cleaned or moved about, and the stocks of Anys's remedies for common ailments have slowly depleted.

The door still sticks as it always did on opening, and as he enters he feels his face breaking fine lines of cobweb. He hears mice running and then the muffled, musty silence of a cluttered storeroom. The smell is like a punch in his stomach, it is so like her and so strong. A marvellous compendium of aromatic, bitter dryness, sweetness, faded concentrations.

Of course nothing is changed in here, except that everything is two years older – the bundles of tansy, lovage, alecost, dyer's camomile, hops, sweet briar leaves, hanging heads down from the crossbeams are dusty and stale, spent, grey with dust and webs.

On the trestle at the back of the room there are bundles and stalks laid out as if abandoned mid-preparation, and these have something of the charnel house about them, dried, nibbled, balding.

The surfaces are covered in mouse-droppings and dust. He opens pots and smells the contents one by one, reading the labels on each in her looping, hesitant handwriting.

Simple waters, compound waters. Calamus root, warm and woody, almost like ginger. Grey gum benzoin, like lava rock and smelling of old beeswax. Dried mugwort, silvery balls of flowers. Frankincense, blond as sugar. Aloes like a dark green coal. Orris. Resinous mastic. Musk ambrette, soapy, sweet and sparkling like fish scales. Ambergris. Oil of spikenard, as used by Mary Magdalen. The pin-sharp smell of turpentine.

Some herbs she bought fresh from the simplers to dry or preserve or to make into oils and waters, and some she tended herself. In his mind's eye he can see her bending diligently over her small patch where she grew a modest assortment of the most useful herbs. He pictures her turning a large leaf of elecampane over in her hand, the breeze blowing loose bits of her hair across her mouth as she spoke.

'Softness on the back of any leaf is a clue, Henry, that it may be good for coughs. I don't know why.'

Anys loved the fact that it was a lady's duty to fill the gap left when the monks, with their ancient, secluded gardens, were ousted, their living knowledge scattered to the winds. She had little sheaves of recipes, in her own and other people's hand, copied out and passed on. She spent hours each week in here, the tip of her tongue sticking from the corner of her mouth as if tasting the air in her concentration. She would have loved this garden he is making now, she would have employed its constituent parts thoroughly, quietly revelled in it.

His chest feels very tight, he rubs his chest, tries to breathe.

He touches her pestle and mortar, fine hair sieves, assorted baskets and folded white linen for gathering. A little book of recipes dense with her handwriting. In a mousetrap down on the floor against the wall, a small mummified mouse carcase is lying rigid in its jaw. He creaks open a wicker chest and it is like opening onto the dead, full of dead breath, crumbled remains, but in one corner a nest of live baby shrews, pink as ham, their squeaking so highly pitched he can hardly hear them. A chafing dish, the distillatory itself, the limbeck assembled with the spout as if ready for heat at any moment. He remembers the mild, absorbed expression that she wore whilst working, humming as she watched for that first precious trickle of distilled fluid from the spout, jar poised to collect it; the virgin essence. Of all their children he sees that particular look of concentration in Florence, sometimes.

'It takes out only the *soul* of plants, Henry,' Anys used to say, 'leaving the rest behind.'

He admits that she seems saintly in a way that he did not notice when she was alive. He wonders if his memory is objective, knows it does not matter if it isn't.

He unstoppers bottles of oils and tinctures, aromatic waters, and most of these smell fresh and useful yet. He feels a small stirring of something that might be anticipation, breathing in these potencies. For so long he has been poring over words to describe these substances, that it is startling to face the living, aromatic force of them. Nothing can properly summon any sense of their vibrancy, the diverse intensity of their characters. He finds dried cherries, puts one in his mouth and chews. They are still good; sour and granular, better than raisins.

He sits down and absorbs the idea that he should clean this still-room out, dust off the jars and begin the task of replenishing the stock. Jane would be well-disposed to help, her flourishing understanding of both plants and Latin would be an asset. Perhaps the table could be moved over there, to receive a better light, and new hooks could be bought, new twine, the shears sharpened … he must make a list at once and send a boy to Somerton.

He hears a noise, and realizes that it is himself whistling a tune very softly under his breath, and begins to assemble the ingredients, wipes out the mortar, grinds everything until the digestive powder is soft and even. Above all, he decides, he should direct Frances towards this renewed enterprise. It should be her obligation.

# II.

*Of ANGELICA. The roote is great and thicke, blacke without, and white within, out of which, when it is hurt or cut, there floweth a fat or oylie liquor like Gumme, of a strong smell or taste.*

HENRY LOVES THIS GLORIOUS FLAT BASIN of wetland that is the Levels. He stands on the fresh quiver of peat, the half-solid sureness of a soil in the making. It is almost a miracle land, perfectly balanced between worlds, between the seasonal inundation of saltwater from the Channel, rich streamwater from the hills and then the draining away and by June the hot sun, beating upon the new and plentiful grasses, that is so good for cattle. There is so much to praise in a soil so blessed. He looks at the cows grazing, at the yellow flags, the vivid green of rushes, the blue flash of a kingfisher. His heart swells with the joy of looking at a fertile land at the peak of its season.

Already it is the twenty-fourth of May, the day after Rogation Sunday. There are flies mildly juggling the air and the sky above is blue and thick. The cows graze across the field, time moving slower in the heat, their legs yellow with the powder from buttercups. The meadow is like a soft fur of grasses.

Looking for specimens he finds lady's smock still flowering, vetch, huge dock leaves, mint, *langue de boeuf*, burdock that is large but still low, comfrey, camomile, water angelica, St John's wort, white archangel, feverfew, alehoof, and cress in the ditches like green sharp little ladders spiking up.

A week later he goes back for more specimens and already the hay has been cut.

It is a bright day with some cloud cover. Silvery green maylight and a relentless wind now; dead-straight like it's been drawn with a ruler. How quickly the summer disintegrates even as it is arriving. Everywhere are blown bits of rose leaf, grasshoppers, ash, supple grasses, skylarks, yellowhammer, swifts. He takes shelter behind some old hawthorns, stiffening nettles with buttercups, thistle, foxtail grasses on fine tough stalks. He sees boys running in the open after hats on the bare, cut meadow after it's raked. On his way home he sees a nest of blue tits in a hollow fence post and thanks God for the blessing of children, of sons.

# III.

*Of ARISTOLOCHIA. Carolus Clusius saith, it groweth about Hispalis a Citie in Spaine, now called Civill, and that he hath found it amongst the bushes and briers there.*

H E HAS HAD AN UNEXPECTED LETTER from Simon Cressing, carrying abominable news. Joan Young has entered a formal bill of complaint against Henry to Sir Nicholas Bacon, Lord Keeper of the Great Seal, in the Court of Chancery. She is taking Henry to court over some matter she has fabricated to do with unlawfully misplaced or secret deeds she says that he has hidden or kept from her, to do with land at Mudford, not the manor, some meadows and pasture. Henry scratches at his beard, trying to work out what she means. There are no secret deeds or conveyances.

*She is publicly implying that there is an unsavoury flavour to your dealings with the estate, that you are freezing her out of what she says she has rights to. That you are not of good character. But we will bat it back,* Cressing writes, *say it is slanderous and untrue. While the threat of litigation is never to be taken lightly, nothing will happen for years. Chancery is notoriously slow. The purpose of this action is to unsettle you, to vex, trouble and disquiet, and cause expense. Unless they take it to the Court of Requests, or even Star Chamber, we need not worry for the moment. We will enter a defence and see what happens next. There is power in patience, Henry.*

Henry stares, irritated, at the letter. 'I know how these things work, Cressing,' he says aloud. 'I was Undersheriff before Elizabeth was Queen. My father was a Justice of the Peace, and escheator for Devon and Somerset in several terms.' He looks out of the window. 'God knows I saw enough family feuds and wranglings across the county.' He shakes his head. 'It is a black, black business to be bubbling up between kin. Never did I think I should be the subject of one like this.'

Frances comes into his study.

'Joan Young hopes to serve me with a subpoena from the High Court of Chancery,' he remarks, and is about to pass the letter to her, when he sees a note at the very bottom of the paper. It says, *I must warn you – she has married her proctor.*

'Dear God.' Henry is shocked.

'Proctor? What do you mean?' says Frances.

'Her lawyer. God knows how she has done it, but she has entrapped that poor man William Phelips.'

'But why were we not told?' she exclaims, sitting down on the desk. 'Your sister Alice will be upset to hear it. Does your brother know?'

Henry shrugs. 'I have not seen him since I refused him yet another loan. How exceedingly ingenious. Now her own lawyer has a vested interest in her affairs beyond his fee.'

They are interrupted by the arrival of the molecatcher. John Parsons the bailiff is over at Langport, so Henry must go out and deal with this.

The molecatcher's mind works in long tunnels of recollection, Henry thinks as he strides up to the orchard. He has never met a man who can work his way backwards in time with so much recorded detail as a stimulus to inconsequential strings of local history. His prodigious memory is contained in a large forehead that bulges from under a crop of sand-white hair, and his long pink hands are tipped with overgrown, broken fingernails. Henry is always disconcerted by the molecatcher, by the sense that he is being woven into the man's rambling chronicle whether he likes it or not. He is a man who never forgets a fleck or particular that he has observed, and is never shy about spouting it all back in its entirety, should any part of it prove relevant. Listening to his tongue wagging on, Henry wonders if everyone secretly prefers to talk instead to those with poor memories, where a new conversational corner in familiar territory is always there to be rounded. This man however must live in a continuum, with never a sense of a fresh day unfolding. Time is all one and the same to him.

'No mole, no cost to you, sir,' he never fails to assert, scrupulously paving the way for a worst-case scenario, where no mole is caught. Henry escapes from his monologue and lets him get on with it. But there is always a sack of soft, smoky corpses to examine and count gingerly the following day. He could employ some other man, as plenty enough of them pass through the vale with their enquiries. But the fact is that the man is extremely good at what he does. He thinks like a mole, he knows just where they run. He predicts with accuracy where tomorrow they will be. He knows to leave those digging in the low-lying marshy parts of fields, being good for the drainage, in favour of upland invaders, where they are not welcome.

Henry always suffers bad, guilt-ridden dreams the night after the molecatcher has been, as though he is not playing fair, as though the moles have more claim on his garden and orchard than he ever would, but he knows this a childish reflex.

'How has Joan done it?' he asks his wife as they retire to bed. 'Did she make herself very needy, very in awe of his special skill as a church barrister?'

'Probably. And the distant glitter of an additional inheritance on the horizon must be quite an incentive to marriage,' she says drily, unbuttoning her chemise. 'Besides, she is still a handsome woman.'

Henry looks up. 'Handsome? What on earth are you saying? She is an icy, dried up, money-grabbing shrew, Frances.'

'She is attractive for her age though, quite well preserved.'

'I have never seen that. Are you serious?' He is genuinely mystified. How hard it is to be objective.

# IV.

*Of SOW-BREAD or CYCLAMEN. The roote of
Sow-bread dryed, and made into powder, and taken in
the quantitie of a dramme with Hydromell, called also
honied water, purgeth downewards grosse and tough
flegme, and other sharpe humors.*

H ENRY AND FRANCES ARE ATTENDING A DINNER, a gathering
of small-to-medium landowners, some elder sons, a handful
of wives, all of the Somerton district, some of whom he knows
through his work previously as captain of the local fighting band
trained to stave off the Spanish. He would have liked to arm them
with six-foot quarter staffs, not the genteel mother-of-pearled swords
they had strapped to their belts like schoolboys. No doubt some of
them would have proved excellent swordsmen, but if he was honest
he'd felt that an iron-tipped beast of a weapon could have stood most
of them in better stead in combat, if frank retreat was not an option,
and he includes himself in that.

Their conversation is local, gossipy, but he can see that across the
table Frances is enjoying herself. Henry's right-hand neighbour, who
has heard of his translation, asks him to explain his project.

'But what I can't understand, Lyte, is how you can identify each plant and say with any surety that the name you give it in English corresponds to that in the original,' he says, when he has finished.

'You have outlined my principal difficulty,' Henry replies, delighted to be able to talk about it. 'There are many regional variables in name and appearance. It is without doubt the most difficult part of the enterprise. Plants are like men in that respect; some men's countenances being very mutable.' He would like to know why this is; how a man's looks could alter so on different meetings, sometimes so markedly that he would be hard pressed to recognize them as acquaintances, unless other clues gave them away, such as a familiar jacket or dog, or greeting, or all three acting together on a man's appearance in such a way as to create a distinguishable picture out of parts. Perhaps that is precisely it, he thinks. We are all made up of a myriad, combining our corporeal selves with our environment, our territorial conditions, peripheral objects, associations, reactions and contexts. Our habit as such is that we as humans separate ourselves quite willingly from our environments, unlike—'

'And what, when it is printed, will I learn from your great book, Master Lyte?' Mistress Yate interrupts.

A thin man whose name Henry won't be able to remember at all on his return home leans over and chortles. 'Sweet cecily is a powerful incitement to the arts of fondness, Mistress.' He winks. 'Candy the root and give it to your husband, or your lover.'

Across the table Frances is giving him a hard stare, as if to say *be quiet over there, do not join in*. But everyone knows Mistress Yate is not faithful to her husband, and who could blame her, Henry thinks, her husband is a dry little man with a fierce cough and no sense of humour. He asks the serving boy for more wine. Enjoying the sound of his voice and the way that Mistress Yate sips from her cup and listens attentively, he finishes his point.

'You cannot correctly identify a plant without considering its habitat.' He squints at the portraits above. 'Man however is itinerant, unsettled. It is that single fact which proves us different from the animal kingdom; our cultivation of a deliberate severance from nature.'

'I'm not itinerant,' somebody says. 'By God's nails I'm fixed to the bloody estate, and the wife.'

His host is amused.

'Oh, no Master Lyte, you are forgetting one thing, which is that, unlike ourselves, animals do not have souls.'

'And where in the Bible does it say precisely that?' Henry demands. He has forgotten that he is not amongst his Lime Street friends now, that he needs to be polite. His voice is loud and solitary. No-one else is speaking now but him.

'Show me the part where God and God alone says that they do not possess a soul, and only then will I believe you.'

A sharp little noise of collective indrawn breath flies across the trestles. Henry doesn't know if he imagines this, or if it is just the way his mind translates the palpable shock he can see on people's faces. He drops his gaze to his glass and scrambles mentally to retrieve the moment. He feels giddy. He can feel himself clambering down from his point of view, and then lurking resentfully at its foot, unable to retract or let it go.

'How readily shocked these people are,' a voice says unhelpfully from one quarter of his mind. 'Idiot,' another says, more accurately.

'Is the malmsey very *strong*?' the wife of Master West asks, peering about, as though it might be to blame.

A frosty silence has descended over the supper, he can almost feel it glittering down upon them, and his host turns deliberately away from Henry Lyte to his own wife. 'The scientific mind at work.' He raises his eyebrows.

Henry is caught out by his own enthusiasm. His euphoria at sharing his idea with a crowd drains away, to be replaced by an embarrassment that slides unpleasantly into the pit of his stomach and swills about in there, ruining his supper. He chews on with the veal until his plate is empty and thinks of something to say that will improve the situation he now finds himself in, but it is too late. He swallows. Wine. More wine. The serving boy fiddles with his glass at the sideboard for far too long and then it is filled again. Then he is grateful for the song that someone has started over at the other side of the trestles, and he fixes a smile on his face as he listens, his mind racing through all the details of what he'd ended up saying and rewriting them, over and over.

A servant forgets to close the door, and through the passage he can see that outside lies a moonlight good enough to ride home by, at a gallop. But Frances is here too, and the kitchen staff are taking an age to produce the sweet dishes and they can hardly leave before the voider course is served. Henry begins to long to get back to Lytes Cary to examine his lilies. He takes refuge in the thought of them, the anticipation. Madonna lilies by moonlight are akin to no other thing, heady with milky, musky scent and blue-white. He has one bloom fully yawned open to its dewy, yellow throat, and three with their heavy heads almost ajar. He must stake them tomorrow himself if Mote is still busy with that summer pruning of the cherries. There are good dry stakes of withy in the shed.

By the time they have made their escape and stepped down from the horse back in the yard at Lytes Cary, the moon has shrunk to a white radiant disc in the sky, surrounded by colour. Their shadows are crisp on the ground. Quite aside from the disaster of the evening, he is glad to be back. The stable boy comes out as instructed, rubbing his eyes, to take the reins.

'Are you coming to see them?' he asks Frances quickly before Lisbet or Old Hannah hears their arrival and opens the door; but she shakes her white face, no she is not.

'I saw the lilies earlier today, Henry, I can hardly spoil my shoes for them.' Her voice is small and cold. Henry knows she is annoyed with him for making such a scene at supper with his speech. He wishes she could have walked with him to the garden anyway, in the hope that her disapproval might be softened by its stripy, preternatural beauty, but he hears the latch click behind her, and then the murmur of voices retreating down the passage into the house. Even as he approaches the garden, past the chapel, and around the side of the house, he can smell drifts of honeysuckle coming through the gate, and then there they are, like prizes, like angels, utterly vast and white and still before him against the darkness of the wall.

He bends his head and breathes deeply. If only more men would take the chance to drink in the smell of lilies in the night in June, he thinks. There can be nothing so delicious. Nothing that could make a man so contented. He feels dizzy with love and tenderness for his garden. Above him is the clicking of bats, and a pale moth looms and flutters near the grass. He tilts his face to the moon and closes his eyes to its whiteness, bathes in its unflinching gaze. The air is warm. He feels enveloped, cupped between the sky and the earth, and once again he has that sudden sense that it is his mother Edith both above and below him. She is the flying, star-studded ethereal horse of his boyhood dreams, flying like bright, extraordinary vapour through the air, and at the same time she is also the green, solid, nurturing soil dark beneath his feet. He looks at his flowers again and sees that the lilies are between those things, a natural, burgeoning, celebratory expression of where they meet, their interchange. He feels the wholeness of things, and the interactions of the universe working smoothly around him.

'Who are we to say what does and does not have a soul, when God exists in everything? And how can it be blasphemy,' he adds in a whisper, 'to call this worship?' These seem, on balance, to be reasonable questions. He smiles. His lilies really are quite perfect.

But then he is dismayed to see, on closer, more objective inspection, the glistening threads of dark, wet, unwanted marauders creeping over their surface, silvery trails in the moonlight giving their presence away. He gets down on his knees and counts them as he picks them off, soberly at first and then with an increasing temper and begins to step systematically on each one until it is a pulp under his boot.

*Twenty-four, twenty-five, twenty-six.*

He can't see any more, though he is turning all the leaves up to the thin light, and feeling round the stems.

Twenty-six slugs wasting away at the greenery of his lily leaves, gnawing tattered holes in all their waxen flawless trumpets. It is an outrage.

'How dare they. How dare they, with their base, bastard, ignorant ways.' He hears his voice rising in a fury, as he squashes the remaining one into oblivion. 'Damn them all for that!'

He looks up at the blue-black sky winking stars and sees the bats have vanished, which he is sorry for as he had no intention of disturbing anything tonight. He looks up at the windows of the house and sees the mild glow of the chamber as Frances gets undressed for bed, and feels ridiculous, out in the moonlight shouting in the flower beds like a drunk or lunatic. Another light has started up on one of the cottages on the far side behind the stables, and now one of the dogs is barking over at Tuck's. He hopes he didn't wake any children, asleep at the top of the house. Or any of the servants. Or Tobias Mote, as he'd never hear the last of such an outburst. For a moment he thinks he sees a movement over by the garden door, but then there is nothing, probably a cat. An owl calls. There is no doubt though, he thinks as he heads into the house and bolts the back door very quietly, that his spleen feels clearer for it.

As he drifts into sleep it occurs to him that at last the good folk of the borough seem to have forgotten all about the whispered talk of *death* and *wife* behind their hands.

# V.

*Of GENTIAN. Whereof each Flower being spread*
*abroad, shineth with six narrow leaves like a starre, and*
*they grow out of little long huskes, in which afterward is*
*found the séed, which is light, flat, and thynne, of a*
*darke evill-savoured redde colour.*

H<small>E CAN'T BELIEVE IT</small>, but William Turner is dead. He has just had word from London. A July death, just like his father's two years earlier, but buried at St Olaves, Hart Street. He feels unspeakably hollow.

He remembers a discussion long ago, soon after his return from Oxford. His father had sent him over there to hear some sense about his forthcoming trip abroad, how he might use his connections to good effect. Dr Turner had a headache and was even grumpier than usual. Henry, like most young men, had been finding ways to disagree with the older man's wise council. The room was oppressively plain, there was never an easy way to find comfort in Dr Turner's house, unless one crossed the boards to browse the rows of many books and absorb the rich smell of their leather, or stood by the window and looked out at the garden. The part of Henry Lyte which enjoyed things pleasant to the eye baulked at that visit on that day. He itched to be gone but it was over a month before his trip into foreign places could even begin. The names Leiden, Bologna, Montpelier were like honey on his tongue. He could almost smell the promise of them, the thyme on sunbaked rocks, the cob-brown supple skin of foreign women. The need to be away from there and on the move was crawling on him like lice.

He'd wished he hadn't come into Wells, that he'd gone for a furious ride on the moor instead with the wind in his ears, but he'd brought the wrong horse to do that; he was not in the mood after all for a gentle meander, a plod through the reeds with a tune on his lips. Not that he disliked whistling. Indeed usually he liked the neat cheerfulness of this town, its market-bustle and shouting traders with their piles of local goods, the same old wily faces in the main street, the same plants growing from the low wall by Penniless Porch, the same beggars if he looked closely. His brother Jack was happy enough living here, when he wasn't in debt. But on that day Wells felt small and dull, stone-bound and hunched inconsequentially at the foot of the cathedral, as though it didn't at all deserve this misplaced, magnificent hulk of an edifice looming above it, its nave stuffed with the desiccating remains of bishops and its arches whitened with pigeon dung.

He was longing for somewhere bigger, more expansive, somewhere that *breathed* with its arms wide and its countenance to a bluer, Continental sky under which anything might happen. He had once tasted the strangeness of olives for himself and he knew how much more was out there to be discovered. Passion lay out there, of many kinds. How on earth could he wait a month? It was impossible.

'Stop twitching, Lyte!' Dr Turner had barked suddenly, swinging his wiry frame out of bed with a creak of rope, and lurching to his feet. His clergyman's robe was crumpled up with being in bed.

Dr Turner wanted to know what the exact purpose of his future was to be. Dr Turner wanted to get to the bottom of his plans for his trip. Dr Turner insisted on knowing what contacts he had lined up to meet, people from whom he would glean the best sorts of learning. Henry didn't like this cross-questioning of his ambitions.

'Go abroad by all means, look at the world from another angle, meet men of learning and weigh up what they say. But make it come to something of use to the world. Travel for travel's own sake is at best a bit of harmless dabbling in what you do not understand and at its worst is,' he'd spat, as if mentioning the devil, 'self-indulgence.'

Henry had wrinkled his brow.

'Do not let it breed a smug superiority in you as it can in other men. Be humbled by your travels and what you see, and put what you see to proper use when you return.' Some sparrows started up chirping and chattering in the eaves outside the window.

'What kind of use would that be?' Henry was sulky about the way this afternoon had turned out.

'To be of service to your fellow citizens. We are on this earth, young man, to effect wholesome change upon it.' Dr Turner thumped the bed and a cloud of dust exploded into the air like spores. 'One must effect change!'

'But I am not ...' Henry had hesitated, 'and it pains me to say this, Doctor, but I am not a radical.' A small unpleasant tweak of something like guilt had started up in him even as he said it. It is a disquieting thing to be faced with the sight of one's own limitations. He didn't like the sound of it being said out in the open, like a poor excuse. 'Not a radical at all, Doctor, not like you. If I held a position of power, I could probably wield it to great effect. But who am I? Once I return from my travels I will be nothing but a small landowner in a damp corner of England, full of concerns for my crops and the state of my father's buildings that will become mine in the course of time.'

Dr Turner was watching him closely. 'But there are many subtle ways by which change can be brought about. Not everyone has to shout and bluster like I do. God knows I shall be no use to any cause when my head is off, bleeding away into the dust. Picture a strong plant in your mind. Most of its effort has gone on underground, working concentratedly at its mat of roots long before any growth of aerial greenery, or show of flowers.'

Henry considered. What if it did turn out that he had lived his life lazily, that he had not begun to deserve what God had bestowed on him at birth?

'But I am young, sir,' he'd protested hopefully. 'I have my whole life ahead of me in order to—'

'One day,' Turner says severely, 'you will look up from your life and you will find that you are no longer young and that parts of the way the world works are still not to your liking and you will have done nothing about that.' He took up a sheet of paper black with notes. 'I have a headache battering my temples. Go home and reflect deeply on what we have talked of.'

Henry did not want to leave without explaining himself. 'My desire is to—'

'No more!' Dr Turner had his face to the ceiling. 'The wretched bishop is on his way. Send him up if you happen to pass him.'

Henry Lyte wakes up with his face to the table, and it is twenty years on with Dr Turner dead and buried, and the room here at Lytes Cary darkening as today's sun goes down. There is a patch of stiffness on his lips that he finds to be dried ink where some has spilled, and outside the window is the regular hissing snip of Tobias Mote cutting the edge of the lawn with his iron shears. He looks at his pile of half-finished work and remembers again how there is an urgency to life. It terrifies him, how little he knows. There is so little time.

'What is all that black on your mouth?' Frances asks, when he emerges from his room and goes to see how long before they are to eat. He touches his lips; he had forgotten.

'Laziness.' He says it almost as a joke.

'What?' she looks confused for a moment, and then she is gone back to the parlour and thinks she has misheard him, he supposes.

'Ink,' he calls after her. 'Just ordinary ink, made of iron, tasting of iron.'

# VI.

*Of PEONIE. Tenne or twelve of the redde séedes,
drunken with thicke and rough red-wine doth stop the
red issues of Women.*

HENRY STANDS IN HIS GARDEN AND THINKS OF THE SEA. Winter has been and gone, and spring is supposedly attempting its reappearance, bulbs pushing out of the wet expanses of weeded soil. He thinks of the low-tide coast at Burnham criss-crossed with mud-horse fishermen, sliding out for miles over the flats on their withy contraptions, going for shrimps.

Henry likes shrimps. Little fat, salty buds of sea-flesh. He wonders what it is for supper. It is Lent, and the lack of meat is beginning to bore him at mealtimes. Sometimes as a boy it felt as though it was always Lent, or Friday or some other cause of abstinence. Old Hannah does try, but she is not, it must be said, a woman of abundant culinary imagination. He closes his eyes and recalls the rich, fresh food in Italy, the smell of olive oil and garlic frying on the open streets, the tang of citrus, sweet black grapes piled upon the tables, and the abundance of wine and debate. He opens his eyes again onto a grey-green English spring, the north wind scouring unfairly at the new growth on the shrubs. His chilblains are itching. Shellfish would be good. He is tired of salt herrings, and even of eels.

He is envious of other people's travels. Thomas Penny is just back from Zurich, settled in Leadenhall Street in London and sending out letters filled with exotic tales, bits of foreign plants, seeds. Henry looks forward to Penny's letters, providing as they do a cheerful contrast to the lawyers' correspondence piling up upon his desk. At least they have a date now for the inquisition, the legal meeting in which his father's lands are formally declared. This means that in general things are moving forward. Amongst the other concerns, he would like to be able to reassure his tenants that it is all in hand.

As if to prove Henry wrong about his low opinion of her culinary scope, Old Hannah returns from Somerton market with a bunch of glasswort from the marshes to serve with the interminable salt cod. For the rest of the day after dinner Henry finds himself dreaming of its succulent delicacy of flavour, of its melting, tender, finely swollen stems, of pulling out the tough little stub of stalk. Eating glasswort is like eating the green sea itself.

On his way from the stables he sees there are kittens swarming like snakes all over the yard.

'Too many cats!' he bellows. His daughter Mary looks beadily at him. At ten years old now, she is fond of animals, and can play with her little tabby in her chamber for hours on end or lie face downwards on the bank of the Cary staring at speckled trout and other frogs and fish nudging about the weeds. He cannot imagine what kind of thoughts slip through her mind as she observes them at their business, sucking the fronds of her hair. She is a passive child.

But these cats are mangy, scrawny barn creatures – more rat-like than feline; coiled springs of disease and bad-temper that dirty the flowerbeds and knock over bottles in the outhouse. They gather at the kitchen door by the slops bucket and whine for buttermilk and sour scraps that could be better used, he's sure. And there are too many of them. Lytes Cary is beginning to be overrun.

'But Father – when did you last see a mouse round here?' she says.

'There are always more mice than there are cats to catch them – it is one of the unwritten laws.' He ruffles the top of her head. 'Of which there are many.'

When Mary learns that he had ordered Richard Oxendon to take the newest kittens down to Cary Bridge and drown them in a sack, she does not speak to him for days, her mouth fixed in a stubborn line across her face. Henry Lyte is concerned that his daughter feels revulsion for him, and it pains him not a little when she mutters, 'It is bad luck, Father.'

'Mary, I—'

But the door has already slammed behind her.

'What did you expect?' Frances points out gently to him that night. 'But I shall be stern. We have been too soft with her if she speaks to you like that.'

In the morning Mary and her stepmother are late for prayers and her eyes are swollen with crying. She says, *good morning, Father*, as bidden, but her face is turned from him and her gaze is flat and will not meet his own. He wants to beg her to listen to him but knows he must not. Perhaps more than the lives of those kittens was lost in the river, that it may not have been worth it.

Five days after Easter, the inquisition begins. It is held at Ilchester, at the office of a barrister called Stephen Brent who is currently escheator. Henry is not looking forward to it, but intends to attend at least one of the days. As he rides down the Fosse Way in the early spring sunshine he anticipates how the hearing is likely to be both interminably dull and sharply painful, to be reminded of his father in so much material detail. He slips in at the side of the office and sits down on a wooden bench in full view of the front of the room where, beside the escheator, he can see Simon Cressing sifting through documents. His lawyer is a smooth and well-presented man said to have a fortune waiting for him in Gloucestershire on the death of his father, and an attention to detail that extends from his clear legal mind to his fondness for finely wrought shoes. The latter is why he never visits Lytes Cary if he can help it. He is good, and he is very expensive. On the other side of the desk sits William Phelips, who is wearing his ecclesiastical court robes, presumably to point to his authority if it were ever in doubt. Henry looks at him curiously, Joan Young's new husband; his reddish, over-long hair, his prominent knuckles. He is not in the least aged, as he had assumed.

The officers are slow with the business, breaking off for pies to be brought mid-morning. There are a lot of lists of lands and other matters to be gone through, field after field and detailed rental costings and income to be looked at. Although he makes himself concentrate on the proceedings for a good few hours, Henry finds his mind drifting. He wonders if his presence tomorrow will be strictly necessary. Probably not. He eyes the door, which is open a crack and a strip of yellow sunshine is slanting through invitingly. He wonders if the bench would creak very much if he was to lever himself up now and inch away. Nothing new to Henry is being said. It is all very tedious, despite its pertinence to his position, as they work through the consolidation of land undertaken by the father to free up capital, through the inventories of what is left. But it is halfway through this session when he receives a shock, as several things happen in quick succession for which he is absolutely not prepared.

Firstly, it becomes abundantly clear that the inventories have revealed that his father had spent all the money he gained through selling off land and other property. Nine hundred pounds in the eight years he had been married to that woman. *Nine hundred pounds.* He is incensed. That woman had begun to suck his father's coffers dry from the moment she married him.

Secondly, it transpires that, two weeks before his death, John Lyte had taken out a mortgage against Mudford, in order to release cash as a lump sum to pay off his debts and legacies owed. He knew he was dying. He did not die suddenly at all – he was in London to see doctors. Questions begin to explode in Henry Lyte's head. Just at that moment he suddenly feels the prickle of somebody's gaze at the back of his neck, and turning round in his seat encounters the chill and level glare of Joan Phelips herself, enshrouded in a dark purple shawl on the bench immediately behind him as if she had manifested there. All the progress of spring seems to shrink away from her. She looks shiny and mottled and hard, like a polished stone. A chilly sweat breaks out all over him.

'Madam! I did not—' He keeps his voice low and civil. 'I did not expect you to be here.'

Joan Phelips fixes her eye above his head.

'I must stress, madam, that I intend to ensure you are well-provided for. I will honour my father's—'

'*Well-provided?*' Joan screws up her face as though she has tasted something very bitter. 'I mislike your claims, sir,' she says. He can see the tip of one wooden tooth glistening in her mouth. 'There are many who express surprise that I should be so unprovided for. Your father would turn in his grave to hear you speak like that. I am a woman of some means, and seek what is mine by right.'

'But you will not want, madam.'

'I shall not,' she hisses. 'Neither shall I be reduced to living in that unspeakable place called Mudford, without even the rental incomes to dignify my position. It is filthy, dingy, *agricultural* in the worst possible way.' Henry wonders if she is aware of how much she is spitting as she talks, or if it is deliberate. Joan Phelips gathers herself up then and leaves the room, and over the drone of the officers at the desk, like a bad dream he can still hear her footsteps tapping on the flags like shod hooves, as hard as iron, going away down the endless, echoing corridor for minutes after she has surely quit the building.

'She seems very intent on causing grief to you personally, Henry,' Cressing observes later at the end of the day. 'I'm afraid this is not proving to be the open-and-shut case I had predicted after all.'

'So if my father knew that he was dying, why did he not draw up a will?'

'Why indeed.'

'You are not suggesting that there may have been one, that has been purposefully destroyed?'

'I would not put anything past that woman.'

'But there would have been witnesses, surely?'

'She is very persuasive,' Cressing says, looking over at Phelips. 'The only other explanation is that your father left this mess deliberately, for you to sort out. But why would he have done such a thing?'

Henry says nothing to that, he will have to wait in misery to see what kind of vast dense document the escheator's clerk can produce in his cramped hand, out of all of this tangle.

# VII.

*Of POLEMONIUM. The root of Polemonia drunken in water, provoketh urine, and helpeth the stranguarie and paines about the huckle bone or hanche.*

'WHAT HOUR IS IT?' Henry Lyte wakes to the sight of his wife dressing with unusual rapidity and purpose. Frances has got out of bed very animated this morning. She opens the chest, takes a clean pair of sleeves out of the coffer and pins them on over her dress. Henry yawns.

'Today,' she announces, 'Jane and I will be found in the stillroom.'

*At last*, Henry Lyte thinks, but does not say it. Those roses have been opening already for a fortnight; pink dewy blooms unfurling to the sun then going to waste by the next afternoon and petals dropping flaccid from the bush. He wonders what can have goaded her to trouble with them. Last year nothing was done with the roses at all and an invoice for expensive rosewater from Hartley's in London appeared on his desk. The window is open and a breath of June air comes in. Perhaps it is just that she has the green spirit of summer quickening her spleen. Perhaps, indeed the countryside is becoming part of how she is. He props himself up on an elbow and looks at her with more attention. Perhaps she is with child again.

She slams the lid of the chest shut, and dust spins in the first rays of early morning sunshine reflecting on the looking glass propped by the window. It must be scarcely six o'clock, he thinks.

'There are tasks to be done which I have been slow to address,' she admits briskly, as if he had spoken aloud, 'but for the whole of this week, sire, I am occupied as a woman should be. Pray for our success in there,' she adds, and sweeps out of the room. He can't tell if she is mocking him.

Moments later and he can hear women's voices down in the garden beneath the window of the bedchamber. He stands and watches as they unfasten the freshest, newly opened flowers from the shrubby rose bushes and place them face upwards in a single layer in wide baskets at their feet in the grass. How tall Jane is these days. He feels a twinge of guilt that he does not notice her more often.

Henry prays and then goes to his manuscript. After dinner he goes to the stillroom to see for himself how they fare. The potential of these flowers and herbs to enrich her own life and that of those around her has finally dawned on Frances.

'Why didn't you *say* I was supposed to do this, Henry.' She bustles about, being efficient, surrounded by petals and steam.

Henry says nothing. He is quite happy to sit back and watch the result he had been hoping for unfolding right before his eyes. Jane, too, is delighted to have another woman in the stillroom with her. They have the fresh roses spread out on the baskets, taking each head and chopping off the bitter white claw at the back of the petals.

Today they are making syrup of roses. Tomorrow or the following day will be the day to heat up the still for aromatic water. There will also be rose sugar, rose vinegar, melroset made with honey. He breathes in deeply. This surely is the smell of happiness.

Outside Henry can hear Johnny prattling in the garden on the grass with the nurserymaid.

In the parlour that evening Henry sits reading a letter from Moffat, Frances is resting, the girls are in bed.

'We shall have to hire a new nurserymaid,' he remarks. 'She is too soft on them. They are lacking in discipline. I went in there after Johnny had so naughtily caused that jug to spill, and she was lying there tickling him.'

'Mmm,' Frances says.

'Can you see to that?' Henry looks up. Sometimes she forgets just what her duties are. She is with child again of course, a cogent distraction.

There is a scent of roses and verbena around the house. Henry basks in the pleasant aroma, and the way that the house is beginning to look cared for, homely. Outside a pinkish light gives a benevolent cast to the garden.

He notices that there are droppings on the carpet, yellow mouse urine on his papers.

'This mouse problem!' he exclaims, to no-one in particular. He thinks perhaps that Mary was right about the cats, after all. There must be a perfect ratio to be achieved, some kind of balance between the quantity of cats and the level of mice causing trouble. He tries to remember which herbs deter rodents, thinks of the sheer mass of pages of his translation he would have to work through to find out.

He shakes his head.

'Do you know, Frances, sometimes I can't believe that no-one has done this before.'

'Done what?'

'Simply listed all these kinds of plants in the English tongue.'

'Not Doctor Turner?'

'I am collecting two thirds more than he did. It is most peculiar that there is nothing else in print which lists them. It is the most curious oversight.'

In his edition of Clusius he is noting down all English names beside the plates as he finds them out. At the back of the book he has listed other points not included in the translation.

*Ambrosia – Pena hathe sen it growing in London gardings.*
*Driapteris root made into powder is given with Bran Salte and Brymstone to kill worms in Horses.*

Slowly, his translation is coming together. Over the next few months, he begins to feel it taking shape, and he will shortly have to think of a title. Meanwhile the year grows colder, and by the middle of Advent his daughter Hester is born.

## ❧ 1570 ❧

# VIII.

*Of ELDER. The gréene leaves pound, are very good to be laid upon hot swellings and tumors, and being laid to plaister-wise, with Deare suet, or Buls tallow, they asswage the paine of the gout.*

COMING BACK FROM THE ORCHARD Henry tries to creep past Widow Hodges. If he tiptoes, she will not hear him. He watches her intently as he inches by, how she pricks up the stakes one by one into a tall shape that resembles a many-legged, unwieldy spider and fits a hoop to contain them as she works.

'I'd give you instruction if you want,' she calls abruptly, feeling his gaze. Henry is caught out, stops. 'So's you could make a basket for yourself. Best way to appreciate a thing is to have a hand in it, Master. That's waling, that is. Not so hard if you pay good mind to what you're doing.' Her hand flutters out for new rods, picks them up, tips them in. He is almost mesmerized, watching her fingers deftly weaving the rods. 'It's all in the thickness of the rods, a good basket is an even basket, where the randing or slewing is steady and tight. Try it.'

'No, no, I couldn't.'

Henry looks in admiration from the pile of damp willow rods, to the complex, knotted thing that is her basket.

'There is a magic in that.'

'And use, Master. It's fit for purpose. God gave us withies to carry things about in.'

She smiles.

'Mistress Hodges, what was it that was wrong with your daughter's mouth? What did you see when she was born?'

'Her mouth,' she repeats, her smile fading, as if trying to think. Henry wonders if she has forgotten what she relayed to him the day of Johnny's birth, then her face sets, and he is not quite prepared for what comes next.

'It was what was inside her mouth, Master. Terrible to see. It pains me now to have to tell you what we had to do.' She sucks in her breath. 'When a child comes out with teeth they are surely the spawn of witches. What I had seen was that my Benet was one such born cursed with ready teeth. It's one of the known signs; set there already in the gums with nothing but evil to hand. That gives a newborn child a very old cast to the face, you'll understand, Master, to any looking on her but the mother, and a mother does not see her child for what it is, does she.

'This was unmistakable. I was sore afraid for my little girl, because if it became known about the village that already she had teeth, then at best she would be hounded and mistrusted all her life, at worse she'd be drowned or pulled apart limb from limb by a fearful mob who had took her for a demon. For one seven-day lest anyone should see we shunned visits from our good neighbours, kinfolk; I feigned milk fever, sent little Richard to stay with my husband's aunt, and our own door stayed shut as we prayed until it came upon us what to do.

'By Monday, with the Sabbath over, I had the answer. My husband was not willing, God knows he did not want to do it.'

'I held her little head tight between my hands, and then my husband, who was a blacksmith by trade, put iron tongs into her tiny mouth and broke the witches' teeth out, one by one.

'He tried to be merciful, truly he did. The blood didn't come with the first one, and then when it began to well up in her mouth her crying was more like bubbling and choking. We had to leave off a few times to let her swallow. It was harder to keep her still, my fingers wedged in her mouth so that her jaw could not clamp shut against the tongs, her tiny tongue soft and wet. I was afraid to squeeze her so hard that she'd be dead.

'I had to make myself a brute. I was a brute, wasn't I, clenching open my daughter's head upon my lap for someone to break off all the teeth she had been born with.

'What a pair we were.

'It was so far from being the blessing that we'd seen at birth. The true horror of the red blood came to me over and over with every crunching wrench, every choking, screaming swallow in her fluttering throat. I shall never forget it. I was dripping with sweat all over by the time we were done, could hardly hold her, and for weeping. What a way to begin living. It was the only time I'd seen something like tears in my husband's eyes. Afterwards he flung his tongs to the back of the hearth with a great, forceful clattering rage, and hid his face. I had to stuff a piece of linen in her mouth to stop the noise she made afterwards, like I was smothering her, so that no-one would come round. It felt as bad as murder. I was sick to my core with what was happening. What we will do for our children can amount to strangeness, Master Lyte, once we get going. *But it is done from love*, I kept on sobbing to her, wishing she could understand as I rocked back and forth with her bundled to me, and my heart burning and thrumming in me as if I was on fire. She wouldn't feed from me for hours, like I had betrayed her, so that I began to think what if I had caused her instead to starve to death.

'I picked all the bloodied bits of teeth up from the floor, and much later, when from exhaustion she was got into a merciful sleep, I dared to steal a look at them, and they were not like teeth that humans bear, but flimsy hollow things, more like the stuff the fingernail is formed from, and without full roots. They made me shudder to see them, it was so clear that they were far from natural teeth indeed I could not touch them again, but swept them into a piece of cloth and next day buried them by the barn. Even that very act felt like sorcery, and later I knew they were too near by our dwelling and I should have taken them far afield, in open country.

'Indeed a few days hence I went to dig them up but I could not find them in the earth where I had laid them, though I combed the soil over and over, so that my neighbour called out had I gone mad for raking over the garden so much. I knew they had dissolved into the earth and burrowed their way back down to hell where they had come from. I didn't like that they were so much in the soil about us. I began to have thoughts that we should leave that place, and start afresh. But my husband couldn't speak of it. His family had abided there since the time of King Edward, he said, holding Benet but not looking at her countenance, although her mouth healed over quick enough.

'My husband never spoke a word about it afterwards, but there was something quite gone out of him, and our door stayed closed against the street. He was a good man but took badly to drink. It was not long later that he took sick and died of tumours, as though the demon had wormed its way inside of him and swelled up as foul corruption in his belly. I lost my son Richard too, when he fell under a cart.'

For no reason Henry has an sudden image come to him of many sloes in a jar, bleeding their purple into the liquor.

'It's all right, Master,' she says, hearing his silence. 'I'll not expect you to say a thing about it. Only now I've started, I can't stay myself talking.'

Henry clears his throat.

'It seems to me, you berate yourself too much, madam. You did what you thought best.'

'Best? Best?' she murmurs. 'Guilt. It's a terrible thing, isn't it, Master. Now if you'll excuse me, I've got handles to peg.'

She begins snipping off ends, dips her bodkin in the greasehorn and a smell of tallow rises up. She upends the dome of her basket base and opens a space to the side of the sticks with the slippery bodkin, rams in a stake. One by one she works her way across, always turning the basket, turning and feeling, turning and feeling.

'It's like spokes on a flower, isn't it, Master.'

'But she survived that, didn't she?'

'She survived that well enough. But how much more there was to come. We should never think to change our destinies. If only we could see what lies ahead. That's our undoing isn't it? Ignorance.'

'And fear. Ignorance and fear, Mistress Hodges.'

*❧*

Between *asarabaca* and *dragon arum*, Henry Lyte goes to the window and looks out at the progress in the garden. He sees that Tobias Mote is stooped over the low hyssop hedges, weeding near the middle of the Knot. The light from the low sun in the west is slanting and golden, and his long shadow pitches across the clipped bushes as he straightens to hurl out clods of dandelion and unwanted stones onto the path.

It is as though he were much bigger than he is – indeed it seems to Henry from his private viewpoint here inside his study that Tobias Mote is like a giant, towering over the miniature arrangements of green below him.

Even his spade appears vast – thrust upright in the soil nearby like an alarming giant's tool.

Not for the first time he feels a stab of envy for that man's disposition – his centredness, the way he seems to belong to the garden in a way Lyte never could, as if he had grown from the very soil beneath his feet. Other, mythical giants were surely not as intrinsic to the soil as Tobias Mote must be. Enceladus shaking under the earth's crust occasionally in furious, incidental tremors. Others, not Greek, whose names he can't recall, crouched clumsily in hills awaiting their changes in fortune. But Mote has none of the maladroit stupidity of giants, nor their inconsistency of temper. He is limber, supple, standing there with the sunshine shining on his back.

Henry suddenly feels self-conscious, staring at another person for such a length of time. He checks to left and right across the expanse of garden, but nobody else seems to be out there. Susan Gander must have gone home to her family. To the south the sky is a deep mauve, with a flock of chalky white birds flying across it; too far away for him to see if they are geese or gulls, just dwindling flecks into the distance. He glances again at Mote's busy, bent-over form, and sees with relief that the effect seems to have lessened, that he has shrunk again to a normal stature.

'It's just the light,' he says out loud. 'Just a trick of the light.' And then behind him a small child bursts into the study without knocking.

'How many times do I tell you to leave me alone when I'm working!' Henry rounds on him in exasperation.

Johnny is sanguine. 'But you wasn't working, Father. You doing nothing there.' He crawls under the desk and sits cross-legged on the Turkey rug, his eyes very bright. 'I saw you do it.'

'Do what?'

'Nothing.'

'But I was thinking very hard.' Henry Lyte suspects this will not be viewed as a properly mitigating circumstance.

The child looks sceptically at him. 'I've learned my catechism,' he adds like an accusation, as though someone else was not keeping his side of the bargain. 'Who were you talking to? I heard speaking but it's empty in here, only you Father.'

# IX.

*Of BRIONIE. Brionie or the white Vine, do grow in moist places of this country in the fields, wrapping it selfe, and créeping about hedges and ditches.*

WINTER AGAIN. There is one occasion of human drowning; a familiar tale comes in about a man wandered off the road at night, into the water during flood time. While it is not a common occurrence, there can be one a year. Sometimes it is said to be deliberate. Last year a woman stepped where there was no bridge, out of despair, rather than any misguidance. They found her downstream a month or two later, swollen beyond all recognition but for her shoes that were made by Munden's shoemaker's in Glastonbury. *Winters can be long and dark*, Lisbet had said, shivering as she served boiled meat and cut it up on the children's plates.

'A traveller is fine on the Levels so long as he does not stray from the causeway,' Henry said briskly. It is a discussion that crops up every year.

'But is the causeway clear to all who travel on it?' Frances asks.

'If foreigners do come ... then, sometimes they veer away unknowingly.'

'So it can be impossible to get across. It is not amenable to being walked on, is it. Man is not supposed to occupy that land. By the laws of nature Lytes Cary manor should be a house with a view over an estuary. Down at the Ten Acre Field there would be a landing stage with small boats tied to it, and mudflats at low tide, and fishermen's nets would be drying all over the grass, and lobster pots.'

Henry laughs, helping himself to more pippin pie. 'Your tone is hopeful. It sounds as though you've thought this through. That's quite a picture.'

'I think about it all the time. It haunts me, Henry. It would be so much better than that unstable hinterland, that false deceitful earth, that lays itself out there instead, inviting living souls to occupy it, in order to be swallowed up when they are least expecting it. They shouldn't be there.'

She drops her voice to a whisper so the servants don't hear. 'When I wake up I can taste salt in my mouth.'

Henry laughs again, more grimly than before. 'You city girls. You have such a fixed idea of what the countryside should be.'

Later, about dusk, he goes for a walk and stares out at the flood plain, sees the moon come up, the reflection of the huge yellow moon lying shuddering in the water at his feet. And for a second he can't look at it because it seems full of sickness, full of luminous, terrible death. It's a spasm in the water.

And then he blinks and it is just a large bright moon rippling mildly in shallow water. A duck quacks softly behind him, settling down for the night. He looks about and sees it is a pleasant enough scene; the reeds, the lit sky, the dark slope of the hill, and even as he stands there the moon is becoming hard and small and ordinarily bright as it rises.

It is about this time that Henry Lyte begins to have bad dreams in earnest. Perhaps two or three a week, when the nights are fitful right through and in the morning he has a dirty, uncomfortable feeling in his chest, like a tidemark inside his flesh where a surge of something has receded.

# X.

*Of WOODBINE or HONISUCKLE. It is good for such
as are troubled with shortnesse of breath: and for them
that have any dangerous cough: moreover, it helpeth
Women that are in travell of childe, and dryeth up the
naturall seed of man.*

**T**ODAY THOMAS FELL DOWN THE STAIRS into the hall and made his head bruised in one place, but he seems fine. That child is remarkably clumsy. If anything is going to befall any of the boys it is bound to be Thomas. He must mention again to Frances to keep a closer eye on him.

As spring approaches the garden is crawling with life. Yellow-blue tits, finches, and small unnameable birds, the colour of moss and bark, that pipe reedy snatches of song from the tips of twigs. Hoverflies hang mid-air in the sunlight, deciding on their next move. As spring begins to gather in strength and force, the woods are a greening cacophony of birds, filled with the soft new leaves of hazel, hardening spears of pussy willow, wild currant.

Henry checks over his garden.

The horehound is tough, he decides. Scorched a little by the snow but otherwise thriving. Even the tender rue has made it through the cold season, squashed by a six-week weight of more than a foot of snow but otherwise unscathed. The furred base leaves of the mother-wort, close to the soil, seem to have been protected by the untidy dead stalks that Tobias Mote had insisted on leaving, despite Henry's orders to trim away all decaying matter last October before the cold weather began. Henry has to admit that his gardener is often right. And the hyssop is only partly damaged, though it remains to be seen if the entire hedge has survived enough to green over by Lady Day. There is a lot to wait for, and a lot to look forward to. Henry feels a quickening in his veins, it occurs to him that it might be a similar sensation to the feeling women must surely get when the desire to have a child comes upon them. He wonders whether there has been any rigorous scien-tific study of the effects of spring on nature and man, and even idly toys with the idea of making some notes towards this himself, perhaps to make a more detailed work once his herbal is finished. It could include an attempt to establish the visible nature of a life-force, not as a counter to the truth of God, of course, but rather as an observa-tional study of what actually occurs.

He begins to feel quite an enthusiasm bubbling inside him for the project, so that by the time he has reached the outhouse where the overwintered pots are kept (except for the oleander, that still lives in the hall during the frosts) it is becoming a fully fledged thesis, with at least forty pages in folio, and detailed plates drawn from nature by Jacques le Moyne or Albrecht Meyer, and in his mind's eye he is even handing a copy to a principal member of the College of Physicians – not for approbation but as some kind of offering towards the celebra-tion of life itself.

The coming of spring had never looked so good nor purposeful.

However later, when he goes inside and broaches this thought with his wife, she bursts into peals of laughter and beckons in Old

Hannah to share the joke. Frances never laughs like that, he thinks, her face is flushed. They are hysterical, he thinks, bemused. Women's affairs are not so far beyond a man's range of comprehension, indeed he may be better placed to make an academic study of it, being at one remove.

He stands uncertainly in the kitchen for a number of minutes, unsure of whether to hold his ground and expand further so that they understand exactly what he means, and then thinks it could be unwise, letting his good, fat seeds of an idea fall upon their stony ground and he retreats to sulk in his study with *wild thyme* to occupy his mind.

After about an hour has passed, there is a warning tap on his door, and Frances enters immediately, bringing with her a smell of frying from the kitchen. Perhaps it is fat pork for dinner. He hopes so – he feels like meat.

'Is there anything you might have noticed, sir, about my person?' she says, standing before him on the rug. Henry casts his eye hastily over her dress to see if it is new and lacking a due compliment, but no, she has worn that red-brown silk since last winter, he recalls. She looks well in it still, he thinks, and can't help a flicker of proprietorial satisfaction, even though he knows that Somerset mud in March is hardly a match for fine fabric like that, and for sure the hem of her skirt is never going to be clean. The dark flint of her eye gleams back at him over the table as though she is winning this game.

'You really can't tell?' she says.

Her hand goes deliberately, gently, to her belly, and stays there.

Then it dawns on him. 'We are expecting another child?'

'Within five months.'

'Five?' he exclaims, dropping his nib. 'You have not told me before?' He is mortified. 'But we have been – supposing there has been damage to the baby?'

'I doubt it Henry.' She turns to leave. 'You are pleased?'

'I am delighted, madam,' he says gravely. When she is gone he looks down at his page and sees he has smudged part of the description of *pennyroyal or puddinge grasse*, pinkish purple ink is all over his sleeve.

It is astonishing how even at the eighth child the sudden knowledge of its existence can still take the breath away. The annunciation of each one provokes a new complexity of feeling, as it will do thrice over at every bloody, terrifying birth. He goes to the window and stares out at the garden for a long time.

# XI.

*Of SOLDANELLA, or SEA-CAWLE. Much like the lesser withywind, saving that the leaves are much rounder and thicker, and of a saltish taste.*

I N SUMMER THE EERIE GREEN GLOW of marsh lights is sometimes seen. Always bobbing out of reach, and usually glimpsed at a distance moving away into the wetter, darker parts of the moor; one had been seen that night inside the house.

'Corpse candles. Only when there is to be a death,' the new serving-girl insists at noon. Henry doesn't remember asking her opinion, he doesn't even remember her name, for goodness' sake. She is worse than Lisbet for superstitious rubbish.

'Nobody is going to die,' he assures Thomas, leaning over the dishes to ruffle his hair, although fully knowing that he is not qualified to say such things.

'And fairly soon,' the serving-girl adds. 'They say.'

Frances has no time for this kind of talk, glares at her and briskly hands out bread herself around the table once she has sent the girl back to the kitchen.

'We are all bound for the grave, and God will take us to him in due course. Keep up your prayers, children and abide by what you have been taught.'

Henry wonders whether she believes everything she tells them. She seems so sure, so firm, at times he almost envies her the textbook nature of her faith. It seems like a safe haven.

Later she goes to Glastonbury to buy cloth for Johnny's first breeches and doublet.

# XII.

*Of SCAMMONIE. The floures be white and round,*
*fashioned like a cuppe or bell.*

Although mote dislikes Henry working in the garden, he doesn't however object to the presence of the weeding women, meaning as it does that his own tasks take up time elsewhere, but there are certain patches of ground that he likes to tend himself, the succory bed, for example, over on the far side of the garden by the wall where the pale salad leaves grow blindly under forcing pots, and also parts of the Knot. He doesn't give a reason, though once Henry heard him mutter, as though some kind of excuse was needed, that the dittany was looking peaky in that quarter and should have a bit of seeing to. This evening Henry goes out in the garden only briefly, to catch some fresh air before darkness falls. The Sorcerer scoffs harshly from the edge of the wood. It flies in short, heavy straightnesses as if pegging out territory.

As he goes back inside the house, he glances up and sees in an upper window a small head looking out. The light is too gloomy or it is too far to see whose it is, but something about it makes him shiver, there is a familiar expectancy to its gaze that he can feel tugging at him as he comes closer to the house, almost drawing him to it, reeling him in. He rubs his chest. He knows that the face must belong to one of the children, probably Thomas, but it's as if it is his own childish self looking down at him. As he approaches the path to the front door he looks up again but the face has gone.

He goes back to the study, eats supper alone much later that night. He is very busy, very preoccupied with his translation, with his garden. He prays absentmindedly, not quite paying the attention to God that he should.

# XIII.

*Of HOPPES. The brewers of Ale and Beere, doe heape
and gather them together, to give a good relish, and
pleasant taste unto their drinke.*

**M**AGDALEN IS BORN ON THE THIRD OF SEPTEMBER. He is
utterly, utterly delighted with her, calls her his daisy, carries
her about in the crook of his arm. Frances is doing well after what is
her fourth delivery, but there is a great fear of sickness everywhere.
The man who comes to collect the interminable malt for his stepmother at Sherborne is talking about previous outbreaks of plague
and the heartache it causes. 'Terrible what families can do to each
other in times of outmost trouble,' he says.

'What do you mean?' Henry Lyte says sharply. But the man is very
busy shovelling. Next time Henry is going to make sure it is in the
sacks already before he arrives. The last thing he wants is to hear
poison from the mouth of Joan Phelips by way of her delivery man.

Sickness lies dormant in the conditions that it likes; slightly saline,
estuarine. He does not like to think that in all that wetness there is no
clean water.

He lies at night worrying about the family.

Accounts are another thing that will keep him awake. Sometimes when he rises it is as if there has been no rest at all. He cannot take sleep for granted in the way his children can, their eyes softly fastened against the dark, drinking the sleep in like water from the well. But there are no certainties. It is his baby daughter Magdalen whom he goes to most frequently, gazing down at the cradle then quitting the room feeling unreasonably vast, bulky, his leather boots creaking the boards as he leaves. The nurse complains about his intrusions, not within earshot of anyone but kitchen staff, but he senses her complaint anyway, her glare a beam of disapproval from the chair in the corner.

# XIV.

*Of MOSSE. The first kind of mosse groweth upon trées,*
*especially there whereas the ground is naught.*

LOBEL'S *STIRPIUM ADVERSARIA NOVA* has been published and
has sold very badly. Some people are criticizing it for its lack of
depth and rigour, but Henry thinks its failure may be because the
market is very bad in England for scientific books, he worries about
that from his own point of view, hopes things will have picked up by
the time he is ready to find a publisher for his translation. When
Thomas Moffat had come to visit with a cartload of apothecaries'
apprentices out on a botanizing trip during the summer, learning the
plant names in unison, Henry had asked him in private.

'What is Mathias's new book like?'

'His *Stirpium*? You've not seen it yet?' Moffat pretended to look
grave. 'Think of the haphazard nature of a butterfly's flight, drawn
only hither and thither by its fancy or a vague trail of scent it follows,
erratic loops of flight, angling about the garden blown by wind and
you'll have a sense of it.'

Henry must have been looking startled, because he had to add, 'I'm
joking! It's a very good, thorough volume. I cannot understand why

it is going so poorly, though. It could be his barbarous style of writing, mangling the language.'

'It could be that it is in Latin,' Henry says.

By mid-September, Lobel has had enough and has decided to leave this godforsaken, heathen land and return to civilization, where they appreciate him and his scholarly efforts. Henry is sorry to see him go. He comes over to Lytes Cary to say goodbye, and they spend time walking in the orchard and garden together. Edith is ill in her chamber upstairs, and Henry has a query for Lobel about something that has been troubling him for a long time now.

'How much of a cure is down to wishing?' he asks.

'None of it.' Lobel is very clear on that.

'Why can praying work, then?'

'Praying is not wishing. Prayer is an acknowledgement of one's dependency on the higher order. Wishing is altogether more vague and wayward, and it can draw on bad influence alike as good. Wishing is like wanting, a base instinct that children should have drummed out of them at a young age. Disease is a message from God, and humbling oneself in the eyes of God may gain his approval, with healing results.'

Henry thinks about this. 'Then why trouble with all the science, with drawing out the qualities inherent in plants that can effect a cure? Why the painstaking work towards understanding their potential, and putting it into practice, with uneven results? If it is all the will of God, then surely it is futile to attempt to reverse his decisions. Why then do the plants exist at all?'

'But you are overlooking one thing, Lyte, which is that the plants themselves are of divine creation.'

'You are suggesting that he has invented some kind of test?' Henry finds this idea frankly shocking. 'What kind of sinister game would that be? I don't believe it. What benign God would create an experiment in which innocent women and children are made to suffer pain and death.'

'In order for mankind to progress? I do not know the answers, Lyte. But a loss of faith will do you no good.' He frowns. 'You might do better to keep these doubts to yourself.'

'I do, I do,' Henry knows this. 'It is just today. It is the anniversary of the death of my wife Anys, and this always raises these same questions in myself. Forgive me. Here you are just off to Antwerp and I am rattling on about myself.' And he changes the subject to lighter things.

Despite his prayers, Edith dies within the fortnight, aged eighteen, on the day of St Matthew.

# 1572

# XV.

*Of SPEREWURT. This herbe is now called in Latine*
*Flammula, that is to say, Flame, or the fierie herbe,*
*because it is very hot, and burneth like fire.*

FEBRUARY. THE SKY IS PEWTER GREY, peppered with birds. Just after the feast of St Valentine, Magdalen dies. She is two. The funeral is at Charlton Mackrell church. Her coffin is tiny. Ralph Let, the gravedigger, stands again by the open grave in the aisle in the north transept and shovels the soil back in on top of his daughter. *My child, my daisy, my well-beloved*, Henry whispers. He would have liked to put in garlands of periwinkle with her, but it is not in flower yet.

On his way out through the churchyard he sees a goldcrest in the tree above, the little slip of yellow on its head like a coronet, tweaking its way through the branches.

He remembers how her first word had come during an outdoor dinner one noon down by the Cary close to Sowey Wood. Her nurse was there because she was still not weaned from the breast, also in attendance were those of the family not with the governess studying back at the house, and a few of Henry Lyte's associates including Thomas Penny because a group of them had just returned from a plant-collecting expedition on St Vincent's Rocks over near Bristol. The conversation had turned from the St Paul's lottery to astrological tracts and then lulled into silence – only by birdsong and the buzz of flies, and people were lying back on the grass with their eyes closed in the sunshine amongst a blissful debris of pie crusts and just enough Rhenish.

'Squiggles!' Magdalen had announced, pointing into the trees, and indeed there were two russet-red squirrels, scrolling jerkily across the tangle of branches. Henry Lyte had sat up, beaming with pride to hear her say it, and had gathered her up in his arms and gone into the woods to show her a patch of campion that were in flower. Her fat little finger had reached out to touch them, and when he'd picked a stalk she crushed it against her mouth in a staining pink mess of petals and pollen as if she could eat it. There is scarcely anything stronger than a baby's grip. He thinks now of the good baby smell of her head, the salty warmth of it against his neck, and his eyes fill with tears.

Behind him in the graveyard hedgerow, dark with ivy and yew, a bird makes a noise like a small key grating in a lock.

# XVI.

*Of HERBE PARIS, or ONE BERRIE. This herbe floureth*
*in Aprill, and the séede is ripe in May.*

**O**N THE TWENTY-THIRD OF JUNE, Joan Phelips has a victory.
Henry hopes it is not the first in a string of many. She has been
issued with letters of administration, an act of probate that gives her
the full power to administer her husband's estate.

'That is a blow.' Henry is not sure that he was expecting this. He sits
down heavily and looks over and over the letter from Cressing. *We
will put in a formal objection of course – an entry for the book of
Cautions*, it says.

What is this *we*, he thinks.

It is a warm day. At noon as they eat in the hall, they are invaded by
early wasps. A nest must have been disturbed in the wall outside in the
courtyard. One particularly insistent wasp hovers over the slices of
beef on his plate, despite being flapped at with a napkin, and settles
down at the middle part where the meat is tender and bloody in its
own juice. It begins to work its waspish mouth upon it, bristly and
urgent, ceasing its buzz until Henry is astonished to watch it chew

away a morsel and fly off with it, a whole tiny piece of pinkish steak clamped between its jaws.

⁂

By November, the garden is battered and flailing beneath the wind and sheets of greyish driving rain, from the west. Most of the trees are bare and stripped of leaves now, except the oak which is still clotted with yellow and gold. And the alder, he notices, is already dotted with tight young catkins as if they had sprouted stiffly overnight, short and compact like unformed fingers. In the stalwart holly, the berries are reddening, and down in the soft, wet ground on the side of the river where it runs wide and broad, the tall straps of the flags are fallen and rotting.

In the afternoon Henry receives a letter from Thomas Moffat in Cambridge, who has recovered from a bout of poisoning from mussels. *I am still alive, Lyte! And I praise God and physic for it.* There is little other news, except that he has had word from Lobel who has set up his physician's practice in Antwerp.

He notices that above the sill in his study there is a butterfly with its wings clasped up flatly in a winter sleep. He peers at its dry barklike wings, its white powdery legs clinging to the wood. He knows nothing of its life. It is Thomas Moffat who would be able to explain about its caterpillar state, the cocoon, and its emergent daily habits during the summer months. At least Henry is able to picture its wobbling, sunlit flight between flowerheads, the straw of its long unfurled tongue dipping in their stores of sweet nectar. He feels curiously, childishly flattered that the butterfly chose his room, unbidden, in which to close itself up for the cold season. It makes his study seem somehow more of a haven. Occasionally during the working day he gets up and goes to the sill to check it is still there, a tiny fragile piece of wilderness. There is much to admire in its absolute submission to a closed, unstarting sleep. After a few weeks he realizes it is likely to remain for the rest of the winter. At first he had thought of himself as somehow its protector, and enjoyed the sense of responsibility he felt towards it, but after many weeks of noticing its unblinking sleep he knows the butterfly needs nothing from him, and only occasionally does he remember its presence.

He works hard on the herbal during these long winter months, buries himself in its detail. Frances does not interrupt him often. Once when she comes into his room, she notices the butterfly too.

'Aren't you the chosen one,' she remarks, without a trace of bitterness in her voice. 'Even the insects coming to you for shelter.' She does not mean to remind him of his failure as a father to protect. When she leaves the room he feels absurdly cross with it for being asleep.

At Christmas the children sing carols, and Henry has to leave the hall because the tune's sharp ache is too much. Even through the closed door he can hear it still.

> *'Oh, the withy! Oh, the withy! The bitter withy*
> *That causes me to smart*
> *And the withy shall be the very first tree*
> *That perishes at the heart!'*

# ❧ 1573 ❧

# XVII.

*Of ACONITUM. Aconite taken into the body, killeth
Wolves, Swine, and all beasts both wilde and tame.*

THIS IS THE COLDEST, HARDEST WINTER for decades, the snow and ice upon the ground lingering even until March. He expects that many of the plants will not survive the conditions. Death is everywhere, stripping and gnawing, and its blanching, deadening grip takes its hold on his family once more. It is Mary who dies on the twentieth of March, the first sunny day.

During the funeral Henry begins to wonder if he has gone mad. He cannot concentrate on what the Reverend is saying, he is so plagued with inappropriate thoughts that stave off death, that stave off the stark reality of Anys's daughter laid out cold before him in the coffin. He closes his eyes against the cold, stone church air and is not praying at all. He feels instead almost nothing but the warm presence of his wife beside him, he imagines putting his fingers to her, between the meaty lips of her, touching the slippery pearl of her until the sap of him oozes into every crack of her being. He cannot sit still for discomfort.

What is the matter with me that I have such unwholesome thoughts at this time? I am the head of a household, he thinks. I cannot afford to unravel. His head hurts as though he has been beaten. Somehow he gets everyone back to Lytes Cary and goes straight to his study and falls asleep at his desk.

An odd rasping in the room wakes him, a tiny noise that he cannot place, and then he sees that the butterfly has opened its wings and is practising flight against the pane. He opens the window and watches it go, fluttering out unsteadily across the grass, over the garden wall. For a moment he worries that the weather is not warm enough, that it will rain, that there will be a sudden frost tonight. And then he forgets, because that at least is no longer his concern.

# THE FOURTH PART

## The Description

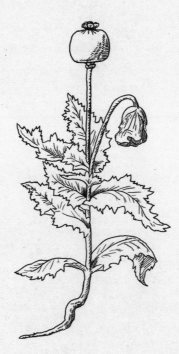

# I.

*Of POPPIE. There droppeth or runneth out of poppie, a*
*liquor as white as milke, when the heads be pearced or*
*hurt, the which is called Opium.*

HENRY IS UPSTAIRS walking past the children's bedchamber. Frances and Florence are making the beds up with clean linen, turning the mattresses, and he can hear from the slop, slop of a brush that Lisbet must be sweeping, or another child.

'Mother?' he hears Florence ask. Henry had insisted from the start that this be the name which the girls give his new wife. They had called their own mother *Mama*, which seemed too intimate and childish to resort to, and they seemed to prefer the formality. He pauses, unseen in the corridor.

'After all this time here, Mother, do you ever miss London?' Henry notes with approval that, at nine years old now, Florence is growing quite able to consider the positions of others, and their accompanying feelings.

'Sometimes I do. Especially when the weather is like this.'

'So you like it here sometimes.'

'Oh, yes, of course I do.'

'And where would you say that your home is, now?'

Henry can't help but hover at the door's threshold to hear what she says. He imagines that Florence is hoping that her stepmother will say *Lytes Cary*, but Frances is very sure in her reply.

'I carry my home around inside me, wherever I go.'

'Is it like a map?' he hears Johnny pipe up, who loves ships, and plans to join an expedition to Cathay or Muscovia or South America as soon as he comes of age.

'Not really, no, not like a map,' Frances says. 'It is more complicated and yet more simple than a map. How does it feel?' She looks at the ceiling to pay this proper attention. 'It feels like a clod of earth, right here at the top of my belly.' She presses a flat hand to her dress beneath her breastbone.

'Where the baby is?' Florence says, because Frances is with child again.

'No, the baby just happens to be in that space right now.' Henry can hear Frances smiling. 'But my home will still be lying in there when the baby has come out.'

Lisbet's voice is muffled, as if bending under a bed. 'My mother was from up-country, Miss Florence, but she always said her home was where her children were. Didn't make a jot of difference where she was and there was no doubt she'd been about a bit, as father was a travelling haulier most of his life. Never stopped worrying he'd done wrongly of her, plucking her out of the Welsh hills like that just for love of her as he was passing through on his way south. She'd squeeze us all tight to put him at ease and say to us, *you are my home. Don't care where I am, so long as you lot are along with me.* And I used to like that. It's what I'll say to mine, when I have babies.'

'And where will your home be when they've gone off and left you?' Frances says, conversationally. 'When they've gone to sea with the Navy or married into a family in Wiltshire.'

There is a sudden lapse of the sound of the besom, and then it starts up again, a little faster. 'I'll be homeless then, won't I.'

'Until you see them again in God's kingdom,' Frances adds lightly.

'Until then,' Lisbet says, in a low voice. And Henry realizes how angry Lisbet is with his wife, just for saying that, just for such a small thing.

❧

Henry's third son Harry is born on December the seventeenth. On his way back from what is becoming a regular visit to make christening arrangements with the Reverend Tope in Charlton Mackrell, Henry takes a detour to see whether work is still going on at the Abbey. It's hard to get a stonemason if you need one, as they're all over there, getting rid of the remains of the Chantry Chapel of the Holy Spirit that had stood there singing prayers for the souls of the dead for three hundred years. The masons are swarming all over the scaffold pressed to its face, scouring at the lias with their mallets and chisels to show its clean yellow surfaces, scouring away the spirits. Among them he recognizes Walter Ellis, an old man now but who'd worked at Lytes on the great chamber when Henry was a boy.

As a seven-year-old – the same age as Johnny is now, he realizes – he'd watch him working the corbels, impressed by his thick tawny forearms and wrists coated with stonedust, mesmerized by the rhythm and pause of the mallet, the blocks of stone slowly pecked away under his chisels, sharp chips flying.

'I'm not making the shape of angels here, Master Lyte,' he'd confirmed. 'I'm just tapping so I can get to the angel that's already in there, my job is to find it. That's what carving's about.'

After that, the boy Henry had wandered the fields, picking up stones and listening hard for signs of life inside them. Were there shapes hidden in every stone? He wished he hadn't forgotten to ask.

When work on the house was done, all the workmen had packed up their rolls of tools and gone. For years he'd walk past a stone on the ground thrown up by the plough and wonder if it had a shape locked inside it. As he got older he stopped bending to pick them up, and instead started to notice that some people were like stones, very closed and hard, but sometimes surprising inside. His father was like that, he has to admit. He misses him. He regrets that his father died thinking so badly of him. If only they could have been reconciled, or if Henry had had a chance to explain himself. Now even prayers for his soul are not obligatory.

People like Lisbet lament the passing of these places like the Chantry, with the new changes that have swept in. Swept in, swept out, swept in again; this century's been like a tidal coast for religious alterations so far. But with our sovereign Elizabeth, it's all settled now. That kind of superstitious practice: it's for the ignorant, the retrograde, the heretic – isn't it?

This question follows him about, though his back is turned. And though they worship at the church of St Mary the Virgin in Charlton Mackrell now, he thinks perhaps he will put new glass in the chapel at Lytes Cary, before the pigeons begin roosting in it. Regret is a useless emotion, he says to himself, as if saying it will make it true. He has so much still to be thankful for.

# II.

*Of MAD APPLES, or RAGE APPLES. The Herborists
doe set and maintaine them in their gardens, as
Cucumbers and Gourds, with the which they doe spring,
and vanish yearely.*

'WHAT IS THE MOST ARRESTING THING YOU EVER SAW?'
Frances asks him one night, as they prepare to retire. The baby has stopped howling in the room next door and there is a lulling peace. She puts down her comb and peels back the linen on the bed, strokes it flat.

'How do you mean?'

'What single image comes to mind? Tell me what startling sight shocked you into something that you wouldn't have done otherwise?'

Henry Lyte laughs. 'Why in heaven would you need to know?' She is such a peculiar woman, he thinks. Frances comes and leans her arm across his shoulder. She smells of hair grease and apples. She is not heavy, in fact it is almost as though she were *acting* her leaning on him.

'I am just interested, Henry.' A coil of her unpinned hair hangs gleaming in the corner of his eye, like a snake. 'Can a wife not ask such things of her husband? If she wants to know what kind of significant changes he might have experienced? Your beard is going grey,' she adds, looking at him up close as though she had not seen him for a while.

'That is the sort of question to ask a man before he gets to the church door, not afterwards,' he says, trying to make a joke of it, putting his hand to his chin. Of course he knows his beard is greying. He is getting older by the day, as we all are.

'What was the first thing that sprang into your head? It's not hard, Henry!' She is like a terrier with her questions.

Henry doesn't like to be pinned down. 'Oh, probably when I first cast my eyes on you. You were very animated, very glossy, there in the passage at your father's house with the dogs yapping all about your feet and you glorious and preoccupied in the middle of it, shaking your slender arms at them as if you were dancing. Then you looked up and noticed me standing there.'

Frances looks at him, her eyes black in the candlelight. She doesn't believe him. Can it be that she actually wants to know? You'll have to do better than that, he thinks to himself.

'Well then, what about watching my mother's coffin walking past me at St Mary's. That was a day. Or maybe the comet that everyone saw that same year.' He feels dizzy to think of it, can almost smell the memory of that comet it is so strong – and it is the irrational, bitter smell of moths and grief together.

She seems satisfied with this, climbs into bed without saying anything.

Still later, awake in the dark, Henry can't remember whether he'd said that it was the sight of his mother's coffin, or that of his first wife Anys. Why can't he remember things properly these days? It must be something to do with getting old. Time stealing parts of him away in the night to feed upon, making off with memories and little bits of his more youthful body like a stoat dragging warm rabbits, just leaving the stiff parts behind, the aches and gaps in his head where a memory was, things he needed to keep. He had been young at the graveside, bowing his head. He remembers the familiar jolt of seeing the earth under the floor inside the church opened up for the burial. The shock of the coffin because a coffin is like a door shut tightly in all directions, and he knows how the body softly collapses inside it, the worms making quick work of her beloved flesh on the persistent bones. As children once, quite by mistake, they'd dug up a dog that was buried a month.

He realizes that he didn't reciprocate. He didn't ask Frances what is the most arresting thing *she* ever saw. There is one other thing that he hasn't properly remembered; how Anys was still alive when he first set eyes on Frances.

The draught from the stone corridor blows under the gap in the door and the candle struggles to one side and goes out. *Dead passing through*, he thinks to himself, which is what Lisbet says every time that happens. If the dead do ever pass through Lytes Cary, it would surely be along the corridors; the places of transition, movement, change. But he knows that Lisbet would say, 'No! They come in looking for warmth, and it's the hearth they go to. Come into a chamber unexpected, Master, and you'll see something like a shadow out the corner of your eye by the firedogs, bending over, and maybe the logs are burning just a bit brighter, as though they'd been turned or the ash tapped away ...'

He shivers. It is cold tonight. He tries very hard not to think of Anys in the cold ground up at St Mary the Virgin, and his daughters with her now. He tries very hard not to think of his father, buried in London because of his visit, in haste because of the heat of July. When he thinks of it like that, his death seems too much like unfinished business.

# III.

*Of GREAT NIGHTSHADE, or DWALE. The fruite or
berries of this venemous Solanum are ripe in August.*

J OHNNY IS IN THE PARLOUR, and Henry and most of the rest of
the family are arguing around him. Everyone is talking at once.
There is an unusual smell, slices of apple browning on the Turkey rug
and an opened crate in the middle of the chamber. A small silver
monkey is clinging to the curtains, chattering angrily and baring its
teeth.

'I have objections, Johnny. Look – it is shitting everywhere. No, it
has to go.'

The boy's face is stricken. 'Please.' He turns to Frances. 'Mother, say
something.'

'He does mention that it is housetrained,' Frances says doubtfully,
the explanatory note, which accompanied the monkey, open in her
hand.

'It's just frightened, Father,' Johnny pleads. 'Remember when you
first had Blackie, after the second day everything was fine. It's like a
puppy in its age. Better than a puppy.'

'What was your godfather *thinking*, sending you a gift like this without asking my permission. God's flesh! A monkey!'

Johnny stands up straight. 'Father,' his eyes are very large and serious and track him round the room, and his voice comes out so clear and firm that Henry is taken by surprise. 'That monkey cannot go back inside that box.'

If he had burst into tears Henry knows it would have been easy to put his foot down. But this small squaring-up to him is different – this appeal to his humanity takes his breath away. His small son is right. Now that monkey was here, there is nothing to be done but make the best of it. It would be cruel to make it travel any more. It has travelled enough.

Even the monkey seems to pause as they wait for his final word on the matter.

'One week's trial,' he announces, despite his misgivings. 'And if it proves to be unmanageable, it will be returned expeditiously, do you hear? With no ceremony whatsoever.' He tries to look strict amidst the gasps of joy and jumping from the children, and finally his face breaks into a grin at the ridiculousness of it all – at having a monkey here at Lytes Cary.

❧

Back at his desk in the study he goes on smiling. Henry understands the fascination with the exotic. He has just discovered tarragon, and is utterly delighted with it. He has persuaded Old Hannah that it is not the Devil's food, and it has been appearing in salads since last week. It is hot and pungent. He makes a note in red ink this time against Clusius. *Tarragon – the Lytell firye Dragon of the Gardinge.* As soon as this herbal is done, he plans to concentrate on collecting specimens from other gardens. Plants that are curios, not native, which might need solicitous care to survive the different climate here. He has had one perfect success with amaranthus, or what is known here among gardeners as purple velvet flower.

The monkey likes fruit, and little bits of meat, and it steals manchet rolls from the bread-tub in the kitchen, scuttling across the flagstones, lifting the lid and helping itself, which makes Old Hannah very cross. Monkey-owning Johnny has found sudden favour with some of the servants however. Lisbet in particular is often just checking whether there is anything to be done in the children's room, straightening the beds, cleaning the windows again with a little smear of verjuice, sweeping the boards and strewing more wormwood than is strictly necessary. She likes the creature's naughtiness, the way it teases her, and that room has never smelt so well-attended. The monkey itself has a strong, exotic odour of its own, though clean enough in its habits just as Johnny's godfather had said, and grooming its own fur. Johnny has a bristle brush borrowed from the laundry, which he uses to brush the monkey's back where he can't reach. He adores his new pet, its tail that curls around his neck as he sits on his shoulder all day long, except at prayers or mealtimes, scratching and picking in his hair. Henry has never seen a child so proud and happy. When they go out together round the garden, Johnny ties a leash about its neck and holds on tight. He has called the monkey Harlequin, which has been shortened to Nin because that is what little Hester calls him in her baby language, but Henry can still only think of it as the Monkey.

Other servants refuse to have anything to do with it. Bridget who works in the dairy for part of the week doesn't like the way Nin creeps behind her, and jumps up to pull her hair and cap. She doesn't like its shriek, nor its chattering, nor the way it nimbly scales the brickwork of the chimney breast and sits there, in the cobwebs high above their heads, flicking crumbs. She is afraid it will turn the milk sour and gets very annoyed if Johnny brings Nin near the kitchen offices.

'Get that creature elsewhere,' she says, flapping her cloth, and crossing herself once he is out of sight. 'Little devil, roaming about. He'll bring no good. You can smell that about him.' She sniffs the air where the monkey has been. 'See?'

# IV.

*Of WHEAT. Men sow their winter corne in September,*
*or October, and the summer corne in March, but they*
*are ripe altogither in July.*

THOMAS PENNY HAS COME DOWN FROM LONDON for a botanizing visit. Every time he sees him, Henry is startled by what a
fleshy, large-palmed man he is, yet so practical. It is late August, and
his guest is interested in seeds this time. After three days the Reverend
Tope gets wind that they have a visitor up at Lytes Cary, and invites
himself for supper.

'I have heard that our gracious Queen Elizabeth loves gardens,'
Reverend Tope says. It is about the extent of his horticultural knowledge. 'Does she love gardens like this one?'

Henry is not sure where this is going. 'I have heard of course like
anyone else of Lord Dudley's garden at Kenilworth, or Cecil's, but
something about the idea of these gardens leaves me cold. They seem
very little to do with the joy of plants and everything to do with
imposing unnatural order on natural things.'

'But is not all gardening an artificial determining of natural things?'
Penny says, rubbing his big lips. 'If you were to leave your Knot alone,

within months the hedges would be choked with vetch and bindweed, self-sown alder trees bullying their way through the matted creeping buttercup and cinquefoil. It would be tattered and seedy, rotting growth not cleared away. Slugs would multiply, and mice, and moulds. The mints and balm and tansy would be rampant.' He points to the sheltered bed by the wall where the more tender specimens are set. 'There would be no foreign delicacies coaxed into being; no ammi, no cumin, no oleander.'

'No oleander!' Henry says. 'Then there would be tiny blessings in this world. I love to visit other men's gardens and see the balance set between what is best in nature and skilful structures made by man. But I want to celebrate the plant itself. That is my first joy in any garden, to see and touch and smell the plants.'

'I had assumed that the unusual nature of your planting was largely due to the virtues of the plants. As a herbalist, perhaps like a garden in a monastery.'

'By unusual you mean unfashionable.'

'Well …' the Reverend Tope slips one and then two chunks of sugar into his mug of sack, stirring it surreptitiously with the tip of his knife.

'Men can be divided into two camps; swiggers and slurpers,' says Penny, annoyed, but Tope is oblivious to insult.

'Would anyone like to circulate the garden?' Henry suggests, to avert an argument.

Tope indicates his plate, still half full. 'I shall decline in favour of this, Lyte, if you don't mind. Not keen on wasps,' he adds. His face is florid.

Henry and Thomas Penny get up and stretch their legs in the day's last few rays of sunshine.

'Your Reverend Tope is part of what is wrong with the church,' Penny mutters, bending to pass under the apple tree. 'He is too softly paunched, too attached to the more corporeal things in life, too …

Catholic. He is walking proof – waddling proof – that the Reforms did not go far enough.'

Henry tries to be more charitable. 'It is just that he lacks a particular spiritual enquiry. He was made that way.'

'He is far too comfortable.'

'And you are not?'

'I believe there are certain responsibilities, sacrifices. And I do ask religious questions of myself the whole day through. I try. I try to be rigorous.' Henry thinks of the large figure of Reverend Tope still helping himself to slivers of mutton, licking his knife. 'Does he strike you as a man tormented by unanswerable questions?'

Henry laughs, despite himself. 'But he is like many clergy these days. There has been so much confusion that it seems easier to lie low, go through the motions required by sovereign law.' On their way to the garden they pass Widow Hodges's cottage but her door is shut.

'That man stands up before you on a Sunday and demands you follow his example. How can you stomach that?'

Henry shrugs. 'I've told you before. I am a moderate. He dutifully spins out the most recent good sense he has been taught and I hear him. It is an official channel I am happy to respect. Besides, we are lucky – in some parishes these days there is no parish preacher and a man would have to walk miles to hear a sermon.'

Penny tuts. 'Where is the fire in your blood, Lyte?'

'I am too busy to stoke myself up with your kind of questions.'

'Nonsense. Every thinking man is in possession of a question. He nurtures it like his own child, feeding it up, raising it to proper standards. What is yours, Henry Lyte?'

'I have no question. I am like most people. I have ideals and vague hopes and then I fail at them.'

'You are not failing with your translation.'

'Not yet.'

'I mean, why bother with your translation at all? Most of us who might need to refer to this work of Rembert's can already do so in the Latin, the French or the Flemish.'

'Scholars, yes, but the ordinary man or woman cannot!' Henry replies quickly. 'Too many die through unnecessary ignorance. Knowledge does not need to be the entitlement of the privileged few, so that they can make easy money from those less privileged. It must be distributed more evenly amongst the population. There are many who would benefit from understanding of the virtues of plants, from sound guidance as to their appearance, uses and cultivation. It would provide a counterpoint to those street quacks who though knowing nothing themselves still go about cheating people of their wages who cannot afford their false remedies but who turn to them anyway. This book is not intended to replace the training of doctors but is to supplement the status quo. It's simple enough, any one of us could do it.' He glances over the grass to check on Mote. 'Besides, I like plants.'

Penny looks satisfied. 'So you do have red blood in your veins. It is good to see you passionate, Lyte. For all your talk of moderation and failure, you seem to me to be a radical.'

'Ridiculous.'

'Sometimes the most subversive amongst us are those working quietly away without noise, unnoticed until what they have is ready. I think you are one of those.'

'You make the way I work sound like sleight of hand.'

'I mean you are a true radical in the sense that you go hard against the established order, but you do it very quietly. I think that is a clever way to work it. If that is not radical, I do not know what is. Noise is not change, remember.'

'It can be.'

'Oh I give up! You are a disputatious old mule. Take the compliment and run, sir.'

Henry changes the subject. 'My main concern now, Penny, is that the illustrations must be good. There has been a strange and inappropriate inversion until now – the written knowledge has been deemed superior over the identification of the plant under discussion. Illustrations in herbals so often do not show us what the plant actually looks like, indeed on occasion can be utterly wrong. This is either a profound oversight, or is a wilful or deliberate bid to mislead in order to keep the field clear for those in possession of prior knowledge. Turner began the change with his herbal in English, and what an uproar that caused. English herbals to date had been only in Latin, and never with clear identifiable illustrations. My version of Dodeons is bigger, longer, broader, with more plants and draws more precisely on the scholarship of other herbalists. And there must be excellent plates!' He ticks off the points on his fingers. 'There is so much to do in the fight against sickness. We have withheld true knowledge from many people, we have maintained a culture of obfuscation, and we have imposed an arrogance on our approach to the natural world. By which I mean we have not gone out into the field and studied closely what we see.'

He stops and touches the tall plant beside him. 'Take this gromwell, its perfect seeds, have you ever seen such things?' He likes gromwell. It is a quirky, savage-looking plant, spiked and sturdy, as though it embodies entire armies along its length. The seeds are like none other; he gathers some into the crease on his palm, rolls them about.

'Isn't this the trouble with humourial theory?' Penny says, as they make their way back. 'I am a physician and in the eyes of the College am not free to criticize or even question this teaching. It does not require us to look. Whilst Galen is still king – the Godhead, even – we will not progress as we could do. My own feeling is that Paracelsus has some of the answers, he certainly believed that many clues to a plant's virtues lay in observation of its particularities.'

Reverend Tope's ears prick up at the mention of *Godhead* as they enter the hall, and he turns away from his discussion with Frances, towards the profanity, frowning. But Tom Coin brings out the distraction of nuts and pies from the kitchen when they are seated again.

'Sometimes, Penny, when I am out in my garden or in the fields,' Henry confides, 'I think if anything, we are just earth.' He takes a mouthful of plum pie and points at the rest on the plate, chewing. 'We are earth, walking about, eating it. We are composed of the soil, but free to wander. When we dig, we dig at ourselves.'

'No!' Penny tilts back his large form on the bench alarmingly and signals for more wine. 'Surely we are water, Lyte? Pulled by the moon like low and high tide. Do we not bleed wetness when we are cut? Do we not spit water? Weep it? And the water inside us – think of the infant that swims in a woman's belly before birth. Think of the tide-mark rippling on the infant's fingertips. Look at the crown of a baby's head from above and you see a whirlpool, a swirl of soft growth.'

'Not water, please Doctor Penny,' Frances murmurs. 'Especially not water in the same breath as babies.' She leans across for the custard pot and spoons out more than she needs.

'Mother is afraid of water,' Florence says, lighting candles with a spill from the fire.

The Reverend Tope's baffled face eases. 'My dear lady. Then we are one and the same on that score, I have a horror of boats and of floating in general. Unnatural way to get about. If one must get to the other side of a lake – then ride round. You can't go wrong on a horse.' He slaps his boots together. 'All four feet.'

Frances pretends to concentrate upon her child. 'Florence,' she admonishes. 'You should have been going to bed hours ago. Up you go. Say goodnight to your father, our guests, and be gone.'

'But Mother—'

'Now!'

And to the Reverend's relief, the ensuing moment of family hubbub means that the thread of this unsettling, perplexing, wildly unsuitable, ungodly conversation about being *earth* or *water* is lost, and he can regain command of the topics.

After a further hour has passed in this way, Penny begins to droop at the table. He stretches and yawns, vastly, until Henry leaps to his feet to bow and bid everyone a good night.

'You should get up to London more, Lyte,' Penny says at the foot of the stone stairs on his way to the guest chamber. 'We'd enjoy having you.' Henry worries that his debate is not intellectual enough for his friend. He feels provincial; for allowing his instinct to speak where analysis was called for.

'And was I rude to the Reverend?' he asks Frances as they prepare to retire.

'Not so that he'd notice.' She gives him a rare, teasing smile. 'That man's skin is like ox leather.'

When the cold weather comes again, Frances sees the monkey needs something to stop it shivering other than draping itself against Johnny all night and day, and she stitches it a little red waistcoat.

'I suppose it will be a miracle if that creature lasts another winter,' she says, as if the thought had just occurred to her.

# V.

*Of RIE. Rie bread is heavy and hard to digest, most*
*méeteth for laborers, and such as worke or travell much,*
*and for such as have good stomacks.*

I T IS MAY THE THIRD, about seven of the evening. Henry is riding
over the edge of the high Mendip from Bristol after a day's botanizing in the hills. His saddlebag is filled with plant specimens,
including what he hopes is spignel or meum – he needs to have a
second opinion, but it seems likely, and if so makes his day's work
very satisfying indeed. There are many herbalists who know of the
existence of this plant, indeed Dioscorides describes it very clearly,
but not many who can claim to have seen it for themselves. All those
parsley-like plants are very difficult to identify correctly, but he feels
quite sure about this one; his bag is aromatic with its scent. Laid out
before him the Levels are bathed in blue mist, the sun feels high for
this time in the evening but of course it is May now, and approaching
the highest, lightest point of the year. At the far-off mouth of the land,
to Henry's right, the sea is a burnished sheet of gold. He has never
seen it so bright, at first he almost thinks he has imagined it, that it is
glare in his eye, a golden chimera. But it must be the sea reflecting the

sun at a certain angle, at a particular point in the tide, perhaps because the sea itself is full of mud and particles, all of which conspires to make it into an expanse of bright yellow gold to the horizon and to left and right as far as the Quantocks and beyond; bronzed and finely crinkling, it looks close enough to touch, and if he could his fingers would surely be dusted with metal. The sea looks glorious, sacred. He feels lit up by its beauty. His spirits soar as he rides down the side of the hill, until the sea disappears behind the lower-lying trees and hills of the horizon viewed from the Levels.

Dodeons says that the true meon is yet unknown. He thinks he might add a note on Mattiolus and Turner's verdict on spignel. Turner calls it hartswurts. But now Henry thinks he has the very thing itself in his possession: an actual, living specimen, riding on his horse with him, plucked by his own hand from the top of the Mendip. And the mayflower is out, the bluebells, the new growth of the wayside brushes softly at his legs as he rides by.

It is the perfect time of year.

As he winds down the hill he comes upon a little low cottage hard by the path and tucked against the outer paling of the wood. A woman is there, sitting outside her rough door holding a suckling baby across her chest, and with her free hand skillfully shelling peas into a bowl. The baby startles at his step and turns its head toward the noise, so that even though after a moment he averts his gaze, Henry Lyte cannot help but catch sight of the woman's wide clay-brown nipple jutting out, wet with milk.

A thirst catches in his throat all the way home, and at night when he closes his eyes he pictures the scene again, over and over; a course of milk dripping from the firm pouch of her breast onto her kirtle and the breast's heavy quiver as she moved to cover it.

He cannot sleep till he has lain urgently with his wife. It was without doubt the most vivid, sudden sight. Afterwards Frances angles her warmth away from him so that it is too awkward to lie with his hand on her thigh, and she falls promptly asleep, leaving Henry alone in the dark bed surrounded by thoughts.

There is some kind of irony, he thinks, that the peak of this most base of earthly acts should be like turning to water, vapour, spirit. Like a glimpse of death, perhaps. Or like briefly reaching the spirit world and being returned from there within seconds when the mistake is discovered. He shivers and wishes that the thicker coverlet were over the bed. He begins to imagine he is feeling the cold as though it were an actual thing creeping up his limbs. Once a strong thought has been made it can be hard to shake off; the layers between the worlds in the mind are too thin, too unreliably porous. He begins to picture the layer separating the worlds as we know them like a shifting stratum of river mist, grey and indistinct, unconvincing, tattered with holes and shreds. When he kicks back the blanket and goes to root for another in the chest his wife stirs and wakes.

'Is that you, Henry?' she whispers across the chamber. 'What are you doing?' And the woken hoarseness of her voice is like the opposite of all his fears and makes him feel foolish, so that when he climbs gratefully back into bed he arrives at sleep quickly, pressed against the crook of her animal warmth and her hair's familiar smell as living proof of life itself.

# VI.

*Of BARLEY. The small common Barley is very well like*
*the other, saving that his spike or eare hath but two*
*rowes or orders of cornes.*

A VERY HOT DAY. Susan Gander and the other weeding woman are in the garden outside his window working along the herb beds. In a minute he will call Mote's boy or Hannah, to take out small beer from the kitchen for them, it is thirsty work. Frances is busy with Lisbet in the orchard – one of the hives of bees has swarmed, collecting as a huge, crawling teardrop of bees hanging from a lower bough of the Catherine pear. He can't hear the noise from here but he knows it well – a heightened frenzied whine, the surrounding air vibrating like a darkness. Lisbet has run for the skep and drum, but it will be Frances that catches the swarm, shakes the branch to dislodge the heavy, preoccupied mass into the basket. Henry was surprised when she ordered silk gauze for herself and announced that she was going to learn the skill, but she has a temperament well suited to bee-keeping; cool, unflappable.

His pen goes on scratching over the page. He returns to lady's mantle, or great sanicle. He wonders if it is wishful thinking on the part of Dodeons as he translates, *ladies mantel pounded and layed uppon the pappes or dugges of wives or maidens, maketh them hard and firme*. He notes that neither Dodeons nor Clusius bothers to give a name for sanicle in English. Just to emphasize the point, he adds a note in purple ink, *there is a greate plenty of bothe thyes kindes of sanicle growing in Somersetshire at Haredge Wood by Aishyewike in the Fosse.*

He looks outside again. In the distance the workers in the field are weeding the barley crop by hand; little dots of industry, bent to their task. Darnel is a wicked plant, though it has several virtues, there are few plants he knows of without any, only the wretched, poisonous, pointless oleander. *They lay it to the forehead with Birds grease, to remove and cure the headache.* By eleven o'clock they have inched less than a quarter-way across Easter Field.

At first he does not notice the disturbance by the Knot, and then he sees Susan Gander standing rooted to the spot as if fixated by a thought, but with the other woman's arms about her shoulders. Then Henry sees that Susan's face is drained of colour, and the other woman staggers as she tries to take the sudden weight of her collapse. It all happens very slowly. Henry rushes out of the room and into the corridor but it is a long way round, and by the time he arrives in the garden, a huddle of women around Susan Gander closes ranks and waves him away. Frances is there with her gauze taken off, kneeling on the ground beside Susan who is sitting hunched with knees apart. Henry can see Susan's knuckles taut as she grips her hand. Frances's other hand rubs the woman's lower back. He can see her nodding as if in answer to a question, and then grimace as they get her into a standing position and begin to lead her away in small, stiff-legged steps. Now he can see the great livid stain of blood down the back of her skirts. After an hour or more Frances returns.

'Your weeding woman has miscarried her baby,' she says, coming out of the ewery wiping her wet hands on her overskirt. 'Poor creature. There can be little so bad as being brought to bed of a dead child.'

The life of an infant bleeding away into the earth, by the hyssop. He wonders, inappropriately, if that patch of soil will be enriched. He imagines the grass growing lush and thick there.

'And as John Gander's not due back from Bridgwater till late tonight, I've left Lisbet in the tenement at Tuck's with her, she can't be on her own with a two-year-old like that.'

'I thought you should know that they've been saying that she must have looked upon the monkey, that it provoked the baby's loss in her, the sight of it.'

But he is not really listening; some kind of memory is stirring in him. 'Oxycroceum.'

She turns. 'Sorry?'

'To expel what is left in the mother. There is a recipe for an emplaister.' He tries to remember the preparation in its entirety. 'Oxycroceum, root of asarum, wild nep, oil of dill. There must be all of these in the stillroom, and her recipe is written down. Anys always—' he checks himself, 'my first wife kept it well-stocked. Perhaps you should seek some out and take it over.'

Frances finds the key and goes without a word. It isn't often that he mentions Anys by name, just once or twice by mistake. On the desk he sees his gallipots of ink are low, takes down the big bottles from the shelf and fills the purple, then the black, letting a measure of each thick dark liquid pour out glistening across the lip.

Afterwards he pushes the two wooden stoppers back into the necks, and then sits for some time examining the bottles, turning them slowly round without seeing them at all.

# VII.

*Of KIDNEY BEANE, or GARDEN SMILAX. Hath long
and small branches growing very high, griping, and
taking hold fast when they be succoured with rises or
long poles. The fruite and cods boiled and eaten before
they be ripe doe provoke urine, and cause dreames, as
Dioscorides saith.*

H E HAS SET THE BOYS UP with archery practice on the lawn.
They tie the monkey's leash to a garden stake nearby and it sits
on its haunches, fascinated for a while until it gets bored with not join-
ing in. Johnny is instinctively quite good with a bow, though Henry
pretends not to notice this. That boy might make a fair stab at life, he
thinks, watching him pull the string taut and release it. The arrow flies
with a thump to the target, and Johnny looks over proudly at him, his
face clear with joy. The boys like to set up a lettuce on a stake and shoot
at that until it is tattered on the ground, but Henry disapproves of waste.

'You're going to eat that salad, are you?' he shouts at them, until
they pick it up and give it to the rabbits.

Afterwards he gives them a guided tour of the garden, pointing out instructing facts and characteristics, the monkey off its leash and chattering on Johnny's shoulder.

'The Tower may have its lions and leopards and polar bears, but pay close attention to your own natural habitat and the rewards are smaller but probably more satisfying,' Henry says. He stoops to pick a single plain pink head of mallow, with the intention of showing them its delicate, veined petals, but Thomas and Johnny have run off and are whooping with laughter.

They think he is out of earshot. 'Who needs a menagerie, when you've got Father to explain the garden to you!' Thomas says. 'He'll start on about rich pickings in the hedges next.'

Johnny's laughter bubbles out of him as he runs.

*Do I repeat myself so much that my spawn do not trouble to treat me with respect?* He smiles, forgetting to tell Hester, too, to calm herself. She has green marks on her skirts from sliding in the grass. The light is bright and the wind from the west ruffles the tops of the trees. The little flower in his grip wilts forgotten as he watches his children. Is it wrong to enjoy their happiness? Some would say so; that use of discipline, humility and the rod is the only wholesome way to bring up children. But what does a boy learn from being striped by birches, but how to brew up anger?

'Look out for dragons!' she shouts, running after her brothers and pelting them with buds of sticky goosegrass. At six years old, Hester is far too infused with storyteller's nonsense, he thinks. Perhaps they should not have that man from Somerton again telling tales at Christmas in the hall. It's a little too pagan, but there again, what harm can it do? Henry Lyte watches his daughter as she runs, her hair coming loose, and tries to feel disapproving.

Mote is nowhere to be seen in the garden, but he is probably in the outhouse playing at cards, which is his new obsession. Tobias Mote knows all the games; gleek, new cut, primero.

Sometimes he and the garden boy play a quick round while Henry is at dinner. He knows they do, because of the way they stand up quickly and pretend not to grin, as he comes back to make sure they are getting on with work after their maslin bread and cheese is finished. Why else would they not come to dinner in the hall with everyone else? Mind you, Tobias Mote has always preferred to eat his own meagre dinner outside at noon, even in winter, long before he took up playing cards.

'I'll have hot food enough when I get home to my wife,' he's always said. 'What I like at noon is a bit of a breather.'

Henry is not sure what to do about the card-playing. He later mentions it to Frances.

'Well,' she replies. 'It's not like he's going off to see the cockfighting in the village. I wouldn't pay it any heed. And if he is proving such a problem, just get another gardener.'

'He's not the cock-fight sort. Is he?' Henry hadn't thought of that, wouldn't put it past him.

Frances rolls her eyes.

The flavour of what is left of the day is slightly tainted by what Tobias Mote, in a fury, brings up to the house an hour later.

'Master!' he shouts in the hall at the top of his voice. 'There is something here for you to see.'

Speechless with rage and indignation he lays out the fragrant corpses in front of everyone who gathers, wondering what the noise is about. Five, six, seven, eight fat blooms of amaranthus, just entering their prime and snapped off cleanly, their thick green stems bleeding juice. He is visibly upset. His hands are shaking.

'There now,' he says, grimly triumphant. 'That is what comes of having unnatural things about, running free. I've always said that foreign ways are not our own. I've a mind to hand in my notice over this.' He points at the severed flower heads. 'Call it what you may, but the devil did this. Just lying there bitten clean off as I found them. Ruined. There you are.'

And he leaves the hall, a trail of mud after him.

Henry has no choice but to take Johnny away into his study and give him the hiding that he deserves.

'Does Nin have to go back,' he whispers in horror afterwards, tears streaming down his cheeks.

Henry hangs up the rod, considers, feels very depressed about the way this glorious summer day has gone.

'That creature is never to be left unattended again. It is to be kept shut up in a coop when no-one is playing with it.'

Johnny sniffs. 'But it will be—'

'That is my final word on the matter. And if you want that pet, you will leave my sight this instant.'

# VIII.

*Of the CICHELING or FLAT PEASON. The first kind is
of nature and qualitie like unto pease, and doth meanly
nourish the bodie.*

ONE MONTH LATER, and Henry has returned from Wells
uncharacteristically animated.

'What is this humour that has come home with you? Have you
purchased something of note?' Frances is amused. 'Or was it just a
lavish dinner with your brother that has put those bright red spots
upon your cheeks?'

'Wait!' Henry struggles to remove his coat in his enthusiasm. It has
been a warm ride. 'I am going to fetch up something from the cellar.
There is a pipe of best sack from Malaga that I have been saving for
good news. Don't tell a soul yet, especially not Jane or Florence – I'd
like to announce it at supper.'

'How can I tell anyone, when I know nothing?'

'What? Oh, I see. Lobel has found a printer for the translation! Of
the new herbal, my English version. He is called Henry Loë, a most
excellent book printer. I have heard of him already of course, he is
very good. On a large work like that, with so very many pages as it will

surely have, the workmanship is paramount. He works in Leiden or Antwerp, I forget which. And the best news is that he has persuaded the Bavarian doctor Leonhard Fuchs to include his illustrations, fine woodcuts to be printed from the blocks from his octavo edition of his herbal printed in 1545. They are simply the only ones that would do, there are more than five hundred and without them the project's worth would have been greatly diminished …'

Outside in the orchard he can see the monkey swinging from the Ruddick pear, but Johnny is there with him, cross-legged on the grass in the late, low sunshine. And he is struck by how very fitting it seems – how this creature from such a different habitat could look so right here at Lytes Cary. The monkey dangles out a long arm and breaks off a pear and squats on the branch, eating the pear and dripping juice. It is finished in a flash and the monkey eats another one, more slowly this time, as if taking time to relish it. How wrong Mote is. This monkey is not incongruous at all.

'I'm pleased for you,' Frances says, and comes to him and lays a cool hand on his. 'You're breathless. Will you need to go to Holland?' Her hand looks very white and slender against his ruddy fingers that have been clasping reins for twenty miles.

'Peter Turner had the letter with him, as he'd come straight from where he'd been staying in London on his way back from Cambridge. I must write and tell Rembert at once,' Henry says. 'I will not need to go to Holland, but the book will be printed there because the wooden blocks on which the illustrations are engraved are so many and of great weight.' He goes straight to the garden to expend some energy.

The year could never be fuller than it is in August. The land is a gift, he thinks. He runs his fingers up a rusty stalk of sorrel to hear the popple of dry seed. The comfrey is still in flower, feeding small bumble bees even at this evening hour. There is a sweet smell in the air, of fruit and sunbaked grasses cooling. Looking up at the sky he realizes, with that familiar gentle annual desolation, that both the swallows and martins have gone. The marsh woundwort is big and drooping, soft, bleaching in mottles. Cuckoo pint berries are dropping misshapen from the fat stem. At the foot of the garden wall stiffened dark harts' tongue ferns sit like augers. And then the sun is lower, dimmer, and suddenly the day has gone unsteady with approaching death; browning towers of foxglove seeds toppling and stripped, the dyers camomile balding in the bed; patches leaning, dragged by bindweed.

'It's a pity that summer has to end,' he remarks to Mote as he fetches a spade.

Mote is noncommittal. 'Always a lot to do, this time of year.'

'I mean all that decay,' Henry says.

Mote brightens. 'Good for the compost. That's how gardening works, how anything works. I'm off home for my supper now.' He shrugs. 'We're all bound for the worm eventually, Master. Our souls leave the body, soon as its purpose is over.' He turns at the garden door on his way out and makes a tipping motion. 'Into the soil we go.'

This is precisely what Henry does not want to remember.

When he thinks of Anys he tries to imagine her as a soft, fine smoke drifting about the room as a gentle spirit. But so often instead the unwelcome picture that comes to mind is her familiar shape turning to carcass, rotting, buried in the ground. Digging helps to counter this, he has come to realize, being with the soil, turning it over, keeping it tilled and sweet with compost and planting, smelling its goodness, its crumbling, just-damp texture, its layer of clay beneath the topsoil, its fanning mats of roots woven throughout, as fine as hairs, turning the minerals to immediate, burgeoning purpose and holding it closely together against wind and rainfall. He likes to see the actual colour of it, the brown, the grey, the black; not the dead spadefuls in his head, but the light is going now. He blinks to concentrate, and when he straightens up and stands into the night breeze starting up from the south he feels his face is wet. With tears of sadness, or excitement that this project is coming together or simple relief; he doesn't know which.

# IX.

*Of LUPINES. A pessarie made of lupines, mirrhe, and
hony mingled togither, moveth womens naturall sicknesse
or flowers, and expelleth or delivereth the dead birth.*

THE EVE OF ST BARTHOLOMEW. Thomas fell off the mare today in the Slait Field and banged his head on a fence post, so that it bled a little. They carried him in but on inspection he seemed to be otherwise well, and went back out to play in the yard with strict instructions not to gallop. But overnight he is brought down by fever, and Lisbet is busy carrying water and freshly mixed up cooling plaisters to the sickroom.

'He must have been bitten by mosquitoes down on the marshes,' Frances says, grey with being up all night. 'When he was with you.' Henry had taken the children across the moor yesterday, to order duck from the wildfowler George Colt.

'I worry about that boy,' Henry says, ignoring her. 'We must keep a lookout for his health and well-being, he does not have an inner common sense like Johnny has.'

In truth there is little anyone can do but wait to see if he gets better. It seems a mild enough fever, but the hot plague is running high over towards Bristol, with thousand dead, they say, so far this year. Henry goes to his study and works. After an hour he wipes his quill clean and goes outside.

'Do you have to make that noise everywhere you step?' Henry asks. He has a headache, and the presence of Mote seems insistent. He has taken to wearing his tools hung from his waist, clanking about the garden, his knives rattling against his thigh.

'Noise?' Mote pretends he doesn't know what Henry is talking about. 'You mean these? I need two kinds, don't I, Master. A pruning and a grafting blade. Two knives together are always going to make some kind of noise, striking against each other as they do. Lucky I keep the saw in the shed, isn't it.' He winks. 'See that on every handle? T. M. That's my initials.'

'In case you forget?'

'Something like that,' Mote says, easily.

Henry shivers when he thinks of what happened in France on this day three years ago. The West Country is full of displaced Huguenot silk-workers, coming in through the ports, grubby with travel and fear. He thinks of all those who were burnt at the stake for their beliefs.

What do I believe in? he thinks warily. In plants. In the power of living things to be complicated by the spirits. But like anyone else he prays later for his son to be spared. He looks in on him as he goes up to bed. Thomas is asleep, but looks flushed and damp. He will help him with some Latin tomorrow, he is sure to be better.

# X.

*Of the VETCH. They sow Vetches in this countrey, in the fields, for fourrage or provender for Horses.*

Henry bursts into the kitchen to speak to Frances. 'I have had a reply from Dodeons,' he says. 'He would like to try to source some more plates for the herbal – so that every single plant is illustrated, which means over three hundred more will be commissioned. Three hundred! This is thrilling news.'

Letters are vital, they are the life-blood of a scholar working in morose isolation as he does. Nothing could progress if exchanges did not happen. To be sure the boundaries between one man's idea and another man's published matter can be unpleasantly blurred. But it is not for glory, or autonomy that a man might devote himself to study, but the advancement of knowledge to the good of humanity. Active debate with wine and friends, or speedy volleys of correspondence, there is no better substitute for a vigorous contribution to the scholastic climate than a shared idea.

Frances is packing for Johnny's day on the Levels looking for late-flowering arrowhead and frogbit with Henry. Thomas wants to stay behind to help with the horses.

'You watch out for deep water where you don't expect it and do not drink any of it down there on the moors.' She hands Johnny his pack of bacon, loaf and apples. 'Here's your labourers' lunch.'

'Don't worry, Mother,' he says. 'I'm always safe with Nin. Monkeys have a great deal of luck and he uses it to keep me safe. Having Nin means I'm safe every day.' Henry sees him beam at Frances and wave goodbye.

Johnny likes to talk about the New World as they walk, which is his favourite topic, and in turn Henry tells him a little of his own travels as a youth. The monkey refuses to get down and put his paws anywhere near wetness, clinging to Johnny's neck and occasionally squeaking. But mostly they are all three quiet, sharing the silence in their own thoughts.

Sometimes Henry feels mired by his environment. The clay, the wet, the expanse of oozing flatness laced with rivers and ditches. Sometimes he feels he will take only one step wrong and the soil will receive him too readily, gulp him down under the quivering surface to nourish the layers rotting into peat, the dead grasses and rushes living, dying, rotting into a floating platform of threshold land barely claimed from the water, the old shape of the estuary where the sea once lay as a matter of course.

Soon in winter the soil will flood over with both fresh and salt-water, and be replenished by that. The eels will move in and the winter birds on migration with their cries like lost souls. But it is a halfway place, between the land and the sea or a near-land that is soil at its most endangered, most newly made. Indeed sometimes down on Carey Moor, when his boots are sinking into a brownish black it is like the end of the earth. This is what it might be like if the sea decided to reclaim its own, forever. And it might, one day. The eels know it is really a place of water. The water-plants, the flocks of winter birds that pour in from the south. The cow-men, like his own man Oxenden, moving their cattle and kine away and up onto higher ground, once the brief summer is over. And there are always drownings on the Levels in winter – lone travellers weighted by baggage, their feet pressing too deeply into the edges. It has been known, come spring and with the water all draining back to the sea, for submerged carts to emerge, covered in silt just feet from the tracks, whose drivers had fallen asleep, not knowing it would be the last sleep they were to enter into, or where they were careless, or lost, or mistaken about the direction. It is easy enough to make errors of judgement when travelling in fog or darkness.

Yes, the moors change and soften once the best of the year is over. In any season but summer the soil on the Levels is like a jelly of mud and roots, quivering at every step, sucking at the ankles of those who cross to the other side, who choose not to go round.

They are late getting back to Lytes Cary.

Frances is in the parlour playing her virginals like she is punishing the keyboard, drumming and drumming, scales and marches, the notes hard as minerals. She looks up and rushes over when they walk in. Johnny is muddy and tired, the monkey asleep in his arms like a baby.

'What is the matter with you!' She is furious. 'I thought something terrible had happened. I was about to get Tom Coin to ride out onto Carey Moor to see if you were lying injured somewhere.'

'This has become an obsession, Frances. It's not healthy.'

She blinks rapidly. 'But I *like* the music.'

'Not the music, Frances, I mean your aversion to the moor.'

'And your own engrossments are healthier than mine, are they?'

'What do you mean?'

'Running over the marsh looking for leaves, scribbling in your book about plants, out in that garden of yours, that *Knot*.'

'Why do you hate the garden so much, Frances? It's a perfectly good garden. It's far from paradise but it has roses and all the things that women like. It's so,' he battles for a word, '—*unreasonable* of you to hate it.'

She turns to him. 'Why should that matter to you? It's as though your heart is trapped out there inside that wretched Knot.'

He is astounded to see that there are tears in her eyes. Why on earth is she crying?

'It's nothing but *plants* in your head. It's … it's unnatural.' She slams the door on her way out but it bounces open. Old Hannah is standing in the corridor to see what the fuss is about and Henry knows he must say something to preserve his dignity.

'My wife is upset. She speaks out of turn but she is never rational when she has slept poorly.' He moves on smoothly. 'Will you make up a caudle for Johnny and ask Lisbet to take him to bed. And will you remind me tomorrow that I must send a parcel to my sister Ashelye over in Damerham? It has been quite a while.'

# XI.

*Of FENUGREEKE. The seed of fenugréeke, is hote in the second degree, and drye in the first, and hath vertue to soften and dissolve.*

WHEN THE MONKEY IS LOST, Henry's first callous thought is that it was inevitable. He tries not to point that out, and refuses to go on looking for it after an extensive search of the estate has thrown up no clues at all. After one week there is nothing left to be done about it.

'It will be long gone now,' he says. 'At best it has run away. We cannot waste any more man hours in searching for a household pet that should never, frankly, have been here at all.'

Johnny is blank with misery. 'All my luck is gone now,' he says, with a chilling surety. 'Nin was my luck and now he's gone.'

Henry thinks of the monkey escaping, struggling through ditches, on all fours running with his tail curlicued above him, a silvery streak across the moor living on stolen orchard fruit and chicken's eggs, or flicking small fishes out of brooks, sleeping in hedges, the red waistcoat becoming tattier and frayed at the hem.

He imagines him getting as far as the other side of Glastonbury, still hoping for the jungle, still finding only the chilly English woods, spitting out mushrooms, ripping handfuls of tough red berries from the hawthorns until a peddler takes him for a showman's monkey and they fall in together, working the taverns and fairs until Judgement Day.

The monkey's loss has left its mark. Johnny is disconsolate and refuses to pay proper attention to his studies, no matter what he's threatened with. He spends hours hunched with his feet up on the sill in his chamber, facing out across the fields, in a hopeless vigil that only a child could undertake. Henry is too busy with his work to chastise him overmuch, and besides, soon enough he will be at school in Sherborne, where enforced learning will hit like a bolt from the blue.

And then of course there is a hard frost overnight on the fourth of October, which is, anomalously, the Feast of St Francis, and then the following night too. Johnny stands shivering in the doorway before prayers, his nightshirt clutched about him. Henry stands with him a moment, their breath white, but they do not talk about it – there is nothing that can be said.

He thinks for years afterwards he will find himself still scanning the edge of the reeds, hoping to catch a glimpse of Nin. He knows he will do it to the end of his days. Why should he believe otherwise; unless someone produces a little monkey carcass for him.

# THE FIFTH PART
## The Names

## ❧ 1576 ❧

## I.

*Of SWEET TREFOYLE. All the hearbe is of a very good smell or savour, the which looseth his sent or smell seven times a day, and recovereth it againe, but being withered and dryed, it kéepeth still, the which is stronger in a moist and cloudie season, than when the weather is fayre and cleare.*

WINTER IS DEFINITELY MOVING IN. When he was a young man, he rejoiced in the thrill of the cold and darkness, but now he feels the gradual loss of light acutely. Each year the drag into wintertime seems more aggressive, a near-physical sensation of being pulled under, as though the advance of old age were like being drowned infinitesimally slowly in the dark patch of each year. And it can only get worse.

As he goes through the chapel chamber on his way out to the orchard, he glances up at the stained glass in the window. The low, late winter light is shining through it brightly; the depiction of his father and his mother Edith kneeling on skulls and looking toward the sun. He always feels close to her here, draws a comfort from it – as though she is embedded in the substance of the house itself forever.

As he leaves the porch, he sees something out of the corner of his eye that makes his stomach turn, but when he bends to examine it he sees that it is not, as he'd first thought, a dead bird stretched out wet and rotting unnoticed by the door, but just a clump of blackened hart's tongue fern, the long leaves torn like feathers, draggled wings.

The crust of leaves underfoot is crisp with icy, crystalline snow, dead black stalks of knapweed and dark green grasses sticking out of it. The beginnings of sunset is reflected from the western sky onto the white hills, blazing with pink like an apricot's flesh.

A heron flies past, greyly vast on bowed creaking wings. It is cold out here. He imagines the flesh of his toes freezing to ice and crumbling away with each step inside his boots. He remembers a poor woman who stumbled into the yard out of last year's snow, all dazed tattered and crusted with ice, no speech coming out of her at all, and cloth binding her feet, which when they unwound they found to be all blackened and thick like plums.

The children are outside playing, trying to make a snow bird on the lawn.

'This snow isn't proper!' Hester laments, holding a fistful out to show him. 'It just won't stick, Father.'

'The next snowfall might be better,' he says. 'The wind will swing round a little to the east or west and the clouds might let down a different kind of snow just a little bit spinier for squeezing together and building objects.'

'But that could be days, yet!' Thomas wails.

His father shrugs and goes on with his walk. Yellow patches of urine dot the snow, and brown cones of molehills have erupted above the snowline and then frozen hard again. There are chunks of ice spinning down the river. Beneath the pear trees, the surface of snow is pock-marked with drops. Something makes him glance skywards and he sees the keen, swift outline of a hawk scouting above the orchard.

On his way back to the house he goes by the bee garth and puts his head to the back of each skep to check the bees are still living through this weather. He bends into the pocket of resinous waxy smell that surrounds them. The warmth of the bees has melted the snow from their roofs, and he is satisfied with their low throbbing that is like a large wild creature breathing, or like a heart coursing warm blood in the veins. They are still alive in there, even in the grip of this most icy of winters; to have survived so far at least is a sign of hope. Henry's heart swells. He loves to think of those bees in there, sustained on honey they have made from flowers he planted. He too feels embedded in the substance of Lytes Cary, intrinsic, he feels as though, alongside his mother and his father and all the ancestors before him, he earns his place here.

His chilblains are itching inside his boots. Even as he stands there some dead bees fall out of the skep. One blackbird sees them and edges closer, one hop at a time despite Henry's presence, too hungry to be cautious.

# II.

*Of MELILOT. The floures be yellow and small, growing
thicke togither in a tuft.*

H E IS ENGROSSED IN HIS MANUSCRIPT when the sheriff's
officer comes, and does not hear the knocking at the door.
Lisbet brings the packet and hovers by the door as he takes it,
surprised. It is a large, official-looking seal, and the hand is ominously
neat and flowing.

'Everything all right, Master?'

He looks up. What on earth is she doing still standing here, with a
shovel in her hand. 'Aren't you supposed to be with the kiln, turning
malt today?' he says. He waits until she is down the corridor before he
breaks the seal. No. Everything is not all right. This is a letter from the
Court of Common Pleas.

He reads it over and over in disbelief. It is like a swarm of old spite
rising up into his face, the words crackling, crawling, spitting at him
from the thick legal paper. He sits down and reads it. He stands up
and reads it, then puts it aside, his chest tight. He feels sick.

This is catastrophic. There is no other word for it. His stepmother has
brought a writ of dower against Henry at common law. His father's will

was never proved, and there is no evidence his father ever wished her to take such a modest settlement as her jointure for life. Ten years have now passed since his father's death, and she is free to begin pursuing Henry for one third of all his father's manors and land, which includes the manor of Mudford Terry. One third – that contains also Lytes Cary.

Surely for all his threat and bluster, goaded by her, his father would never have wanted Henry's stepmother to oust him from the family seat. *Her claim is for a third of all his land.* Henry will not share a single inch of any dwelling with that woman Joan Young, no, *Phelips*, whom he never called Joan Lyte. This family would have to move out, and so displaced, where would they go? In the meantime her vile presence would bring to Lytes Cary the worst sort of meannesses. He pictures the lack of feast for the tenants, dust gathering in the Great Hall, her particular grey chill seeping up the stone stairs and down the corridors like a perpetual winter. To be sure she would pass eventually, and at least in death could not keep him any longer from his patrimony. But his life is now, he thinks. Now! Not in twenty years' time when he is beyond caring. And with so much to be done here – in many ways the garden is only just beginning. My *life* is here, he thinks. He suddenly wonders whether his brothers felt like this when he inherited the management of the estate, with the prospect of full inheritance upon his father's death; Bartholomew, dead now, and Jack, with his weak head for figures … He storms out to the garden, stares angrily at the plants, *his* plants he loves so much.

At the base of the marshmallow, there are some very new green shoots. The borage is blackened slimy rosettes like old seaweed. The motherwort is tiers of seeds left on the stalks like burrs. And amongst the stubs of the stems of alecost are almost imperceptible green bluntnesses, building up under the surface.

The Sorcerer is doing rusty hysterics in the orchard, over and over. Henry Lyte grabs a fistful of soil and flings it over the wall in the bird's direction.

'Demented bird!' he shouts. 'What kind of *chicken* are you?' It is the worst and perhaps the most ridiculous insult he can think of. The sudden silence is disconcerting, and he glances back at the house to see if anyone could have noticed his outburst.

He goes inside, and in great anguish of mind writes a flurry of letters. *Madam*, he begins, *I implore you to … as you are born so void of decency … You durst not … A witch could not more evilly …*

An hour later, he sits, exhausted, looking over the pages that can never be sent.

He writes to his brother Jack, outlining everything, hoping for what – some kind of familial solidarity? Then he goes back out to the garden and paces up and down the path, freezing in the cold without a coat on.

She has a house, he thinks. What can be wrong with Mudford Manor? Only that it does not have someone worthwhile to torment nearby. And for the first time he considers if his father's marriage may have had its obstacles to happiness. Joan Phelips has ever craved a quarrel for her cause, as other women might thirst for steak during their confinement. This animal need in her has always sniffed the air for juicy conflict. Up in the orchard a magpie flies off with something in its beak, and he has a fleeting image of Joan Phelips's bony form hunched over Lytes Cary like a carrion bird with a piece of pink meat, tearing at it with her teeth, a kind of devilkin trying to wrest a piece of his own flesh from him.

And it has always felt like this, he realizes. She has taken it upon herself to make his life a misery since he was twenty-seven, and a resentful, restless witness at his own father's wedding, trying to swallow marriage-cake with the reproachful shouts of his mother's dying filling his head. How that cake had stuck in his throat as he toasted the happiness of bride and groom. Despite all the food he had eaten in foreign lands as an eager youth travelling for self-improvement; betrayal tasted to him, for years afterwards, like almonds and saffron.

She resented Henry above all the others; Bartholomew, Alice, Grace, Dorothy. For he was the obstruction preventing her from acquiring Lytes Cary itself.

Joan Phelips has always been inching, clawing towards this moment of seizure, a decades-long calculation maintained against his father's passing.

Henry turns to the house and imagines each room at Lytes Cary filling up with liquid; dark fluid creeping over the flagstones and up the walls, and he cannot tell if it is fluid that has spilled from him, or from the body of the house itself, or if it is the unspilled, unformed blood or tears of his descendants who should yet be born there.

Henry Lyte is not given to violent thought, and suspects that Reverend Tope would say it was blasphemy.

He chides himself aloud for having thoughts like this, and tries to hum. He breaks a sprig of rosemary from the main stem and pinches a leaf. The scent is woody, resinous. He keeps taking breaths of it until the sprig is limp and dark between his thumb and forefinger, and night has come. At supper he does not mention the letter. Not to Frances, nor to anyone.

# III.

*Of TREACLE CLAVER. Thrée leaves drunke a little
before the coming of the fit of the fever Tertian, with
wine, do cure the same.*

**F**EBRUARY THE TWENTY-FIFTH, St Matthewtide. The first
naked, knotted strings of dog's mercury push up blindly, then
foliate themselves abruptly, and then the curled spears of ramsons
emerge, till there are creeping tiny armies of them breaking out across
the middle wood. He is not keen on ramsons, neither for their smell
or woodland floor dominance nor by June for their cowardly collapsed
yellow stench, rotting for weeks in the woods like the gamey, onion
smell of death. Simon Cressing says that it could be a while before the
case gets to court, that they have time to decide how to proceed.
Henry does not like the idea of his personal affairs being decided upon
in Westminster Hall. He, the upstanding son of a Justice of the Peace.

But in the meantime the buds are breaking open on the wych elm,
and are like furred white pearls dotted over the perfect domes of
pussy willow in the hedge.

The woodpecker flies off towards the copse. He is envious of that
Sorcerer, the way he must see things with some distance, always

outside, always moving to a better vantage point. *Lucky bird, getting the best views.*

'Not like a hawk, mind you,' Mote says beside him, and with a start Henry realizes he must have spoken aloud.

'That bird,' Mote nods his head at the retreating woodpecker, 'flies like it's tethered to something, like it's trailing an invisible string off its tail and can't get free.' Henry has to admit that it does. 'And you can't get much distance when you're tied to the earth like we all are.'

Henry looks at him warily. Mote is not usually so philosophical.

'But a hawk, that's different.' He points above them, high into the blue sky, and Henry can just make out a speck up there, circling on the air.

'Don't suppose we look like much, do we, down here,' Mote says, unnecessarily. There is a pause while they both watch the buzzard spiralling easily towards the east, over the lower pasture. It has seen something, some small unsuspecting mouse or rabbit, and is descending for the kill. Henry feels a chill pass over him as the bird swoops down, claws first, out of sight. Mote is still in this odd contemplative mood. 'They bear the souls of men who've died away from home,' he says, scratching his head. 'That's why they're always searching like that, keeping an eye peeled.'

'Good God, man,' Henry can't stand any more of this. He rounds on him. 'Are there not things that need attending to? It's just that the last time I looked, there was a pile of onion sets to go in, raspberry canes to be cut back, and if you're still short of tasks, a shed to be cleared out of broken crocks and swept.'

The gardener shrugs and walks away, not overfast. Henry hopes he didn't sound too shrill. He doesn't know why he is so tense. Sometimes these days he feels almost overwhelmed by that sense of imminent disaster.

There is a great noise coming from the kitchen. Old Hannah is shouting at one of the kitchen staff. Henry can't hear the words but they are punctuated by a clattering of implements. She doesn't often lose her temper; something must be off, or mouldy, or missing, or burnt. Everything feels out of kilter.

He goes to the bee garth to check them over. There is one bee-skep out of the six that since the cold snap last week has had no sound or warmth radiating from it. Three days of frost so cold the pond was hard through, and then a thaw. This time surely spring must be starting up. Henry stands behind it and listens closely, willing there to be a faint hum, some sign of the presence of life but nothing, just the rushing of his own blood in his ears. There is a sharp, mousy sourness to the smell emanating from the hive now the freeze is over. When he breaks open the skep to try to understand what went wrong for this particular colony, he finds a soft cluster of dead bees huddled in a tight ball round the dead queen, loyal even beyond the end. He breaks open the brood comb too, and pores over it in the greenish-grey February light for clues. And then he sees the healthy white eggs, some capped grubs, and the nearly formed bees inside the cells almost ready to come out. If she was laying eggs, she must have thought that it was spring! He groans aloud. If only the colony could have held on for one more week, eking out the last scraping of winter store honey until the yellow catkins were loose and ripe enough to yield some pollen, or some early crocus for the nectar, then these bees would not have starved to death. What very bad luck. He feels a fleeting grief for them, their death hinged on the decree of a queen misreading the intentions of spring.

Henry Lyte shivers. He can just hear the gurgle and suck of the river Cary slipping by unseen in the reedy shadows somewhere on his right. Cary means 'heart', and it feels somehow sinister that this cold black gurgling heart should be snaking round his land. Inch by inch tonight's darkness accrues, and the day's light is seeping away, and all the goodness with it.

*What is darkness?* The science part of Henry Lyte's mind asks him, knowing about the sun and the roundness of the earth. But another, older part answers back. *It is a place for melancholy, sleep, forgetfulness, not-seeing.*

# IV.

*Of WOOD SORRELL, or CUCKOWES MEAT. This
herbe groweth upon the roots of great old trees.*

U P IN THE ORCHARD Henry has reached a point of contention
with Tobias Mote. Henry has read of an intriguing method for
curing a canker about the roots in plums and pears, and wants to try
it out.

'All due respect, Master, but your book is wrong. If we do that we
will waste the rootstock. I know pears. If there's one thing I know, it's
pears. And I cannot do what you're asking of me. If we go about it in
this way then those young grafts will die for no good reason other
than your being misinformed.'

'But this volume is the *definitive* guide to tree-rearing and grafting.
It has the newest—'

Mote shrugs dismissively. 'There may be some kind of pear I have
never clapped eyes on that thrives on this kind of treatment but it is
not a common one.

'To be blunt I think this gentleman, Master, has made this book
with the thought of money in his head. And if he has run on
further than he should have, in order to fill up pages, then what is

omitted, well, if you'll beg my pardon he may be talking out his arse.'

'And I suppose you have read it, have you?'

'You know I have not, Master, I can mark out my name and that is good enough for me. But I know about what goes in them and know that there are some sorts of knowledge that cannot be put in books. It's all very well, men sitting inside writing books about what goes on outside, but just because it gets printed, bound, made into a fair thing all leather-tooled and its name done in gold, doesn't mean it's talking sense.'

Henry suspects that Tobias Mote is getting at him. He tries a different tack, containing his temper.

'Look, I have been all over Europe, and I have seen many different ways of treating trees, and I would say that there are most likely to be many different ways to—'

'It's all very well, Master,' Mote interrupts, 'dotting about and trying things from books, but when I work I am drawing on not just my own experience but my father's too. The work of our hands, on this soil over seventy years. *This* soil, mind. They know what they're doing here. While you was off roaming about, I was here at my father's side, learning what field the cows liked best, then learning from old man Colleyns how to use a pruning knife, learning how to work this *particular* land, Master.' He almost spits the last words out.

'So this is what this is all about? Your claim to this land is more valid than my own?' He can hardly believe his ears. The man is deluded if he thinks his right to this ground is so simple as that.

'Mote! I order you to treat those roots according to this diagram. That is my specific instruction.'

'I do not care if you dismiss me for this, Master, for I will not do what I know is never going to work. It would feel like a wound, doing that to a tree. It would be cruelty. I say no more on the subject.' And to Henry Lyte's astonishment, he sees his gardener put down his tools at the foot of the ladder and walk off. He walks off, just like that, over the grass, lets himself out of the gate and is gone.

'All right,' Henry says to himself. 'I'll show you.' And right in the middle of the orchard he chooses three trees on which to perform his experiment. He spends the rest of the day with a mattock and then a trowel and then his bare ungloved fingers, clawing back the earth and exposing the root systems. He is astonished by what he sees. The roots are a web of meshed threads stretching far, far out and down. Henry breaks a lot of them, it is impossible not to. He has a faint feeling of unease, almost a nausea, as he did at university one time when he went with a friend who was a student of medicine to see a dissection as part of a lesson on anatomy, sensing that he was looking on what no man should be allowed to see. He glances over his shoulder and Widow Hodges is standing by the gate, her head cocked as if straining to hear what he is doing. But he goes on with it anyway, lets the drying-out process that his book recommends begin, and when he looks up again, she is gone.

There are plenty of other matters to put his mind to. He doesn't see hide nor hair of Tobias Mote. It's as if he too has vanished into thin air.

He does not know if he'll come back to work tomorrow. He thinks of sending a message over to his wife to give notice to quit, but he knows he cannot do this garden without Mote.

'Find another gardener,' Frances says, busy with the children at suppertime. 'Eat neatly, Thomas, you are wearing your good coat and I do not want it covered in greasy spots. Have you washed your fingers?' She passes the dish of roast capon, and Henry takes a large piece; it is Lent in ten days' time. 'There must be hundreds of farm hands used to working the soil round here.'

But Henry knows what he has.

'I'll wait a bit,' he says. As if there wasn't enough to worry about, without losing his right-hand man. Yes, that is what he is. Tobias Mote is absolutely necessary to the garden's success. If he is honest with himself, he might even say that Mote is intrinsic to the very garden itself.

That night Henry dreams he sees Frances grabbing at a likeness of Anys standing over the bed. In the dream Anys is putrid, semi-solid, muddy from the grave.

When he wakes on the third day following the orchard argument, Tobias Mote is out in the garden with his rake in the seedbeds before Henry is even risen. He can hear his tuneless whistle and the hiss of earth and small stones against the iron prongs as he sleights the soil. After an hour Henry goes out and they go to the kitchen garden to discuss in which bed to sow parsnips and plant out the garlic. Neither of them mentions what they quarrelled over.

# V.

*Of OUR LADIES THISTLE. It flowreth the same yeere
it is first sowen, and when it hath brought forth his
seede, it decayeth and starveth.*

WEEDING IS ALL A STRUGGLE, inching across the soil. The aching back, the resistance, the interminable pull, tug, shake. Weeds maze the mind with their multiplicity. It is impossible to have clear, sequential, rational thoughts whilst weeding, he has discovered. They make him too angry. He resents them for their successful abundance.

It is hot for May. By the afternoon Tobias Mote is pushing handfuls of silverweed into his boots.

'What are you doing?' Henry asks.

Mote puts a boot back on and closes his eyes with bliss. 'Good and soft on the blisters I have from forty miles of walking to my brother's place and back on Sunday. Works a treat.'

Henry looks dubious. 'I suppose it could palliate the broken skin, but it is better for internal bleeding or bloody flux, *and such as are squat and bruised with falling from above.*'

'Squat and bruised!'

'It's what Rembert states. My task is to translate what's there.'

'My father taught us to stuff 'em in our boots, and all I know is how it works for us!' Mote says cheerfully. Why does he always have to have the last word.

In the middle distance, Henry spies a cart inching up the track from the Ilminster road, the driver's head a red dot behind the horse. The cart has spiked wheels, and he frowns to see it churning up the track like that. By the time it has drawn into the yard, Henry Lyte has forgotten all about it.

'Where's barn to, chief?' the cart boy nods at his load.

Henry Lyte is still thinking of silverweed and for a second stares uncomprehending. The cart boy's hat has a distracting hole in it, so that red wool hangs frayed across his forehead.

'They said dump the seed wheat in his barn,' the boy repeats stonily.

'Over there,' Henry Lyte points at the obvious hulk of the largest outhouse. He can't even remember ordering seed wheat, let alone twenty quarters of it. He looks about. Is there nobody else to take this in? Where are they all? The yard is empty of anyone useful, though he can see a child hiding behind the horse trough and in the far distance the cowman is carrying something heavy, probably a bucket.

Is he letting the house slip? If he can't even keep an eye on goods coming in at the gate, then what bigger matters might lack attention. He must arrange a meeting with John Parsons his bailiff, for this afternoon perhaps. There is that uneasy feeling of a thing unresolved, coiling right in his belly again. He leaves the cart boy letting the load out over his tailgate and goes quickly inside to check his ledgers for unpaid accounts, anything lain overlooked in the last month or so. He scans up and down the columns of handwriting. *Settled with Reynolds March twelfth. Thirty-two lbs beef Mistress Davey. Received of Roberts new kneading board, ash.* Nothing out of the ordinary. Henry Lyte thinks, worries, chews his thumbnail. The knock at the door of his study makes him jump in his seat. 'Master Parsons for you,' Lisbet says and shows his bailiff in.

'Of course.' Henry clears his throat.

$\approx$

That night he cannot sleep at all. He thinks of his stepmother choking, binding, twisting, clogging; stealing the nourishment from the very soil at his feet. He gets up and wanders the house, gropes from darkened room to room, until each is lit greyly by the dawn light. He sits in the smallness of the larder, not eating anything, surrounded by the comforting smells of smoked sausage, kicking his heels against the barrel of saltfish.

He can feel it tightening, tightening about him. Surely lack of sleep will turn a man mad?

# VI.

*Of GOOSE-GRASSE, or CLIVER. All the hearbe doe
cleave and sticke fast to every thing that it toucheth: it is
so sharpe, that being drawne along the tongue, it will
make it to bleede.*

I N THE KNOT, the hyssop hedges have burgeoned, so that there is
less room between them. The Knot itself seems to have swelled. It
is more constricted, there is less room to move about inside it. The
wind ripples across the garden, so that the hedges knock about as if
the Knot were alive. How overgrown it is; the last few summer days
have produced a surge of growth.

Henry pushes his way to the centre, his legs soaking with wetness,
and stands with his arms folded tightly.

The hedge is spreading its tendrils outwards. He should be very
pleased about its success. But this morning there is something about
his Knot that makes him feels oppressed, squeezed, as though things
have grown larger than they should be, more out of control.

He wonders whether he should attempt to settle out of court – pay
Joan Phelips off with a little more than his father intended her to
have. He gets the iron shears and a whetstone, sharpens the blades

to a shining keenness, oils the pivot and then trims the hedge methodically, evenly, keeping an eye on the shape and the angles. He begins with the outside edges and works inward. It takes four hours, but he's doing it very thoroughly. And when he's reached the last quarter, finished it and straightened up, aching, he feels the world is more in order.

# VII.

*Of WOODROW. Woodrow is counted a very good*
*hearbe to consolidate and glew together wounds.*

J UNE AGAIN. A beggar couple come to the door asking for alms.
The man had an bad accident with a scythe, losing a hand, and
has been unable to work since last harvest, he says. Henry offers to
look at the hand, to see if it needs treatment or has infection spreading if it cannot heal, but the man refuses to unwind the bandages. The
woman is strange, jerky, doesn't stop talking.

A few hours later, items are found to be missing from the kitchen.
A leather jack, a whole carp and three cooked merchet loaves that had
been cooling on the rack. There is a great argument about who left the
door open whilst the woman was prattling, and let the man in unattended for a drink. No-one will own up to it.

'I expect he was thirsty,' Tom Coin, who may have been responsible,
says sulkily. 'It's been a hot day. There were windows open.'

Old Hannah is very vexed about the loss of the carp, which is hard
enough to catch in that murky pond and now she has to come up with
something else for tomorrow's dinner.

Frances does not says a word about it, but gives Henry a look as if to say *I told you so*. One of the girls has a bad dream in the night, of thieves breaking in and looming over their beds.

'For goodness' sake,' Henry says loudly, crisply, at noon the next day. 'Nobody died!' A silence follows like a dropped pot. He hears Jane's knife clank against the pewter. With one accord, the entire household has turned its many heads towards him, hands paused halfway to mouths, lips parted mid-sentence. Even the ale being poured at the far end of the table seems to hover for a second in the air. Henry feels their astonishment and reminds himself that stolen property is a serious matter, and if the master does not seem to think it of importance there is something peculiar afoot. He should know better than to make light of it; a thief can hang for less than the amount that disappeared from the kitchen yesterday. Most citizens would agree that they should hang, that the punishment meted matches the crime. For lesser crimes there are the stocks, ducking, but theft of property is wicked, extraordinary and punishable by death. In his head his thoughts are running, *how can I be concerned about a missing fish when it is my entire estate that is at risk.* But his outward reaction is inappropriate. It is not at all what a former undersheriff should say in front of subordinates. He should have respect for the law. They will begin to notice his distraction, begin to question his authority. He reaches across for some more bread and adds, moderately, 'They are unlikely to return, and if they do, they will be apprehended and justice served.' He holds up two fingers, one after the other. 'Nobody is to worry and everybody is to be vigilant. It is simple.' He cuts a sliver of bacon and chews it down. He hopes that will be enough, and yes, something along the table relaxes again, the natural order of things is restored, and chatter starts up around him as if nothing had happened.

Only Frances glances at him once or twice, he feels her scrutiny but does not turn to look. She feels crystalline, as hard as salt beside him, not at all what a wife should be. A wife should prop, support, soften, meliorate, receive. She should accept his word as the last, not sit there bristling with unspoken queries.

❧

Nightfall is late at this part of the year. He stands in Gore Field and takes in the night sounds, watches the ranks of sheep out here, white in the darkening light.

'People in London don't think of sheep in the dark,' he thinks aloud, irrelevantly. 'Out in the dark sleeping in pale white huddles, or grazing by moonlight. I'm not sure they think of animals sleeping much at all. In the dark for them the countryside ceases to exist.'

He goes inside and sits with Frances in the parlour, where no fire is lit as it is too warm, just one candle. He goes to the window and looks out, fearful. Moonlight harbours, and also conceals. In moonlight he always expects to see a figure; some kind of confirmation that his fears are rational, justified. He has to force himself to look, his heart rate tripling in speed as he cups his hands against the glass.

*See. Nothing.* Just the gaping white flowers hoping for moths, like white bowls floating. The solid rock-shadows, the blue glinting drops of water, winking diamond sharp as he moves his head.

He squints, his breath is fogging up the panes.

'What is the matter Henry?' Frances asks.

The present is crawling with the past. And one would think by moonlight almost anything could be made visible. All going on once the dark has come and then going on in the moonlight because it can, it does. With terror he looks to see what's out there – it's almost worse that there is nothing. He wipes the fog away and goes on looking. *Where is it?*

'Where is what, Henry?'

'If I knew that,' he snaps, 'it wouldn't signify. Look for yourself – all blue white and inky shadows, stark with nothing – in the way that ice smells of nothing.'

'But ice does have a smell,' Frances objects.

Henry rounds on her. 'It does?'

She hesitates. 'It is like dust, very cold dust.' There is a pause whilst Henry absorbs this, remembers that she is right, remembers being a small boy holding a frozen pail at the chicken hutch, smashing the trough ice for the pleasure of hearing its shattering squeak, seeing the trapped brown ripple-edged oak leaves stuck in time, his face close to snow and breathing in that smell of winter, his breath melting back the fur of frost to the shrunken wet patch beneath.

'So now you are agreeing that it is out there, it is only that I do not see it.' Henry breathes slowly and calmly.

'No, Henry.' She slips from the chair. 'I am going to fetch a drink and then you must sleep. What a hot night this is.'

# VIII.

*Of BUCKS-BEANES. It is also good to be taken in like
manner of such as spit bloud, and are liver sicke.*

IN THE MORNING the air is still oppressive and thick. Frances
pours out ale for him. 'You did not sleep well last night, Henry?'

He looks sharply at her. 'I slept very badly, as I often do these days.'

'You were counting in your sleep, aloud, Henry.'

'I was?'

'Very low numbers.'

He drains his mug. 'Sometimes the simplest calculations can be the hardest.'

'Where are those children, we will be late.'

'I dreamt of the coast and the sand all covered in flies, droves of flies running before the incoming surf, black clouds of them rising up and settling on the dwindling sand as the tide thunders in, and the water black with flies too, thick and gritty with drowned fly-bodies.'

Frances shudders.

'You did ask,' Henry says. 'Are you ready for church? Did you manage to settle with Hannah for the beef?'

Frances finds her gloves.

'Have you seen my hat?' Henry demands.

'Which one?'

'The hard one, the beaver. The one I always wear,' he adds testily. *What is the matter with everyone today?* Then he finds it on the chest in the hall where he left it yesterday, which makes him feel crosser. The last thing he wants is to start losing his mind, with all this going on.

This summer is packed with thunderstorms, rolling over and over the house persistently, unproductively, ridding the air of nothing of its thickness, its too-warm malignant soupiness, smelling of dust and dank, overripe fruit.

Before a storm, everything waits.

When they get back from church, Henry looks at the fish gasping in the muddy, weed-choked pond that needs days of rainfall to fill it again and feels some sympathy for them.

At noon he looks at the bitter lettuce on his plate, hears the crickets rasping outside the window, and sees creeping up the hedge the evil shiny bryony; indeed the hedgerows are crawling and flickering with birds. In the sky the swallows are like flies, he thinks, flecking and darting above a piece of meat. He is finding he has a loss of appetite, finds most food distasteful. Even the light greasiness of eel-flesh is too much for his palate.

Henry tries to read in the evening but his eyes are too sore from tiredness to continue, or the candle too poor with its dim flame swerving away from the draught.

It is tightening about him.

'What is?' Frances asks, coming into the study unexpectedly.

'Now look what you've made me do!' he says. On page two hundred and sixty-one of Clusius, *Clematis*, there is a splodge of red ink, a pen dropped.

He sits there getting more and more irritable. By eleven o'clock he should be in bed, but still ploughs on, making mistakes quietly to himself.

# IX.

*Of ORACH. Afterward commeth the seede, which is
broad, and covered with a little skin or rime: the roote is
full of hairie strings.*

**T**ODAY HENRY LYTE IS OUTSIDE and finds the neatness and
difficulty of his garden is too much. The weeding woman Susan
Gander packs up in the gathering drizzle and leaves to cook her
husband's supper. The baby lolls asleep on her back as she tramps
down the path to Tuck's. The other woman, *what is her name?*, is shaking the last of her limp, gritty weeds into the barrow to take to the
compost, and for some reason is eyeing him over the Knot. Her eyes
are very black. When she rubs her filthy hands on her apron and calls
out politely, 'Night, Master,' he finds he has still forgotten her name,
is distracted by his loss of memory for a moment and then finds that
she has gone.

He rubs his head. He goes to stand in the Knot with his boots
against the wet brush of hyssop and looks across at the intertwining
shapes and they seem small and nightmarish. It is a contradiction of
constraint and unmanageableness, mapped out into absurd and
meaningless zones of conflict. Mats of dying-back early perennials,

stubbed with dead-headed stalks are dotted between unresolved tracts of blank brown earth, clotting into lumps speckled with unwanted gravel and some new shoots of growth; nigella and marigold perhaps, he can't remember what they sowed. He looks at the grid of his always unfinished patch and feels hostility flexing inside him. He looks at the sky and feels no better at all, and begins to stride towards the river, taking the distance in sharp biting steps.

He stops hard by the river, leans back on the trunk of the largest willow and takes deep breaths until his heart slows. There is a pinched feeling in his hip. A cart is crossing the bridge on the highway but no-one can see him on this bank behind the withies, and it is soon gone. He shuts his eyes and then opens them and begins to watch the water sliding by; the soft tug of water fondling, dragging at the reeds, the toppled browning sedges, the crusted mud bank peppered with holes, the plop of fishes surfacing for crane flies, and he feels something slacken inside him. He looks up at the willow and sees its yellow, supple shoots springing faithfully from the cut limbs, the deep cracks of its bark. And when he hears a noise and puts his hand to his own face he finds his cheeks are wet, that he is sobbing.

He is there for a long time, very still. After a while, a kingfisher lights on a overhanging twig of alder above the river, its plumage darkened with rain. Henry holds his breath, it is so close, sitting oblivious to him less than five feet away. The whole dagger of its head is poised, waiting for fish. The muddied water's surface is textured with rainfall, rippled circles cross-hatching, blebs of bubbles dragged by, and limp drowned rounds of leaves turning under the surface. If this rain keeps on, the river will be deepened by a foot at least by the end of the day, pouring down off the Mendip, and further downstream below the weir, mingling with the salty tidewater as it rises. The water must bring with it a taste of the hills, traces of salts and minerals from the higher ground over the lias. Ten minutes later and the kingfisher is still intent for fish. It shoots out a white splash of dropping and moves to another twig above the water.

That night at supper he enjoys the eels the man has brought, with some relief and return of appetite. Already skinned and filleted, he has only to part the pale, delicious oily flesh with his knife. But he is grateful for the need to examine his plate for the odd occasional translucent bone, lift it away with the tip of his knife and push it aside. Even the rich taste itself requires some concentration. It is not a fish to eat without due attention.

For some reason the Reverend Tope is here for supper, but Henry Lyte only has to bow his head occasionally against the flow of his guest's talking and keep an eye to ensure that glasses of Canary wine are set at his elbow with regularity, rinsed, returned to the sideboard and filled again. For at least an hour he has had no distinct sense of what the Reverend has said to him, only that it is about the state of his neighbour's fields, the weather, paying perhaps more than sixteen shillings towards queensilver this year, and so on. He has a sensation that is not unlike being adrift on a small green sea, bobbing pleasantly along. He even clears his throat as a matter of course at intervals to show he is paying attention. Frances chitters brightly whenever silence threatens, which is not often, as the Reverend has been known to hold forth for several hours at a time, even without such good refreshment to encourage him.

Henry considers the practicalities of defending his territory, what he would have to do should the law prove his enemy. It occurs to him that beneath the flagstone upon which the Reverend's foot rests so lightly, is a large square hole, filled with serviceable swords and daggers kept oiled and sharpened against the unexpected. A good sword's blade should pass soundlessly through an apple as though it were butter, with no pressure applied from the hilt.

They reach the next course, which is a tansy, a bittersweet milky egg dish tasting of herbs, that Henry likes, along with the children.

'A favoured pudding!' the Reverend bellows, and is quietened for several full minutes in order to consume one, two portions spooned onto his plate and then the monologue resumes again.

Henry Lyte notices his wife has floated dried rose petals in the fingerbowls of water, like little pink boats.

# X.

*Of SOWTHISTLE. These do grow of themselves both in gardens amongst other herbes, and also in the fields, and are taken but as wéeds and unprofitable herbs.*

**H**ENRY FEELS MORE ENERGETIC, less skewed, for several days. He spends time collecting seeds and roots for re-stocking the stillroom. The drying racks are almost full, but he needs to bring in angelica. Lisbet helps him, scrubbing the roots clean of soil as he lays them out to dry on linen spread out on the trestle.

He likes angelica, its resinous, carroty taste. A fat or oily liquor like gum comes out of it when cut. He slices into the black root to show Lisbet.

'Here.' He holds some out, the paleness exposed. 'Smell this.'

Her face lights up. 'Oh yes, I remember that, Master. When my old Da was bit by a dog over at Bridgwater docks, the woman put it on him, against the mark like this, and it did not go bad.' She smiles. 'My Da was a big man.'

'Some call it the root of the Holy Ghost,' he adds.

'They do?' Lisbet drops the stems and wipes her hands on her apron, back and forth. 'Well then I've just remembered something else. Something from the back of my mind, Master. These stems and others like it, hollow ones with tops like that, like the kecks and cow parsley on the wayside, and cowbane, and hemlock at the edge of ponds, my mother always said all of us, my brothers and sisters, we was to stay away from them, as by way of their hollowness they'll lead us down to the otherworld given half a chance, they'd lead us down to the place of the dead.'

Henry looks at his lovely pieces of garden specimen with its joints and ribs laid out on the stillroom table. 'There is some sense in that instruction for children,' he says. 'So many of them are poisonous, even to the skin. These plants are full of watery acrid juices. Not for nothing is cowbane called *dead tongue* by country folk. It renders those who swallow it without a voice. Even the smell of hemlock can make you ill or giddy. So in a way, this folklore has good sense to it.'

'Being hollow, you see. How could I have forgotten that,' she says to herself, not listening to him at all. The preoccupying angelica smell is very strong in the chamber. 'Straight down to the dead.'

There is something he could ask her. 'You know about these things, Lisbet,' he begins.

'I do? Like what?'

'Such as how a spirit might show itself to you.' Her eyes widen. 'No, don't worry, I've not seen anything alarming, indeed nothing at all. I am …'

'A spirit could climb upon your back sir, and make you carry it about until you did its deathbed wishes as you should have, Master.'

'Is a spirit heavy?'

'It has what they call half-heaviness. It drags at you, though not with a living body's strength or weight. It stands to reason, for a corpse will have started to decay inside the grave, to progress only *part* of itself on to the next place. There has been talk of men having to lump spirits about with them on their backs, as toads do carry each other. Think of that, Master! Never turn your back if the dead are in the room with you.' Her eyes are very round. 'They are all falling apart by that stage. Some spirits have been known to come back to the living in tatters, but they've still got the strength to pull you into the grave with them or squeeze you to death, if it's the last thing they'll do.'

'Tatters?'

'Rotting away, things have gone on so long. It's best to act swiftly with spirits, do what they want if they're asking you something.'

'But what if you don't know what it is that they're saying to you, how to comply?'

Lisbet looks confused. 'Then they wouldn't be coming, would they Master.'

'No,' Henry says. 'Of course not. Can you take this pot back with you to the kitchen.'

'Master.'

She is gone.

# XI.

*Of GROUNDSWELL. The lesser Groundswell hathe
gréene leaves, which be also muche torne, and deepely
jagged upon both sides.*

**H**ENRY LYTE IS STRUGGLING with a particular kind of plant in
the herbal, *Thapsia*. Although he has the Latin and the Arabic,
still he cannot say what name it has in the English tongue. He cannot
ask Turner because Turner is dead. He has written a swift note to
Lobel in Antwerp but there may be no reply for over a month and he
thinks besides he may be away or else the letter is lost to the vagaries
of the post. He rode to Bristol yesterday to see if Bredwell was about
but he seemed to be away, his servant was unhelpfully evasive as he
stood there on the doorstep. He will have to wait till Penny comes
down from London, which he plans to do soon.

His body is stiff and sore after the ride to Bristol. He wants to feel
exerted, limber after exercise like that. But he is too bent from being
at his studies, his neck craned over books lit by nothing but one
candleflame's poor, uneven light. Too much time spent in scholarly
pursuit is bad for the humoreal balance, he has decided, and for the
eyesight. He should have more red meat, perhaps. More beef. Surely

it must be almost suppertime, he thinks peevishly. He tries to stretch and hears his joints cracking like his father's used to do.

'Why do I feel as though I am merely *existing* in my body, rather than using it to its full capacity,' he grumbles. 'This book is wearing out the very bones of me. I am brittle, Frances, where I should be lithe.'

Frances, almost twenty years his junior, sees no reason to be sympathetic. She nods at the window and says tartly, 'There's plenty to do in October. Why don't you join the cartman out there, then. Or they could do with another pair of hands grinding the crabbies.' She puts her sewing aside. 'Just make sure you do not start another book.'

She can be very caustic with her speech, he thinks, aggrieved.

In bed later with his wife, he gathers her to him out of habit, slides his hands under her back but he does not feel worthy of any response; his spirit is sluggish and old, and is failing tonight. He pictures some other couple, both youthful, rosy skin-to-skin and sharing the wonder, the dewy freshness of the body and its pliant joys. Now he feels stiff and unfit for pleasure, as though at some point he grew into his body wrong but went ahead with life anyway. His spine feels rigid, every limb feels unkempt, dirty with neglect and stiffness, with too much sitting. His mind won't leave his thoughts alone even for a moment to allow him to enjoy this moment in the marital bed, like time off he's earned, like a pause for bread. The thoughts go on rattling about his head like he is nothing but a husk, a dried old seedhead.

'You are out of sorts, Henry,' his wife says crossly, rolling away from him, and she is right.

# XII.

*Of PURCELAINE. These two Purcelaines are full of Juyce.*
*The root is long and of a wooddie substance, and liveth*
*with his stalke, and certaine of his leaves all the winter.*

**H**ENRY GOES OUT PAST THE AVIARY, and the fog has thickened. Everything is damp, dripping. Even the grass on the higher ground squeaks with water underfoot.

It is easier to feel afraid in fog, afraid of spirits, as though the dead in the air's moisture can brush the skin of the living. Fog is the weather of the dead, of the past muddying the present. Under cover of fog the earth creeps out of itself and ventures to places it wouldn't otherwise attempt. Fog is the breath of the collective dead, the ancestors rising like wet old vapour from the earth, to be abroad, sidling into cracks and clouding across open spaces brashly populated by the living. Fog is obfuscating, making uncertainties, distortions, shifts.

There is a snort of horses in the next field, and one looms white over the willow hedge, its tail high and spooked.

'It's all right, it's only me,' he mutters.

The next day the fog is still pressing about Lytes Cary, though less insistently; as though it may have done with them for the time being. Henry goes out to the orchard and finds that a strange foggy wind has blown up. There is one blackened leaf spinning on its stalk not coming loose from the Norwich pear, tapping against the bough. Looking up he sees a lilac-grey sky pressing down, and behind the house there is a vaporous fur of trees on the ridge.

He spends much of the next day thinking rationally of the compound nature of soil, of its diverse characters, how little we understand of the way it works, the way it yields up a nourishment to the plant that is not just water.

It is only when he steps out of the house again to stretch his stiffened legs that his irrational response begins in earnest. It is close to twilight when he reaches the lower fields beyond the willows. He sees the carcass of a rabbit or coney stretched out, and begins to pick his way between the ankle-snapping lumps of clay protruding from the sodden herbage. Suddenly, as in a bad dream, the wet ground seems saturated with the dead – souls seeping about his leather shoes, clutching at him with the greenery. He thinks of the soft rushes soaking the dead up, drinking them in. When he goes into the house his shoes are claggy with them, he tries to wipe as much as he can away on the rush mat at the door but their footprints follow him across the hall and almost to the parlour, where to his wife's dismay he takes them off and his hose, and goes barefoot. When he takes the stairs to their chamber he walks on tiptoe to shake them off, but later as he lies in bed at night, he is unable to sleep because he can feel them crawling on him, so that he has to get up and go to the ewer and pour out water and scrub his hands and face again and again more thoroughly. The splashing wakes Frances.

'Why on earth are you washing again, Henry?' she says, sleepy, from the middle of the bed. 'You are very peculiar tonight.'

'I forgot something,' he says, rubbing his face. 'I forgot how the mud here can cling.' And when he returns to the bed he also forgets to blow out the candle. The Castille soap is a homely smell, and he is grateful for Frances's forearm stretched out on his chest. He arranges the bedhangings so that he can glimpse through the parting into the lit chamber. The dead settle down when there is more light, he thinks groggily, too tired to pray, but satisfied that they will leave him alone now in the clean sheets for the remains of the night. When you can get it, sleep is truly a limbo, a respite from the filthiness and confusion of the day.

# XIII.

*Of BROOKELIME. Groweth also sometimes by running
streams, and brookes hard by the water.*

**THOMAS PENNY HAS COME AT LAST TO VISIT.** He fills Henry
in on recent news; Moffat has been expelled from Cambridge,
and all the unsold copies of Matthias Lobel's disastrous *Stirpium
adversaria nova* has been bought up by a well-known printer called
Christophe Plantin, remade into a new version, and it is a runaway
success. Henry tries to listen, but as soon as he can, gets him out in the
garden.

'You know, Penny …' he begins at once. 'You are a physician. What
do you think to this – lately I have been having something in my head
that I can't dislodge.'

'Headaches, visual disturbances?' Penny prompts gently.

'It's ridiculous, but I can only mention it now because we are away
from the house. I wasn't going to at all, but then last night it happened
again. It sounds extremely absurd to say it aloud.' He grimaces. 'A kind
of voice.'

Thomas Penny's face takes on an immediate and surprising
compassion.

'God's words come to us in many ways,' he suggests. He puts his hand on Lyte's arm. 'Is something troubling you? Are you anxious about some aspect of your faith?'

'It is not like that,' Henry says. 'Nothing so abstract, indeed I find increasingly the warmth and gentle patter of regular prayer something of a comfort, even a distraction. That internal predictable speech of communion in its fixed arrangements … But what I am speaking of, it is more like …' he touches the back of his head experimentally, 'something's *in there*.'

A pigeon's flight whistles overhead.

'It's a voice saying something very old. It's like a very old small wound in the shape of a voice that is still festering, very dark, like a rusting nail in the flesh, in the matter of the brain itself.'

'And how exactly does it speak to you?'

'Usually I can't quite hear what it is saying, it's garbled, jumbled.'

'And you are quite sure that the words are meant for you to hear?'

Henry hadn't thought of that.

'It's a woman,' he adds, almost as an afterthought.

'A woman!' Penny is taken aback.

'Do you think I'm going mad, Thomas? Be frank with me.'

Penny considers for a long moment. A bird's shadow flies over them, a jackdaw.

'No. I would say that on the surface, you seem quite yourself, if anything. What I have seen so far. Forging forward with your occupations and family duties.'

'Then have I been seized?' Henry Lyte interrupts.

Penny shakes his large head. 'Possession is a very unscientific notion,' he says firmly. 'You have no demon, not in any sense of it that I know of. My professional advice would be that you should aim to have fresh air, sufficient invigorating exercise, enough participation in the delights of Venus that keep a man's cullions in working order, but not an over-indulgence. You are too preoccupied, Lyte. Get on with busying yourself about your herbal. You see,' he suddenly grins, 'this is what happens when you bury yourself in the countryside – the dark thoughts take over because you have not enough resistance to them, shining in your life. A mind alone at home, no stimulus beyond your own – it is hardly surprising that a man might begin to go a little inward. The fineness of your mind getting mired in …' he looks around at the wet fields, 'mire.'

Henry begins to protest now. 'My life is nothing like that, Penny. How you city dwellers put out standard notions of what a country man does with his days. Indeed, some nights I fall into bed exhausted with plans for a complicated harvest or grafts or sale of land. It's not all rose arbours and watching the fall of leaf through the windows, you know! Nor yet is it a vale of mud. For us the land is our living and our being. It is yours, too, of course, but you people seem so wont to forget your dependence on the countryside. You study it, dipping in and out of field trips, but as something *other*, something exotic, fascinating, when it is actually our lifeblood, our integration with nature that is so vital.' He looks into the distance and fiddles with a reed between his fingers, peeling the fibres from the pith and adds quietly, 'I'm sure you are right, though. What is there to fear.'

'Do you speak with your wife about these dreams? No? Your chaplain, perhaps.' Henry pictures the corpulent figure of Reverend Tope forking in a great mouthful of pie and laughs loudly in some relief. 'I could not!'

'Then perhaps addressing them in prayer may cause their dispersement.' Penny adopts a soothing tone that he must use on his more stubborn and resistant patients.

Henry Lyte knows he will not do this. 'I'm sure you are right,' he repeats.

They go on with their wet walk, their coats wrapped about them against the autumn chill. Henry's coat is getting so old and worn that he will soon need a new one.

'I should be glad if we do not speak of that matter again.' Blackie wags her tail as they near the porch. 'There's a good old girl,' he says, bending to pat her. 'What is it that drives a doctor, Penny, besides the money and the prestige? Is there a conscious need to heal?'

'I have a great desire to help, to mend, make balanced what has become disordered in the body's humours. Well, to be frank, Lyte, I have not examined it too closely before, but I could say it is like a gnawing in me, an obligation.'

'You see I have that desire too, but I am not qualified, all I can do is write my herbal.'

'Which will be of considerable service.'

'Do you think so?'

'Finish it and your troubled conscience will leave you alone. Principled, hard work is a great assuager of guilt.'

Henry looks sharply at him. 'What do you know of my conscience?'

'Only what you have told me.'

# XIV.

*Of EARTH CHESTNUT. The root is round like a*
*wherrow, or rather like a little round Apple, browne*
*without, and white within, in taste almost like to*
*Carrots.*

HE REALLY CANNOT SLEEP. The winter moon's cold stripes laid all over the floor of the bedchamber, everything is checkered, rigid, utterly still except for himself, rearing and turning under the damp sheets as though his torture was movement and his imprisonment the moon's shadows. Why can't he sleep? He counts to sixty, seventy, three hundred, tries to think of his garden. When he closes his eyes to pray, instead he has unpleasant little shreds of thoughts coming to him; a child – he can't see which one – running away from him and falling over, a single white cloud moving too slowly across an otherwise unblemished sky, and weeds, weeds, all tangled in with the pieces of meat Frances is serving him, dripping from the spoon, fine bitter strings of weeds in his mouth as he tries to swallow, his plate swimming with ditchwater.

He opens his eyes and the taste in his mouth is almost intolerable, he wants to spit to be rid of it. He swallows and swallows. Fully awake now, he begins to feel that there is something about the chamber that is not as it was. There is a faint, familiar smell that he cannot place. He strains his ears. There is … what is it? Something *breathing* out there. He hopes it is not a rat.

He swings his feet out of bed to go to the pot and is disconcerted to find that the furniture is not quite as it was. The table was *here*, and the coffers are moved too, and where is the Turkey rug by the bed? His feet are on bare, cold boards. What is that smell? He doesn't look behind him because he has a sudden, unaccountable fear that the bed won't be there if he does. There is a movement at the far end of the chamber, like a piece of moonlight shifting about, flickering on the limit of his vision. It cannot be. Dear God. When he sees what it unmistakably is, his heart chokes shut and rips open again several times, every slow, terrified beat is red-raw in his chest. Perhaps he is dying, too, or dead. *My love*, he whispers hoarsely, because before him a pale shape of Anys is there, full-sized in her bare feet, caked in mud from the waist down. He grips his arms in anguish. Her face is grey-blue in the moonlight, with a pearly membranous sheen, as though she were made up of tiny lights that are winking out, extinguishing all over her. The chamber has filled with a smell of oldness, the mustiness of old dried petals, the closeness of air inside thick walls. This is what the past smells like when it has run its course, gone over, spent its last breath. She is fading already. He thinks her lips are parting very slowly as if to speak to him, dear God please no. Dear God may she not speak to him. A spirit's voice does not come from the throat but echoes from the hollow body's core, as from an empty jug, rattling loose teeth from the jaw. He panics, screams.

'Frances!'

Why doesn't Frances wake up.

'Frances!' He cannot see her in the shadows of the bedcurtains.

When he turns back Anys has gone. He is abandoned in the dark, his heart pounding.

## The Knot

The same words judder round and round his head like bats in the sky. We measure ourselves against time by the marks that we leave in the earth. We notch, we dig, we score, we bury – and we unearth again.

*I'm sorry*, he says.

# XV.

*Of MALLOWS. Mallowes are temperate in heat and*
*moysture, of a digestive and softning nature.*

H E SUPPOSES THAT HE MUST BE ILL. Everything seems to him
to be moving with unnatural smoothness. When he raises
himself up in the bed to look at the orchard out of the window he sees
a bird swoop between trees like lead swinging on a plumb-line. Lisbet
rolls up to his side as if on wheels and stands in a strange, bent shape
over the form nearby, pouring a string of slow water from a jug.

With deep discomfort he recalls Dr Turner's words. *Truth-telling is
spiritual physic.*

'We are all unreliable witnesses, to be sure.'

'Are we, Master?' Lisbet looks worried, and goes away from the bed.

'I have made too many mistakes,' he says to himself. 'I have not told
the truth, even to myself.'

But what is truth? A slippery thing. It is a shape-shifter, a protean
myth. There are no truths from the past, only layers of mutable read-
ings and recollections and broken isolated fragments pieced together
differently with each retelling or reworking. The past is a monster
made up of all this, crouched just offstage.

He struggles to remember the facts as they were. His head hurts with the effort of it. He wishes it would lie down and be simple.

'All I want,' he begs, the sweat pouring off him, as he twists in the bedsheets, 'is to remember.' He is vaguely aware of his wife being close to the bed, or her white face passing. But which wife is it? He couldn't be sure. He falls asleep and dreams he has backed out into the courtyard and is scanning the upstairs windows. Yes, there she is. He can see Joan Phelips's shape up there in the south range, going from chamber to chamber, her head ducking back and forth as though she is looking for something. Everything is all muddled up.

When he wakes he feels all of the sickness to be shrunken and lodged in his spleen like a congealed, concentrated lump, and knows it for what it is. Guilt is a destroyer of men.

'We need to get all that nasty matter out of you,' he hears Frances say. And she keeps bringing more hot plasters smeared on the leather that she lies against him, four, five times a day. 'We need to draw it out.'

This seems about as likely as drawing down the moon. That's exactly it, he thinks one night, tossing and turning in the candle-light, he doesn't want to be paranoid but he definitely has a piece of wet, malevolent yellow moon lodged under his cheekbone or at the back of his skull. Where is it from? Was it there at the start of all this? Did somebody plant it there? The yellow moon oozes parts of itself down the back of his throat from time to time, but won't come out. When he mentions this certainty to Frances she doesn't reply but goes to the window and pulls back the curtain onto the night to reveal the cool, white, immensely untouchable moon in the sky drenching down over the sill, the bottles, the edge of the nearest willow tree.

He gazes at this real moon gratefully, her precise blue rim that is absolutely nothing to do with him, then closes his eyes and lets himself be laid flat by the stream of her whiteness.

'That is the trouble with sickness,' he begins apologetically, still with his eyes shut, 'how it makes one insular and shamefully apt to invent a false scale of things,' at least he means to say this, but has fallen asleep, and doesn't see Frances fastening the window.

Later when she brings him the bitter wine to swallow that she has, it occurs to him, brought for several nights in a row, he tries to raise himself up to see what it is.

'It's fine,' she says. 'Stop worrying.'

'But what is that stuff? Where did you get it? What can I taste in there?'

'I found the recipe amongst your notes,' comes her startling reply. 'And made it up myself. Let's just see if it works, shall we?' She will not discuss it any more. Now that he knows what it is, he feels easier. He lies back and feels the landscape stealing through him.

The next day he is considerably better.

The day after that the children are allowed into his chamber to tell him which bits of the catechism they have learnt by heart. Hester tells him that one of the ducks has begun laying – her first of the year. 'A duck's egg, Father!' They are delighted with their piece of news.

He has been ill for over two months, it seems, and spring has come.

Two days after that, he gingerly puts on his clothes that seem to hang upon him, he is so thin, and goes out to the garden. Its existence booms around him as he focusses on one object of interest at a time. A blade of grass, a ladybird, a small, nodding flower of pulmonaria. All these things in his garden, busy with him or busy without him – it makes no difference to them. The air is gently spiky with birdsong. He feels washed and empty, and sits on the grass bank without a thought in his head, feeling clean and smooth and useless. Frances sits with him, though they don't speak. The Sorcerer laughs from somewhere in one of the orchards.

'Where is everybody?' he says after some minutes when it occurs to him that there is no-one gardening in here at all.

'I sent them away. Just for an hour, so you could have some peace.'

'Oh,' he says, surprised.

'You should go inside and eat something,' she says. He feels cold, out here, but doesn't mind. It is good enough to be almost well again.

'Why did you not say that your father's wife had served you with a writ of dower, Henry?' Her voice is very quiet. 'I found the letters with your notes.'

He looks at her. He cannot think how to say that it would have been an admittance of failure as a husband to provide security for his wife and family, an admittance of fear.

'If she is to have a third of my entire estate that would mean she takes all the income from the Mudford land, Frances, and she would move in here, to Lytes Cary. The loss would be more than the manor house.'

'Is there a chance you could lose this case when it comes to court?'

'I would have said no at the outset, but I am not so sure now. I am sorry, Frances.'

'Suggest she takes Mudford with all its appurtenances and income, Henry. See if that is enough to satisfy her. Let it go. When she dies it will come back to you and then to Johnny. I am not qualified to give you counsel on your affairs, but I do need you here with me. Look what all this has done to you – you have been very ill. Let her have it. Let her walk away with it. She has no scruples. It is not worth the fight.'

'Give it to her? Of course I will not do that.'

Henry is so tired. Inside every blink there is a flash of light – as if from some other world behind this exhausting one. Inside again he thanks God for the fire on his face and falls into a deep slumber.

# THE SIXTH PART

## The Temperament

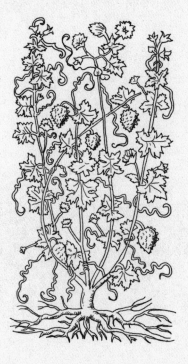

## ❧ 1577 ❧

# I.

*Of GOURDES. The rinde or barke of the gourd burned
into ashes, doth cure and make whole the sores and
blisters that come of burning.*

IN SPRING THE FRENCH CHERRY TREES are bright with unwelcome pairs of bullfinches, picking off the buds.

'We should get those boughs netted over,' Mote announces, 'I'm fed up with that noise.' And he does not wait to hear agreement but goes off to enlist help. Henry Lyte can see him up in the orchard propping his ladder and shouting directions to the boys as they tie in weights and throw the nets. Clearly it is quite a business.

Henry goes to his translation to look back at the entry for cherry and mazars, and is reminded that the distilled water of cherry is good to be poured into the mouths of those with the falling sickness. This July, when the fruit is ripe he should make sure that Frances makes some to take to Susan Gander's eldest child, who is afflicted with this. As it turns out, the devilish finches are unperturbed by the nets and move on instead to the cornel tree in the hedge by the long barn. Keeping fruit is a battle.

One month later and it is April. Henry's strength is returning, he is making longer walks every week. Today he goes up behind Lytes Cary with his eldest son.

There is a mild breeze catching the top of the rise and ruffling at the new growth of docks and nettles.

'Just think of all those who have lived here before us, Johnny,' he says. Johnny studies the ground at his feet earnestly. He has already caught the sun and small freckles dot his nose and cheeks. Henry has a sudden conviction that it will be a good summer. That thick white blossom down there in the orchards will lead to an abundance of pears. The lambs will grow fat and strong and gain a fair price at market, and the field crops; the barley, wheat and vetch, will yield highly. Having made that wish he has the usual qualm at tempting fate, so familiar it feels almost like belly-ache, but it is not a crime for a man to dream. What farmer doesn't wish for a good year ahead of him. Dreaming is what takes a man forward, makes him stretch for new things.

'Would it have been right here, the settlement from ancient times?' Johnny asks.

'It is a good spot.'

'Sometimes I look for bones with Thomas, but we've never found any except small ones, of rabbits maybe.'

'I found a very old bone outside the chapel, once,' Henry says.

'The chapel here at Lytes Cary?' Johnny is excited. 'Is it human? Can I see it?'

'Remind me later,' Henry says, 'I have it in a box somewhere.' He had forgotten all about the bone, which he had found unearthed after a prolonged spell of heavy rain had given way to a very dry summer, and some creature, rats or badgers, had dislodged a part of a bank at the back of the chapel. The bone was dark yellow-brown, and gave off a strong sense of something lost, of being separated from the rest of something else. It was probably a fingerbone, he'd felt, from a very long time ago. His instinct had been to bury it again immediately, but some incautious spirit of enquiry had instead made him carry it into the house, where it had lain on his desk for many years, perturbing him each time his eye fell upon it. It gradually become familiar and then ignored, and was finally tidied up with a bundle of curios from his youthful travelling days and put to the back of the shelf.

'Who will live here on our land after us, in a hundred years?' Johnny says suddenly. 'Who will it be, coming up here to look out over the hills and the Levels.'

'It's strange,' Henry says, 'how one never pictures the future of a place beyond oneself. I think about how the world will be for you – for all my children – but I can't form a ready picture of what that might look like. It goes against the grain of human nature, I suppose. Nobody likes to imagine the world passing us over, moving on to the next; fluidly, unhampered by our flaws and limitations, just sweeping on ahead of us and into the blue distance. I suppose we all like to be players, big and central in the foreground of our own affairs. Thinking too far ahead feels strained, thin, unnatural, none of our business.'

'Your pear trees will be there for years and years after you're gone, Father. The Catherine pear is very old already. Grandfather Lyte must have planted it.'

Not for the first time Henry wishes that his father could have met Johnny, if only he had waited just a few more weeks before he died. The horizon today is far away, the sky blue and limpid meeting the darker streak of hills. If this ground were higher, they would see the sea. The hawk can, of course, spinning above them on its ribbon of hot air, rising. Down there in the distance he notices Widow Hodges standing outside her cottage, then she goes inside.

'I'll look after your pear trees, Father,' Johnny says. 'Though I shan't like to think of you gone.'

Henry touches Johnny's yellow curls. 'That will be a comfort to me in my old age, and perhaps yours.'

'Especially the Sugar pear. That's my best-loved one, because it is so juicy.'

The breeze gets up momentarily so that all the new leaves hiss and flap. It's coming from the north-east, and for a second he thinks he does catch a faint smell of salt or weed from the coast, like something rotting, washed up by the tide. Henry shivers and rubs his elbows. Why is it that death always shadows any fundamental thought? Death is always lying in wait, just out of sight, like a man fishing for trout lies on a river bank with his hand already submerged, inching to his prey infinitesimally slowly so that it cannot see the end advancing in the water until it is too late.

Above them, very high now, the hawk mews. Johnny is cold too, despite the spring sun.

'Come,' Henry rubs his hands together briskly, 'we are standing still for too long. You have Latin to learn and then target practice if you can find those arrows. And I have the whole of *vetchling* to translate.'

As they go down the slope of the field he thinks of how there have always been people living at Lytes Cary. Sometimes workers dig up bits of pot they believe to be from Roman times. Once, a little irides-cent glass bottle, an inch high. He was surprised at how Frances's face lit up with delight when he showed it to her. She'd gone immediately to soak it in water and clean it up, and had kept it on her windowsill. A few times since then he's found her standing there gazing at it, turn-ing it over in her hands to catch the light. A pretty enough object, he supposes, but quite misshapen and worn and he can't imagine what its attraction must be for her. On the whole Frances's fondness is for new, sleek things. She does not like holes, or chips, or fraying or unravellings of any kind.

# II.

*Of RAMPION. In the top of the saide stems groweth a
great thicke bushy eare, full of little long small flowers,
like crooked hornes of a blew colour, purple, gray or
white.*

H<small>E IS OUT IN THE WOODS WITH</small> J<small>OHNNY</small>. The trees nearest the water are a clotted mesh of alders, new leaves striped and cupped upright to the sky.

'Here is a plant that I do not understand. It is held by some to be one of the standegrasses, or orchids, but there is no consensus – look at its root.' Henry scratches one up. 'See? The roots are not a pair of cullions like orchids as we know them, but are made up of threadish strings.' He presses it back into the soil. 'The lack of name in English is holding me up.'

'Name it yourself then, Father,' Johnny suggests, with that plain way of getting to the unthought-of but obvious that children have. 'What could you call it?'

They squat down together.

'We have to consider what its distinctions are.'

'It looks, well, *ordinary* to me, Father.'

'Such a term is useless in botanic study,' he says. 'One should never describe something without first looking very deeply.'

Johnny puts his freckled face up close to the plant and absorbs it, then another specimen. His eyes flick between the plants.

'There's a green stalk, father,' he says eventually. 'And greenish flowers carried on top like tiny chicks or goslings, and at the bottom is what, at first, I took to be a waybread leaf.' He checks again. 'Always in pairs.'

'So I should call it two-leaf, perhaps, or double-leaf.'

Johnny screws up his face. 'There must be another name for leaf, Father.'

'Foliage? Blade?'

'Blade is good, but two-blade sounds like something sharp, or like a weapon.'

'Twain? Or is that worse. The high Dutch word is "Zuey".'

'That's it!' Johnny interrupts. He grins broadly, three milk teeth missing. He tries it. '*Twayblade*. It doesn't sound like anything else, does it? You'd never forget that plant if you knew its name.'

He gets up and brushes the loose earth from his breeches. 'Soon I'll be going abroad, Father,' he announces, 'when I'm grown, right across the ocean to the New World and there will be many plants to name that no-one has ever heard of. You could come and visit me. It will be weeks, months even on the ship, but there would be most likely porpoises to look at. We could eat a thing called pineapple, which is not like an apple at all. There might be elephants. Perhaps I'll cross the Indian Ocean too, make it to Malay, bring you back spices.' There is a small silence suddenly as they both remember that was where the monkey came from.

'I'm sorry about your pet,' Henry says.

Johnny's eyes glisten. 'I did love that monkey. But Mother says a man needs to have his heart broken before he's truly grown.'

Henry's eyebrows rise. 'That seems rather a harsh thing for a mother to declare.'

'So do you think I am man enough now to go to sea?' he pleads, wiping his nose on his sleeve.

'You've a while before your schooling's over. But sometimes what we dream as children is what makes us men.'

There are three jays in the ash tree. Pinkish and hefty, they sidle up and down a branch together, scolding.

'Bully birds,' he points out to Johnny as they return to the house. 'No subtlety at all.'

# III.

*Of RADISH. The wilde Radish is stronger, and more biting than the garden Radish. It is good against the Lethargie, which is a drowsie and forgetfull sicknesse.*

**T**WO LETTERS TODAY, one of them confirming identification of the *agnus castus* shrub, which he is pleased about, as it means that section is almost finished. Thomas Penny has also rather ludicrously sent back the bit of specimen, which is now of course a dried-up and unidentifiable crush of brown leafy pieces that sprinkled out all over him when he opened the letter. But he wishes him well and says that he should consider being in London, where these matters could be settled so much more quickly. Perhaps he should be. Lime Street would be a hive of advice if nothing else. But it is entirely possible that he might not want to talk about plants if he wasn't surrounded by greenery. He would hate to be in the city for too long a time, after a spell in London he begins to feel stifled and too tightly sprung.

He reads some of the letter out to Thomas Moffat, who is here to visit before his trip to Basel. Just occasionally, when the weather is fresh and bright and windy and smells of change, Henry gets itchy feet and longs to see more of Europe and beyond. He thinks of foreign

340

countries out there across the channel, great plains of land teeming with other kinds of life and ways of living. He is envious of Moffat, who hopes to lodge with Felix Platter, famous botanist.

'A good letter,' Henry concludes. 'And then he ruins it all by asking if my garden is any nearer to being done than the last time he saw it.'

'You know he has lost his stipend from the church, for being too nonconformist?'

Henry nods. He looks out of the window at the blue sky, filled with the flashing dots of swallows. 'A garden is never *done*, any more than a child in its progress through life achieves a point when it's *finished*. A ridiculous idea. Does an artist say "my painting is done", or does he more likely say, "take it away; I can do no more to this for the moment without killing its spirit"?' And Henry sounds quite wistful as he thinks of his sheaves of notes; his collations of other wider-ranging botanists that would be such an addition to Rembert's scholarship. There is so much more he could be including with the herbal. But then it would not be the plain translation he had planned for, talked about with his printer.

'I am very near the end. I am well along with the sixth part of the history, *Contayning the description of Trees, Shrubbes, Bushes, and other Plants of wooddy substance, with their Fruits, Rosins, Gummes, and Liquors.* I have done most of the trees. I have done oak, linden, clammy cherry, birch. There are various pines to do, yew, *cassia fistula*, and then I'm almost there. Some gaps to fill in, and waiting for replies to a few queries by letter.' He puts his hands behind his head and leans back, yawning. 'You know, my translating has progressed considerably these past few years. Now when I'm working, on the whole the interpretation of the French comes to me almost in a twinkling. It's like it pours through me instantly. I do not have to drag the meanings from one side of my head to the other, kicking and screaming, in order to render them suitable for English palates.'

'I think you should hurry up and send it off, Lyte, before you go mad.'

'My madness is passed, Moffat. It crawled out of the soil and grabbed me by the throat and squeezed the life out of me for a while, but I am still here, aren't I?'

Moffat looks sceptical. 'There's room for improvement, frankly, but it could be worse.' Then he bursts out laughing. 'What on earth is that?' He has spied something sticking out of Henry's gardening shoes, which he is not wearing. He goes over and peers in. 'Your shoes are full of wilted leaves, Lyte! You really have gone crazy.'

'Silverweed is very cooling to the feet. There's nothing like it. Try it yourself.' Henry counters. 'Your scorn will shrivel to nothing in the face of reason. Once they've been crushed beneath the foot for quite a time they begin to smell of newly sliced apple flesh,' he adds, but this makes Moffat laugh even harder.

'You are an eccentric country boy through and through. It's why I trail all the way down here, despite the mud.'

'Besides, a garden is a different matter. It is always growing.'

'So if it is not a work of art, what do you call it?'

He looks out at some of the components of his garden readily obvious from the window; the leggy vervain, the honeybees dotting the air above the hyssop, the broad yellow heads of elecampane.

'A garden is a deliberate gathering together of living things, partially governed.'

'That reminds me. Can I borrow some leaves from your almond tree, Lyte?' he asks. 'I thought I'd go out and see what the Somerset insect life is like in August.'

'What do you want with my leaves? Do they eat them?'

'Almond leaves in my specimen box, chopped up into vicious little pieces, they'll kill an insect with their fumes. By the way, does your great book have a title yet?'

'I thought to keep it simple. Something like *A Niewe Herball*, or *Historie of Plantes*.'

'Like Turner's.'

'Like Turner's, but better.' He grins. 'I can say that; it's not my own work.'

❧

At supper Henry shows Johnny how to carve. 'Time he was learning the niceties of life,' Old Hannah says, approvingly, 'it's the kind of thing that she thinks counts, unlike Latin. Johnny is pleased to be given this temporary grown-up duty, and hands out ragged slips of beef.

At the end of the meal he takes one bite from his pear and lets the rest drop from his fingers back onto his plate. He fidgets on the bench. 'Can I leave the table, Mother?' he asks.

'But your plate is not empty,' Henry intervenes.

'I'm full up,' Johnny says, and hiccups.

'Would you do that with your meat?'

'No, Father.'

'Why?'

'It is a sin to waste good meat.'

'Where did that pear come from?'

'The orchard, Father. Please can I—'

'By whose grace did it grow?'

'Yours?' he hazards.

'God's! By God's grace!' He wipes his knife on his napkin. 'Come.'

He strides so fast that Johnny's little legs have to run to keep up, all the way through the grass to the near orchard, where the great Greenlock pear is dripping with ripe, dusky fruit.

Henry takes his knife and butchers a pear longwise into quarters, and it lies there, the four pieces of its pale flesh glistening pinkish wet in the evening sun.

'Does it not strike you to be like a body?' he demands. 'Look at those veins running from the stalk to core. Look at those blackish pips nestled in its central organ. You know it is four months since its blossom was set. It has sat, swelling, through so much weather and survived magpies and late frost and wasps. Those are the pips containing the sleeping essence of life for it all to begin again, there is life, Johnny, life itself. Does it not make you queasy with shame to think that you cast such perfect anatomy aside like rubbish?'

'Yes, Father.'

'Eat it! Go on, let it slip down,' he insists. 'You are eating the whole effort of growth. It has taken months, indeed years for the tree to arrive at that particular pear you threw aside and squandered.'

'It is delicious, Father,' Johnny says, swallowing with effort.

'Was it perfect?'

Johnny nods, and Henry rubs his head. Although he knows his son is being obedient he also sees he licks his fingers carefully as if to catch every precious clear drop. He will not waste a pear again.

'Now, I must get back to work,' Henry says, and Johnny runs away from him towards the stables bent at full tilt, as if released from captivity.

# IV.

*Of SKIRWURTS. The juice of the root dronken with*
*Goats milke, stoppeth the laske.*

**H**ENRY HAS OPENED the Book of Common Prayer and is about to begin, when a child whispers, 'Please may I be excused a minute, Father?' Johnny shuffles his feet with embarrassment at having to ask.

'What, now? We are in the middle of prayers. What is the matter with you. No! You can wait, like everyone else.'

Johnny looks at the floor.

Henry goes on with the prayer, even perhaps a little slower than usual, giving due weight to the words, taking some kind of solemn pleasure from their resonance and pattern, so familiar now. This immersion in prayer is almost like sleep; a between-worlds state, hanging these words in the gap between ordinary life and what exists in the afterlife. It is speaking to God, and also like speaking into an empty space, with its echo of men, though the dust and the pattern of prayers are settling again since this book of Elizabeth's came out. It had been a very dark and clouded atmosphere. For almost a genera-tion there had begun to feel something almost experimental about worship, after all the chopping and changing that has gone on throughout this generation; to the Book of Prayer, the creed and collects, the litany, as though there has been a great deal of thought put to the *method* of addressing God, at the expense perhaps, of true purpose. As a young man, he had felt oppressively aware of the tampering of men with the litany. It felt too human, too constructed. So many had died in its contention, and now it felt like man's blood-ied fingerprints lay on every page of every Bible. Perhaps blood and prayer will always be conmingled. But although the nature of worship has altered so much since his youth, the Queen's book that he has in his hands has been part of daily worship for eighteen years now, and there is clarity and surety again.

He becomes aware of a disarrangement in the room's reverence; a sudden ripple of noise to his left, a general lack of concentration, and one of the servants is stifling a titter. What on earth? Johnny's face is flushed crimson, and a dark patch has spread over the front of his breeches.

'Deuce!' Henry exclaims.

Frances steps forward. 'Henry, perhaps you should—'

He shakes her hand off his arm. Does she think he cannot manage his own household, his own son, his servants? He has been paying too close attention to his work and too little to the discipline beneath his roof. The household is falling apart. He has to restore some proper order. Henry dismisses the company with perfunctory speed, shuts the door behind them as the last one shuffles out, and rounds on his son.

'What kind of incontinent *infant* are you that you cannot hold your water?'

'I'm sorry, Father.'

'There is no excuse, Master Lyte! These are matters of basic decency that you should have mastered long ago. What is wrong with you that you cannot organize your own bodily functions. You are eleven years old, far too old to be pissing at whim.' Henry is shouting so loud that he is spitting. 'And before the entire household. Do you have no common pride that you would do that in front of your mother, sisters, the servants?'

Johnny's face is streaming with tears of distress. 'But Father!'

'In my day, boys your age were signing the muster rolls eager for battle, not wetting their beds or their breeches. You'll be soiling yourself next, will you?'

'No Father,' Johnny tries one more time to make his father understand. 'It is that—'

'Get out of my sight. If you do it again I will birch-rod you, like the little boy you are.'

Johnny hangs his head and steals out of the room.

❧

Henry goes to his herbal, Frances taps on his door and comes in. 'Henry, I am a little concerned about Johnny,' she begins. 'It is just that he—'

'*Comforteth the harte* would be better here,' he decides aloud, to show her how busy he is. 'But what in heavens does *oeillet* mean? And there is nothing between those verbs.'

She tries again. 'He seems to be having trouble with passing water.'

Henry frowns. 'Nothing that a good box round the ears wouldn't solve overnight.' He dips his nib and has it poised over the page. 'It is just the natural indolence of the boy, he needs to harden up a bit, he is too babied, madam, like some kind of milky tot. If he cannot be trained to control his basic urges, he must be made to. That, I believe, is up to you.' Sometimes Frances does forget which are her responsibilities and which are his. He looks up and sees her face.

'Perhaps I too have been too soft in the past myself,' he says. 'He is an agreeable, biddable boy in most respects, it is easy to forget that parental obligations are to drum certain niceties into our children, no matter how uncompromising that may seem. To do otherwise is a dereliction of duty. Now is the time to stop all that nonsense before he is utterly spoilt.'

Clusius has made a pig's ear of *gillyflowers*, he decides. And after several hours trying to make sense of it all he restructures gillyflowers to suit himself, which works much better, and then tips in *floure Constantinople* just afterwards. Only then does he allow himself to leave his pens aside and retire to bed.

# V.

*Of SMALLACH. Smallach hath shining leaves, of a darke greene colour, much divided, and snipt round about with small cuts or natches.*

THE THREE PEAR TREES ON WHICH Henry had performed his experiment at the heart of the orchard have sickened. Their output at harvest is naught. They have made no fruit, the leaves have withered and dropped away long before autumn.

Tobias Mote shrugs when it becomes clear that there is no way of saving them. 'It was to be expected,' he says, expressionless. It is as if the trees are cursed. Henry has cursed his own trees, caused the rapid decline of them for the sake of experiment. Next time he will be a better husbandman, applying some sense to his thirst for progress.

They are dying, and so the woodman cuts them down with the axe, and the stumps are dug back, and the grass has begun to grow over the old wounds. Henry broaches the subject of what to replace them with.

Mote is adamant. 'No, there should be no planting on that spot again.'

'Why?'

'Cankers and disease – it's like a bad luck or poison that gets into the soil and won't come out, not in our lifetimes.'

And this time he does not argue, though there is no reason that he knows of not to set in some healthy whips of Catherine pear or feathered maidens as he'd imagined. So at the heart of his orchard is nothing but a grassy space. He plans to have the leadworker in Ilchester make a sundial.

'So that I know what hour is passing by. I do like to see the grey finger of time's shadow circling the dial,' he says to Frances. It should remind him of the need to keep on moving forward with his plans, to take nothing for granted, even out in a sunshine shining through the many healthy trees that are left, with those fat white geese keeping the grass down. 'After every summer there is always going to be a winter, and we all know what that means, though how many of us do anything about it.'

# VI.

*Of STONE PARSELY. It is also called of some ignorant*
*Apothecaries Amomum. It is very excellent against all*
*cold passions of the sides, the kidneies, and bladder.*

**A**T NOON TODAY, the household is assembled to eat and Henry
is about to begin grace when Hester pipes up, 'But Father,
Johnny isn't here yet.'

To make the point he makes them wait, it is cold in the hall. The
child arrives late and stands behind the bench, looking sheepish.

'What is the matter with you?'

Henry turns to his wife. 'Your son's self-discipline seems to be
deteriorating.'

Frances says, 'There is something that—'

'Madam!' he says, glaring. Dear God, she is not going to start
answering him back in front of the servants, is she? In a fury he
hammers through grace and then makes the household stand in
private prayer. Gradually his heart rate slows to normal, and the
obedient stillness in the room indicates that control of the situation
is restored. He will give them two more minutes to consider the state
of their souls, he decides. Any longer and Old Hannah will instead

351

start to fret about the state of tomorrow's loaves she has left rising in front of the kitchen fire, and other parts of the unfolding of the day will start to go wrong. There is always so much to be done. He can't help it but his mind fastens upon plants. *Stitchwort in May*, he thinks. Its starry timidity belies its power. He remembers, *men have written, that if a woman drinke the seed of stitchewort three daies together, fasting after the purging of her floures, that the childe which shee may happen to conceive within forties days after, shall be a man childe.*

What happens next means that he will always associate the little white flowers of stitchwort with the smell of fear, because at this moment Johnny collapses, falls to the floor.

The new doctor from Somerton diagnoses the stone.

'But he is young for that, surely.'

The doctor shrugs. 'It is more common than one would think. I have seen it often enough in London.'

'Bladder, kidney?'

'I would say bladder. A kidney stone being passed down could have already killed a child this size. And the pain seems to be manifesting in the abdomen. But your son is fighting it quite strongly.' The doctor looks hopeful, Henry thinks, watching him for clues about what to do, what to say to the rest of the household.

Johnny lies in the white bed gazing up at them, relieved that at least he is no longer in disgrace.

'Twice a day give him fennel water or fennel juice in good white wine. You have these things? I can arrange—'

'We have fennel here.'

'He needs to drink copiously, if we are to flush this *calculus* out of his system. Throughout the day give him the root of marshmallow boiled in wine to drink. I'm sure that you have this too? Every lady grows mallow if they tend any herb at all.'

Despite the circumstances, Henry can't help his pride rippling. The man clearly doesn't know where he is. At any other time Henry would offer him a tour of his garden – he may be very much intrigued at such a remarkable source of herbs in his region. But Henry has a lot to do today, and he has to let the doctor go on a promise to follow up his patient's progress in a day or so. He can surprise him with the extent and range of his herb garden then, perhaps, when there is more time.

'Right!' Henry rubs his hands together. 'You are under control, my son.' He ruffles Johnny's hair. 'Drink up the nasty stuff that your mother will bring you, like a man. And public accidents will be a thing of the past.' Johnny looks rueful.

'I am off to get on with *tamarisk*.' He whistles all the way downstairs. He is relieved. That was quite a fright, but the man is sensible and knows what he is doing. It is about time that Somerton had a good doctor. Henry sits at his desk and feels almost cheerful. He works concentratedly so that he almost forgets to stop for supper at six.

When he looks out of the window there is a little owl, sitting on a post in the garden in broad daylight. Lisbet would say that that was not a good omen.

# VII.

*Of CHERVILL. Chervill eaten with other meats, is good
for the stomacke, for it giveth a good taste to the meats,
and stirreth up meat lust.*

JOHNNY'S CONDITION HAS WORSENED OVERNIGHT. The doctor examines the flask of his dark, thickened urine and looks grave. He prescribes a powder of blended herbs that includes gromwell seeds, dropwort, dried saxifrage and tormentil.

'There are other medicines at our disposal for this condition, such as marsh pennywort, sanicle, wild parsnip, pignut.' He coughs. 'And I didn't like to mention this earlier, Lyte, but as you may know there is an operation for the cutting of the stone which has some measure of success. We may yet be fortunate, the stone may be very small and pass of its own accord, but other outcomes should be considered.'

A small needling chill is confirmed in Henry as he hears these last words, that sharpening of senses that comes with recognition of danger.

'Can it be that serious, doctor? My friend Turner had the stone for a great part of his life, and it was not that which killed him, but disappointment. Surely there is no need to operate? He is a healthy child! He will get better. He—'

The doctor indicates the jar of urine. 'It is now very cloudy indeed, there is undoubtedly infection starting up. Its darkness may indicate the presence of blood, which as you must be aware is not a good sign.'

Henry looks around. 'Frances? Frances! Where is my wife?'

'She's in the kitchen, Master,' Lisbet says.

'She should be here!'

'I am, Henry,' Frances says quietly, coming into the room with the next dose of fennel prepared in a cup.

'I know two good specialists in London. Either would be ably equipped to operate on your son. It is quick – the patient tied and propped, and there is a fair chance of success in the hands of a skilled lithotomist.'

Henry looks at his son, damp and crumpled now with pain and the beginnings of a delirium. This child would not survive a day's journey to London, strapped behind him on a fast horse, and a cart would take too long. No, the distance is against them. For a moment he thinks of how Frances had pressed him and pressed him for them to move up to London. He has never felt so far from anywhere as the thought of London at this moment. Think of the jolting he would have to endure, it would be an intolerable way to end a life. *I would not treat a dog like that, let alone my son.*

But what if this man is right? Supposing that an incision could, in five excruciating minutes flat, cleanly bring forth the obstruction from the neck of the bladder, in a gush of fluids, and that there would be no festering, none of that unpleasant consequence that seems to follow so much surgery, and all would heal over with the swiftness of new growth that only youth can produce? It seems unlikely. Is it his weaker self, he wonders, that is clutching at straws? He has no sense of what is real anymore.

'What shall we do?' Henry asks his wife, once the doctor has gone. They stand by the bed watching Johnny sleep. 'I know these surgeons, how they can botch and mangle. Just look at him, how small he is. It is a gamble.'

'Yours will be an informed decision, Henry. I know nothing of the hazards of medicine.'

'But what does your woman's instinct tell you?'

Frances does not reply. There are two spots of colour on her cheeks, as if she were feeling something very intensely, and will not share it with him. If only he could understand her more clearly – his own wife is incomprehensible to him.

'I have the receipt for the doctor's powder,' she says. 'I will be in the stillroom grinding seeds if anyone needs me.'

'Tell Tom Coin to take a bow and arrows down to the moor at once and shoot a duck.'

'What kind of duck?'

'Any. Tell him to take it to Hannah that she can cut the grit from its gizzard, rinse it then bring it to you.'

That night he dreams of saddling his horse in haste and searching the Mendip for spignel plants. In the dream he cannot find the place where he dug up the specimen he'd found last May. The root, he remembers even in his sleep, is exactly what they need. He remembers writing, *the same layed upon the lowest part of the belly of young children will cause them to piss and make water*. But of course when he wakes he knows that it is no longer the season to find such a thing.

# VIII.

*Of SHEPHERD'S NEEDLE. Yée may finde it in this
country in fat and fertile fields.*

IT IS THE TWELFTH OF NOVEMBER, the day after Martinmas. The
first day that all attention has not been spent on Johnny in his bed,
as there seems to be some improvement. Today, Henry has been able
to return to work on his herbal, though his mind has been partially
turned to the quietness upstairs, the creak of boards as Frances or
Lisbet goes in with a bowlful of medicine for Johnny. He has a hope
that this new medicine will work. They have begun to apply it topi-
cally, wettening the place with rags soaked in the preparation so that
the combined properties can work directly at the calculus by penetra-
tion of the skin, instead of filling the bladder with the excess fluid that
is causing so much discomfort to him. Certainly Johnny has not cried
so much today. He has been able to sleep a little, and the other children are under strict instructions to play on the other side of the
house, and to go about their business quietly and with due considera-
tion. If the improvement continues, and God knows how fervently
Henry is praying for it by the hour, then in a day or so Henry will
spend time at his bedside, perhaps reading sections from the gospels,

or some Virgil, or some of his collections taken out of the New Testament. Listening can be very soothing, and Johnny has always been so keen to learn. He would not like him to fall behind with his studies, when he is due to go to school.

Henry makes a note of where he has stopped work for the day, stretches, and stands up. He could go and see his son but there is no sound from the room above, Johnny must be sleeping. It makes him happier to think of him asleep, oblivious of pain. Ignorance is bliss, of course. He rubs his hands together, stiff from holding the pen, the pages. How dark it is already. November evenings draw in very fast, and it is almost time to light candles. He puts on his cloak and hat and goes out to the garden for a breath of fresh air before supper. Mote has packed up and gone home an hour ago, and Henry is glad to be able to spend a solitary moment out here.

There is a swift, chilly sunset going on above, just a few windblown streaks of orange and a deep, clear bluish-green sky settling down for the night. There could be a frost, but most likely a mild one. Henry goes to the beds and walks the path, stopping to bend to some late-leafed, soft sage, hanging on raggedly despite the bracing nights, sheltered by this taller, woody bush. Scent in the dark is so much stronger. Idly he runs his cupped hand up a sprig of rosemary to catch its aromatic tang. He breathes it in, fills his lungs with it. In the far distance of the great parlour Frances is playing at her instrument, up and down the scales, some quadrilles, then something in a minor key. An owl calls. He has to admit, he almost feels a sense of peace. Perhaps this truly is the beginning of an improvement to things.

The next few moments pass very slowly. Even the tawny owl cries from the wood seem hollow and soupy, drawn out.

Henry is not sure what it is that makes him realize that there is something odd about the light. A sudden awareness of a whiteness of gaze that is not moonlight, or lamplight or starlight cast at his back or on the ground, but a malevolent, freakish glare.

He turns suddenly and what he sees fills him with dread and realization that some part of the world, possibly his, is on the cusp of something very bad. A monstrous light, its head half as wide as the moon, has risen above the south-western horizon. Blue-white, trailing an arc of brightness. It can only be a comet. He cannot believe it. *Not again, surely.*

His throat tightens.

He hears the scrape of feet on the path beside him and sees that Mote too has been drawn from his dwelling at Tuck's Cary. For what seems like over an hour they stand without speaking as it goes on rising at a crawl into the sky. It points to the sea, the double tail fanning away eastwards for an arm's length. It is vast. When Henry turns to the face of the house he can see parts of the comet's terrible white light reflected in every window, as though the house itself has gone blind.

With an iron will he does not allow himself to run as he goes inside, but panic is bubbling in him now. The light it casts feels poisonous, ill-meant.

When he looks again at the sky from inside, he sees that the land is lit up most broadly and horribly with a cold, vast pool of comet light, beamed down. The shadows it makes are terrifying, flat, splayed out. Brighter than moonlight, it is more like sheet lightning frozen into permanence. Henry feels like falling prostrate to his knees before it, begging God to spare his son, begging him to show mercy. The whiteness is so sharp it is almost keening, and seems to fuse readily with the staccato notes still coming from the great parlour like a vicious spell.

Henry goes into the parlour and watches her, speechless. Between those tasks that she cannot let slip, and breaking off to go up to the boys' bedchamber to change Johnny's bedsheets or take him physic, she is playing the virginals on and off all day. It is astounding. It seems on the whole she is sending Lisbet instead to sit beside the bed.

How can she play that thing when her child is lying ill in bed above her? What kind of mother lets herself be flooded with those notes of music, lets herself concentrate on something so spurious, frivolous, as music. She is playing dances, letting her fingers run up and down the keys in neat little scales and chords, almost bouncing, as though there was nothing at all wrong at Lytes Cary, as though their first-born son were not in pain, alone in bed up there struggling between sleep and agony and death.

Why is she not up there, holding him tight, holding him fast to this earthly world like all mothers should, until the will of God is absolutely clear. She is unnatural. In the corridor the comet's eerie light falls on the floor in the diamonds of the panes.

He takes the steps upstairs two at a time, his heart racing.

❧

'Mother? Oh!' Johnny says, seeing Henry.

'The child refuses to pass water, Master,' Lisbet says, getting up from the bed. Johnny's face is deeply flushed, and his breathing is too fast. 'I cannot do it Father,' he wails. 'I can't.'

Henry does not like that look of fear in his son's eyes, the red water-ish staining around his shirt discarded on the floor. When he sits down he realizes his legs are shaking. He pours from the jug on the form by the bed, spilling some, and takes a sip himself, then drinks down the whole cup. Johnny's gaze has been fixed on his father since he entered the room.

'You'll be fine soon enough, son,' he says, patting the slender arm sticking out of the sheets. How hot he is. He tries not to notice the unmistakeable smell of infection about the bed. The air is close and thick and sour. Henry knows Lisbet doesn't want the window left open as an invitation to bad spirits. What she doesn't know is that the world is about to change, that anything could happen after a comet.

He cannot see any inch of this little boy that he would not give up his own life for if it would help. He strokes his hair out of his eyes, his head wet with sweat from what is stewing in him. He gathers him into his arms and buries his face in his small, damp neck, after all, he is not contagious, but Johnny writhes free and says that he does not want to be held, that it makes it worse when he is trapped like that. His hand rubs his lower belly constantly, trying to distract his body from the pain. 'My hand aches, Father,' he whimpers pitifully, 'can you do it for me?'

So Henry pulls back the shirt and tries to rub away the hurt, lightly stroking at the horror of his boy's swollen, hard belly, and tries not to think of what is inside the container of this skin, the bleeding, over-flowing, festering vat that his son's bladder has become.

'You are too rough, Father,' Johnny says, almost inaudibly. 'You are pressing too hard. Nothing makes it better.' And he curls on his side and cries, not like a child at all but like an injured animal that has been too long in the snare.

This is inhuman.

Henry gets Tom Coin out of bed to ride for the doctor again, even though it is late. 'Make him come,' he barks at him. 'Insist. Tell him cost is not the obstacle.'

Tom Coin is staring, far too slow.

'Immediately!'

# IX.

*Of CHARLOCKE. Charlocke groweth about old wals
and ruinous places and oftentimes in the fields, so that it
should séeme to be a corrupt and evill wéed or enemie.*

**T**HE DOCTOR ARRIVES, a decent man pretending not to
be inconvenienced, though his buttons are done up wrongly
and his hair tousled at the back. He takes one glance at Johnny
and suggests either a dose of henbane or opium, to be given at
intervals.

Henry allows this to sink in, gives himself some moments to
consider which one, knowing that even this could be the choice of
death itself. What kind of sleep, what kind of death: in some instances
they are one and the same. He holds the two deaths in his head,
weighing them.

'Have you thought any more about cutting for the stone? I can
arrange a lithotomist …'

'He is only a child.'

Henry thinks of the baleful, fetid stink of henbane; its hairy, sticky
leaves, inky-veined cream flowers each with a centre so utterly dark
that it seems to harbour something vanished. He thinks of the opium

poppy, its crumpled petals like silk, the milky sap oozing from the pricked pods, going brown as it congeals and concentrates.

The doctor rummages in his bag for a piece of cloth, which he unwraps to reveal little round cakes. Henry knows that these will be of blackened leaf mixed with wheatmeal and then dried hard. If they are less than a year old they will be very potent. He tries to imagine Johnny chewing one of these tough, offensive mouthfuls without gagging. He imagines his pupils dilating, his eyes black and dazed, then sliding into the swirling, vaporous nauseous sleep of those on the brink. There is henbane in the garden, so these dried doctors' cakes could, in theory, be discarded in favour of something wetter, juicer, more easily swallowed; leaves freshly boiled in wine, say or vinegar. But what of opium, the other choice? It is one poison against another.

What would Turner say? He goes downstairs quickly to his desk, the doctor politely insistent at his heels, and takes the first and second volumes of *A New Herbal* from the shelf. Galen, even Dioscorides, did not always have it right. But Turner was like a father to him in many ways. He led him when his own father would not. Turner's voice is like a living man's reassurance in his ear, countering his own deficiencies. What kind of a father cannot protect his children? His hands shake as he turns the familiar dog-eared pages. At least he can select the right sleeping draught to soothe his son's pain.

He looks up. 'And what kind of henbane is this?'

'Caked in this form I have shown you, it is a very precise dose.' The doctor's cordial manner has stiffened a little during the wait.

'But is it black henbane? Yellow? Surely not the third kind, red. It makes a—'

'Ready-made from the apothecary at the sign of the Three Doves in Bucklersbury, London,' he says crisply. 'I bought it myself in June. It is absolutely of the finest quality.'

Doctors do not like to be cross-questioned, do not like their expert opinion challenged in any way. But this time Henry Lyte is not going to be cowed by any doctor, no matter where he trained, no matter how respected by the College of Physicians, no matter how successful he claims to be.

'What *kind* of henbane is it?'

'Black,' the doctor says, but his eyes slide away from Henry's direct gaze and suddenly, instinctively Henry knows that he is not going to take any advice from this man.

He shuts the book.

'Syrup of opium,' he says. 'And there will be no operation. If God will take him from us, let him go in peace.'

'But what if—'

'No. We both know it has gone too far, that the infection has spread. He has suffered enough.'

# X.

*Of WINTER CRESSES. It doth mundifie and clense*
*wounds and ulcers, and consumeth dead flesh that*
*groweth too fast.*

WHEN JOHNNY PASSES AWAY THE NEXT MORNING his mother is not with him, where a mother should be. She is downstairs in the parlour playing at the virginals. It is Henry that holds his slack little body in its urine-soaked shirt and sees the life roll out of his eyes. He is barely conscious as he goes. Henry hopes upon merciful hope that he did not die in a passive agony.

Frances looks up from the keyboard when she hears Henry's footsteps and fixes a rigid gaze upon him as he walks towards her, and although she is not looking down at the instrument she is never pausing for a moment, hammering out the tune as loud as she possibly can, or so it seems to him, like she is making a shield with it, staving him off. He feels a rush of hatred for her, sitting there like that making music. *Music*, for Chrissake. Why does she not stop? Her face is ashen white, her fingers mechanically going on with the chords, though at half speed now and faltering, hitting wrong notes in a cacophony of silver muddle. What is wrong with her?

'Your son has died, madam,' Henry imparts loudly, coldly, over the noise.

Only then does she break off her extraordinary melody, and she stands up and faints.

Henry is so disgusted with her that he does not stay, leaving Lisbet to unbutton her ruff and collar and chemise and administer plain water to her lips or whatever she will, he does not care. He has to leave; if he remains in the room with her he might slap her. Unlike many husbands, he has never struck a woman in his life, but at this moment, he feels in danger of it, indeed he itches for it. Johnny deserved more than that from her. Well might she collapse, a mother acting so untowardly, frankly it is the very least she could have done. Where was a mother's love and tenderness when Johnny most needed it. Was it that she had no heart, or that she was too weak to face the trauma of her son's pain. He will loathe her for either of those reasons, can she not prove otherwise, for the rest of his days.

Outside Henry can hear the noise of the Sorcerer as he shrieks heartlessly from tree to tree.

*How many of them dead now, Henry Lyte?* mocks the Sorcerer from the orchard, *Five, five, that's how many.* But even Henry, in the stubborn bluntness of his distress, knows that there is no arguing with the will of nature once its mind is made up.

Three days later as they enter the churchyard, a heron flaps by like a vast grey ghoul. Ralph Let the gravedigger has dug the graves for many members of his family now. The Reverend Tope preaches the funeral sermon like he almost means it. Henry is surprised by his compassion, later shakes his big, pink familiar hand gratefully, grips it tight with both his own.

It's the mealy mouthedness afterwards at the feast from men and their wives that he only half knows that he can't stand. Why should he listen to it being God's pleasure to have taken his child from him, God's will, God's preference or desire, God's good grace.

'They were only trying to be kind,' Frances says, turning to him when the last guest has gone. 'You did not need to be so rude.'

'Kind? And by what means did you recognize that *particular* emotion?' He is glad to see her flinch. 'I am sorry if it offends God that I am not more grateful to him for his special attention to our family, that I do not find comfort in it. If I do offend God then so be it.'

He looks at what has sat on his plate for more than an hour. At least caraway does have a mournful flavour, he thinks. A warming taste, but one that carries a tugging, underlying sense of loss or distance at the back of the tongue. He finishes the piece of cake though it almost chokes him to do it, and then presses up the last stray crumbs and licks them from his finger. He hates wastefulness, of course. He feels bleak with rage.

# XI.

*Of IBERIS. Iberis hath round stalkes of a cubite long.*

A FEW WEEKS LATER and Henry is riding out of Wells. As he passes the tippling house by the smithy down at the bottom of town he feels a sudden thirst come upon him and does what he does not do usually, goes straight in.

Henry edges past the spittoon and takes a bench. The man in front of him wears the smock of a day labourer, perhaps. Henry Lyte cannot imagine this vacant, dirty space filled with talk or the clatter of roundels. The world in here is a joyless, unsavoury place filled with draughts, lice and nothing to do. Henry Lyte swallows beer. He has a gnawing in his belly that may be disregarded hunger or just the aching of his spleen.

Partly to fill the silence and partly because he has an almost incontinent urge to tell anyone what has happened, he says, 'I have lost my lad.'

The man raises his eyebrows and drains his cup to the silt at the bottom. But when he gets up to go out he passes a penny to the serving-boy and nods at Henry sitting in the corner. Henry downs this unexpected stranger's drink with grim relief, and finds it makes it easier for him to order one more, and then another. By the time he notices the light is failing out there, the hedge-hops are twining in his head with quite a vengeance. He goes out to the open yard behind that stinks of old and copious amounts of urine, and empties his own bladder in a hot and forthright rush and wishes, as he does each time, that little Johnny could have done the same. He edges away from his own steam and leans his head on the rough cold wall for steadiness a moment, then unties his horse and heads out on the Glastonbury road.

All the way home his head bounces forward of its own accord, he feels a numbness creeping on him, a kind of deadening of the flesh. He wonders if he will fall under his horse and be mashed into pieces by the hooves and be left for dead and his mare find her way home without further mishap.

What is that? Something familiar looms up. He hiccups, his face warm from something. He slides to his feet, makes an attempt to speak.

'Master?'

The boy pries free his hold on the halter and leads her away into the pungent fug of the stables. He wants to follow her in and lie down at once, but he staggers across the terrain of the path towards the porch one step at a time and then to his unwarmed bed and lies there spinning in what he vaguely senses is an undeserved near-stupor. Where is Frances? he thinks and can do nothing about it as his legs are separate from his effort. He latches onto one solitary thought circling over and over in the whirlpool of his head: there is no point at all to this feeling of panic that he has. The danger is all over, the thing he dreaded so has happened and the panic is of no use to him. No use at all.

He wakes with the familiar plummeting recollection of loss, and a raging headache that spreads right through his body. He goes to his study, lays out involuntary pieces of his day and proceeds with them, one at a time. He sits there at his desk while his heart is being ripped from its threadroots.

❧

He knows it will never leave him, this kind of grief. The organ of grief itself must have begun to grown when Johnny was born, swelling with quick, wet love like a small fat fruit is set after the blossom is over. He thinks of how many other such fruits we carry inside us that do not need to reveal themselves. In any cluster of set fruits on the bough some are destined to drop at the will of nature, and some of those that do not must be pulled clear in order for a few to reach maturity. Their success depends on the death of others. He doesn't know why he is thinking like this. These truths are irrelevant. There is no doubt though it will be all the better for Thomas, second son, next in line, who will now inherit everything.

❧

His anger about it all comes out in curious ways, when he does not want or expect it. Impatience with a middle-aged woman with too many baskets trying to push past him at market – it is an accident that his hose is snagged, but he turns on her, knowing that his anger is disproportionate, but still going on with it, seeing her indignation turn to a swallow of fear, gripping her scant cargo of eggs and vegetables, a glance sideways for assistance or escape from this madman that Henry can see in himself but does not care about. One man, a cloth merchant not from round here, steps in and lays his hand on the sleeve of his coat, suggesting he should take a breath and head straight home. Henry stares right into the man's eyes as he speaks, sees the blue of them, their glisten, the sty on one eyelid flickering.

He keeps control of himself for a full two weeks after this incident, though seething inside. For more than a month he snaps at everybody, especially the servants. He shouts at the occasional letters of condolence that still arrive, refuses to answer any of them. He swears quietly, venomously at the floor from time to time. He still scarcely speaks to Frances. He is especially angry with his father, for being dead, for dying with so much unsaid. Why wasn't he here? Couldn't he have waited to die? Couldn't he have arranged his affairs properly before quitting this life, leaving him to clear up the mess that ensued. Couldn't he have seen Joan Phelips for what she is, a money-wangling heartless bitch with a thirst for whatever lies within her reach but belonging to others? If he could, in this frame of mind he would have blamed Joan Phelips for the loss of Johnny. But the truth is he can blame no-one on this earth, not even himself this time. Just as Simon Cressing had predicted, there is still no date for the hearing from the Court of Common Pleas. What do these legal men do all day?

The comet shines on till the feast of St Thomas Aquinas.

❧

Spring begins to tip towards summer.

This evening Henry walks up the hill and looks out at the Levels, slowly purpling into dusk behind Lytes Cary. This is the kind of long, far-reaching view that the Sorcerer sees all the time, he thinks, or the hawk. There are chimneys smoking as far as the eye can see – smoke coiling up from every dwelling, plumes in the cool air, hundreds of them. He can hear sheep, dogs, children, church bells, shouting.

And he decides, right here, that he will try to settle out of court.

He goes back to the house and writes to Joan Phelips at once. This is far more than his father had ever planned for her as jointure. His offer is simple enough laid out on paper – if she withdraws her claim for a third of his lands (which she may not get) she can have Mudford Terry, and accompanying lands in Broadmerston, Adber and Trent with their income for life.

# XII.

*Of DITTANDER, DITTANY, but rather*
*PEPPERWURT. It is very good against the Sciatica,*
*being applied outwardly with some soft grease, as of the*
*goose or capon.*

ALMOST IMMEDIATELY, as though she has been waiting for this for years with her reply at the ready, she sends a message back, via his lawyer. *I have good news, Lyte,* he says. *The plaintiff has responded positively to your offer. She will agree to what he is suggesting, and it shall not have to go to hearing, with one exception. She will have Mudford Terry, not just for life, but for her heirs forever.*

Her heirs forever.

On signing his own lands away like that, Henry feels suddenly that he needs to speak with his brother. It is none of his business in a way, but Jack knew his father as well as Henry did. He begins a letter but gets up abruptly, saddles a horse and rides to Wells in the rain instead. He arrives at his brother's house dripping wet, but a woman who must be a servant tells him that he's out.

'I shall wait,' Henry says.

'He's gone overnight though, Master,' she says apologetically.

'I see.' Henry turns away. 'Will you tell him that his brother Henry called, on an important matter?'

'Well if he's your brother then I can tell you that he's with your mother, Master, you could catch him there.'

'Our mother? At her grave?'

'No, Master.' She looks confused. 'In Sherborne.'

'You mean my father's wife,' he says, and does not mean to sound so bitter.

'He is gone to discuss the arrangements. There is so much to be—'

'What for?'

'Oh! Did you not know? He is shortly to be wed to Mistress Franny of Chilthorne Domer, or is it Trent, I can never remember.' She looks excited now. 'He even went down to the cellar and chose a pipe of good wine to take for the Phelips.'

There is plenty of plain estate business to be going on with back at Lytes Cary. Kelway's and Squire's account for ploughing the grounds, wages, rates for the poor, one half-pound of cumin to chase up in rent for Cary Fitzpayne.

Henry works on with the herbal. If he wasn't so worn out, he would be amazed that his mind still goes on translating without being touched by the pain the rest of his body feels inside. The words just keep on coming. Only occasionally does he stumble. Here at quince, for example, there is an unfamiliar term in this phrase. He tries to conjure the word. What is this *sang louts*. Sanglot? No this is to sob, that can't be right. Ah! The casting up of blood. That would be more like it. See how a word can twist this way and that?

'You are talking to yourself again Father,' Thomas says, by the open door.

'Have you been there long?'

'Only a while,' he says.

'You can come in while I work if you like, if you are quiet. Shut the door behind you.' He puts his quill down. 'You know, I am nearly done with this book I am working on.'

'At the last page?'

'Not so many to go now, perhaps about fifty kinds of plants left. Mainly trees and shrubs.'

Thomas borrows a book from the shelf and sits on the rug at his feet.

❧

Frances has found there is refuge in sleep, going early to bed to be possessed by shallow, slippery dreams that still seem to go on for hours beside him once he comes up to bed for the night. Sometimes she sleeps on her back as white as wax in the candlelight but weeping, her body quivering soundlessly, her unwashed hair wet with tears. Henry lies poised in indecisive misery unsure if he should wake her from it, but afraid to disturb her solitary dreaming lest it should damage her still more.

Sometimes Frances cries out in her sleep, with her eyes wide open, which is worse. 'What is it chicken? Come here my sweet son, don't be afraid,' and she turns and turns, looking for children in the bed, so that despite himself Henry wants to take hold of her.

Each morning she remembers nothing of the night, or if she does she gives no hint of it. She appears to slip calmly through her day, speaking when necessary, performing all of the duties a housewife should with a dull but firm efficiency, except that she will no longer lie with him, making his nights a confusion of grief and thwartedness. Her fine, pale body so close to his and so far away. His hands itch to touch the smoothness of her, run his palms on her skin, taste the salt of her, understand her like that. He can smell the grief on her breath, in her sweat.

One day outside the dairy, Henry overhears Bridget remarking on the strength of Mistress Lyte. The rattle of spoons against the side of a dish drowns out the reply, but then there is a pause for whispering, and he is sure he hears someone hiss above the slop of liquids, 'You are too mean spirited!' but he cannot be sure.

A wave of defensive indignation goes over him on her behalf. It surprises him, but Henry knows that she suffers. He wonders whether her guilt equates to his, and if, because of this, he should try to forgive her. They have both aged about ten years this month alone, he notes. They are lined and tired. His hairline is receding. Clipping his beard, he notices more grey and white hairs than even last month. He feels like his father used to look. A little too stooped to be healthy, drawn at the face, yellowish skin tone. Death goes on feeding on the youth of all those involved in a family loss.

# XIII.

*Of INDIAN PEPPER. Amongst the leaves grow floures*
*upon short stems, or colour white, with a gréene star in*
*the middle. The séede or graines are of a pale yellow*
*color, broad, hot, and of a biting taste.*

**H**ENRY IS OUT IN HIS GARDEN. Not working in it; he has not had the heart to do that for quite a while, but having a look.

The lady's mantle has a silvery sheen or fur of early morning dew; the ruffs of the leaves are compressions of green, collecting balls of silver water like mercury in each hollow. Every tiny reddish-tipped tooth on each edge of leaf has a ball of dew on it. There are froths of cuckoo spit on a few stems. He examines the mallow, its downy, pert young leaves. The borage is softly bristling, rasping to the touch. Its leaves taste of cucumber, loose-woven to the bite like something knitted. The fat purslane is like spoons on stalks, clappers spread wide. The calamint's spade-shaped leaf is flourishing, and the thin, minty spears of pennyroyal. The untidy knotgrass looks vulnerable to being trodden on, he must get Mote to tie it back from the path, such a thinly cumbersome plant. The white horehound with its dingy little flowers is covered with honeybees. The scent of horehound when brushed is like sea air and a sweet dustiness combined. The rue is neat, like a plant printed on a pack of cards. Henry has to admit, his garden gives him welcome solitude, fresh air and consolation.

It is with great surprise then, when later that afternoon he comes across Frances sitting in the centre of the Knot. He never sees her in the garden, and it pulls him up short at the Knot's edge with an exclamation and when she looks up, her face is dull and wet with tears.

'Oh!' she says, wiping her cheeks. 'You startled me, Henry.'

'I'm sorry,' he says, across the low hedges. 'Were you praying?'

'Praying? No, I find it hard these days to submit readily to the will of God.' She sounds very tired.

Henry watches a treecreeper tweaking delicately up the trunk of an apple tree by the garden wall, its sleek brown body tapered to a fine bill like a sable brush.

'Are you well, madam?' He feels awkward, talking across the hedges like this, but he knows he should ask.

'Why are you so cold with me, Henry?' Frances says suddenly. Her voice is very far away, almost a whisper, as if it doesn't belong to her, or anybody.

'Cold? No.'

'You have been for a long time now.'

Then he hesitates. 'Well at first … at first, I was angry with you for playing at your instrument, when Johnny was … I could not understand how you could play it, why you wanted to.' He brushes the new growth of hyssop with the back of his hand. 'But none of that seems to matter anymore.'

Frances looks puzzled. 'But why were you angry?'

'I suppose I could not understand how a mother could put aside the care of her son in order to play music like that. It really doesn't matter now.' He doesn't want to talk about it.

Frances still frowns, as though she can't understand what he's saying to her.

'But Johnny loved me to play to him. He loved music.'

'Did he?' Henry looks at her. He didn't know that.

'Johnny said that when there was music, he could imagine some kind of magic going on downstairs. He said it made him feel less frightened. In those last two days, he whispered that it hurt so badly he wanted to die, Henry, because it was eating him up from the inside, it was burning like acid. He said he thought that each musical note my fingers struck was like a butterfly, flying up the stairs towards him, gathering in the room about him.

'When there were enough butterflies to bear his soul away, he said, he would be gone and it wouldn't hurt anymore, up there in the blue sky going to heaven.

"*I will go to heaven, won't I Mother?*" he asked me.

"Of course my darling," I said, holding his hot little hand in mine, making sure he couldn't see me weeping. I knew these were the last chances I would ever get to feel the pliant softness of his knuckles between my hands; his wristbones clad in child's living flesh for just a few more days. I would have laid down and died for him myself if I could, and yet all I could do was play that instrument for him. I tore myself away from his side and sat before it. It was so horribly meagre, but it was all he wanted, not even water, especially not water.

"*And will you play to me for hours, so there are enough butterflies to get me there? Play faster, Mother, more notes, it hurts less when you play faster.*" I vowed I would play until my fingers bled if I had to.' She shakes her head. 'I won't play again for a long time.'

Her voice is so quiet he can hardly hear her. 'But why did it happen, Henry? Why was he allowed to die? It makes no sense. He was a good little boy. He was—'

'Even nature makes miscalculations sometimes,' he says, thinking of the death of last year's bees. 'Just because something is natural doesn't mean it's right.'

'Why did you not grieve for the others like you have for Johnny?' she says suddenly. Her voice is light and odd. 'Because he is not the first child we have lost.'

Henry feels the world turn on its axis. The light is different. The air is different. His reply is blunt, the only thing he can think of.

'I have no idea,' he says. 'It seems there is no way to govern what happens inside us.' It sounds like an excuse, the kind of careless throwaway comment made by a younger man than he. But it is true that Johnny was his favourite child, his son and heir. He presses his hands together. There is a hole inside him, there is nothing to be done about it. He looks across at Frances, and wishes somehow there was a way to pool their separate griefs. He steps into the Knot and winds his way towards her.

She squints at the sun. 'You know what has surprised me the most?' she says, as if she has read his mind. 'It was to find out how there are so very many sorts of grief. I mean, in the same way that one discovers a different love for each of one's children. That every grief is singular.' She looks at the apple tree. 'That each bereavement has a different *taste*.'

'Taste?'

'In the mouth.' She hugs her elbows.

'The human heart is infinitely complicated,' Henry replies, and breaks a piece of hyssop from the bush. Even as a platitude this sounds extremely vague. He pulls leaves away from the stalk.

'But I don't just feel my grief in my *heart*; do you?' Frances says. 'It's everywhere; in the tips of my fingertips, on my tongue, bubbling up at the back of my throat, in my bowels. I feel it red-raw sometimes, it's like I am opened meat on the butcher's block. Or like a sharp bite, the shock of its jaw clamping down when I least expect it. Or it comes softly, sweetly flooding through me in great waves of tenderness; treacherous happinesses that lure me out onto mistaken ground and then leave me abandoned.' She looks down at her feet in the grass. 'Or I am like clay, feeling nothing. Which is no better, is it?'

Her attention fixes upon something in the distance.

'How fast everything grows. How long will that tree live for, do you suppose?'

'Three hundred years, perhaps?'

'Longer than all of us. I wish that I noticed things more.'

'I would say your gaze is acute, madam. Much finer than mine.'

Side by side, they survey the garden. Everything converges at this point, all paths, beds, intersections. The roses are pink and white, the lavender a haze of blue and bees.

'I have been so jealous of this garden,' she says, very clearly. 'So many times I sat and watched you dreaming of your plants, saw how you ached for your first wife, how you wanted her back.'

'No!'

'All your mind has been taken up with it, with her. Every slip tenderly planted, every root, every seed committed to this earth; all for her.'

Henry turns her around to face him here in the centre of the Knot, the warm smell of blue-green hyssop rising all about them like breath.

'You are the mother of my sons,' he says softly, cupping her wet anguished face with his hands, looking into her eyes. 'You are that world, the one I have now. We are bound together.'

She is so motionless as he holds her against him that he thinks she must have fallen asleep on her feet. But when he stirs, she is also ready to walk back to the house. They mention supper as they walk, Thomas's schooling, the supply of wool to be sent to market.

❧

At least now he can be sure that the opium had given Johnny some relief. He would have wept to hear this, if he could only remember how to weep. Now at night he will be able to picture, in his sleeplessness, how the sickroom slowly filled with butterflies; first one or two, zigzagging about the chamber, settling on the bedsheets, on Johnny's fingers, then tens of them, then hundreds, flitting between bedpost and sill and jug and coffer, multiplying with every chord and ripple of musical notes that floated upstairs from his mother's music.

He imagines the bedsheets becoming powdered with the sheen from the scale of beating wings, the soft rush of air about the bed darkly metallic like the dust on a goldsmith's bench. When the air was thick with shoals of orange, blue, crimson, purple, velvet brown and black and yellow and emerald; it would have coruscated, rustled; as one idea assembled out of many intricate and fragile parts. How strangely heightened the chamber would have smelt; of insect-bitterness and nectar.

And then, amassed in sufficient numbers, the butterflies would have begun drawing off Johnny's soul for transportation as he had hoped, drawing its silvery, shimmering threads out of his wracked, spent little body, working the spirit free from its eleven years of weight, between the dancing of their tens of thousands, the soft hair-line spindles of their legs, the dry tugging of their flight, with an improbable collective ease. For them it made no difference whether the window was open or shut, they would have passed through the stone walls of Lytes Cary as if through smoke, a host of flickering colours bearing one soul away.

That is how death should be.

He thanks God for this. He thanks Johnny for this late gift, this way to forgetting the blackened turgid flesh of his own child, the smell of the soft quick rot of infection with its yellow-brown discharge seeping from him, the soaked feather bed they had to burn.

This new, bright image he clings to gratefully. And that night, when at last he finds sleep, he dreams briefly of a sea of flowers.

# THE SEVENTH PART
## *The Virtues*

## ❧ 1578 ❧

## I.

*Of the ROSE. The juyce of Roses, especially of them*
*that are reddest is of the kind of soft and gentle*
*medicines, which loose and open the belly. It is good to*
*be used against the shaking, beating, and trembling of*
*the heart. The wine wherein dried roses have bin*
*boyled, is good against the payne of the mother or*
*womens secrets, eyther poured in, or annoynted*
*with a feather.*

HE HAD ASSUMED THAT WHEN THE MANUSCRIPT was finished and packed and sent off to Holland he would feel a great sense of achievement or satisfaction. But he is surprised to discover that instead it is one of the oddest, most melancholy days of his life. A small loss when compared to the loss of loved ones, of course, but he feels formless, unanchored. He puts on his coat and goes out to the river and watches the water slip by. Moffat swears he will put the package into the hands of the Dutch postmaster himself. Emmanuel van Metteren is a reliable, upstanding man who will see that it gets to Loë quite unscathed. So no, he is not worried about its safe passage, but he is faintly bereft; emptied.

It is very quiet back at the house. Florence, who is now fourteen, has just started a position as a lady's companion on the Devonshire border, and since Thomas was sent to school in Sherborne, there has been no noise of his own boys playing, only the tenants' children in the yard or on the track. Henry is missing everybody. Sometimes for a second he forgets that Thomas is gone, forgets even that Johnny is dead, and cocks his ear for sounds of their rough and tumble. There is Harry of course, but Harry is only five and does not burst into a room with muddy knees, carrying a bird's nest or some other hedgerow trophy to show him, or ask inquisitively, 'What's that book you are reading, Father?' as Johnny always did.

# II.

*Of FRAMBOYS RASPIS. They plant it in Gardens, and it loveth shadowie places, where as the sunne shineth not often.*

A S HE WAITS FOR HIS BOOK TO RETURN COMPLETED, he watches the general softness of the decay of autumn tip into winter. The grey-brown, sagging grass turning to mush underfoot, the leathery leaves. There is always the needling tough grass that will outlast the winter, where all the thistles are winners and the other plants rotten and spent in their old age.

And then at last, late in November, a battered message arrives from Antwerp. He feels a small private pleasure, holding the letter in his hands, then rushes into the parlour to find his wife.

'I have confirmation from Loë!' he says. 'It has been at press this month, and we should see copies shortly when the binder is done with it; as soon as van Metteren can arrange to get one safely to me. The rest he says will be shipped directly to Gerard Dewes at St Paul's churchyard in London, where they are to be sold.'

Frances doesn't look up, she is busy hemming undershirts. Plain sewing keeps her thoughts at bay, she is never without it now.

'What's that?' she says. 'What will be ready?'

'The book.'

She turns properly to look at him. 'The book?'

'The *Niewe Herball*!' What on earth else would he be talking of?

'That is good news, Henry.' Then she tries harder. 'It surely is.'

She bites her thread, ties it off, and then suddenly he sees her eyes open up as an idea, a purpose, comes swimming towards her. She throws her sewing in her lap.

'A feast!' she exclaims. 'You must welcome your book with a feast at Lytes Cary!'

'I don't know, Frances …'

'Oh but you must!' Her face is quite disconcertingly radiant with delight and relief.

'But who would come?' He starts to explain. 'Lytes Cary is such a distance from anywhere. Difficult and damp. Moffat for instance finds it too cold in the hall in June let alone the coldest part of winter. And even when it's stopped raining he hates the way the hedges collect water and soak his doublet when he brushes by them. No one will come, and if they do, it will be a disaster. The bedrooms will be cold and musty. Or the drive will be frozen and someone will slip as they get down from their carriage and break their collarbone. Or all the carriages from London will be mired on the way with broken axles and lame horses and not even arrive, and everyone will return to the city furious with me for inviting them out during nasty weather. It's out of the question. The summer, frankly, is the only time for city folk to visit the countryside in groups. Let's wait for another, more amenable time.' He can see she isn't listening. 'Besides – who would we invite?'

'Everyone,' she says. 'Absolutely everyone. Get Peter Turner down from Cambridge, all your botanizing friends from Lime Street, any other naturalists you can think of. Thomas Penny obviously, Thomas Moffat, that man Stephen Bredwell whom you do not like and his friend from Bristol too, they can travel together. William Clowis. The

Garets. My mother. That little protégé of Lobel's you talk about called Jimmy something …?'

'Jimmy Cole.'

'And who is it you met who has just started gardening for Lord Burghley? The one you promised to exchange seeds with?'

'John Gerard.'

'That's right, him. And get Mathias Lobel back from Antwerp—'

'Delft,' he interrupts. 'He is in Delft now – remember he is appointed court physician to the prince of Orange, William the Silent.'

'Wherever he is, no doubt he sometimes comes back anyway. We can even invite Clusius across from France, and Rembert Dodeons himself – and see what we end up with.' She rubs her small bare hands together. 'Your brother Jack, it is time you spent some time together. And there are the locals.'

'Many of whom would not like to come,' Henry adds, remembering the disastrous midsummer supper ten years before. 'You usually refer to them as uncivilized natives, I seem to recall,' he says.

'Mistress Yate is always interested in discussion of ideas, she will come. Especially since that boring little husband of hers has died.'

'And where, pray,' Henry enquires, 'would all these people sleep?'

'The children will give up their beds, and people can share, and we can borrow bedding. We can turn the kitchen offices into a dormitory. Some people can put up at the inns at Kingsdon and Charlton Mackrell. There'll be plenty of space.'

He is not sure. 'No-one will come. We'll end up with the Reverend Tope slouched at the top of the table, belching and eating his way through the most part of the victuals. Which will be just as well because otherwise we would be wading our way through delicacies till the following Michaelmas.'

'Have faith Henry! They'll come because it is something worth celebrating, and because we will have been preparing the best feast this part of the West Country has known for a ten-year.'

'Not hard,' he points out dryly. 'Somerton is not known for the vibrancy of its social circle.'

'And if it took place at some point during the twelve days of Christmas, the hall would be filled with greenery, the children would be at home, people would be in the right humour for a little bit of triumphant pageantry. See – it's getting better and better. But what could we do for entertainment?'

'Mummers?' he says sarcastically. 'A hobby horse, winding up through the frozen, dreary garden? The men of science would scorn me forever. That would not be a way to bring a precise piece of scientific work into the world, old rituals dragging at its tail, like a painted half-dead corpse of the past. Although, if we flung in a bit of reference to the stars, perhaps we'd satisfy the Paracelsians …' He has a sudden thought of a small child dressed as Sirius, weaving across the vegetable patch through the winter cresses. 'And the garden isn't ready.' Henry adds. That at least is indisputable, and he spreads his hands wide in front of her. 'So you see the whole thing is simply impossible. Next year,' he suggests, firmly.

'It will be wintertime, Henry, with not a green shoot in sight. Not a soul will need to come out to look over your garden. But finish it, if it matters to you so much!' She seems to think this would be achieved without effort. 'Buy in some statuary. Wheel out some pots. And the hall can be made as warm as it is for the tenants' feast at Christmas – we'll ask Parsons to get his boys to drag down some of that fallen elm on the corner of Twenty Acres. It will be seasoned enough, it fell years ago didn't it? Before I arrived.'

'The elm tree came down before you were here.' This is something he can't deny. How different it was, all those years ago when the elm was standing. The elm was older than any of them, than his father even. The elm would have been a sapling as Edward came to power on the death of Henry of Winchester. Before the manor house was built, before the chantry chapel even – there would have been settlement here, a daily movement of people's lives crossing this soil, passing this tree. For a moment he thinks of that time as silt; fine, sifted remains lying undisturbed at the bottom of everything.

'You see Henry, why should you object so much to the idea of a feast?'

'I do not.' He sighs. 'As it is clearly a certain fixture in the calendar just be so good as to inform me of the date.'

*What are my objections?* he asks himself as he retreats back down the corridor into his study to be alone with his letter and his news while he still can. Why has the thought of a celebration for his book stirred up that unsettling thing at the core of him? Like something unpleasant is rootling about in there under the surface and he can't quite see what it is yet – as though he has forgotten something. He sits down at his desk and looks at the part of the iron grey sky he can see through the window. Perhaps is it simply the expense that makes him recoil from the prospect. Or is it the over-public nature of an announcement to the world that his modest work is finished – does it smack of grandiloquence or boasting? Maybe it does a little, he thinks, but that is not his problem with it. No. It is because *things happen* at a feast. That convergence of bodies, minds, threads of lives knotting together – all of which form a moment that is a kind of phenomenon, a point of change or fastening. His life has no need of disturbance at this time, its smoothness and unembellished regularity, is fine quite as it is. Feasts provoke unnecessary things. In his own experience of feasts and their consequences, history has almost always borne this theory out.

And besides, he thinks, there is the garden and the state it is in. *Finish it*, indeed, as though it were some kind of manmade object waiting for its function to begin, after the final wax and polish. Crafted it may be, a contained piece of wild land coaxed and planted up and ordered into symmetry, but a living garden is never finished.

# III.

*Of SPANISH BROOME. Out of the twigs or little
branches steeped in water, is pressed forth a juice, the
which taken in quantitie of a little glasse full fasting, is
good against the Squinancy, that is a kinde of swelling
with heat and paine in the throte.*

THE PREPARATIONS ARE INTENSE, and largely nothing to do
with him. New plate for the table has to be ordered from
William Hornblower, and a set of silver spoons, and a large gilt salt
and various drinking glasses. Henry dutifully notes down the cost of
each; white plate is worth five shillings and sevenpence, parcel plate is
more, and gilt the most at seven shillings. He yawns, stretches, leaves
Frances to decide, though he does put his mind to what wine and ale
will be drunk, and arranges delivery from the merchant in Langport.
Frances waits until Old Hannah starts to grumble in earnest before
hiring some kitchen boys to grate breadcrumbs and mind the pots
and stir things as bidden. John Hunt the butcher's wife Emmot is due
shortly too, a tolerable cook.

Replies to the invitations are coming in steadily; many acceptances,
some polite refusals, some of those with genuine regret. Nothing

from his brother Jack though, not a word. The kitchens are brimming with the smells of bubbling syrups and suckets and gingerbread and onions and marmalades and meats and comfits. Frances has made conserve of quinces, with damask water and ginger, and persuaded Old Hannah to lay gold leaf patiently upon the slices. Much of the winter's butter has had to come out of storage, and more has been purchased, along with the finest white flour, for all the spice cakes and marchpane. A source of eggs has been established, though expensive at this time of year. Additional dried currants and prunes, oranges, citron and almonds arrive. The prospect of Christmas dwindles into insignificance, though the tenants will still have their feast on St Stephen's.

Frances corners Henry with her lists and runs through the bill of fare and its variants endlessly until Henry's head reels. 'Oyster pie, minced pie, marrow-bone pie, gigot of mutton, several conies, chine of beef, capons, perhaps a pig roasted. If it is to hang we should get the butcher in this week. And for cold baked meats – what do you think? Hare? Boar? Gammon of bacon? A shield of brawn?'

'Excellent.'

'And the roast wild fowls should include woodcock, bittern, shoveller, crane, served with galantine made with the blood of swans?'

'It will depend on what George Colt can get.'

'Or sauce?'

Henry eyes the door.

'Small things on a trencher to pop in the mouth are always agreeable, nuts, jumbles, Genoa paste, suckets I have made already, other sweetmeats, baked wardens. Piles of pippins and pears from the store, medlars and honeyed plums. Fresh salads are difficult at this time of year, but there are the preserved salads with vinegar which we can start with. There is fresh cress outside, of course, and parsley under the cloches, and savory, and we have artichokes in oil and can do kidney beans with herbs. Fish! Smoked eels, perhaps a pike, little shrimps and crayfish. What kind of seafish boiled in broth? I like tench. And sturgeon. Do you like sturgeon, Henry? Henry!'

But he is gone.

Outside for a walk, he passes Widow Hodges who is working away beside her cottage in the cold air.

'Morning, dame,' he greets her briskly. 'Baskets going well?'

'Well.' She shivers. 'My soaking trough keeps freezing over. I've had the fire on boiling up water, but even so the colder it is the longer they must souse. In warm weather when God smiles on us, the rods are biddable enough for working after one week, sometimes less. Winter is our punishment, isn't it Master. The colder the frost, the greater our sins.'

'It is a cold season,' he agrees.

She reaches for her picking knife, begins snipping off the ends at the sides of her basket. 'I like doing borders best, finishing off is very satisfying, when it all goes as it should. A good basket can't unravel, can't work its way undone. A good basket is a firmly fixed vessel, perfect from every aspect.'

Henry can't help wishing the same could be said for his herbal. He is nervous about its imminent arrival, which should be any day now. Supposing he has made mistakes, or the printing is of poor quality. What are people going to say of it?

'It will be a feast to remember, yours, and these wickers at the heart of it. I think of that as I work at them, Master. They've fair boding woven into them.'

Henry's heart sinks. 'Good, good. Glad to hear it.' He had forgotten that Frances had commissioned new, shallow baskets for the serving boys to carry bread in.

'I have that notion green inside my head,' she says, her blank eyelids flickering. 'The good thoughts get into the baskets along with the withies.' And she breaks into a blackened grin that he has to turn away from it is so open and unguarded. It disturbs him, thinking of her twist and knot and cut with his feast in mind all the time.

Everybody's doing it. When he returns from his walk, inside the house Lisbet is running round getting bedding aired and ready, her cheeks very pink. The kitchen boys are at the far end of the kitchen doing something he cannot see, with their backs to the door. Old Hannah, sweating profusely, is making batches of jumbles beside the oven now that the bread is done. He can smell baked meat pies that are cooling in rows on the racks, and as he goes through the Hall he hears her admonishing Tom Coin for tasting something. 'They must be perfect, you little weasel, get your grubby hands out of there!'

'Can nobody think of anything else?' he says aloud, in irritation. He goes to the parlour and peers from the window, looks enviously at the peace of the empty garden where nothing is happening.

He notices that on the outside of the garden wall, Widow Hodges has inched her three-legged stool further along and out into the path, as if following the sun as it swings round with the morning.

'Doesn't that old woman ever feel the cold?' Frances says brightly, coming up behind him.

'She gives me the creeps,' Thomas remarks from the hearthside, who has come home from school in Sherborne for Christmas. 'It's like she's listening to everything, like she *knows*.'

Thomas rubs at his neck. He is afflicted with a scaly rash that his mother slathers with ointment despite his protests. 'You can't be all red-raw for your father's feast. Do they not treat you at school if you are unwell?' she asks.

'No, but if we itch too much we get the rod. Roger Hook had the lice and scratched right though arithmetic and they took him off and when he came back he couldn't sit down for three days. He didn't scratch afterwards, so you could say he was cured, couldn't you?'

'You could,' Frances says dryly, and she flicks a look at Henry across Tommy's head which means, *and that is what you pay so much for?*

'A bit of discipline.' Henry says, noncommittal. 'It didn't do me any harm. Right! I'll get over to George Colt's for the wildfowl, I'd send someone else but I've a fancy for fresh air.'

'Take me with you, Father,' his smallest son pipes up. 'I like rowing.' Harry is only five, and still in skirts.

'If you make yourself very light in the coracle. We don't want to get stuck. Wrap up, I'm going this minute while your mother is distracted.'

Harry follows him down to the other side of Pricklemarch Bridge, where a couple of small boats are pulled up on a slight, willowed rise beside the shimmering moor fields.

'Why does he live out here in the water, Father? Is there nowhere dry for him to go?'

'He is the sluicegate keeper. What use would it be if he lived a mile inland and the river began brimming over? He needs to be right by the sluices, to be the eye on the ebb and flow.'

Henry wades them a few feet out and then jumps into the coracle and punts. It is moderately cold and their breath is white about them when they speak, which is not often. Fine ice is wrinkling up and cracking all the way. The floodwater here is not deep, often less than a foot under the shallow keel, but it makes any distance impassable on foot, and useless for grazing. He punts them between the gateposts at Outdrove and out onto the open space of Rushmoor. Harry screws up his eyes in the bright December light to see the ducks fly up, and the angular, odd flight of snipe.

By the river the reeds are thick halfway across, so that they have to struggle through. Henry wonders if he has lost his way, and then there they are. A boy is getting a boat ready at the staithe as they draw up.

The door is wedged open. Inside, the air in the lower floor chamber is muffled with rows of hung ducks and pale goosander. There is a strong, gamey smell of bird-blood and weed and feathers. In the corner there is a stool and a soft pile of pluckings not yet swept up. Pieces of down swirl about as they enter, and settle on their clothing. Harry puts his gloved hand over his nose to stop out the smell.

'Didn't know you had a son,' Henry says genially, when the wild-fowler climbs down a ladder. People with dwellings on the Levels live upstairs in winter, little fireplaces in the upper chambers. Floodwater can rise in the night. It has no regard for the time of day.

George Colt nods back through the open door at the Mendip, the high hill-line circling the Levels to the north and east.

'He's from up off,' he says, as though this explained everything. 'My brother's boy Samuel, though sometimes I don't think we share much, bloodwise. Up off, it seems they don't know much about the ways of water. Still, a man's got to have some sort of a boy to carry on the family ways, hasn't he Master Lyte,' he says, nodding at Harry, who has been staring fixedly at George Colt's feet since they arrived.

'Is it true you've got webbed toes?' he blurts out. 'My brother Thomas swears you have.'

George Colt's stare is impassive. 'Oh yes,' he says, 'we've all got those, down here. Can't do without them.'

He pulls out two sacks. 'Your birds are here. Six teal, a dozen Jack snipe, mallard, two brace of widgeon … I got most of what was wanted. They're not plucked, that's what she said, wasn't it?' He's putting his coat on. 'You'll have to excuse me but I've to get the sluice-gates open as the tide'll have turned shortly. Very high tides we're having at the moment. Always makes us a bit heedful when it's winter like this and if a storm were to brew, well. There's not much of a seawall down there between us and the rest of the blue, it'd slip in here, easy as pie, given half a chance. I saw you had a bit of trouble getting through. Can have a lend of my meak, if you want,' he offers, holding out the implement with its long sharp rind of blade for cutting reeds. 'Just to get back with. I can pick it up from Lytes on my way back tomorrow. Wouldn't mind getting these feet up on dry land for a minute or two. Wouldn't mind getting a sight of your feast coming along, neither.' He winks at Harry. 'I'll say it'll snow within the week, can smell it coming, can't you?'

They load the sacks of birds into the coracle and punt unsteadily back through the icy, crinkling water, until reeds and the cold rustling of last year's dry flags surrounds them again, swallows them up. They get out and Henry drags the boat the last few hundred yards towards the high ground above Outdrove, his small son wading beside him. They leave it tied to a willow stump. Old Hannah shrieks in horror when she sees them so covered in mud as though they'd emerged from a primeval swamp, and practically snatches the sacks of limp birds away from him, such is her indignation at the mess dripping on the scrubbed kitchen flagstones.

'Master!' Lisbet calls out as they go into the passage. 'Nearly forgot. There was a letter come for you.' She fishes for it.

The letter is warm from being inside her kirtle. Henry looks; the erratic sloping hand is his brother's. What can he want with him? It is all … He scans its contents. 'Ah.'

'What is it, Father?' Harry is shivering with being wet.

'Your Uncle Jack writes simply to say that our stepmother Joan Phelips has passed away.'

'Dead?' Harry, his marsh-soaked boots in hand, runs his toe along a crack in the floor. 'Who is she anyway – do we know her, Father?'

'And that, along with a portion of her not inconsiderable wealth, she has left the manor of Mudford Terry alias Woodcourt to her kins-woman Franny, who of course is now my brother Jack's wife. She had many relatives, but it was Franny whom she chose to be her heir. So. It is Jack who has Mudford after all, because a wife has no property of her own while her husband lives. Of course.' He sees it all now, folds the letter shut. 'They plan to move in without delay.'

By finding a way to give it to his brother she has had her final revenge. One last, taunting gesture; dangling the manor of Mudford under Henry's nose but out of reach, for perpetuity. How very satisfying for an old woman as she waited to die, knowing that even from beyond the grave she can go on reminding him of how she had the closing word, how ultimately she was in charge of these affairs.

'Well, that's it then,' Henry says. 'It is all over.'

'Shall we go upstairs and get changed, Father?' Harry says.

But Henry is surprised to find that he feels nothing at all. In fact, as he climbs the stone stairs with Harry's cold little hand in his, an image comes to him of Mudford Terry as it might be one day, once they are all gone. An oblong of mown grass bound by hedges, nothing more; no manor house, no walls, no shelter. Just a faint green footprint in a field, a scant ghost where a building once was.

# IV.

*Of CAMMOCKE or REST HARROW. The roote is long
and very limmer, and doth oftentimes let, hinder and
stay both the plough and Oxen in toiling the ground.*

MATHIAS LOBEL AND REMBERT DODEONS have both sent
word that they are unable to attend, as Henry had expected,
but other guests are starting to appear in Somerton, at local inns.
Lytes Cary is filling up, bags and packages stacked up in the porch and
on the stairs, the stables busy with other people's horses.

'A friend of Master Bredwell's has brought his hawk and wants to
know the best place for hunting in the morning,' Lisbet garbles,
breathless with fetching and carrying.

'Tell him nowhere near the chicken run or the coney garth,
obviously.'

Moffat is due shortly, and the lute-player from Bridport has
arrived a day early, a well-fleshed man in a foreign style of dress, as
though he is just come lately from Seville with his Dorsetshire
accent. He has taken a fancy to Lisbet and hangs about, making her
flustered. He came highly recommended, but Henry wonders if he

is going to be a pain. He'd better play well enough to justify the trouble he is causing, he thinks, as Lisbet drops what seems to be a crock of butter in the cross-passage. It is mayhem here, truly it is. Frances is in her element, directing in the kitchen, in corridors, in the great porch. A length of the huge trunk of elm has been burning in the hearth for one day already, kept gently smouldering, mild flames licking up its sides, across the many rings of its life. Nobody will be cold in here in three days' time, and how many of us there will be, he thinks. Through the week people have been arriving from London and elsewhere.

Henry considers the space of the hall, thinks of the configuration of the trestles. 'Of course,' he points out, 'assuming sixty people do turn up, there will be no room in here for dancing.'

'Dancing? This feast is going to be an exchange of *ideas*, Henry!'

The day before the feast, Frances bans everyone from walking through the hall, so that the space can be prepared. Any of the Christmas greenery that has wilted is removed and replaced; ivy, holly, rosemary and bay, and then the floor is swept before the strewing can begin, clean rushes first, and then Lisbet walks about with armfuls of dried herbs; throwing meadowsweet and lady's bedstraw, lavender, more sprigs of fresh rosemary straight from the garden that Henry did not have the heart to refuse her, spikes of lavender cut in the summer, dried mint and pennyroyal. A sweet, aromatic hayish savour fills the air, and they cannot begin to lay the linen cloths on the trestles until the dust has settled. In the meantime, an argument ensues about who is to be responsible for the wine.

'Tom Coin can serve,' Henry says.

'He never will! He talks too much. He will fumble it, and spill wine on our guests.'

'But so might the hired boys,' Henry points out. 'He can manage it.' Tom Coin makes a vast effort not to look hopeful before his mistress.

Frances wavers. 'You will have to spend an hour in the cellar with me, learning diligently which wine is which, and how to pour. And you will have to *remember*, Tom. Do you hear?'

He nods eagerly. 'All right. But!' she raises her hand. 'Your apron must be spotless.'

She has everything in hand, Henry thinks, leaving her to it. If nothing else, this has given Frances diversion from her great sorrow, and lifted her spirits admirably. Florence too is enjoying herself.

# V.

*Of AGNUS CASTUS. Some write that if such as journey or travell, do carry a branch or rod of Agnus Castus in their hand, it will kéep them bothe from chafing and wearinesse.*

In the bleakest month when the earth is hard and unyielding and allows no growth, how satisfying to spread out the new, bright plate that is like the sun. Sunshine is the light towards which all things grow, a bringer of life. On the white cloths spread on the trestles, the new plate glitters and glistens in the candlelight. In the end they'd spent over fourteen pounds on plate, a handsome sum. All the candles are of beeswax, not a drop of cheap tallow in the hall today, and about each flame is a pool of scent – an aromatic sweetness that is a warm, honeyed accretion thick with stories.

'What is it, Father?' Florence slips a hand under his elbow, and he realizes he must be speaking aloud again; middle age is creeping up on him. He clears his throat.

'Well, stories of flowers and journeys and tastes and directions taken by honeybees,' he says. This daughter has almost grown into a woman, he realizes with pride, a tall lovely woman stood beside him.

'I wish I were a bee,' says Florence, 'in and out of those blossoms all day, sucking at the nectar and flying about.'

'You would have to be very unselfish,' he points out. 'Everything a bee does is for the good of its hive.'

'Not like us, then, Father,' Florence says. 'Not like you and me.' And she gazes at him with her eyes as green as lovage. 'I like your book though.' He is glad she has remembered how they share a kinship. He kisses her hair. 'It is good to see you looking so well,' he says.

She goes again to the little table at the side where the volume is sitting in state ready to be admired or judged, he is not sure which; opens it with the creak of new binding and leafs through gently. *Woodbinde or honisuckle hath many small branches,* she reads aloud from the crisp black text, darting glances at him, *whereby it windeth and wrappeth it selfe about trees and hedges. Woodbine is hote and drye almost in the thirde degree.* She turns a page. 'I really am delighted for you, Father,' she says.

'Would you like a copy for yourself?' he asks, on impulse. 'I understand if you should think it a cumbersome thing, apt to take up room and gather dust. But you may find it of some small use, one day when you have your own household to run, your own garden?'

She looks startled.

'I will save one for you.'

'If only Mama could have seen it,' she says quietly. Henry finds himself glancing into each shadowy corner of the Hall. 'She would have liked your book too.'

An hour to go. He goes upstairs to wash and change, glad of the refuge of his own bedchamber from the hubbub outside. Frances is ready, pinning on her starched ruff.

'How do you like me?' she spins about, a dazzling whirl of emerald velvet, its beetle-darkness shot through with flashes of gold thread.

He looks. It strikes him that the dress has made her waist ribbed like the stalk of an umbellifer, like a green piece of cowparsley before the season is over. He wants to say that what he likes is actually *inside* the dress, and that though it is undoubtedly lovely he can't help thinking instead that under the stiff bones of that bodice is her supple white waist, and of the softness and freedom of her fine bare skin as it would be on an improbably perfect night against his, for example. Or perhaps this is the point precisely of a lovely garment – that it enables a man to more easily dream of its contents. He clears his throat.

'You are very fine,' he assures her gravely.

All this sumptuous dressing up is like play-acting, a bit of theatre. *The squire and his lovely wife – see how well they look.* He supposes he is as complicit in the display as anyone, with his luxurious hose and slashed sleeves puffed like gourds, laid out waiting on the bed. When he kisses Frances on the mouth she tastes of apples.

# VI.

*Of LICORISE. They use to make a kinde of small cakes or bread in some Abbeyes of Holland against the cough, with the juyce of Lycorise, mixt with Ginger and other spices.*

GOING DOWN INTO THE NOISE AND TUMULT of the hall, he has to admit that Frances is magnificent. He doesn't mind at all that he feels drab beside her despite his new garb, she is poised and shining, a woman who knows what life is worth. They greet their guests at the door, and Moffat arrives, shivering uncontrollably.

'The weather Lyte! I cannot believe you people live like this.'

'Look at that,' Henry exclaims, 'the man has had a haircut!' He claps him on the back. 'Come and sit beside me in the warmth, get some wine in your belly.'

There is a clank as Moffat puts down his baggage by the door. 'You brought your collecting bottles? Do you ever stop thinking about insects?'

Moffat sits himself down beside Penny and puts his arm about his broad shoulders, laughing.

From the high table, Henry glances up and down at the faces; most familiar, some familiar by association. So many people came. Amongst this throng of sixty or so are some of the country's finest minds, he thinks with satisfaction, all gathered together to sup and be merry here at Lytes Cary, in a deafening crush along the trestles exchanging ideas, discussing new botanical finds, medical opinion, sharing whatever it is that herbalists dream of at their desks. It will be remembered as the Lytes Cary Dinner of 1578, he thinks, where the plants were sovereign.

Thomas Moffat stretches his hand across to a young man whom Henry has not met but has heard a lot about.

'May I introduce my good friend Henry Lyte, botanist,' he says with a flourish, 'to James Cole.'

'I am no botanist.' Henry bows. 'Merely a translator.'

'And a modest one at that! Have you seen the work itself yet, Cole? What he has done for Rembert's disquisition, you will agree that meticulous is not the word.'

'Since when did neatness itself deserve praise?' Henry says.

'I do not mean neat, and you know it for you are grinning from ear to ear.' Moffat throws his bread at Lyte. 'You have crumbs in your beard, sir.'

'You're an excitable fellow,' Henry laughs. It is so good to see everybody.

Opposite, Thomas Penny is wheezing with asthma that has worsened since his last visit. He struggles to raise his voice above the din. 'You know, that boy is fifteen years old and already has exemplary self-taught Latin and a zeal for botany and learning that I have not encountered in any other youngster.'

'The new generation,' Henry says.

'Yes, look out for your daughters. Oh and remind me, Lyte, I must bring Clusius to see your garden if he comes to London. He is due. It would be ludicrous if you do not meet the man, having spent so much time translating from his French. He likes rarities.'

Henry shrugs. 'If he is passing.' Charles l'Écluse did not reply to his invitation to the feast. Henry and his translation are small fry in the eyes of the great man Carolus Clusius, no doubt. Any letter coming all the way from Vienna, where he is now employed by the Emperor to work on the imperial gardens there, may have got lost in transit of course, but Henry thinks it more likely that there simply wasn't one.

'I was sorry to hear of your losses, Henry,' Penny adds. Henry raises his glass to him in a small private toast, grateful he's mentioned it. 'To absent friends.'

By the time the first courses start arriving, he can see that along the tables the *Niewe Herball* is doing the rounds, being passed from hand to hand, pored over, examined, discussed. John Gerard, he notes, has held it for a long time, Henry wonders which pages he is so interested in. And then the food begins to be presented in earnest, and the herbal is put aside in favour of more immediate things as the serving boys trot out one after another until before every trencher there is a myriad victuals. It is a spread. Old Hannah and her bought-in troupe of helpers have done them proud. Beside him Frances beams at how it is all working out in the kitchen with the arrival of every new dish. Occasionally she bends to whisper instruction to the oldest serving boy or Lisbet. Tom Coin scurries up and down with the wine glasses from the sideboard, pouring carefully, not spilling a drop. Even the amorous lute-player is very good.

It is only later, when appetites about the hall begin to slow to a satisfied pace, with the wine flowing plentifully and the candles some way burnt down, that the discussion goes on.

'Tell me, Bredwell, what do you think on it?' Henry calls him over to a seat beside him. Stephen Bredwell sucks in a little wine and pulls a face as though it is too tart for his taste.

'You have not made allowances for the class of plant that you describe. I am aware that it is a …' he pauses, '*translation*, but it seems to me you would have had ample opportunity to distinguish more tactfully between the vulgar and the cultivated, in terms of use.

'Could I?' Henry says.

'But you have included *weeds*, alongside finer specimens grown by skilled and knowledgeable herbalists. The College of Physicians will not thrill to the idea of the common man getting his grubby paws on a volume such as this and having tools at his disposal lying in the wayside and in ditches. *Ditches*, Lyte!'

Henry looks deliberately enquiring. 'So what is your verdict?'

'It's just,' Bredwell pauses again, 'not hierarchical enough.'

Henry Lyte grins broadly and claps him on the back. 'Good, good,' he says. 'I'm glad you said that – it's the best reaction yet.'

Henry turns to Moffat. 'I'm not satisfied with the church's idea that only God can heal, that it's only his choice. Why then did he create all these potent plants that grow so plentifully all around us? So many of them are not cultivated or costly specimens. They grow freely on waysides, in the humble plots of labourers, in woodlands, orchards. Knowledge should run freely between men and women, readily available to those who care to know, who have their eyes and ears open. Shouldn't it?' Stephen Bredwell leans forward as if he has not heard correctly.

'At its very least my translation offers to the literate householder an alternative to paying blindly for what they cannot afford. It offers some modicum of self-rule.'

Moffat's eyebrows rise in delight. 'Incendiary language, Lyte!'

'And I'm aware that each volume is in itself a costly item, far out of the reach of the poorest amongst us. But it is cheaper than an exclusive education. It can be read by capable women who have not been taught any other language but their own. It can be handed down and loaned to others, recipes copied down and sent on to sick relatives, tenants, neighbours. You once asked me what my question was. I am sure now. Mine is, *By what equitable means can suffering and death be fought?* And I hope that it is the dream of many others. Imagine a world where good health is a universal possibility!'

He helps himself to a spoonful from the dish nearest to him. 'But we shall see what kind of life it has.'

Thomas Moffat is laughing at the expression on Bredwell's face. 'You sound so serious, Lyte. But I like it. I do like it.'

'I think in fifty years we will not recognize the cultural climate.' Henry nods at James Cole sitting opposite him. 'You are the future now, young man. And our heavy, expensive folio editions will be outmoded by your inexpensive, expertly written compact tracts that everybody reads.'

'There's no doubt that more lives will be saved as a result,' Penny says.

'Turner taught me that change is brought about by insignificant people taking a step. The more of us the better. At least, that's what I now understand he was telling me, though it has taken me more than twenty years to realize it.'

'Should we be worried that there will be a devaluing of knowledge?' Penny says. 'A dilution, a coarsening, debasing, bluntening, once it is in the hands of those who did not train so exclusively and deeply?'

Moffat takes a pear and bites into it. 'Maybe it will slowly make scientists out of all of us, or better still it might provoke out of the population some new kind of science.'

'And we will be – defunct,' Henry says.

'At first we will appear simply fusty, a little moth-eaten, then we and the baggage of our ideas will be crumbled to dust.'

'I would never have thought that when I began this project so many years ago. But the quickening pace of change has already begun whilst I've been engaged, you can feel it underfoot, in much the same way as you can feel the spring starting up, and walking on the earth is like walking on a living entity.'

Moffat agrees. 'Which is precisely what it is. Old Mother Earth or God's kingdom, call it what we may. I'll admit it, especially when I leave the city there are times when I am torn between science and the truths found in folklore.'

'There are plenty who see folklore as received wisdom, passed down in the bones, in the blood from father to son, mother to daughter. It's not science though, is it, not progress.'

Henry smiles. 'The trouble with folklore is that sometimes it's right.'

'Don't let your Reverend Tope hear you say that.'

'Or Lobel.'

'Or my mother – she'll hand you over as swift as lightning to the Queen's officers on a charge of heresy.'

Henry goes to the sideboard to get more wine for the company.

'Change won't happen all that quickly.' He looks down the table at his herbal. 'This book will be the main authority on herbs in England for a good while yet. There's no-one at work on something comparable.'

The jug is empty, and there are no more on the side. He looks for Tom Coin but he is not to be seen. He'll have to fetch it himself.

'Excuse me gentlemen, but we are in need of more claret.' And Henry winds his way unsteadily out of the hall. It is cool in the passage, and before going to the cellar he opens the front door and steps out into the great porch for a breath of air to clear his head.

# VII.

*Of the WHITE THORNE, or HAWTHORNE TREE.*
*The white thorne most commonly groweth low and*
*crooked, wrapped and tangled as a hedge.*

I T IS DARK NOW, A SMALL ICY MOON illuminating bands of cloud advancing from the north, above Lytes Cary and stretching to the east and west as far as the eye can see.

Out in the yard, a thin dusting of snow has fallen, and a few flakes are drifting down, catching the moonlight and flashing colours like crystals. The air is blue. It is so exquisitely beautiful and still that he cannot resist stepping outside, just for a moment to stretch his legs, despite his fancy ridiculous velvet shoes.

He stands listening to the muffled din of the hall going on without him for some moments. He walks round the side of the brightly lit house to go to the garden. The thin layer of snow quiets his footsteps and bounces an eerie light up from the ground. The plants are dark against its whiteness in the moonlight. Approaching the garden gate, he catches some kind of movement to his left and almost jumps out of his skin.

It is Widow Hodges. Henry can't understand what on earth she is doing out here.

'Deuce, madam, what are you doing, working out here in the dark? Surely you don't do this every night?' He is horrified. 'It is cold!'

'Oh no. It's just that I had a mind to listen to your feast, Master. Darkness means nothing to me. In warmer weather if I cannot sleep, I often sit and make baskets until the birds begin to sing again and the place begins to stir. So tonight I wrapped up warm in my blankets as you see me now. I heard the man had arrived with his instrument, and it's been a while since I caught a bit of music.'

'You must come inside and sit by the fire then, dame.'

A look of panic crosses her face. 'Oh no, Master. Not in there with all those people.'

'Then I shall send out something hot for you.'

'You are a good man, full of kindness like your mother.'

Henry wishes that were true. 'Why do you find it so difficult to sleep, Mistress Hodges?'

Her rods of withy whip about as she weaves and talks. 'Noise of rats or the drumming of rain: there's many a reason for staying awake, you know that. Besides, guilt is a terrible burden to bear, but no more than I deserve. We can never escape from the past, can we, Master. It just goes on collecting inside us no matter what we do to staunch it.'

'Have you always been blind?' Henry asks. 'I remember as a child the day they sewed your eyes shut, but could you see before that? Why did they do that? Do you know how the world appears to others – or were you born that way?'

'Oh yes, I remember the way the world looked. It looked good enough, until some certain events took place in it which I bore witness to.'

'Do you mean what happened with your daughter's witches' teeth?'

'No, not that.'

There is a pause, and then what she says next makes Henry's blood run cold.

413

'And what I did was why I put my own eyes out, Master.'

'You blinded *yourself*? Sweet Christ.'

'I didn't deserve God's gift of sight for what I'd done. The second eye was the harder. I'd practised in the air like this: stab, stab, quick as fish leaping upstream, so as to get the blade in twice before I fainted. But I didn't reckon on how it didn't push in nor come out so easily as I was ready for. It was the liquid, the knife going all wet and slippery as well as hot. I could hardly get a grip upon the handle. And such a smell as I never came across, all down my own face.' She rocks backwards and forwards, a tiny movement.

'Why did you do it?' Henry says.

'I didn't want to die, I deserved worse than that. It would have been too easy just to die. No, suffering was what I wanted. And the mess and horror of it filled up my mind. Afterwards I had a lot of new learning about the shape of the world. I was covered in bruises from making mistakes about the house. I don't know why I'm telling you all this now. I haven't spoke of it for years. It's just that music reminds me of something in my head. You wouldn't know about that, Master, but wrongdoing's a terrible thing to eat away at you.' She trails off.

'Like a canker.' Henry says, bitterly. 'I admire your courage, Widow Hodges.'

She snorts. He notices she has completed one whole round of wicker while they have been talking. 'Feelings are beside the point, Master, it's our acts, isn't it, that make a difference to anything.'

'And what was it that you did that was so bad, dame?'

'I don't hate myself, that would be too easy too. Sometimes there'll be something that'll make me laugh. But even as I'm laughing I'll know I don't deserve to.'

'Did it mitigate your guilt, has it eased your remorse in some way?'

'Taking away God's gift of sight was a sin too,' she admits, her fingers running lightly up and down a length of willow as though feeling for flaws. 'No-one should try to undo the will of God. No,' she whispers, finally. 'No, it made no difference. How could it.' When she turns her face to him it is a sight he knows he will not forget.

'Did she suffer? That's what I don't know, Master Lyte. I was not there to share her suffering. I was not there to make her final days more tolerable, to give her succour and the love and tenderness that she deserved, as any child should have from its mother. For do you know what I did? I did what no mother should ever do, what goes against the grain, what is inhuman.' Her voice breaks. 'It was a bad plague time upcountry. She was nine years old. Every place had it, dying was commoner than living. We stayed in our house and thought to let it pass us by. There was only the two of us, why would it seek us out? We kept the windows shut tight and ate what there was in the store of our house for two weeks. Only once a day did I creep out to the well and back. She went on laughing and playing and being the girl I loved so much, there was so much light in her, Master, yet there was a day when I saw that she had the bubies there all blackening in her, bubbling up in the skin of her chest, and something in me could not keep still. You'll understand that all about the dead in our town were mounting. The dead cart coming past every day. The smell began to be bad, you could not sleep for the sounds at night. And now it was my little Benet that lay in the chamber, stinking, crying out for water, and I could not go to her.' She is weeping now, has put her basket aside. 'It was as though she had become a monster to me overnight. I pushed a mug of water through the crack of the door towards her on the bed, with a long stick I'd fashioned. Can you imagine that, Master, not going to your children to comfort them? I should have held her, washed her, given her what I could. She did not even hear me say goodbye, for I did not say it. I walked away from my own child and left her there to die alone, quite by herself. I walked and walked without pause for days, I did not stop to sleep. I cannot sleep since. I have never slept a full night for the rest of my life since. I shall never know why I did what I did.

Only later did I learn that not everyone died of contagion, that sometimes a body was saved, with the sickness passing through them.' She wipes her nose on her sleeve. 'You see, you are repulsed by it. Any man would be.'

Henry looks at the darkening sky, the clouds edging the moon's brightness, and tries to say something.

'God knows there have been many who have done the same.'

'I disgust myself every day that comes.'

'She would probably have died, if you were there or not, Mistress Hodges.'

'But she was left, she was left.' Henry turns his face away from her raw, blind anguish in the moonlight. 'And it was I that did that.'

There is no sound from anywhere.

'I pray for a cure.' She sniffs. 'Is there a cure for the plague in your book, Master?'

'Well,' Henry recites quietly from the relevant passage. '*If anybody be infected with the pestilence or plague, they give him straightaway to drink a dram of the powder of this root with wine in the winter or in summer with the distilled water of scabious, blessed thistle or rose, then they bring him to bed, and cover him until he have sweat well.*'

'Is that so,' she breathes.

'And you yourself as carer would hold in your mouth a piece of root to protect your own body from the infection.'

'Who would have thought.'

'I don't sleep either,' he says suddenly.

'You? Why not?'

Henry swallows. 'We have more in common beside the inability to sleep at night, Mistress Hodges. I have my own burden.' He looks up into the night. 'I made my first wife suffer needlessly.'

Above them the sky has clouded the moon over, and he feels a momentary, gentle brush of snow against him in the dark, like something passing. The old woman's teeth are chattering fiercely now, so that Henry leads her into the cottage where a scrap of fire is still glowing in the darkness.

'A mild, contented sort of woman, wasn't she?' she says, opening the blanket to let the heat get to her as he coaxes the flames. 'Everyone said so.'

'Anys did not deserve what happened to her. But at the time of her last confinement my mind was elsewhere. I was not unstinting in my prayers. I did not believe, perhaps, that she could be taken from us. God knows that Doctor Turner had warned me against complacency in life.

'Two years before, the midwife warned us that another confinement like the last could be the end of her. Anys should apply honeysuckle as a poultice if we would go on lying together. But we went on with our lives as usual, did not trouble to meddle with the way of nature, and were blessed with another conception. I was hopeful this time, the child seemed to lie on the right and was exceedingly active, which meant it could be a male infant.

'The midwife's views were very forceful. She said Anys was too frail to bear another child to term. She listed any number of savage herbs that she could take, made up a pessary of wool dipped in the juice of rue and tried to administer it when I was out one day, which I discovered, by chance returning in time to put a stop to what I thought at the time was her evil. As I threw her out of the house she berated me for allowing Anys to become with child. *Were not three healthy daughters enough of a blessing?* she shrilled through the keyhole. Anys was at this time five months gone. It was the first time I had seen her cry.

'When her time came, I would not send for the midwife, though Anys begged me. I sent instead for a Doctor Driffield, staying in the district, and whom I had heard to be very advanced and forward with his medicine. He seemed young and was expensive, but I felt he was the superior choice given the risks that had been outlined to me in no uncertain terms.

'Her travail was long and fraught, the doctor intervened constantly, so that she ran out of strength by the second day.

'I sat outside the chamber and could tell I had made a mistake. The doctor did not call for clean water, good old wine, he did not use the herbs that the midwife had administered successfully during Anys's previous labours. He referred constantly to his book that he carried with him as if he had not attended a birth like this before. But still I did nothing. Why?

'She wept and called for the midwife several times by name, but I refused her, over and over. I wanted the best medical care for her, you understand, she was at risk, and I wanted to protect her, pay for her care. It was a double birth, of course, as it transpired. Anys was carrying twin babies, side by side in the womb. The babies were delivered alive, with great pain and difficulty and she lost much blood, and the afterbirth came away but in part. She became very ill with a milk fever shortly afterwards, which she battled valiantly but became weaker and weaker. She was never to rise from her bed unaided again. Once or twice she struggled to the window of her chamber to look out over the garden, leaning on the sill with her white wrists as thin as the bones inside them. But she was to die a few weeks later.'

'And the babies were well, I recall, at least—'

'My fifth daughter at first survived the birth, but she was not spared death as it claimed her a few weeks later, outliving her mother by days. What was it all for, I wondered?'

'Rest her soul,' the old woman murmurs.

'Florence was the other, of course, she had come from her mother first, fighting for her life. Since then no day has passed when I have not felt death lingering like a physical entity, waiting in the shadows at the sides of our lives, waiting for all of us; one by one it will get us in the end.'

'I remember the time of your wife dying,' she says, when he has finished.

'You do?'

'I remember all the talk of it, and how the funeral was on a cool September day, though the drizzle stopped just long enough for the coffin to be got to church. It wasn't long after that the frosts started, was it, and an exceeding hard winter that followed.'

'What was the talk? Did everybody say—'

'There is always gossip, Master. Folk have little else to latch on to – and your adversity was as good as anything to pass the time of day with. You should not dwell upon those circumstances, it was never your fault, but a jeopardous labour.'

'But I did kill her. I killed her. I wanted a son.' The words rush out of him, the breath squeezed from his lungs. 'It was I that caused it. I know it, my father knew it.'

The old woman reaches about for him in their different kinds of darkness and finds his hand.

'No, Master, you did not. It was nature that took her from you.'

&

At first Henry finds he cannot return to the house, but goes on into the cold, darkly white garden and stands shivering in its very centre. He closes his eyes. Within its symmetry, his body is adjusting to some slight but vital changes. He can almost feel the knot of history forming and re-forming inside himself.

Then he turns to go back, and as he rounds the corner of the house he sees in the torchlight from the great porch that the snowy path is already criss-crossed with trails of animals and human footprints, as well as his own. Perhaps a cat, a fox, small rodents, their tails dragging, a stable boy. There are tracks everywhere.

He feels lightheaded.

He puts his head into the kitchen and directs the nearest boy to take out something hot to eat, at once, to Widow Hodges in her dwelling. He goes down quickly into the vaulted sepulchre-smelling cellar and then, wine in hand, re-enters the raucous heat and noise of his own feast, the thickened smell of strewing herbs and drink and smoke and bodies like a wall he passes through. Frances looks relieved to see him appear.

'Lyte!' Moffat calls over. 'Where the devil have you been? You've been gone over an hour. You have missed the banquet course. There was sugar paste in the shape of flowers and leaves. We saved you some, it's very good!'

Henry stands tall at his place on the dais. Moffat chimes his drinking-glass with a spoon vigorously for him, with no regard for the cost of their Venetian qualities. The lute player stops his melody. Unevenly, a silence falls, and then he speaks.

'Firstly, I would like to thank you all for coming here today. I should like to give thanks for the extraordinary love that I have from my family and friends, and give thanks to the plants. Secondly, I should like to propose a toast.' He makes sure that his voice is loud enough for the ancestors to hear, those at rest or otherwise, and holds his glass high.

'To the past,' he says clearly, 'and to the forgetting of the past.'

'To the past!' the assembled guests chorus raggedly back at him, not caring what he means. 'To the forgetting of the past!'

Henry sits down in his place, he is suddenly exhausted. Moffatt leans across. 'What was that all about?'

'You mean you haven't heard?'

Moffat holds out his glass for more wine. 'I doubt it.'

'That we are all free men, loosened from our bonds and making progress.' Henry Lyte feels a surge of something close to happiness. He knows this sensation will not last, but just for once feels that he is allowed to enjoy it for its duration. 'Do you know, it's snowing out there,' he adds.

'What are you rambling on about? Congratulations on your herbal, by the way.' Moffat says. 'I hope you're proud. You should be.'

Henry helps himself to a piece of what is left of the sweetmeat, goes on talking with his mouth full.

'That anybody could have done it is the truth. Sometimes all it takes is for someone to speak out, to begin to change the course of how things seem. Even very ordinary men and women could do this in their lifetimes. Tiny changes, here and there.' He breaks off another sweet bite. 'Isn't it so?'

Moffat looks curious. 'You're very exuberant, suddenly. Or overexcited. Or tense. Or drunk. But I'll drink to changes, whether you're right or not.'

Henry Lyte glances into the corners of the hall. Nothing. And with the darkness outside he can hardly see the armorial glass above him.

'Why do I have the feeling that no-one will remember the date of my birth, Moffat? I doubt even that the place of my burial will be known in the end, and why should that matter? Why should anyone need to know the exact location of the place where my earthly body has broken down and gone back to the earth? My children, perhaps some grandchildren, will know and after that it will not matter. I know that one day my contribution to English botany will be largely forgotten. Most of us are forgotten in the end,' he says. 'But I suppose small parts of us are left as traces, the shape worn into the stair by the flat of our feet where we tread every night as we go up to bed, the smoothness on the handles of tools. Our bones will make a faint chemical difference to the soil they are buried in. Our smiles may crop up in the smiles of our children's children. But ourselves and our ideas will be usurped, improved upon, forgotten. And that's as it should be. In the meantime, look!' he says, raising his glass to the illustrious company, to the ancestors, across at his children, his wife. 'Just look how far we've come!'

# THE EIGHTH PART

## The Dangers

## ❧ 1607 ❧

## Epilogue

*Of WITHY or WILLOW. All kinds of Withy delight to grow in moist places, along by ditches and waters, but especially the Oziers.*

HENRY LYTE WAKES TO THE FAMILIAR SOUND of mice in the panelling behind his head. Something is different. He lies with his eyes closed, trying to work out what he feels has changed. Is it the light? The weather? Has a tree fallen down in the night? Have thieves broken in and stolen the horses? Maybe it is just that he is getting older, every day inching to the grave. He is seventy-eight years old now, though his third wife's children are still young; Gertrude and Rafe. He has a host of grandchildren, mostly Thomas's boys, and Thomas has run the estate himself for fifteen years.

He reaches for his stick and takes a while to pull himself up from the bed, stands a moment, then goes to the trap to see what was last night's catch. A field mouse this time, with a soft pale underbelly and a bright brown coat, its jaws unmovingly ajar to a pool of darkened mouse-blood. Henry prises open the spring with his old man's fingers, removes the little carcass – stiffening already – by the tail, and shuffles to the window to drop it into the dormant tangle of the garden.

He leans against the sill and peers down after it. There is definitely something odd about the air; charged, he thinks, not unlike the air before a thunderstorm. But it is a bright sunny morning for – what is the month? January. January the twentieth, in the fourth regnal year of James. Frances is dead, and so are Thomas Penny, Thomas Moffat. He is left here, aching, exceedingly old, still clinging on there is no doubt. Perhaps someone will bring him a little bite to eat. He is not sure if he feels like getting up just yet today, goes to the bed, sits down and eyes the chamber pot.

But where is everybody? The house is eerily quiet. There had been a scuffle of activity about an hour ago, probably children clattering down the corridor, some shouts out in the yard, an argument perhaps; and now – nothing. It feels late; later than usual. He is annoyed with himself for feeling apprehensive, suddenly. It is just that … He begins to wonder if he should try to make his way downstairs unaided.

Now he can hear footsteps, running almost, getting louder. And when the bad news comes hurtling up the stairs, he recognizes it immediately, as if he has been waiting to hear this all his life. Thomas has burst into his chamber. His face is white and flat with shock.

'The sea,' he chokes. 'The sea! Father, it has breached at Burnham and many other places and it's come for us. There has never been a thing like this. I saw …' He breaks off, gasping for breath, pouring with sweat. 'Father! I've seen pieces of ships and a windmill rolling by, and drowning cows, the pieces all bundled up at the front of the wave, like splinters, and dashed inland. The wave didn't break. It was like a wall, perhaps ten or twelve feet high with great gobbets of hay churning behind it, whole ricks of peas, and I saw a dwelling-house tumbling along, Father, and there were rabbits everywhere running up for higher ground, they were so thick beneath me I was treading on rabbits, trampling them down, so that my horse wouldn't go unless I got down and pulled her through them, her hooves all bloodied and covered in fur. The wave never stopped, Father, just drove on ripping trees down like they were nothing. And in the water I began to see that there were little dots of men, and I saw that about the water were people clinging, floating, and that the noise in my ears was their voices screaming. Fish were jumping out of the water all around, and on the banks I saw a women's hair just stood on end with terror. And I could not stop, Father, but rode straight home to warn you all, and we must leave. We must leave at once and move uphill.' He is shaking all over. 'The servants are gone. Everyone says that this must be the Second Deluge, a punishment upon our heads.'

'These punishments do not exist. I stopped believing in them long ago.' Henry has to lie back on the bed and press his eyes closed to think clearly. So Frances was right. Eighteen years after her death and she is right.

'What are you doing, Father?' Thomas says, shaking him. 'Don't go to sleep!'

Henry suspects that in his panic Thomas thinks he has died in front of him. 'Is that what the young think of the old?' he says. 'That in the midst of all this they cannot grasp what is happening?'

Thomas's gaze is wild. 'What?'

'Well they cannot. Who can? There has been a peculiar smell to the air since dawn.'

'There has?' Thomas is bewildered. 'Father! Listen to me, we must leave at once.'

'I am not leaving Lytes Cary. You go on if you please, with your wife and children, take Dorothy and my children, but I am too old now to run away. For someone who fears death so, I have lived for a remarkably long time. And I cannot think that the water will rise as far as the house.'

'You don't understand, Father. The Levels are deep underwater right up to Glastonbury, the sea has claimed its own again, as Mother always said it would. Do you remember, Father, all her bad dreams? I have seen dead bodies lapping at the edge of Kingsdon. This is not like anything we have seen before. I implore you to believe me, Father, if you had seen what I have already with my own eyes you would be packing your saddlebags and calling for horses. Where are your papers, the deeds, other things that should be kept safe?'

'I am infirm. I am going nowhere. Is the water still rising? If I drown here I drown.' He struggles back to the window, strains to see out to the moor, and yes, the glare of sheets of saltwater lying all over the land is astonishing. This is more than the annual, shallow inundation, surely. This is a reversal, a loss of land. How extraordinary, he thinks, his heart racing. All that threat of man's invasion from the sea during the time of the Armada – and then this! The sea itself.

Outside the Sorcerer flies from the holly to the high ash, to the willows and back again, not comprehending what it sees.

'I will not leave you here,' Thomas says. He stands in the room getting hold of himself. 'Lytes Cary must send out boats, lend out useful men, food and fresh water.' He turns to go.

'Thomas!'

'Yes, Father?'

'Nothing. Only that … you are a good son.'

Later that morning, Henry gets dressed and is carried downstairs and helped out to the water's edge. The river Cary has disappeared, swallowed up into the murky, despoiled lake stretched out for miles, lumps of rises and higher ground jutting, black and crawling with birds and small animals.

'What's that floating out there?' Henry says, and they watch, and as it bobs closer they see that it is a loaf.

'Deadman's bread,' one of the children says, putting her little hand in his, and a pair of ducks flies in steeply from overhead, splash-lands and begins to squabble over it.

He does not want to but this makes him think of soft parts of bodies drifting slowly along and sinking into the silt beneath. He knows he will never again be able to eat eel or any other scavenger fish or crab. He does not like to imagine how fat and prosperous they will become, how there are always those who benefit from tragedy, feeding on pieces of death down there, the loss of others.

There will be worse to see than that, and he is right. By the evening the bottom field is littered with swollen cattle drifting in batches, and a man mercifully face downwards, until the children can be taken away back to the house. Dead, sodden poultry; a pig, its sides gashed. A morass of branches and timber and the debris of barns and dwellings, and the expanse of water carries the roars of stranded cattle quite a distance away. In some of the trees and hedges there are drowned sheep, hanging. In spring they will be bare bones up there, he thinks, like pale horrendous nests made of ribcages, hind legs, and then exposed to the drying winds and sun of summer they will come loose and clatter down again.

The servants begin to return with stories from nearer the coast. At Huntspill, as the great wave drew back even as it advanced, four new-laid coffins were sucked out of their soft, loosely mounded graves, to be smashed open like pods, and their contents spilled, to sit swilling, turning in horrible circles at the edge of the wetness miles inland. There is talk of thousands of dead. Grim, unspeaking men in boats are hauling in dead bodies all the time, to be put on to carts and laid out in market squares and churches all round the rim of the Levels. One of the drowned brought out at Lytes Cary is Samuel Colt's little girl, her hair like dark snakes of wetness, dripping up the path as they carry her.

His head is filled with a clamour of voices from his past, as though stirred up like this muddied water. He can hear all Frances's fears, borne out and doubled, tripled in height and length and depth. He hears his father, disapproving, distant. He hears his mother, Anys,

Johnny, Magdalen, Old Hannah. One voice that he does not hear is Tobias Mote's, who left his employ in the end to work up country and Henry has not seen him for these past ten years, though he thinks of him often. He does not hear Lisbet, who went off to marry the lute-player she'd met at their feast. He does not hear Joan Phelips.

The voice of the Sorcerer though is very insistent, always with him, not ageing at all, living an unfading existence, the green spirit of the unbroken present. As a child, hiding away from his brothers inside the hedge, Henry had watched the Sorcerer out on the lawn, licking ants from their homes, its grey tongue shooting out for their little, bitter bodies, and he felt for them and saw the deep unfairness of the world.

It is always like this here on the edge of the Levels, he thinks, we begin and end each year with the threat of saltwater, the sea a hand's-breadth away. It seems impossible that these fields will ever drain and burgeon with plants and cattle and dwellings again, and yet the earth will be refreshed by silt and death.

Outside the house, Henry stops and leans on his stick to watch a hawk spinning slowly above Lytes Cary. He wonders as he always does what it can see from its better vantage point, how the land looks from up there. Like everything, he supposes it must be biding its time, watching for movement, changes; waiting for spring.

# Author's Note

**H**ENRY LYTE DIED IN 1607 at Lytes Cary, Somerset, on 15 October at about four o'clock in the afternoon. Trobridge of Taunton supplied the blacks and he was buried in the parish church of St Mary at Charlton Mackrell. His estate and husbandry implements were left to his son Thomas. As there is now no visible stone to mark his resting place, most visitors to the church would miss the fact that the earth beneath their feet in the north transept contains the remains of a distinguished contributor to the progress of English botany.

His scholarly translation of the *Cruÿdeboeck* by Rembert Dodeons, first published in 1578 as *A Niewe Herball or Historie of Plantes*, was the standard work on herbs in English during the latter part of the sixteenth century.

Thomas Penny died before him in 1589. Henry's wife Frances also died later that same year, and he married again and had three more children; Gertrude, Henry and Rafe. Thomas Moffat died in 1604. And in the year of Henry's passing, there was a devasating tsunami or storm surge that flooded the Somerset Levels, drowning thousands – just as Frances had always feared.